South University Library
Richmond Campus
2151 Old Brick Road
Glen Allen, Va 23060

D1778568

AUG 3 0 2012

Wonder in Shakespeare

Wonder in Shakespeare

Adam Max Cohen

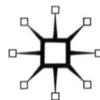

WONDER IN SHAKESPEARE
Copyright © Adam Max Cohen, 2012.

All rights reserved.

First published in 2012 by
PALGRAVE MACMILLAN®
in the United States—a division of St. Martin's Press LLC,
175 Fifth Avenue, New York, NY 10010.

Where this book is distributed in the UK, Europe and the rest of the world, this is by Palgrave Macmillan, a division of Macmillan Publishers Limited, registered in England, company number 785998, of Houndmills, Basingstoke, Hampshire RG21 6XS.

Palgrave Macmillan is the global academic imprint of the above companies and has companies and representatives throughout the world.

Palgrave® and Macmillan® are registered trademarks in the United States, the United Kingdom, Europe and other countries.

ISBN: 978–0–230–10541–6

Library of Congress Cataloging-in-Publication Data

Cohen, Adam Max.
   Wonder in Shakespeare / Adam Max Cohen.
     p. cm.
   Includes bibliographical references.
   ISBN 978–0–230–10541–6
    1. Shakespeare, William, 1564–1616—Criticism and interpretation.
  2. Wonder in literature. I. Title.

PR3069.W65C64 2012
822.3'3—dc23   2011027849

A catalogue record of the book is available from the British Library.

Design by Newgen Imaging Systems (P) Ltd., Chennai, India.

First edition: January 2012

10 9 8 7 6 5 4 3 2 1

Printed in the United States of America.

Debbie, Hailey, and Lauren.

Contents

Acknowledgments ix

Part I Wonder in Shakespeare

Introduction 3

Chapter I.1 Wonder, Amazement, and Surprise: Beginning a Stunning Story 9

Chapter I.2 Resurrections of the Living and the Dead: Natural and Spiritual Bodies and Souls 17

Chapter I.3 "Die to Live": Various Forms of Empathetic Wonder 41

Chapter I.4 The Metaphorical Use of the Prodigious Birth Tradition 53

Chapter I.5 More of a Prodigy than a Prophecy 69

Chapter I.6 Wonder, Awe, and Admiration: Shakespeare's Cabinets of Curiosity 85

Chapter I.7 Transalpine Wonders: Shakespeare's Marvelous Aesthetics 97

Notes 109

Bibliography 117

Part II Six Responses to *Wonder in Shakespeare*

Acknowledgments   125

Introduction   127

Chapter II.1   Embodying Wonder   131
               Maura Tarnoff

Chapter II.2   The Aesthetic Resurrection of the "Death-mark'd"
               Lovers in *Romeo and Juliet*   139
               Janna Segal

Chapter II.3   The "Spectacle of Conversion," Wonder, and
               Film in *The Merchant of Venice*   149
               M. G. Aune

Chapter II.4   God Save the King: *Richard II* in Wonder-land   165
               Rebecca Steinberger

Chapter II.5   A World of (No) Wonder, or No Wonder-wounded
               Hearers Here: Toward a Theory on the Vanishing
               Mediation of "No Wonder" in Shakespeare's Theater   175
               Kristin Keating and Bryan Reynolds

Chapter II.6   Passing for Truth: Wonder Tales and
               their Audiences in *Othello*   195
               Joshua B. Fisher

Bibliography of Works by Adam Max Cohen   215

Contributors   217

Index   219

Acknowledgments

That this book exists at all is wonderful. My book's experience is like a play. Some parts have wonder either in delight or despair, and other parts do not amaze or astonish. Also my book tries to be wondrous in different ways. Shakespeare's books and this book, I hope, can be enjoyable or traumatic to actors and to lovers of language. For years I have been interested in reading accounts of how wonder is displayed in Shakespeare's plays. In this book I show that Shakespeare covers a wide range of emotion both in tragedy and in comedy. He is never limited to only one emotion in his plays. My book was a fascinating product to research. I hope you find your own wondrous responses.

I would like to thank Hailey Cohen, Lauren Cohen, Debbie Cohen, Leslie Cohen, and Dr. Max Cohen. They have been remarkable in the recent era. My mother Leslie helped me to edit my writings, and my father Max has helped to keep me alive and informed each day. As I lost my vision my parents stepped forward and helped me present myself as a scholar. They also helped me write and deliver my work. Thank you to Dr. Heather Henri, Brian Henri, David Henri, Andrew Henri, Robyn Cohen, Mildred Krupsaw, Dr. Stuart Bauer, Lee Bauer, Jay Bauer, and Eric Bauer. Thanks to Dr. Patrick Wen, Dr. Arthur Day, Jennifer Key, Greg Carter, and my students from the University of Massachusetts Dartmouth.

Among my colleagues I would like to thank M. G. Aune, David B. King, Michael Carlozzi, Bruce Boeherer, Dan Vitkus, Bryan Reynolds, Kent Cartwright, Rebecca Steinberger, Joshua Fisher, Katharine Maus, Anupama Arora, Jerry Blitefield, James Bobrick, Christopher Eisenhart, Shari Evans, Stan Harrison, Tracy Harrison, Catherine Houser, Joan Kellerman, Richard J. Larschan, James E. Marlow, Jim Nee, William Nelles, Morgan Peters, Jeannette E. Riley, Edwin J. Thompson, Judy Schaaf, Lulu C. H. Sun, Robert P. Waxler, Patricia White, Diane Brown-Couture, Michael Couture,

George Vafiadis, Carol Murchie, Stephen Fulchino, Barbara Fulchino, Corinne Marlow, Karoline Szatek, Matt Tudor, and Lerman family. In addition I would like to thank the Shakespeare Association of America, the Group for Early Modern Cultural Studies, the University of Massachusetts Dartmouth, and the librarians and staff members at the Folger Shakespeare Library. I especially want to thank Brigitte Shull and Lee Norton at Palgrave Macmillan for helping to bring my near-death experience to a wondrous triumph in my lifetime.

PART I

Wonder in Shakespeare

Introduction

In early November 2008, after I had just received tenure from the University of Massachusetts Dartmouth and was finishing the final draft of my second book entitled *Technology and the Early Modern Self*, something strange began to happen: I lost my ability to read. This was very frustrating. One evening I tried but was unable to read bedtime stories to my two-year-old daughter Lauren, and my four-year-old Hailey had to ask my wife Debbie to read. Prior to the Thanksgiving break I saw my local eye doctor who told me to take it easy. He said I was working too many hours on the final revision of *Technology and the Early Modern Self* and that the headaches and vision loss were the results of working too hard. I tried working less and playing with my girls more often during the evenings, but my daughters love to read so interacting with them meant suffering terrible frustration. For my three Shakespeare classes at UMass Dartmouth I tried enlarging pages of Shakespeare's texts on the computer and using giant printed emails, but these attempts did not work either. The old technologies on which I had relied were ineffective and new ones were unusable. I began to feel a creeping terror and a dizzying sense of dislocation. What kind of Shakespeare scholar can not read? I had become partially blind. How could I learn to read again?

When I went to my eye doctor a second time he recommended a study of my brain using magnetic resonance imaging, an MRI. It was a Wednesday, and I requested an immediate MRI testing so that I would not have to cancel my Thursday classes. The doctor's assistant contacted an MRI clinic forty miles away in Brockton, Massachusetts, where I was told I could be seen that afternoon. I liked the timing because it gave me an hour to eat. I drove to a restaurant and did my best to order but did not get what I really wanted because I could not read the menu. After I ate I asked the servers to help me plan my drive to the MRI clinic. They did their best but the normally forty-five–minute drive took me over an hour and a half because I had to drive slowly, stay in the right lane, and try to monitor the other cars with my impaired vision. The technologies on which I had so often relied—cars, the modern highway, my own sight—had become somewhat unusable and my relationship to roads and cars became dangerous and terrifying.

Somehow I found the MRI center and was relieved to make it safely inside the building. However the technological invasions, dislocations, and redefinitions had only begun. For forty minutes I laid inside an enormous, all-encompassing machine that weirdly whined, bellowed, and hissed as I held my breath. I was terrified regarding what this cyborg-like machine might find within me. After forty minutes the radio, which had been tuned to ESPN, turned off, but the machine continued for more than another half hour. These exams were not supposed to go this long. After an hour and fifteen minutes they took me out of the MRI machine and gave me a package containing copies of its images. Then they left me alone in another room. I opened the package containing the images and learned that I was suffering from a massive brain tumor and was likely about to die.

In an emotional free-fall I heard the phone in the room ring, answered it, and listened as my father Dr. Max Harry Cohen, a cancer surgeon in Bethesda, MD, told me I needed to go immediately by ambulance to Brigham & Women's Hospital in Boston and that the family would fly to Boston early the next morning to meet me there. Dad also said that my father-in-law Dr. Stuart Bauer, a pediatric surgeon at Children's Hospital in Boston, had arranged a meeting for me at the hospital with Dr. Arthur Day, the best brain surgeon in the area. After hanging up I was terribly concerned. I was alone with my horrific news, and I felt everything about me and my life was collapsing, spinning, lost. I worried that I might soon die. I began to cry, not for myself but because I knew that if I did die I would never again see my two young daughters. It would be a terrible loss if I could not see them grow up, go to school, fall in love, and experience other forms of joy. I love my wife Debbie very much, but the possible loss of my two young daughters was my greatest sorrow. Everything that mattered most to my identity, such as my kids, wife, and work, seemed to be going, going, gone.

When I arrived at the hospital my doctor wanted to avoid an invasive surgery because my tumor was growing in a terrible location. It was way too close to the middle of the brain. To try to remove the tumor would damage the brain's areas that enable sight, speech, and comprehension. But as the evening progressed the tumor continued to spread. It was killing me. The doctors decided to try to cut parts of it out since the game was nearly over and I had basically lost. Miraculously the doctors managed to remove my tumor without destroying all the sensitive components of my brain. They saved my life and retained most of my sight. I would only be partially blind, and I might even live a while to see my children grow up a little bit. What a relief it was for my family to see me survive that night!

Unfortunately more darkness was to come. After a few days of recovery from my surgery I began steroid therapy and chemotherapy that flooded my body with biotechnological invaders. These radically altered my relationship with the world. For over forty days I could not sleep at all, was often on edge, ate gigantic meals six–eight times a day, and experienced vivid, terrifying nightmares. At the same time I commenced daily radiation treatments in which I was laid prone on a hard flat slab (like Juliet's) within a grid of lasers and told not to move as a mammoth, rotating, loudly humming mechanical beast whirled above me. The Shakespeare scholar who had sat comfortably at his computer, ably directing it to do as he wished was now at a machine's mercy. Before I had controlled my world. Now my world controlled me. Never had I felt so powerless and scared and less like myself. Unfortunately even worse experiences were yet to come.

I want to emphasize the desperation I felt when my doctors gave me radiation for my brain from December 31, 2008, until February 11, 2009. This treatment made me incapable of reading just as I had been unable to read before. Why did I have to lose my ability to read again? I was supposed to be a reader and a writer, a husband and a father, a doctor of philosophy and a Shakespeare professor! Who was I now? What had this invasive toxic cancer and the technologies thrust upon me to remove it done to me and my relationship with the world? I felt like King Lear in the wilderness, Hamlet after his father's death, Caesar as Brutus plunges in the dagger, and so many other Shakespearean characters. I felt like a man whose relationship with his world had suddenly become unmoored. During both these periods of illiteracy I was continually terrified, furious, and frustrated. What a drag illiteracy was! It made me so upset and terrified that I might never be able to read again. I cried every day in early March when I could not read. I felt terrible despair when I could not read.

Not only did I lose my ability to read, I lost my ability to clearly express myself through speech. After my tumor treatments I could not remember simple terms. No longer the confident scholar, I was now an idiot incapable of using simple words to describe people, places, and things. It is incredibly frustrating being incapable of saying words, and even now as I begin to improve I still struggle to express myself clearly. I often ask people to be patient with me as I try to describe things, but my attempts to speak often do not work. I try to spell words but sometimes that does not work either. I try to draw a spatial image with my fingers to express words, but that often fails too. How can I be a teacher, I wondered, if I can not even explain that I want a sandwich for lunch? The technologies and techniques on which I usually relied were unusable, my standard place in the world lost. Like so many of Shakespeare's characters I had been yanked out of a life in which my place was certain and thrown into a maelstrom, an Arden Wood of the mind and spirit, a Prospero's island where I had no idea who I was or where I belonged.

A brain I had thought under my control was attacked by an internal enemy and temporarily overtaken by it. The tumor's cells were mine, but they were not part of my normally functioning self. My body was seized by a radical insider, a tumor that behaved like an outsider. The tumor took over my brain and my brain could not combat it. I had to defeat and remove the tumor, but the tumor was a part of me. Self-defense required an attack on the self. Inner-outer, self-other, safe-dangerous diversities all fell apart, merged, and fell apart again as my whole sense of an intact self began to disappear.

As happens with so many of Shakespeare's characters, I found within this dizzying series of reversals, redefinitions, assaults, and losses powerful insights that propelled me to a fuller and more direct encounter with Shakespeare. My analysis brought me new insights and methodologies that actually strengthened and enriched my scholarship. Due to biotechnical invasions I was unable to read, speak, live, and define myself as I always had, but after an agonizing period of disorientation I was forced to find new ways of doing work until a new paradigm for myself and the world emerged. Having done so brought me closer to my subject than ever, and substantially improved my work, yielding to me a new perspective.

After my near-death experience in December, which kept me from finishing the term, I fought for the chance to borrow an on-campus theater to show my former students great film versions of Shakespeare's work. My temporary illiteracy forced me and my students to engage only visually with the plays. My "disability" thus became an "ability" because I could experience the plays as Shakespeare probably intended. This literary critique differed from most scholarly approaches. We saw film clips, then talked about them, examined their strengths and weaknesses, and explored how they affected us. Watching Trevor Nunn's 1996 film version of *Twelfth Night*, for example, I found myself unable to rely on a printed text of the comedy or a printed critique of the play by a fellow scholar. This forced me to listen to and watch the DVD editions of the play with extreme intensity. I began to think about how many of the audience members for Shakespeare's plays were in fact illiterates, groundlings, similarly struggling to understand their place in an increasingly confusing technological, mechanical, and textual world. From the ashes of my studies emerged flesh and blood people on stage in Shakespeare's time with whom my disability allowed me to connect. My experience with illiteracy gave me unique insights into how the technology of the printing press changed Shakespeare's plays.

Fortunately my illiteracy has faded slightly in recent weeks. I can catch many words now. In fact I can almost read. I cannot read a scene from a published Shakespeare play from start to finish yet, but I can read the occasional word. I can even read the word "Shakespeare." After losing my ability to read I felt stupid for weeks, but now I am starting to enjoy books again. What a thrill it is today, June 5, 2009, to begin to feel that I may soon be able to read like I used to. Only when stripped of the ability to read does one learn the tremendous importance of experiencing a Shakespeare play in performance. Though my situation has been terribly frustrating and troubling at times it has also taught me fascinating information about some of the ways we experience Shakespeare.

Critical studies of wonder in Shakespeare's plays have been somewhat limited to date in that they have focused either on Shakespeare's tragedies—J. V. Cunningham's *Woe or Wonder* comes to mind here—or on Shakespeare's late romances. Recent examples of this second type are T. G. Bishop's *Shakespeare and the Theatre of Wonder* and Peter G. Platt's *Reason Diminished: Shakespeare and the Marvelous*. Initially considered appropriate only for tragedy and epic, the marvelous came to be considered paramount as an organizing principle in comedy, novella, and other forms of discourse. I believe that a similar type of generic expansion is now possible for Shakespeareans. Shakespeare selected subject matter and literary styles to generate wonder in his tragedies, his history plays, and his comedies. Given the ambivalence of the term "wonder," the centrality of the marvelous in the critical discourse to which several of Shakespeare's sources participated, and the extent to which the wondrous came to be accepted as the proper end of tragedy, epic, comedy, the novella, and even lyric, it is reasonable to consider whether the pursuit of the wondrous served as an overarching aesthetic for Shakespeare as his imagination "bodie[d] forth / The forms of things unknown... Turn[ed] them to shapes, and [gave] to airy nothing / A local habitation and a name."

This book departs from most academic approaches in that it stresses asking questions rather than providing clear answers. There is much more in this book than the things that I think. Where possible I provide many varied options to describe what Shakespeare may do. My approach resembles Shakespeare's work by resisting clear finite forms. Instead Shakespeare and I are trying to generate variety among readers and viewers. Wonder is often scary for scholars. Scholars are usually uncomfortable when they are unsure of the storytelling, but uncertainty is necessary within plays and in Shakespeare's writings. Ambiguity is what we avoid, fear, resist, and fight, but I believe in these things. In fact these types of acceptance are what Shakespeare sometimes relied upon when he wrote a play that he helped to perform. My readers will have to do the same to me too. My near-death experience has encouraged me to think in new ways about Shakespeare's plays. My hope is that this book also helps you to study and think about Shakespeare in novel ways, and perhaps even to imagine what Shakespeare may have been like for readers and viewers both old and new.

CHAPTER I.1

Wonder, Amazement, and Surprise: Beginning a Stunning Story

It seems reasonable to begin a sustained study of wonder in Shakespeare's plays with a close look at Miranda. "Miranda" means "wonderful" or "admirable" in Latin, and she is wonderful both as a subject and as an object. Her instinctive response to the rapidly changing tempest-tossed world around her is wonder, awe, admiration, and astonishment, and she is also a wonder to behold because of her beauty, her array of virtues, and her innocence. This chapter will begin by evaluating the young woman who Ferdinand refers to as "Admired Miranda!" and then it will draw a series of concentric circles around her. The first of these will show that the play she inhabits is a wonderland in many different ways; the second will highlight the centrality of one type of wonder mentioned in *The Tempest* and in a variety of other plays; and ultimately I will suggest that homologies existed between Shakespearean wonder and the wonder traditions—both religious and secular—that influenced his culture.

Miranda is best remembered for her response to the appearance of Alonso, Gonzalo, Antonio, and Sebastian during her chess game with Ferdinand in the final scene of the play: "O brave new world / That has such people in't!" (5.1.186–87).[1] Less attention is paid to her very first words upon seeing the three men: "O wonder! / How many goodly creatures are there here!" (5.1.184–85). Her initial response is an undifferentiated sense of wonder, and then she articulates her delight at seeing these "goodly" creatures. While the men are high-ranking and well-dressed, they are not all morally good, a sign that Miranda is easily deceived by appearances.

The wonder of this scene is bilateral, as the nobles marvel at Ferdinand and Miranda playing chess. They are already in a state of amazement before

Prospero reveals the young lovers because Ariel has cast a spell on them to bring them to Prospero, so they are ripe for additional wonders. When Ariel lifts the spell and Gonzalo awakens, his first words highlight his sense of amazement: "All torment, trouble, wonder, and amazement / Inhabits here. Some heavenly power guide us / Out of this fearful country!" (5.1.106–108). This statement highlights the extent to which wonder could be associated with suffering, pain, and sorrow. After revealing himself to the nobles, Prospero comments on their sense of wonder:

> I perceive these lords
> At this encounter do so much admire [wonder]
> That they devour their reason, and scarce think
> Their eyes do offices of truth. (5.1.155–58)

The word "reason" here suggests not only cognitive function but also speech, indicating that the nobles are mute with wonder, a telltale sign of the response and one persistent complication in its definitive diagnosis.

Before pulling back the curtain of the discovery space, Prospero tells the dazed nobles that what he is about to show them is a wonder:

> Pray you, look in.
> My dukedom since you have given me again,
> I will requite you with as good a thing;
> At least bring forth a wonder to content ye
> As much as me my dukedom. (5.1.169–73)

Alonso is the first of the nobles to speak. He is wary of believing that the figure of his son before him is truly his son—a reasonable skepticism given the many spirits he has seen: "If this prove / A vision of the island, one dear son / Shall I twice lose" (5.1.177–79). Sebastian confirms that what they are witnessing is "A most high miracle" (5.1.180), and a key claim in my study is that Shakespearean theatrical wonder offered an alternative, a substitute, and in some sense even a replacement for the venues of religious wonder that were eliminated under Elizabeth.

Miranda's amazed response upon seeing the noble spectators is indicative of her wide-eyed innocence throughout the play. In her first appearance she laments that the storm she believes her father has created has caused the deaths of the ship's passengers and crew. "Be collected," her father tells her, "No more amazement. Tell your piteous heart / There's no harm done" (1.2.14–16). Here "amazement" is being used as a synonym for Miranda's empathy, her heartfelt concern. As this book will show, the plays often present characters who experience and express wonder as if partly to guide—in Jean Howard's words to "orchestrate"—the audience's response.² Put another way, stage characters such as Miranda who wonder at the events they perceive serve as ambassadors or go-betweens for the playwright and the audience. Since admiration is so important to the affective experience of *The Tempest*, Miranda plays a critical role, guiding audience members toward the affective end that the play pursues.

Upon first seeing Ferdinand, Miranda assumes that he is some sort of divine creature. Her sense of awe indicates the extent to which stage wonder and religious awe were overlapping and in some cases indistinguishable affective states during the period: "I might call him / A thing divine, for nothing natural / I ever saw so noble" (1.2.422–24). Shakespeare's allegedly Protestant audience members might have disapproved of this idolatrous claim and Ferdinand's response "Most sure the goddess / On whom these airs attend," in the same way that they would have questioned the idolatrous references in the accelerated courtship between Romeo and Juliet. The key here is that Miranda's admiration is profound.

After the love between Miranda and Ferdinand has been solemnized in the private wedding ceremony complete with the exchange of vows in 3.1, Prospero describes Miranda and Ferdinand's response to the discovery of one another as "surprise": "So glad of this as they I cannot be, / Who are surprised with all" (3.1.93–94). Surprise is a key facet of wonder, particularly when it entails reversals of fortune toward the end of a play. Prospero's relatively muted response to the match between Miranda and Ferdinand mirrors the muted response that audience members may have upon seeing Miranda and Ferdinand together playing chess toward the end of the play. At this point the audience members are in on the joke, accomplices if you will. The muted sense of wonder experienced by the audience here sharply contrasts the intense wonder orchestrated by a play such as *The Winter's Tale*, where the audience members and the stage characters are equally naïve prior to the final reversal.

As noted earlier Miranda is not only a wonderer, she is also a wonder, a source of amazement and admiration. Ferdinand is so astonished by her beauty that in his first words to her he refers to her as a wonder: "My prime request, / Which I do last pronounce, is—O you wonder— / If you be maid or no?" Instead of answering the question, Miranda takes up his marvelous praise first in order to humbly deflect it: "No wonder, sir, / But certainly a maid" (1.2.432–33). Miranda's response is astonishing to Ferdinand because he did not expect her to speak his language. "My language! Heavens!" he religiously exclaims, simultaneously absorbing her beauty, his pleasure at learning of her unmarried and presumably virginal status (*pace* Caliban), and the fact that she can communicate with him (1.2.433).

Ferdinand does not learn Miranda's name until much later in the play, and when he does Shakespeare insists on having Ferdinand address its importance: "Admired Miranda! / Indeed the top of admiration, worth / What's dearest to the world" (3.1.37–40). It is interesting that he compares her to an earthly treasure because riches were often described as wonders and occasionally even collected for private viewing in spaces referred to as *Schatzkammern*, or treasure cabinets. Ferdinand believes that Miranda is a wonder because she possesses the best qualities of all women. While other virtuous women possess flaws, Miranda is flawless. To borrow a phrase from Othello, she is a "world / Of one entire and perfect chrysolite" (5.2.151–52).

The admiring and admirable Miranda lives in a world where wonders never cease. The play's opening scene is an awe-inspiring tour de force of special effects with thunder, lightning, and a ship heaving on the high seas. When Lewis Carroll, the author of *Alice's Adventures in Wonderland*, saw a production of the play on July 3, 1857, he marveled at the technical accomplishment of the opening scene, claiming that the stage shipwreck vividly brought to mind actual shipwrecks he had witnessed:

> The scenic effects in *The Tempest* certainly surpass anything I ever saw there [at that theater] or elsewhere. The most marvellous was the shipwreck in the first scene, where, (to all appearance), a real ship is heaving about on huge waves, and is finally wrecked under a cliff that reaches up to the roof. The machinery that works this must be something wonderful: the scene quite brought back to my mind the storm I saw at Whitby last year, and the vessels plunging through the harbourmouth.[3]

While Shakespeare's company may have been incapable of achieving the same level of verisimilitude in the "direful spectacle of the wreck" (1.2.26) in the second decade of the seventeenth century, Ariel's description of the tempest he creates at Prospero's behest is filled with impressive pyrotechnics:

> Now on the beak [prow]
> Now in the waste, the deck, in every cabin,
> I flamed amazement. Sometime I'd divide,
> And burn in many places; on the top-mast,
> The yards, and bowsprit, would I flame distinctly;
> Then meet and join. Jove's lightning, the precursors
> O'th' dreadful thunderclaps, more momentary
> And sight-outrunning were not. (1.2.197–204)

Editors agree that Ariel is describing the mysterious and terrifying effect of St. Elmo's fire, a type of electroluminescent coronal discharge that emanates from shipmasts, steeples, airplane wings, and other projecting structures during electrical storms. The religious connotations of these apparently supernatural pyrotechnics are clear both in their association with St. Elmo, the patron saint of sailors, and in the Portuguese word often used to describe them—*corposant* or *corpusant*, which means "holy body."

These otherworldly pyrotechnics have the intended effect on the ship's passengers, terrifying them so that they leap from the boat to their expected deaths:

> Not a soul
> But felt a fever of the mad, and played
> Some tricks of desperation. All but mariners
> Plunged in the foaming brine and quit the vessel,
> Then all afire with me. The King's son Ferdinand,
> With hair upstaring—then like reeds, not hair—
> Was the first man that leaped; cried "Hell is empty,
> And all the devils are here." (1.2.209–16)

The "amazement" that Ariel generated by transforming his airy self into fire was a form of terror so profound that it led the passengers to attempt suicide.

Spectacular effects also generate wonder or amazement in the disappearing banquet scene and the wedding masque, which immediately follows it. The appearance and disappearance of the banquet in act 3, scene 3, merit a close reading because they present a purposefully wondrous spectacle, and succeed in generating a range of wondrous reactions including awe, amazement, and distraction, which borders on madness. The characters enter literally amazed, having wandered through a variety of paths to reach their present destination. "My old bones ache," Gonzalo complains, "Here's a maze trod indeed / Through forthrights and meanders" (3.3.2–3). Gonzalo is speaking of literal paths, both direct and indirect, that the nobles have taken, but the statement also serves to describe the narrative structure of *The Tempest*, which is filled with "meanders" such as Prospero's tormenting of Ferdinand and, in this scene, the initial appearance of a sumptuous banquet, which is magically retracted.

Antonio and Sebastian actively plot the murder of Alonso and Gonzalo in the first few lines of this scene, and the conspiracy is marvelous because it involves an unnatural fratricide. At the play's end Prospero reminds Antonio that in usurping his own brother's dukedom he has behaved in a way that is "unnatural" (5.1.79). Intrafamiliar conspiracies such as these intensify the wonder of many of Shakespeare's plays ranging from *Hamlet* to *Lear* to *As You Like It*. The plotting of Sebastian and Antonio is interrupted by music that is described as "Solemn and strange," and music is used throughout this play and many others to intensify wonder. Gonzalo confirms the wondrous nature of the music in this scene when he describes it as "Marvellous sweet music."

It is fitting that Caliban is a sort of connoisseur of the island's marvelous music because he is one of the most prominent wonders within the play. The spirits in "several strange shapes" who bring in the table and dance around it in act 3, scene 3, cause Sebastian, Antonio, and Gonzalo to contemplate the marvels depicted in travel writing, a genre that often included various sorts of monsters, rarities, and prodigies. The play resembles a wondrous travel narrative most closely in its presentation of Caliban, who is explicitly depicted as a marketable wonder by Stefano and Trinculo.

The spirits' appearance with the banquet table and their ensuing dance lead Sebastian to accept the veracity of mythical travel accounts such as the existence of unicorns, and the death and rebirth of the phoenix, while Gonzalo takes this apparition to mean that there really are mountain men with pouches of flesh hanging from their necks and others with heads that do not protrude above their shoulders. Gonzalo's comment that the people of the island may be of "monstrous shape," but "Their manners are more gentle-kind than of / Our human generation you shall find / Many, nay, almost any" indicates the type of utopian view of the savage found in Montaigne's "On Cannibals," itself glossed by Gonzalo earlier in the play.

"I cannot too much muse," Alonso says after seeing the spirits that present the banquet. He claims he has reached the limit of his capacity for wonder. Then as he approaches the banquet table to partake of the food Ariel orchestrates more stunning special effects, which push him over the edge toward insanity. Ariel creates thunder and lightning, descends from above in the guise of a mythological creature with a vulture's wings and a woman's face, and as he claps his wings together he makes the banquet magically disappear. He claims that his goal in duping the nobles this way is to drive them to a suicidal form of madness—"I have made you mad, / And even with suchlike valour men hang and drown / Their proper selves" (3.3.58–60). This madness—a near relative of the suicidal madness that led the men to jump from the boat in the opening scene—is primarily the result of the tension between what one believes to be true and what one sees with one's own eyes.

Prospero asserts that he has amazed the nobles to the point of distraction in order to gain power over them:

My high charms work,
And these mine enemies are all knit up
In their distractions. They now are in my power;
And in these fits I leave them. (3.3.88–90)

For Prospero the presentation of this particular wonder was a power play engineered to conquer the minds of his enemies, to transport them into fits of "ecstasy" (3.3.108). Power and wonder usually exist in inverse proportion to one another. Because wonder is deeply intertwined with awe and admiration, it is traditionally the response that an inferior feels toward a superior, whether that superior is a worldly ruler or a divine being. Thus one of the routine mechanisms that Shakespeare uses to generate wonder is the portrayal of kings and queens.[4]

Prospero's production of the wedding masque for Ferdinand and Miranda in act 4, scene 1, is another power play, but it is a power play of a very different nature. Prospero claims that he is obligated to produce the masque, that he must "bestow upon the eyes of this young couple / Some vanity of mine art" because "It is my promise, / And they expect it from me" (4.1.40–42). Given Prospero's insistence on ruling Ferdinand—especially where Ferdinand's libidinal impulses are concerned—the masque does not appear to be a filial obligation. It seems to be more of an agrarian tour de force, a reminder of Prospero's immense power. Indeed one can hardly imagine a more domineering and intimidating future father-in-law.

Ferdinand's response to the masque indicates its wondrousness. At its conclusion Ferdinand asks if the goddesses who performed in it were spirits, and Prospero affirms that they are spirits subject to his command. He says that he has "called" them to "enact / My present fancies" (4.1.121–22). Ferdinand registers Prospero's immense power by acknowledging that he is endowed with the capacity to generate wonders: "So rare a wondered father and a wise / Makes this place paradise" (4.1.124–25).[5] It hardly seemed a paradise when he was lugging logs around, but he is absolutely correct that Prospero is, like Shakespeare himself, a "wondered father," a creator capable of generating all sorts of divine wonders. The following chapter will discuss Prospero's most remarkable wonders, the raising of the dead, a wonder that has received relatively little attention because it is reported at a key moment in the play but never shown.

Some of Prospero's most remarkable wonders, like some of the most astonishing elements of Shakespearean drama, are literally obscene. They are reported but never presented on stage. Prospero provides an astonishing litany of marvelous acts in the same speech in which he promises to abjure his rough magic. Addressing the spirits who have aided him in his magical manipulations of the elements around him, he claims he has

> bedimmed
> The noontide sun, called forth the mutinous winds,
> And 'twixt the green sea and the azured vault
> Set roaring war—to the dread rattling thunder
> Have I given fire, and rifted Jove's stout oak
> With his own bolt; the strong-based promontory
> Have I made shake, and by the spurs plucked up
> The pine and cedar; graves at my command
> Have waked their sleepers, oped, and let 'em forth
> By my so potent art. (5.1.41–50)

The first few miracles listed here are familiar to us because we witness them in the opening scene. Given his ability to control the elements, Prospero's claim that he has caused earthquakes and plucked up trees is not surprising either. But the final wonder listed here—the raising of the dead, resurrection—is of a different order from the rest. In the Christian context in which Shakespeare wrote, the raising of the dead has special significance.

CHAPTER I.2

Resurrections of the Living and the Dead: Natural and Spiritual Bodies and Souls

Is Prospero a hazy approximation of a Christ figure? Scholars have debated this question vigorously, without coming to a definitive conclusion. Prospero certainly behaves in a deeply Christian way at the end of the play when he opts to forgive those who have wronged him. The key statement he makes when he decides to forgive his oppressors and conspirators links the rhetoric of wonder to that of Christian forgiveness: "The rarer action is / In virtue than in vengeance" (5.1.27–28). Prospero's turn toward forgiveness at the end of the play when all of his enemies are in his power is "rare" on several fronts. Prospero shows considerable vindictiveness throughout the play, so it comes as something of a surprise given his prior behavior; it is unusual in human interactions to forgive those who wrong us; it is a surprise to those familiar with Shakespeare's fondness for the revenge tragedy tradition; and it is generically unnecessary within the comic tradition since villains are punished even in comedies such as *The Merchant of Venice* and *Twelfth Night.* Here the usurping brother and his diabolical conspirator both avoid retribution, and this represents a wondrous and rare reversal at the end of the play.

Prospero's claim that he has raised the dead from their graves is extraordinary within Shakespeare's corpus—a body of texts that included some eighteen plays miraculously resurrected and preserved for us by John Heminge and Henry Condell. The standard theme that we see throughout Shakespeare's plays is what I will refer to as pseudoresurrection, by which I mean either the raising of those thought to be dead but not actually dead, or the apparent raising—in the form of a ghost, for instance—of the actual dead. Influenced by the genre in which the events take place, the topos of pseudoresurrection is central and ubiquitous throughout the plays. Why is Shakespeare so interested in this particular effect? Indeed why do so many of his plays pivot on a pseudoresurrection of one kind or another? As several scholars have noted, Shakespeare's attraction to the idea of resurrection indicates his awareness of one of the central miracles of the Christian faith—Christ's own resurrection, celebrated each year at Easter. In addition, I will suggest here that these roundabout reckonings with resurrection indicate an important form of continuity between his plays and the medieval dramatic tradition, particularly the *Resurrection of the Lord* plays that featured prominently in mystery or miracle cycles and survived in later Protestant renditions created in the mid-sixteenth century.

Shakespeare could not have written a true *Resurrection of the Lord* play because religious subject matter was forbidden to him. Barred from tackling this central Christian wonder head on, he opted to come at it obliquely, indirectly. I agree with Beatrice Groves', claim that "censorship, through outlawing openly Christian drama, unintentionally promoted a subtle and sophisticated engagement with biblical language and Christian ideas in ostensibly secular plays."[1] While the narratives Shakespeare created do not dramatize actual resurrection, the characters on the stage perceive them as actual resurrections. They feel and articulate wonder in response to the resurrections they think that they see, and Shakespeare uses the wonder of his stage characters to generate sympathetic or empathic wonder from his audience members.

Resurrection was a unique wonder within the Christian worldview because it was transhistorical, the alpha of Christ's miraculous personal sacrifice and the omega of the end of days. While the official Protestant position was that wonders ceased after the time of the early church fathers, the raising of the dead was both a cornerstone of the establishment of the faith and its final endpoint at the Last Judgment. Resurrection was also unique during the early modern period because unlike the vast majority of scripturally recorded miracles, it was a wonder in which every faithful and righteous Christian expected to participate. This shared participation is clear in the following passage from Isaiah: "Thy dead men shall live, together with my dead body shall they arise. Awake and sing, ye that dwell in dust... earth shall cast out the dead" (Isaiah 26:19).[2] Similarly, in 1 Corinthians 6:14 Paul says, "And God hath both raised up the Lord, and will also raise up us by his own power."

One of the most powerful articulations of the faithful Christian's coordination with Christ occurs in John 11 in the moments before Christ raises

Lazarus from the dead. Jesus tells Lazarus's sister Martha "Thy brother shall rise again"; she answers, "I know that he shall rise again in the resurrection at the last day"; and Jesus responds "I am the resurrection, and the life: he that believeth in me, though he were dead, yet shall he live: And whosoever liveth and believeth in me shall never die" (John 11:23–26). This passage transcends mere analogy between the risen Christian and the risen Christ; it suggests that to believe in Christ is to guarantee one's own resurrection.

In his *City of God* Augustine linked wonder and resurrection when he described the doctrine of Christ's resurrection as one of the "three incredibles": "It is incredible that Christ should rise again in the flesh, and carry it up to heaven with Him. It is incredible that the world should believe this: and it is incredible that this belief should be effected by a small sort of poor, simple, unlearned men."[3] How were the underdog disciples able to promulgate this remarkable doctrine? According to Augustine, they did so by performing more wonders: "their proofs and persuasions lay not in words, but wonders: and such as had not seen Christ risen again, and ascending, believed their affirmations thereof, because they confirmed them with miracles."[4] Here a certain circularity enters into Augustine's assessment of the establishment of the Christian faith as he acknowledges that one of the key wonders that these disciples performed was the raising of the dead!

> They cured a man that had been forty years lame, even from his mother's breasts, only by the very name of Jesus Christ. Their handkerchiefs helped diseases; the sick persons got themselves laid in the way where they should pass, that they might have help from their very shadows, and amongst all these miracles done by the name of Christ, they raised some from the dead.[5]

Through the performance of miraculous resurrections the early church fathers were able to establish the veracity of the initial resurrection. In Christianity resurrections are diachronic, leading backward to Christ's own fate even as they show the way forward to eternal bliss for the faithful.

In a defense of the doctrine of corporal resurrection, as opposed to the resurrection of the spirit, Samuel Gardiner, a divine who was a contemporary of Shakespeare and is known today mostly for his writings on angling, delivered a sermon on June 9, 1605, in which he asserted that the doctrine of resurrection was the very lynchpin of the Christian faith. He refers to the doctrine as "the hand that holdeth vp religion by the head: the life and soule of it, the first stone that we are to lay in our spiritual building, or rather the foundation that beareth vp the building, the anker [anchor] of our hope, the certaintie of our saluation" (sig. A4r).⁶ To abandon the doctrine would be to

> take away altogeather, our preaching, your beleeuing, burne the Bible, throw downe pulpits, lay our churches euen with their foundations, play the Epicures & belli-gods, and liue as ye list. For the Bookes are found lyars, the Prophets & Apostles haue fed vs with fables, & they are as Fountains dryed vp. (Sigs. A4r–A4v)

While there was little debate during the early modern period that Christians would be raised from the dead at the time of the Apocalypse, there is a very long tradition of controversy regarding the precise nature of this resurrection, and the key terms in this debate are echoed in Shakespeare's plays. This chapter will show that the same types of questions about the miracle of resurrection raised in the Christian foundation texts, commentaries on the scriptures, and elsewhere inform Shakespeare's plays. I will not suggest that Shakespeare's plays are simply holding up mirrors to long-standing debates about resurrection. Instead I believe that they foreground pseudoresurrection in order to generate a unique and powerful type of wonder.

In Gardiner's 1605 sermon defending the doctrine of corporal resurrection against those who suggested that the Last Judgment would usher in only a spiritual resurrection of the faithful, the authority in which Gardiner places most of his faith is Paul, and the text by Paul that is central to his argument is 1 Corinthians 15. Gardiner glosses Paul's defense of resurrection when he writes at the outset of his sermon

> Our Christian expectation is the corporall resurrection, which is grounded on the Doctrine of Saint Paul, who bringeth in bundles of reasons for it by order of iust consequence thus: If there were no resurrection. 1. Then were our preaching vaine. 2. Your faith of none effect. 3. Wee should be found false witnesses. 4. The dead were quite vndone. 5. We were yet in our sinnes. 6. Of all men, Christians were most miserable. (sig. A4r)

This list of proofs is drawn directly from 1 Corinthians 15:12–19, which reads as follows:

Now if Christ be preached that he rose from the dead, how say some among you that there is no resurrection of the dead? But if there be no resurrection of the dead, then is Christ not risen: And if Christ be not risen, then is our preaching vain, and your faith is also vain. Yea, and we are found false witnesses of God; because we have testified of God that he raised up Christ: whom he raised not up, if so be that the dead rise not. For if the dead rise not, then is not Christ raised: And if Christ be not raised, your faith is vain; ye are yet in your sins. Then they also which are fallen asleep in Christ are perished. If in this life only we have hope in Christ, we are of all men most miserable.

There is an important misrepresentation in Gardiner's argument, however. Paul affirms the doctrine of resurrection, but he does not distinguish in these verses between physical and spiritual resurrection. In Paul's complete analysis of the doctrine in 1 Corinthians 15 he clearly indicates that resurrection will entail an important metamorphosis. The risen body will not be the same as the body that walked the earth. In particular, the risen body, which inherits the kingdom of heaven, will be a spiritual body. In verse 35 Paul raises the central question: "But some man will say, How are the dead raised up? and with what body will they come?" Employing an agricultural metaphor, he answers his own question: "It is sown a natural body, it is raised a spiritual body. There is a natural body, and there is a spiritual body" (1 Cor 15: 44). Paul clarifies his position further at the very end of the chapter in a passage that seems to indicate an indebtedness to Ovid's *Metamorphoses*, one of Shakespeare's favorite texts:

> Now this I say, brethren, that flesh and blood cannot inherit the kingdom of God; neither doth corruption inherit incorruption. Behold I shew you a mystery; We shall not all sleep, but we shall all be changed, In a moment, in the twinkling of an eye, at the last trump: for the trumpet shall sound, and the dead shall be raised incorruptible, and we shall be changed. For this corruptible must put on incorruption, and this mortal must put on immortality. So when this corruptible shall have put on incorruption, and this mortal shall have put on immortality, then shall be brought to pass the saying that is written, Death is swallowed up in victory. (1 Cor 15: 50–54)

This emphasis on spiritual inheritance directly contradicts Gardiner's argument in his sermon.

Paul's statement that "flesh and blood cannot inherit the kingdom of God" proved a major obstacle to theologians who wished to argue for bodily resurrection. Augustine devoted a considerable amount of time and effort to reconciling Paul's discourse with the orthodox position, and the result was an impressive routine of mental gymnastics that Augustine performed in a range of texts including *Faith and the Creed* and *Enchiridion*.

Augustine argues that the word "flesh" in Paul's statement does not preclude the resurrection of the body because *flesh* and the *body* are distinct entities. In *Faith and the Creed* he writes,

> All flesh is corporeal, but every body is not flesh. Among terrestrial things wood is a corporeal thing but is not flesh, while the body of man and beast is also flesh. Among celestial things there is no flesh, but simple and shining bodies, which the apostle calls spiritual; but some call them ethereal. So he [Paul] does not deny the resurrection of the flesh when he says: "Flesh and blood shall not possess the kingdom of God," but declares what flesh and blood are to become.[7]

He reiterates this argument in *Enchiridion* where he writes,

> as far as the corruption which weighs down the soul and the vices through which "the flesh lusts against the spirit" are concerned, there will be no "flesh," but only body [in the heavenly kingdom], since there are bodies that are called "heavenly bodies." This is why it is said, "Flesh and blood shall not inherit the Kingdom of God," and then, as if to expound what was said, it adds, "Neither shall corruption inherit incorruption." What the writer first called "flesh and blood" he later called "corruption," and what he first called "The Kingdom of God" he then later called "incorruption."[8]

Other Christian theologians came to the defense of bodily resurrection using different tactics. As early as the second century Athenagoras, a Platonist who had embraced Christianity, authored a defense that would have been available to Shakespeare and his audience members because it was translated into English by Richard Porder and published in 1573 as *Athenagoras, The most notable and excellent discourse of the Christian philosopher Athenagoras, as touching the resurrection of the dead, translated out of Greeke into Latine by Peter Nannius, and out of Latin into English by R. Porder. A treatise, very necessarie and profitable for this our laste ruinous age of the vvorlde, in the vvhiche are such svvarmes of atheistes and epicures, vvhose pestilent infection is more to be feared then papistrie. Therefore vvorthy the consideracion of al men, as vvel for ouerthrovv of their pernicious errours, as staying the faith and conscience of the vveake and vnlearned*. While Gardiner relied on scriptural authorities, Athenagoras utilized reason and logic to make his case. He began by asserting that those who challenged the doctrine did so because they believed that God lacked either the capability or the will to raise the dead. He took up the major objections to the doctrine one by one, confuting each, and presented his arguments in favor of the doctrine. His central argument, first presented in chapters 14 and 15, was the so-called argument from the nature of man, which stated that "Man is soul and body. Soul alone, or body alone, is incomplete."[9] He claimed that the body was the soul's partner in both good and bad acts, so the soul and the body must be either rewarded or punished together at the Last Judgment. This type of argument based on the natural integration of body and soul proved to be an enduring one, and it was embraced by Aquinas, among others:

> Everything craves what belongs to its nature, and therefore desires its parts to be reunited. Since the human soul is united by nature to the body there is within it a natural appetite for that union. The will could find no perfect rest until the soul and body are joined again. This is the resurrection of man from the dead.[10]

Elsewhere Aquinas insisted that the resurrection of the body followed logically from the a priori assumptions that the soul was immortal and that the soul and the body were linked: "Nothing unnatural can be perpetual, and therefore the soul will not be without the body for ever. Since the soul is immortal the body should be joined to it again. This is to rise again. The immortality of the soul, then, would seem to demand the future resurrection of the body."[11]

This notion of the inherent integration between the body and the soul at the time of resurrection reappeared in the *Thomas of India* play performed as part of the Towneley cycle. Responding to speculation that his own resurrection was merely a spiritual or ghostly rising from the grave, Christ claims that his personal integrity will be an example of the integrity of the faithful Christian at the end of days: "My saull [soul] and my cors [corpse] haue knytt / a knott that last shall ay; Thus shall I rase, well thou wytt / ilk [each] man on domesday" (342–44).[12] In a culture that came to rely on the production of raw materials for textiles the image that the soul and the body were knit together was a compelling one. In the York cycle play *The Last Judgement* this same notion is emphasized at play's end. The second angel notes that the dead must bring their body *and* their soul with them to judgment:

> Ilka [each] creature, both old and young,
> Belive I bid you that ye rise;
> Body and soul with you ye bring,
> And come before the high justice. (89–92)[13]

This leads the First Good Soul to reiterate the linkage between body and soul:

Lofed [loved] be thou, Lord, that is so sheen [radiant],
That on this manner made us to rise,
Body and soul together, clean,
To come before the high justice. (97–100)

It was only fitting that the mystery cycles emphasized the corporality of the resurrection because the cycles were initially conceived as celebrations of the Eucharist, the mysterious metamorphosis of the wafer and the wine into the actual body and blood of Jesus Christ. Just as orthodox Christians believed that the Eucharist was the magical metamorphosis of the wafer and the wine into the corpus of Christ, defenders of corporal resurrection insisted that the faithful Christian's body would be resurrected together with his or her spirit at the end of days.

Athenagoras employed one analogy that would prove critical to Shakespeare in his characters' discussions of death and rebirth. Borrowing from biblical rhetoric linking death to sleep, he argued that just as the body and the soul seemed to be severed from one another during sleep, the soul was temporarily separated from the body during death, only to be reunited with it during the resurrection.[14] Many Christians extended this metaphor into the animal kingdom, noting that if bears and other animals could hibernate for the winter before reviving, then human bodies could hibernate during death only to reawaken at the second coming.

Shakespeare's characters routinely state that when an individual dies the soul is divorced from the body, and they suggest that the process is painful. As Cleopatra's fortunes take a turn for the worse and Cleopatra decides to hide in her funeral monument to escape Antony's fury and solicit pity from him, Charmian compares the pain suffered when one's reputation is lost to the pain suffered at death when the soul departs the body: "The soul and body rive not more in parting / Than greatness going off" (4.14.5–6).[15] It is not entirely clear here whether Charmian is talking about Antony's greatness or Cleopatra's greatness. She may be referring to both. In the late eighteenth century Malone usefully compared this statement by Charmian to the following line in *Henry VIII* in which Anne Boleyn laments the indignities suffered by Queen Katherine:

O, God's will! Much better
She ne'er had known pomp; though't be temporal,
Yet if that quarrel [quarreller], fortune, do divorce

It from the bearer, 'tis a sufferance panging [as painful]
As soul and bodies severing. (2.3.12–16)

The description of the separation between the soul and the body as a "divorce," which involves pain or "panging," may be an echo of an earlier passage delivered in a lighter context in *Twelfth Night*—though Viola/Cesario and Sir Andrew believe it is deadly serious. To further terrify Viola/Cesario prior to her enforced duel with Sir Andrew, Sir Toby brags of Sir Andrew: "Souls and bodies hath he divorced three, and his incensement at this moment is so implacable that satisfaction can be none but by pangs of death and sepulchre" (3.4.210–13). The "pangs of death" was an idiomatic expression, but the comparison of death to divorce seems a more artful and potentially more intriguing description, in part because divorce was so uncommon during the period and in part because it suggests a permanent rather than a temporary separation between the soul and the body.

The concept of metamorphosis was a guiding principle in Shakespeare's literary development, in large part because of his fondness for Ovid, so he would have appreciated the fact that Athenagoras compared resurrection to metamorphosis. Athenagoras argued that the metamorphosis required for resurrection was no more wondrous than the routine metamorphoses involved in the human life cycle. If a normal human being could change from seminal fluid (he neglects to mention the ovum) to a fetus to a baby to a child to an adult to an elderly person, it was entirely possible that a dead body could evolve or mature into a resurrected body.[16] In this same vein he argued that resurrection was no less wonderful than the initial generation and development of a human being. Indeed if God could create the universe and all the creatures in it, He could certainly also raise the dead at the appointed time.[17] Athenagoras's treatise amounts to a logical proof of the doctrine of corporal resurrection. Given his classical importance as the first director of the library at Alexandria, his philosophical roots as a Platonist, and the alleged importance of his texts in inspiring early Christian martyrs, he was a particularly appealing figure to metaphysicians such as Augustine and Aquinas, and his influence, through these figures and others, was significant during the English Renaissance.

Debates regarding the nature of Christ's resurrection and the resurrection of the faithful persisted throughout the medieval period in England, despite consistent efforts to highlight orthodox resurrection doctrine in church liturgical drama and other religious practices. Many scholars believe that the postclassical revival of drama in the West grew out of the liturgical dramas that coincided with Easter Sunday. The so-called *Visitatio Sepulchri* was a Latin dialogue sung between clerics representing the angel and the three

Marys at the empty tomb, and this dialogue was later incorporated into the York mystery cycle play depicting the resurrection. Special Easter anthems such as "Christus resurgens" were also integrated into the cycle plays.

The cycle plays themselves consistently emphasized the wonder of Christ's resurrection and the wonders of the resurrection of the Christian faithful to come. When Reformers suppressed the cycle plays due to their basis in the celebration of the Eucharist and their importance to Catholic ritual more generally, Protestant dramatists stepped in to craft Resurrection plays that also emphasized the wonder of Christ's resurrection. In one such play, thought to be written by Bishop Bale between 1530 and 1560, the soldiers commissioned to guard Christ's sepulcher are wonderstruck when an angel descends and Christ rises from the tomb. The stage direction indicates that productions of these plays could also become wondrous spectacles in their own right:

> here they fall
> downe as
> deade in
> hearing the
> gonnes shott
> of[f] & thunder
> Iesus riseth
> throwynge of[f] Death.[18]

The stage direction, which precedes the first soldier's response to these wonders, and the response itself indicates that he is amazed: "The .j. Souldier after his astonishment What a wonder, we shoulde be striken with such feare and dreade / that we could not stande, but fell downe like as deade." The second soldier is no less astonished as he described the angel who "like lightnynge" came down "With clothes as white, as ever was the snowe" (243–49).

The Protestant *Resurrection of Our Lord* play is an important link in the chain between the medieval mystery plays and Shakespeare's pseudoresurrection dramas. It indicates the persistence of earlier traditions, and it also shows that creative reappropriation was possible. Another important post-Reformation dramatization of the resurrection story was Nicholas Grimald's *Christus Redivivus*, first performed at Brasenose College, Oxford, and printed in Cologne in 1543. Unlike the mystery cycles and the Protestant *Resurrection of Our Lord* play, this play was written in Latin and targeted toward an educated audience. Grimald's play is very Shakespearean in its mingling of tragic and comic elements. It combines a Senecan treatment of the resurrection story with a comic underplot in which the four Roman soldiers are skewered as versions of the braggart soldier.

Because Grimald's play was in Latin and intended for the elite it was exempt from Elizabeth's proclamation of May 16, 1559—reputedly written by the queen herself—prohibiting religious plays in large public theaters. The proclamation, which precluded Shakespeare from engaging with scriptural material directly on the public stage, prohibited those plays "Wherein either matters of religion or of the governance of the estate of the commonweale shall be handled or treated, being no meet matters to be written or treated upon, but by men of authority, learning and wisdom, nor to be handled before any audience, but of grave and discreet persons."[19] It is interesting that Elizabeth permitted elite Latin biblical drama, in part because its authors and spectators were some of the same people whose dissident religious beliefs threatened the security of her throne. After a series of scripturally inspired dramas during the first half of her reign, Elizabeth tightened the restrictions against biblical subjects even further in 1589 when her Privy Council created a Censorship Commission to "stryke oute or reforme suche partes and matters as they shall fynd unfytt and undecent to be handled in playes, both for Divinitie and State."[20] Under James the Act to restrain the Abuses of Players made it illegal in "any Stage play, Interlude, Shewe, Maygame, or Pageant" to "jestingly or prophanely speake or use the holy Name of God or of Christ Jesus, or of the Holy Ghoste or of the Trinitie."[21]

There are important differences between the mystery cycle plays and the Protestant plays about the resurrection. For instance, there are no long discourses on the corporality of the Eucharist in Bale's play because that particular doctrine was anathema to reformed church doctrine. Still the thrust of Bale's play is the same. Indeed in many places the Protestant *Resurrection of Our Lord* play follows the dialogue presented in the York and Towneley cycle plays of *The Resurrection of the Lord*, *The Pilgrims*, *Thomas of India*, and *The Last Judgement* verbatim. This Protestant transformation of a Catholic drama is remarkable in part because the feast of the Corpus Christi for which the mystery plays were written was considered a pagan heresy. In much the same way that Protestants such as Bale transformed Catholic cycle dramas, Shakespeare re-presented Resurrection dramas without presenting actual resurrections. He turned to pseudoresurrections because they spoke to the aesthetic tastes of his audiences, they offered a close approximation of the affective and cognitive pleasure of wonder plays, and they were acceptable to the Elizabethan and Jacobean censors.

In the final analysis the ultimate fate of the body and the soul at the end of days was a question of faith. The relationship between faith and resurrection doctrine is clear in the pseudoresurrection of Hermione in *The Winter's Tale*.

Before Paulina cues Hermione's statue to come to life in the final scene of the play she tells the assembly that they must either leave—which they are physically unable to do as they can hardly look away from the wonderfully verisimilar sculpture—or prepare themselves for "more amazement" (5.3.87). The complicity of the stage audience is critical here, as is the complicity of the theater audience, and Paulina's directions seem intended for both audiences. Paulina claims that she will make the statue "move indeed, descend, / And take your hand," only "If you can behold it" (5.3.87–89). She emphasizes this complicity again in the last moment before she brings the statue to life: "It is required / You do awake your faith" (5.3.94–95).

If there were any doubt that Paulina is attempting to generate wonder by bringing Hermione's statue to life it is dispelled when she tells the statue to move, instructing it: "'Tis time. Descend. Be stone no more. Approach. / Strike all that look upon with marvel" (5.3.99–100). Paulina invokes Christian rhetoric when she describes the statue's motion as a resurrection that defeats or cheats death:

> Come,
> I'll fill your grave up. Stir. Nay, come away.
> Bequeath to death your numbness, for from him
> Dear life redeems you. (5.3.100–103)

This description of the conquest of death echoes Paul's claim in 1 Corinthians 15 that at the Last Judgment "the saying that is written" will come to pass: "Death is swallowed up in victory. O death, where is thy sting? O grave, where is thy victory?" (54–55). Indeed it may be more than just a coincidence that Paulina's name is a feminized version of Paul, the apostle who offers the most extensive defense of the doctrine of the resurrection in 1 Corinthians 15. Paul even performs a pseudoresurrection when he brings a man named Eutichus back from apparent death in the abbreviated tragicomedy presented in Acts 20:7–12.

The uncomfortably close connection between magic and miracle working—emphasized in the court of the Pharaoh in Genesis, for example—survived in medieval England and in the early modern suspicion that natural philosophy was a close relative of diabolical magic. Paulina is aware throughout the final scene of the play that she is liable to be accused of sorcery. When she tells Leontes that she can make the statue move she worries that she will be thought a witch:

> If you can behold it,
> I'll make the statue move indeed, descend,

And take you by the hand. But then you'll think—
Which I protest against—I am assisted
By wicked powers. (5.3.87–91)

Paulina's concern is well-founded in part because Leontes has already asserted that the statue of Hermione is a magical marvel, which is capable of conjuring memories of the evil Leontes has committed and generating stupefied wonder in Perdita (5.3.39–42). In Paulina's insistence that her wonders are not the product of witchcraft she echoes Joan of Arc's self-defense in Shakespeare's *1 Henry VI* in the moments before she is executed. Joan asserts that she was "chosen from above" to "work exceeding miracles on earth," and she defies those who "judge it straight a thing impossible / To compass wonders but by help of devils" (5.6.39–48).

Paulina reiterates her concern that she might be thought a witch just as Hermione appears to come back to life. She assures the assembly "Her actions shall be holy as / You hear my spell is lawful" (5.3.104–105). Here Paulina is trying to insulate herself from accusations of diabolism and she is trying to insist that Hermione herself is not a demon but a *true* Christian both in terms of her actions and in terms of her physical being.

Paulina's anxiety regarding accusations of diabolism are understandable because associations between resurrection and diabolism were long-standing. In the *Resurrection of the Lord* play performed as part of the Towneley Mystery Cycle, the Centurion insists that the mass raising of the dead, which occurred after Christ's crucifixion, was a sign that Christ was the son of God. Caiaphas challenges this interpretation, arguing "if that dede men ryse vp bodely, / That may be done thrugh socery" (ll. 128–29). In the *Resurrection* play performed as part of the York cycle Christ himself is described as a "warlock" partly because of his ability to raise himself from the dead. Lamenting that Christ has managed to escape from his sepulcher, the First Soldier wonders, "Alas, what shall we do this day, / That thus this warlock is went his way?" (305–306).[22] In calling the risen Christ a "warlock" the First Soldier is also probably alluding to the miracles, including the raising of the dead, that Christ performed before his own crucifixion.

The apparent resurrection of Hermione is a stunning and awe-inspiring piece of stage business because Paulina is the only one aware of the deception. Unlike *Much Ado* or *Measure for Measure*, where the audience members know that the miraculous reappearances of apparently dead characters are in fact merely masks removed, *The Winter's Tale* builds to a climax in which the audience members are placed on the same blissfully ignorant footing as the wonder-struck Leontes, Polixenes, Florizel, Camillo, and Perdita.

Paulina's resurrection of Hermione is a profoundly Christian one. When Paulina says to the statue, "Come, / I'll fill your grave up" (5.3.100–101) she seems to literally mean that she will replace the empty space created by the removal of the casket with dirt, but there is also a hint here—partly because Paulina mentions her own demise in her final speech in the play—that Paulina will herself trade places with Hermione's corpse in a sacrificial act that recalls Christ's bodily sacrifice through death for the sins of humanity. In an early modern Christian context familiar with the medieval legend of the Harrowing of Hell—a legend dramatized in the mystery cycles—Paulina's claim "Bequeath to death your numbness, for from him / Dear life redeems you" may also have suggested Christ's voyage to the underworld to defeat Satan and rescue his deceased ancestors (5.3.102–103).

Pericles begins with a narrative resurrection as Shakespeare brings Gower back from the dead in order to serve as chorus for his play: "To sing a song that old was sung / From ashes ancient Gower is come" (1.1–2). This reference to "ashes" could either be a generic reference to death—ashes to ashes, dust to dust—or an allusion to the Egyptian myth of the phoenix that was adopted by early Christian fathers such as Clement and frequently reiterated by early modern Christians such as Samuel Gardiner, who argued in favor of the resurrection of the body in his *A Sermon Preached at Paules Crosse the 9. Of June. 1605*. There is certainly a Christ-like aspect to the resurrected Gower because he notes that he is "assuming man's infirmities" in order to "glad your ear and please your eyes" in much the same way that Christ incorporated himself to redeem humankind (Prologue 3–4).

The central resurrection in *Pericles* is Cerimon's raising of Thaisa, and it is a resurrection that highlights important theological and medical questions. Cerimon is described as a doctor, but he is also described as a demigod. Cerimon is not a Christ figure per se, but he need not be in order to raise the dead within a Christian context. Elijah, Elisha, Peter, and Paul all bring back the dead. The fact that Cerimon lives in Ephesus, a city well known for Paul's ministry, gives him the patina of an early Christian apostle. As noted earlier Paul offers the New Testament's most extensive defense of the doctrine of resurrection in 1 Corinthians 15.

In the scene in which Shakespeare introduces Cerimon, Cerimon indirectly suggests his own divinity. The first gentleman "much marvel[s]" that Cerimon is awake at such an early hour, and adds that "'Tis most strange, / Nature to be so conversant with pain, / Being thereto not compelled" (12.21–23). The deliberate subjection of one's person to unnecessary pain recalls Paul's self-denial and, to a lesser extent, Christ's own sacrifice, and the second gentleman later reiterates that Cerimon has not only given his knowledge to help others, he has also suffered "personal pain" (12, 43). Cerimon responds to this praise by expressing his priorities:

> I held it ever;
> Virtue and cunning [knowledge] were endowments greater
> Than nobleness and riches. Careless heirs
> May the two latter darken and dispend,
> But immortality attends the former,
> Making a man a god. (12.23–28)

While Cerimon's intention here may not be self-praise, the effect of this statement is that it aligns him with Christ.

The second gentleman indicates that Cerimon has always sacrificed what is his in order to heal others, and the result is that hundreds of people who might have died now live.

> Your honour has
> Through Ephesus poured forth your charity,
> And hundreds call themselves your creatures who by you
> Have been restored. And not alone your knowledge,
> Your personal pain, but e'en your purse still [always] open
> Hath built Lord Cerimon such strong renown
> As time shall never—(12.39–45)

The sudden arrival of Thaisa's casket interrupts the conclusion of the second gentleman's praise, but it is clear that if he were allowed to continue he would assert that Cerimon has attained an indelible reputation verging on immortality because of the sacrifices he has made to heal others.

Throughout the Old and New Testaments figures who are able to raise the dead such as Elijah, Elisha, Peter, Paul, and of course Jesus himself gain fame throughout the regions where they perform their miracles. Indeed in certain places in the New Testament Christ's miracles seem to be part of an effective public relations campaign to win over disciples and followers. Whether Cerimon wishes to gain a reputation as a demi-divinity or not, his actions have created a cult of fame. This link between raising the dead and the attainment of demigod status also appears in *The Winter's Tale*. After publicizing Hermione's alleged death, Paulina promises to worship anyone who can raise her from the dead:

> If you [Leontes] can bring
> Tincture or lusture in her [Hermione's] lip, her eye,

Heat outwardly or breath within, I'll serve you
As I would do the gods. (3.2.202–205)

After noting that the casket is "wondrous heavy" Cerimon insists that the distinction between a dead body and a living one is not always crystal clear:

Death may usurp on nature many hours,
And yet the fire of life kindle again
The o'erpressed [overcome] spirits. I have heard
Of an Egyptian nine hours dead
Who was by good appliances [medical treatments]
  recovered. (12.80–84)

What Cerimon does for Thaisa is not precisely the same as what Christ does for Lazarus in John 11:41–44, because Lazarus has been dead and buried for four days. His raising of Thaisa more closely resembles Paul's raising of Eutichus in Acts 20:7–12. The passage describes Paul delivering a speech in an "upper chamber." Paul's speech was so long (and presumably so deadly) that it put Eutichus to asleep.

And there sat in a window a certain young man named Eutychus, being fallen into a deep sleep: and as Paul was long preaching, he sunk down with sleep, and fell down from the third loft, and was taken up dead. And Paul went down, and fell on him, and embracing him said, Trouble not yourselves; for his life is in him. When he therefore was come up again, and had broken bread, and eaten, and talked a long while, even till break of day, so he departed. And they brought the young man alive, and were not a little comforted. (Acts 20:9–12)

A similar but far briefer account in which a sleeper was thought dead can be found in Matthew 9:18–26. When Jesus comes to the aid of a ruler's daughter she is surrounded by "the minstrels and the people" who are "making a noise": "He said unto them, Give place: for the maid is not dead, but sleepeth. And they laughed him to scorn. But when the people were put forth, he went in, and took her by the hand, and the maid arose. And the fame hereof went abroad into all that land" (Matt 9:23–26).[23] These passages resemble Cerimon's resurrection of Thaisa in *Pericles* because in each instance the healer recognizes that the individual is not actually dead. Cerimon gives Thaisa a vial of medicine, he asks for music to be played in much the same way that Paulina asks for music as she brings Hermione back to life, and Cerimon delivers his prognosis: "Gentlemen, / This queen will live" (12.89–90). Cerimon does not take credit for her resurrection. He suggests that he is merely helping to bring forth the almost smothered life that lies within her:

> Nature awakes, a warmth
> Breathes out of her. She hath not been entranced [unconscious]
> Above five hours. See how she 'gins to blow
> Into life's flow'r again. (12.90–93)

Still the incident is interpreted by the stage characters, the audience members, Thaisa herself, and ultimately Pericles and Marina as a miraculous raising of the dead.

Because Thaisa's coma was brought on through the trials of childbirth, it also makes sense to consider her fate in relation to the well-established medical discourse surrounding the revival of the so-called suffocating mother, which Kaara L. Peterson has recently highlighted.[24] In Edward Jorden's medical treatise entitled *A Briefe Discourse of a disease called the Suffocation of the Mother* (1603) he describes that the swooning or "syncope" that mothers often experience after childbirth as "the very image of death" (D2r). He also points out classical authorities such as Pliny and Galen who described comatose states brought on by the travails of childbirth.

Wonder holds an important place even within early modern medical discourse. For example, in John Sadler's *The Sick Woman's Private Looking-glasse* (1636) Sadler reports that "Paraeus [Ambroise Paré] writeth of a woman in Spayne, which suddainly fell into a uterine suffocation and appeared to the judgement of man as dead: [during an autopsy] the woman began to move, and with a great clamour returned to herself againe, to the horrour and admiration of all the spectators."[25] This reference to "horrour and admiration" reminds us of Horatio's description of the "woe and wonder" at the conclusion of *Hamlet*. Whether we read Thaisa's resurrection in a Christian context or in the context of early modern medical discourse, it is a wonder when it takes place and it is wondrous when it is revealed to Marina and Pericles at the end of the play.

In *Pericles* the first gentleman is the first character to speak after Thaisa shows signs of life, and his statement, while intended to indicate that Cerimon is a conduit or a channel for divine wonder, also indicates the extent to which Cerimon himself will gain immortal status: "The heavens / Through you increase our wonder, and set up / Your fame forever" (12.93–95). Most early modern English men and women believed that all wonder ultimately derived from God, but the source and the agent were sometimes conflated or even confused with one another.

Shakespeare gives Cerimon a Dr. Victor Frankenstein-like moment as he describes the signs of life returning to Thaisa:

> She is alive. Behold,
> Her eyelids, cases to those heav'nly jewels
> Which Pericles hath lost,
> Begin to part their fringes of bright gold.
> The diamonds of a most praisèd water [luster]
> Doth appear to make the world twice rich.—Live,
> And make us weep to hear your fate, fair creature,
> Rare as you seem to be. (12.95–102)

Wondrous women are often described as rich jewels. Indeed this analogy was conventional. There is nothing conventional, though, about Cerimon's successful attempt to bring Thaisa back to life, and both of the gentlemen acknowledge this. The first gentleman asks rhetorically "Is not this strange?" and the second answers simply, "Most rare" (12.103). "Rare" and "strange" were two of the more popular adjectives used to describe wonders or marvels during the period. Thaisa says little after her revival, but the few words Shakespeare does give her to speak link her directly to Miranda: "O dear Diana, / Where am I? Where's my lord? What world is this?" (12.103–104). She may as well have described Ephesus as a brave new world that has such healers in it.

Augustine is careful in his *Enchiridion* to distinguish between "the cases of resuscitation after which people died again" and "a resurrection to eternal life after the fashion of Christ's own body."[26] Because Thaisa is never completely dead, her revival is not technically a resurrection in the religious sense, so it is no surprise that the word *resurrection* does not appear in *Pericles* or in any other Shakespeare play for that matter. As Cerimon attempts to explain Thaisa's fate he claims that he "recovered her" (22.44), the same word he uses to describe her coming to after her fainting spell. However, Shakespeare invokes resurrection rhetoric at every opportunity in this play and in the other plays in which characters are believed to be brought back from the dead. Pericles is overjoyed to hear his wife's voice, and when he does so he exclaims, "The voice of dead Thaisa!" She qualifies her husband's statement: "That Thaisa / Am I, supposèd dead and drowned" (22.55–57). However, Pericles returns to the language of resurrection when he asks for an embrace: "O come, be buried / A second time within these arms" (22.65–66). Without an actual death, then, Shakespeare is able to take advantage of the wonder of death and rebirth while skirting the fringes of a religious doctrine that was, like all religious doctrine of the period, technically taboo.

The stunned Pericles asks whom he should thank—"Besides the gods—for this great miracle," and Thaisa answers, "Lord Cerimon, my lord. This is the man / Through whom the gods have shown their pow'r" (22.80–83). Here Cerimon most closely approaches the status of a Christ figure because Peter describes Christ in Acts 2:22 and elsewhere as an instrument of divine power. He refers to Christ as "Jesus of Nazareth, a man approved of God among you by miracles and wonders and signs, which God did by him in the midst of you, as ye yourselves also know."[27] The question of agency is particularly cloudy where Christ's own resurrection is concerned. In certain places in the New Testament Christ is depicted as raising himself from the dead, but in others God the Father is presented as the powerful force that raises Christ. An example of the depiction of Christ as a passive subject can be found in 1 Corinthians 6:14, where St. Paul says, "And God hath both raised up the Lord, and will also raise up us by his own power." This verse neatly links Christ's resurrection with the ultimate resurrection of the faithful. It was adopted wholesale in the Protestant *Resurrection of our Lord* play: "Christ is risen from ye deade, by his fathers power/ so let us rise from our oulde life, to walke anew manner" (ll. 319–20).

In praising Cerimon Pericles is careful to distinguish between a human instrument of divine power and an actual divinity. "Reverend sir," Pericles says to Cerimon, "The gods can have no mortal officer / More like a god than you" (22.84–86). However, Pericles's final question indicates that in his mind what Cerimon has accomplished is no less miraculous than the raising of Lazarus or the resurrection of Christ himself: "Will you deliver [explain] / How this dead queen re-lives?" (22.86–87). For Pericles this is not a case of an ill woman recovering; it is an utterly astonishing divinely ordained miracle.

Marina's fate is quite different from Thaisa's. At no point is she actually deceased—though her life and her virtue are in grave danger on multiple occasions. Yet because she was *believed* dead her reunion with her family is consistently depicted as a return from the dead. Like Miranda, Marina is consistently described as a "wonder" even before her apparent resurrection. Gower's chorus introducing act 4 informs us that she is in Tarsus where she has gained so much "grace" through her education that she is "both the heart and place [the focal point] / Of gen'ral wonder" (15.9–11); and in the chorus introducing scene 20 she is again described as a wonder who sings like "one immortal," dances like a goddess to her "admirèd lays," and is so wise that she strikes "[d]eep clerks" dumb (20.3–5).

Marina is not without a hint of self-consciousness regarding the effect she has on others. When she reunites with her father she describes herself as a "maid" who "ne'er before invited eyes, / But have been gazed on like a comet" (21.72–74). Pericles certainly views her as an awe-inspiring comet or shooting star. When Marina tells Pericles her name he first thinks that he is being "mocked" by her, then says she "dost startle" him (21.130, 133). Intense wonder often leads one to question if one is dreaming, and Pericles feels he may be dreaming as Marina names her nurse Lychorida to confirm her identity: "This is the rarest dream / That e'er dulled sleep did mock sad fools withal" (21.148–49). Today a jubilant individual may ask someone to pinch him or her to confirm that he or she is not dreaming. Similarly Pericles is so overwhelmed with joy that he asks Helicanus to deliver a painful wound to him to keep "this great sea of joys rushing upon" him from "O'erbear[ing] the shores" of his "mortality / And drown[ing]" him with "their sweetness!" (21.177–81). In a reversal of the true order of generation, which may also recall the allusions to incest between Antiochus and his daughter, Pericles describes Marina as making him feel as if he is born again: "Thou that begett'st him that did thee beget" (21.182).

From her father's perspective Marina is not only found, she has died and been reborn. She is "Not dead at Tarsus, as she should have been / By savage Cleon" (21.201–202). "I am wild in my beholding" (21.209), Pericles pronounces in an attempt to explain his sense of wondrous bewilderment, and there is a hint that his delight drives him to a sort of madness when at the peak of his jubilation he is the only one capable of hearing the music of the spheres, a music so "heav'nly" that "It raps" him "unto listen'ning" (21.218–20) and induces the sleep he needs to receive Diana's wondrous vision.

The raising of the undead generates wonder in *Cymbeline* as well, where Imogen imbibes a potion that induces a comatose state. Cornelius describes the sleeping potion he created—despite the queen's request for mortal poison—as

> A certain stuff which, being ta'en, would cease
> The present power of life, but in short time
> All offices of nature [all natural faculties] should again
> Do their due functions. (5.6.255–58)

"Have you ta'en of it?" he asks Imogen, and she responds "Most like [likely] I did, for I was dead" (5.6.258).

Friar Laurence offers considerably more detail regarding the potion that creates the temporary illusion of death in Juliet. Faced with the prospect of marrying Paris after marrying Romeo and consummating their marriage, Juliet tells the Friar that she "long[s] to die / If what thou speak'st speak not of remedy" (4.1.66–67). Because of her desperate pronouncement the Friar says that it is likely she will

> undertake
> A thing like death to chide away this shame,
> That cop'st [who wrestles] with death himself to scape from it;
> And, if thou dar'st, I'll give thee remedy. (4.1.73–76)

This notion of "cop[ing]" or wrestling with death may suggest Christ's Harrowing of Hell, a story with important implications for any understanding of resurrection in the early modern period. As noted earlier, it also would have recalled discussions of resurrection in 1 Corinthians 15 and elsewhere in which the resurrection of the dead at the end of days is depicted as a permanent defeat of death. "O death, where is thy sting?" asks Paul rhetorically, "O grave, where is thy victory?" He answers, "Death is swallowed up in victory" (1 Cor 15:54–55).

The "distilling liquor" the Friar gives Juliet has miraculous properties. It causes a "cold and drowsy humour" to run through her veins, and it will stop her pulse:

> No warmth, no breath shall testify thou livest.
> The roses in thy lips and cheeks shall fade
> To wanny ashes, thy eyes' windows [lids] fall
> Like death when he shuts up the day of life.
> Each part, deprived of supple government,
> Shall, stiff and stark and cold, appear like death;
> And in this borrowed likeness of shrunk death
> Thou shalt continue two-and-forty hours,
> And then awake as from a pleasant sleep.
> Now, when the bridegroom in the morning comes
> To rouse thee from thy bed, there art thou dead. (4.1.98–108)

It is interesting that in his description of the effect of the potion the Friar does not say that she will look dead, but that she will be dead, at least from Paris's point of view.[28]

In *Cymbeline* Imogen dies not as herself but as Fidele, a male disguise she has taken on to protect herself away from court. The name, which means "faithful one" in both French and Italian, indicates her fidelity to Posthumus, but it also suggests the extent to which faith and wonder are intertwined. Indeed without a certain level of voluntary belief—whether that belief is described as the suspension of disbelief or something else—audience members cannot share the wonder experienced by Shakespeare's stage characters. This voluntary faith is aptly described by a late nineteenth-century audience member named William Archer in his book *The Theatrical World of 1895*. Archer describes voluntarily suspending his disbelief in order to fully enjoy the proliferation of twins in a production of *Comedy of Errors* by the English Stage Society, an organization under the management of William Poel "largely responsible for the revival of interest in the conditions and conventions of Shakespeare's own stage as a more suitable framework for his plays than the picture-frame stage of the nineteenth century and its realistic assumptions."[29] As Archer writes candidly:

> It interested me to note that whereas I had always conceived it next door to impossible to find or make two pairs of actors even passably alike, as a matter of fact the two Antipholuses and the two Dromios were to me, at no great distance from the scene, actually indistinguishable. Of course, I was vaguely conscious of certain differences between them; but it would have needed a special effort of attention (from which I carefully abstained) to fix the differences in my mind so as to enable me to tell, when one of them entered, whether he was of Ephesus or of Syracuse. I was effectually enveloped in the "general mist of error." To this end the broad brims of the Antipholuses' hats contributed most ingeniously.[30]

This "general mist of error," which was facilitated by the use of hats with broad brims that obscured parts of the actors' faces, seems as good a description as any of what wonder feels like as one experiences the performance of a play.

As Arviragus enters the stage holding the apparently dead Imogen/Fidele in his arms in act 4, scene 2, Arviragus, Belarius, and Guiderius all lament Fidele's death. Though the stage direction reads "Enter Arviragus with Imogen, dead, bearing her in his arms" there seems to be some confusion as to whether Fidele is dead or asleep. Belarius asks Arviragus "How found you him?" and Arviragus answers

> Stark [stiff], as you see,
> Thus smiling as [if] some fly had tickled slumber,
> Not as death's dart being laughed at; his right cheek
> Reposing on a cushion. (4.2.210–13)

He thought Fidele was asleep upon first seeing him, so he took off his boots to keep from making too much noise. After Arviragus delivers a beautiful speech in which he promises to deck Fidele's grave with flowers,

Guiderius puts on a courageous, stoical front. In so doing he reiterates the extent to which wonder could tend toward woe as well as jubilation:

> Prithee, have done,
> And do not play in wench-like words with that
> Which is so serious. Let us bury him,
> And not protract with admiration [wonder] what
> Is now due debt. (4.2.230–34)

Imogen is alone on stage when she awakens, a wondrous moment for the audience. She discovers what she thinks is her beloved Posthumus's body beside her, beheaded, and laments his death. Cymbeline gave Posthumus his name, which means "after death" in Latin, because he was the son of a father who predeceased him, but the name takes on a secondary meaning in the play from this point forward as Posthumus is presumed dead. His ultimate reunion with the royals and with Imogen represents a pseudoresurrection, and his ancestors enjoy a posthumous presence in the play as well when they appear as apparitions to beg Jupiter to cease Posthumus's suffering.

Imogen's miraculous reappearance at the end of the play is one of *Cymbeline*'s central wonders. Disguised in the scene as Fidele, she initially looks familiar to Cymbeline, but he cannot quite place her. When she speaks her assumed name, Belarius, Arviragus, and Guiderius are the first to recognize her. Belarius is dumbfounded: "Is not this boy / Revived from death?" (5.6.119–20). Arviragus claims that the boy resembles Fidele exactly: "One sand [one grain of sand] another / Not more resembles that sweet rosy lad / Who died, and was Fidele" (5.6.120–22). "What think you?" he asks his brother. "The same dead thing alive" Guiderius answers (5.6.122). Despite the identical name and the identical appearance Belarius counsels caution in jumping to the conclusion that their dead friend lives: "Forbear. / Creatures may be alike" (5.6.124–25). Guiderius struggles with the contradiction between the person he seems to see now and the apparently dead Fidele he saw with his own eyes: "But we see [saw] him dead" (5.6.127).

There is a physiological aspect to wonder in addition to its emotional and philosophical aspects. After knocking Fidele/Imogen down in a rage, Pisanio tells Posthumus that he has killed Imogen. Realizing what he has done, Pisanio loses his physical balance, his equilibrium: "How comes these staggers on me?" (5.6.233). In the same way that Pericles feared he would die of joy, Cymbeline fears that his joy will be so overwhelming that it will be mortal to him: "If this be so, the gods do mean to strike me / To death with mortal joy" (5.6.234–35). To intensify the wonder of his response Shakespeare delays his recognition of his daughter until after everyone else has identified her. When Cymbeline finally speaks to her he uses the rhetoric of stage performance to chide Imogen for not including him in the conversation sooner: "What, mak'st thou me a dullard in this act? / Wilt thou not speak to me?" (5.6.265–66). In fact Cymbeline has made himself a dullard, standing nearly mute and incredulous for several minutes. In this way he delivers the most complete performance of wonder.

When he is able to converse with her he turns to holy language in a sort of recapitulation of a baptism that brings Imogen back to life: "My tears that fall / Prove holy water on thee!" (5.6.268–69). When Belarius informs him that his sons Guiderius and Arviragus are also alive and right before his eyes, he describes their return as a rebirth and he compares himself to a mother who through a sort of immaculate conception has given birth to them and Imogen. "O, what am I?" he asks, "A mother to the birth of three?" (5.6.369–70). Just as Thaisa and Miranda depicted their wonder as the discovery of a brave new world, Imogen tells her father that in the discovery of her brothers she has not lost a kingdom but "got two worlds by't" (5.6.375).

CHAPTER I.3

"Die to Live": Various Forms of Empathetic Wonder

Shakespeare employed the plot device of the raising of the undead or the apparently dead in his midcareer comedies as well as his late romances. As would be the case with the later plays, pseudoresurrection generated intense wonder among the stage characters and, by extension, the audience members. The raising of the apparently dead figures largely in *Much Ado About Nothing*. As in *Romeo and Juliet*, the apparent death in this play is a plot constructed by a well-meaning Friar to reunite star-crossed lovers. Ritual figures prominently in this pseudoresurrection plot, as the Friar instructs Leonato to adhere to all the "rites / That appertain unto a burial" (4.1.206–207). Fully cognizant of the fact that his plan is a "strange course," (4.1.212), the Friar links pseudoresurrection rhetoric with eschatology in his simple directive to Hero: "Come, lady, die to live. This wedding day / Perhaps is but prolonged" (4.1.253–54). Because Christ was often figured as the bridegroom of the faithful Christian, this line linked the transvestite male actor playing Hero with the righteous Christian planning for his final reunion with Christ.

The notion of life in death or life through death resurfaces in *Much Ado* in Claudio's epitaph, where he claims that Hero has achieved a sort of immortal reputation in death, which she never possessed while alive:

Done to death by slanderous tongues
Was the Hero that here lies.
Death in guerdon [recompense] of her wrongs
Gives her fame which never dies.

So the life that died with [from] shame
Lives in death with glorious fame. (5.3.7–8)

Claudio conceives this statement as a symbolic revival, indeed more of a metamorphoses from vulnerable mortal to enduring model, but it is also literally accurate: the life that (apparently) died from shame does actually live in (supposed) death with glorious fame. Because Borachio and Don John's villainy has been discovered in the previous scene, Hero enjoys an unspotted reputation even as she is believed dead by Claudio, Don Pedro, and others.

There is a more direct and far more material reference to resurrection in the Song sung after Claudio hangs his epitaph for Hero on her tomb:

Midnight, assist our moan,
Help us to sigh and groan,
Heavily, heavily.
Graves yawn, and yield your dead
Till death be utterèd [fully lamented],
Heavily, heavily. (5.3.16–21)

This song reflects the belief that actual dead bodies rose from the grave until the proper rites had been completed. This belief figures prominently in *Hamlet* as we will see later.

There are several intriguing references to resurrection in *Much Ado*'s wondrous dénouement. After she unmasks Hero describes herself as a sort of phoenix risen from the ashes of her tarnished reputation: "one Hero died defiled, but I do live" (5.4.63). The theater audience understands this to be a figurative statement, but Claudio and Don Pedro do not yet know of her death disguise, so from their perspective Hero truly seems to have risen from the dead. In response to Don Pedro's astonished exclamation, "The former Hero, Hero that is dead!" Leonato attempts to explain Hero's cryptic comment by adding, "She died, my lord, but whiles her slander lived" (5.4.65–66), but even this statement is incomprehensible to Don Pedro and Claudio. Their response to this pseudoresurrection is wonder, and we know this because the Friar steps in and offers to "qualify" or reduce "all this amazement" (5.4.67). The Friar's soothing statement would have been unnecessary if Claudio and Don Pedro had not been so "attired in wonder"—to borrow a phrase that Benedick uses earlier in the play. The Friar offers to explain what has taken place after the wedding ceremony has ended, but this offer does nothing to diminish the wonder that Claudio and Don Pedro feel. If anything the Friar only magnifies the misunderstanding: "I'll tell you largely of fair Hero's death. / Meantime, let wonder seem familiar" (5.4.69–70). Fair Hero did not die, but the Friar does not explicitly state that here, deferring the clarification until after the play has been completed. Nor does his directive "let wonder seem familiar" make any sense. It is impossible for one to regard a wonder as something familiar or common. Thus Claudio and Don Pedro are left in affective and cognitive suspense as Beatrice and Benedick rekindle—with help from their friends—their romantic interest in one another.

In *Much Ado* and in other comedies Shakespeare generates wonder through the supposed resurrection of the apparently dead, but in the tragedies wonder is generated by what we might call the apparent raising of the actually dead. We see the grotesquely material side of this technique in *Titus Andronicus*. Aaron digs dead bodies out of graves and props them up in front of their loved ones' doors in order to rekindle the loved ones' despair. His depiction of this hobby is particularly graphic, and it is made all the more gruesome because we do not see it for ourselves. We merely hear Aaron report the practice. His vitriolic confession that he unearthed dead bodies to torment their mourners serves as the climax of his vitriolic confession, itself more of a rhetorical attack than a surrender:

> Even now I curse the day—and yet I think
> Few come within the compass of my curse—
> Wherein I did not some notorious ill,
> As kill a man, or else devise his death;
> Ravish a maid, or plot the way to do it;
> Accuse some innocent and forswear myself;
> Set deadly enmity between two friends;
> Make poor men's cattle break their necks;
> Set fire on barns and haystacks in the night,
> And bid the owners quench them with their tears.
> Oft have I digged up dead men from their graves
> And set them upright at their dear friends' door,
> Even when their sorrows almost was forgot,
> And on their skins, as on the bark of trees,
> Have with my knife carvèd in Roman letters
> "Let not your sorrow die though I am dead." (5.1.125–40)

Aaron does not actually bring these "dead men" back to life. He moves their dead trunks from one location to another in order to terrorize their loved ones, and then he transforms their bodies into texts, which communicate the need for continued sorrow. By using the first person in the statements he carves into these fleshly texts he creates the illusion that the dead man is speaking to his loved ones, but in fact he cannot.

A very different kind of wondrous pseudoresurrection evokes immense pathos from the audience at the end of *King Lear*. Three times Lear believes that the dead Cordelia shows signs of life. The first two times Lear is disappointed, but he dies amid the combination of horror and rapture he experiences on the third occasion. "She's gone forever," he laments as he enters with her in his arms (5.3.258). To set the stage for the wonder of her imagined revival he highlights the clear distinction between death and life, a distinction that so many of Shakespeare's plays seem to challenge: "I know when one is dead and when one lives; / She's dead as earth" (5.3.259–60). Determined to confirm that his assessment is correct, he calls for a looking glass to see if her breath will mist or stain it. Soon after, he thinks he sees a sign of life from her: "This feather stirs; she lives!" He claims that her resurrection would be a "chance which does redeem all sorrows / That ever I have felt" and the rhetoric of redemption makes sense here because Kent, Edgar, and Albany have all just compared Cordelia's death to the Apocalypse (5.3.265–66). After Lear turns Kent away he thinks he hears Cordelia's voice: "Ha! / What is 't thou say'st?" Then in the final moment before he dies Lear imagines her resurrection once more: "Look on her, look her lips, / Look there, look there!" (5.3.308–309). Earlier Edgar reported that Gloucester's heart "'Twixt two extremes of passion, joy and grief, / Burst smilingly" and the same can be said for Lear (5.3.97–98). He dies grieving Cordelia even as he delights in the fantasy of her revival.

Summing up the entire play in response to Edgar's simple statement, "He is gone, indeed," Kent asserts, "The wonder is, he hath endured so long. / He but usurped his life" (5.3.315–16). This statement neatly links wonder and resurrection, suggesting that the wonder of Lear's latter days was his ability to steal or at least temporarily borrow his life from Death. At the play's end, Lear pays his ultimate debt to Death, but the order of his kingdom is ultimately restored.

Three varieties of pseudoresurrection intensify the wondrous pathos at the conclusion of *Antony and Cleopatra*. After faking her death in order to encourage Antony to rescind his jealousy and ire, Cleopatra reappears to her beloved and miraculously manages to heave his dying body up to her monument, presumably presented using the tiring house balcony. Antony has mortally wounded himself and tells Cleopatra that he is "dying, Egypt, dying" (4.16.19). He asks for her to come down to him; she refuses out of fear she will be captured, and begins to haul him up. She complains of his weight and while raising him offers an intriguing allusion, which suggests that hoisting his body is analogous to the resurrection of the dead: "Had I great Juno's power / The strong-winged Mercury should fetch thee up / And set thee by Jove's side" (4.16.35–37). As Barbara Ardinger has noted, this statement by Cleopatra invokes the resurrection of Hercules, described earlier as Antony's divine benefactor: "After thunderbolts destroyed his funeral pyre, Hercules was transported to Olympus, where he was welcomed by Jupiter and the other gods and adopted by Juno through the ceremony of rebirth."[1] The permeable barrier between life and death is Cleopatra's focus as she ministers to her half-dead lord: "Die when thou hast lived, / Quicken with kissing. Had my lips that power, / Thus would I wear them out" (4.16.39–41). Critics disagree as to whether Cleopatra speaks of cheating or merely prolonging death here, but her reference to quickening certainly suggests that she is attempting to revive Antony. In *Ductor in Linguas, The Guide into Tongues* (1617), John Minsheu noted that to "quicken" meant to "Put life into," and that is certainly Cleopatra's motive here (437).[2] The scene ends with a final pseudoresurrection as Cleopatra faints, is presumed dead, and then recovers to lament her female frailty before confirming her desire to pursue suicide.

While Aaron digs bodies up from the grave and Lear imagines Cordelia's revival, the most common way in which Shakespeare generates the wonder of pseudoresurrection is through the visitation of spirits, ghosts, or apparitions. Today we draw clear distinctions between a spirit or ghost on one hand and a revivified dead body on another, but Shakespeare seems to intentionally cloud this distinction, generating the impression that when Hamlet and Macbeth see the spirits of their father and their friend, respectively, they believe they are seeing a dead body risen from the grave to torment them.

The corporeal nature of the vexed spirit who has risen from the dead seems clear in a conversation between Leontes and Paulina in the final act of *The Winter's Tale* about whether Leontes will ever remarry. The deeply penitent Leontes says that he will never remarry because if he did

One worse,
And better used, would make her [Hermione's] sainted spirit
Again possess her corpse, and on this stage,
Where we offenders mourn, appear soul-vexed,
And begin, "Why to me?" (5.1.56–60)

This seems a clear indication that the early modern (or at the very least the Shakespearean) idea of the ghost was of a spirit who possessed or occupied a tangible corpse in order to torment those who had wronged the individual while alive. It is interesting that we see so many ghostly resurrections in the plays because the official church position on this matter was that ghosts did not exist, nor could human bodies rise from the dead except at the resurrection at the end of days. This official doctrine had little impact on local superstition, however.

The persistent fusion of dead corpse and incorporeal spirit in Shakespeare's plays can be read in a number of ways. It may indicate the early modern English understanding of ghosts, or from a more pragmatic standpoint it may even be a function of theatrical necessity. Shakespeare had to use a flesh and blood actor in order to portray the ghost of King Hamlet and the ghost of Banquo. Instead of attempting to obscure or gloss over this fact, he may be attempting to take advantage of it—much as he takes advantage of transvestism in plays such as *Twelfth Night* and *As You Like It*—to generate additional wonder. While it is astounding to see ghosts on the stage, it is even more astounding to see apparitions that are materially indistinguishable from actual corpses, ghosts that literally matter.

There may also be a theological source for the materiality of the Shakespearean apparitions. They may reflect the consensus view in the persistent debate regarding the corporality of the resurrected Christian. What manner of ghost is the ghost of King Hamlet that appears first to the watch, then to Horatio, and finally to Prince Hamlet?[3] Initially he seems to be an incorporeal spirit, an ethereal presence that "usurp'st"—to use Horatio's loaded term—the physical features and the military accoutrement of the deceased monarch. Horatio confronts the ghost and demands, "Stay, illusion" (1.1.108); he later compares it to other "extravagant and erring spirit[s]" (1.1.135), and Marcellus acknowledges that it is unrealistic to try to strike at it with his partisan because it is "as the air invulnerable" (1.1.126). Even when the ghost's physical similarity to King Hamlet is noted by Horatio and the watch, the ghost is consistently depicted as a sort of symbolic representation of King Hamlet, a "figure" at one Platonic remove from the actual article. Horatio describes the ghost as an "image" of the king (1.1.80); in Q2 Barnardo describes the ghost as "this portentous figure" (1.1.106.2); and Horatio describes the ghost to Prince Hamlet as a "figure like your father" (1.2.199).[4] These references to images and figures suggest that the ghost is an ethereal presence, not a tangible object, a supernatural photocopy instead of a corporeal original. This ghost is closely related to the ghosts that appear to Richard III in his tent before the battle of Bosworth field. Richard calls these ghosts "shadows," which "Have struck more terror" in his soul than "can the substance of ten thousand soldiers / Armèd in proof and led by shallow Richmond" (5.5.170, 172–73).[5] Here Richard emphasizes the difference between the immaterial spirits and the physical bodies of armed soldiers in the field.

When Prince Hamlet finally has the chance to speak with the ghost, the ghost confirms that it is a spirit, not a body:

> I am thy father's spirit,
> Doomed for a certain term to walk the night,
> And for the day confined to fast in fires
> Till the foul crimes done in my days of nature
> Are burnt and purged away. (1.5.9–13)

His mention of the "days of nature" suggests a separation between the spirit realm and the realm of the flesh. The division between the two realms is even clearer when the ghost withholds his "tale" of the sufferings of purgatory because he insists that his "eternal blazon must not be / To ears of flesh and blood" (1.5.21–22).

This harrowing conversation with his son seems to clarify the Ghost's status as an immaterial spirit, but until this speech takes place Hamlet is uncertain about the ghost's true nature. When he first addresses the ghost he does so in a speech that shifts from the apprehension of the immaterial—"Be thou a spirit of health or goblin damned" (1.4.21)—to a reckoning with the explicitly and troublingly material or corporeal, addressing the ghost as if it were the actual corpse of his father risen from the dead and demanding that it

> tell
> Why thy canonized [consecrated] bones, hearsèd in death,
> Have burst their cerements [grave clothes], why the sepulchre
> Where we saw thee quietly enurned [entombed]
> Hath oped his ponderous and marble jaws
> To cast thee up again. What may this mean,
> That thou, dead corpse, again in complete steel [armor],
> Revisits thus the glimpses of the moon
> Making night hideous, and we fools of nature
> So horridly to shake our disposition
> With thoughts beyond the reaches of our souls?
> Say, why is this? Wherefore? What should we do? (1.4.27–38)

Significantly for this study, the first thing that Hamlet, the watch, and Horatio do upon seeing this "dead corpse" that has been vomited up by the earth is experience an intensely terrifying variety of wonder. "It harrows me with fear and wonder" (1.1.42), says Horatio after seeing the ghost for the first time. He tells Hamlet that the appearance of the ghost is a "marvel" (1.2.194), and when the prince sees it and converses with it himself, he responds simply and profoundly, "O wonderful!" (1.5.122).

This is not the only instance in the first act of the play in which the ghost of King Hamlet is either described as or compared to an actual corpse risen from the grave. As Barnardo and Horatio struggle to make sense of the apparition in the Q2 edition of the play, Horatio compares the appearance of King Hamlet's ghost in arms to the prodigious resurrection of dead corpses on the eve of the assassination of Julius Caesar. Horatio says that

> In the most high and palmy [flourishing] state of Rome
> A little ere the mightiest Julius fell,
> The graves stood tenantless, and the sheeted [shrouded] dead
> Did squeak and gibber in the Roman streets
> As stars with trains of fire. (1.1.106.6–10)[6]

Horatio does not specifically claim that the ghost of King Hamlet is a "sheeted dead" who rises from the grave, but he does state that the "like precurse of feared events" have taken place in Denmark among his countrymen, thus the analogy by historical association puts the ghost and these resurrected corpses on equal (clay) footing. The mass Roman resurrection described by Horatio may be pre-Christian, but it closely resembles the depiction of mass resurrection in Matthew 27:52–53, immediately after the description of Christ's crucifixion: "And graues were opened, and many bodies of Saintes which slept, arose. And after they were come out of the graues after his resurrection, came into the holie Citie, and appeared vnto many."[7]

There is an even more subtle ambiguity regarding the materiality of the ghost during Horatio's first mention of it to Prince Hamlet. After Prince Hamlet tells Horatio that he thinks he sees his father in his mind's eye Horatio tells Hamlet "My lord, I think I saw him yesternight" (1.2.188). The exchange that results from this shocking revelation does not initially distinguish between the material or the ghostly body of the king. When Hamlet asks who Horatio saw, he replies, "the King your father"; Hamlet repeats this in the form of a question, and he experiences a profound sense of wonder. We know this because Horatio tells him not to get too rapt, too carried away:

> Season your admiration for a while
> With an attent ear till I may deliver,
> Upon the witness of these gentlemen,
> This marvel to you. (1.2.192–95)

Hamlet's natural response to hearing of this "marvel" is "admiration." Horatio later adds that if Hamlet had seen the figure "It would have much amazed you" (1.2.234). When Horatio provides the details of the visitation, he specifies that the ghost was not a tangible corpse but a "figure like your father," an immaterial "apparition"; but in the early phase of the exchange Horatio creates the impression that he may have seen the king in person, in the decomposing flesh.

Why is there such ambivalence about the nature of the ghost of King Hamlet? I have suggested that the ambivalence may have something to do with persistent doubts about the materiality of the resurrected Christian. The ambiguity may also reflect Christian ambivalence regarding the nature of Christ's own resurrection that dates back to the Gospels. Christ appears in many forms after his resurrection, and this creates some confusion. Christ appears first as a gardener to the Marys and their companions in John; he appears anonymously and in disguise to Cleopas and his companion in Luke; and later in Luke when he appears to his disciples they believe him to be a spirit instead of the physical body of the risen Christ (Luke 24:37). Jesus asks the disciples to look at his hands and his feet and touch him to confirm his materiality: "Behold my hands and feet, that it is I myself: handle me, and see; for a spirit hath not flesh and bones, as ye see me have" (Luke 24:39). When they still refuse to believe they are in the presence of Christ's body, Jesus asks for food and eats broiled fish and a honeycomb to prove his humanity.

The gospels agree that the primary affective response to the risen Christ is wonder, and that wonder derives both from terror and jubilation. Matthew 28 emphasizes the terrible wonder the Marys experience when they visit the sepulchre, noting that when Mary Magdalene "and the other Mary" went to see the sepulchre "there was a great earthquake" caused by the angel of the Lord, whose "countenance was like lightning, and his raiment white as snow" (2, 4). This terrified "the keepers" of the sepulchre. They "did shake, and became as dead men" (4). Here ironically Christ's resurrection is experienced as mortifying. When the angel tells them to go tell "his disciples and Peter" that he is going to meet them in Galilee, "they trembled and were amazed" (Mark 6:7). Similarly the two men at Emmaus tell the disguised Christ that they were "astonished" to hear that the Marys and others found Christ gone from his sepulcher (Luke 24:22). When Christ appears to his disciples in Luke they are initially terrified. He lets them touch him, and then "they yet believed not for joy, and wondered" (Luke 24:41) until he ate to prove his humanity.

The central cognitive response to news of Christ's resurrection in the Gospels is doubt. Mary believes the body of Christ has been taken away, the two men Christ meets at Emmaus believe Christ is dead, the disciples consistently doubt the physicality of the risen Christ, and Thomas, described in John, requires tangible proof of the risen Christ: "Except I shall see in his hands the print of the nails, and put my finger into the print of the nails, and thrust my hand into his side, I will not believe" (John 20:25).

Prince Hamlet has profound doubts about the nature of his father's ghost. Is it a divine spirit? Is it a demon? Scholars who emphasize Prince Hamlet's so-called delay routinely downplay this critical issue, making of Prince Hamlet a weak and indecisive figure, a man incapable of action. This response to an ambiguous resurrected entity has its scriptural original in the character of the doubting Thomas, and a brief comparison between Thomas and Hamlet sheds light on Prince Hamlet's predicament. In the Towneley cycle play *Thomas of India*, Christ appears to his disciples but Thomas is not present. When given the news Thomas doubts Christ's physical resurrection. In order to convince him Christ finally reappears to Thomas and invites him to feel his five wounds. Prior to this definitive empirical experience Thomas refuses to believe that Christ rose bodily from the grave. He asserts multiple times and at great length that what the disciples must have seen was a ghost, not a physical body: "ye sagh hym not bodely / his gost it myght well be" (*Thomas of India*, 193). He even asks how the other disciples could possibly have recognized the difference between a body and an immaterial spirit: "when cryst cam you to vysyte / as ye tell me with saw, / A whyk [quick, living] man from spyryte / wherby couth ye hym knaw?" The sixth apostle answers, "Man has both flesh and bone / hu [complexion], hyde [skin], and hore [hair] thertill [therefore] / sich thyng has goost none" (218–22).

Thomas's dubiousness regarding the nature of Christ's risen body is not only an interesting parallel for Prince Hamlet's doubt regarding the nature of his father's ghost, it also sheds light on Macbeth's haunting suspicion that Banquo's ghost is a material presence, casting Macbeth as an antitype to Thomas. Macbeth describes the ghost not as an ethereal spirit but as a wondrous resurrection of a dead man's corpse. He prepares the audience for the physicality of Banquo's perceived postmortem presence when he claims that all of Scotland's nobility would be under one roof "Were the graced *person* of our Banquo present" (3.4.40; my emphasis). This roundabout way of describing Banquo gains significance when a physical body appears to take Macbeth's seat at the banquet table. The ghost is so lifelike that Macbeth is initially incapable of noting its supernatural status. "The table's full," Macbeth says simply, indicating his perception that flesh-and-blood beings occupy each seat (3.4.44). His accusatory "Which of you has done this?" (3.4.48) seems to assume that some Aaron-like Scottish nobleman dug up the dead body of Banquo and placed it in a chair to torment him. At this point Banquo's ghost moves, indicating that it is not merely a lifeless corpse, and Macbeth responds by telling the ghost not to "shake" its "gory locks" at him (3.4.49–50).

Even though it moves, Banquo's ghost is mute, intensifying Macbeth's terrified wonder. He demands that it speak to him, but it does not. Macbeth is not as lucky as Prince Hamlet in this regard. Macbeth's response to the ghost's silence is to contemplate the topic of corporal resurrection generally. He launches into a pragmatic critique of the physical resurrection of dead bodies: "If charnel-houses and our graves must send / Those that we bury back, our monuments / Shall be the maws of kites" (3.4.70–72). The process of burial is useless, Macbeth suggests here, if the final resting place for even the buried body is the mouth of a bird of prey. In response to this statement Lady Macbeth questions her husband's manhood—a familiar refrain in the play—and Macbeth responds by offering a fascinating historical commentary on the increase in resurrections in recent times. In the good old days, he claims, murder victims remained in the grave, but now they rise from the grave to torment their murderers:

> Blood hath been shed ere now, i'th' olden time,
> Ere human statute purged the gentle weal;
> Ay, and since, too, murders have been performed
> Too terrible for the ear. The time has been
> That, when the brains were out, the man would die,
> And there an end. But now they rise again
> With twenty mortal murders [deadly wounds] on their
>   crowns [heads],
> And push us from our stools. This is more strange
> Than such a murder is. (3.4.74–82)

Macbeth sees a historical sea change in the finality of death. Death used to be an end, but now it is merely a corpse's transitional phase en route to the enacting of vengeance. The speech is also intriguing because it asserts that the rising of foully murdered dead bodies is more "strange"—more wondrous—than the foul murders themselves. This is undeniably true, and Shakespeare was well aware of this, thus the emphasis on the raising of the wrongfully or foully murdered in *Hamlet*, *Macbeth*, *Julius Caesar*, and elsewhere.

During the second appearance of the ghost of Banquo Macbeth again insists on its materiality: "Let the earth hide thee. Thy bones are marrowless, thy blood is cold. / Thou has no speculation [sight] in those eyes / Which thou dost glare with" (3.4.92–94). Macbeth hopes for the corpse's reinterment as he suffers its mute vengeance. The fact that the ghost does not speak further confounds both Macbeth and the stage audience, raising the following question: Are we viewing an insubstantial ghost or are we viewing a body raised from the dead to torment its murderer? The ghost of King Hamlet ultimately clarifies his status for us, emphasizing its immateriality, but the ghost of Banquo does not, leaving Macbeth and the play's audience to wonder about the true nature of this wonder.

While the nature of the figure who rises from the grave to torment Macbeth is left ambiguous, Macbeth's response, like Prince Hamlet's, is unambiguous. Like Prince Hamlet, Macbeth experiences a profound sense of wonder. He tells Lady Macbeth as much: "Can such things be / And overcome us like a summer's cloud, / Without our special wonder?" (3.4.109–11). This is a rhetorical question. Of course "special wonder" is the only reasonable response to what Macbeth has seen.[8] Because Lady Macbeth does not see the ghost and therefore believes that it is only a figment of her husband's imagination, she believes that Macbeth's own behavior is the source of wonder in the scene, and she chides him for what she calls his "most admired disorder" (3.4.109). This exchange highlights the way in which wonder can have several simultaneous sources. It can be generated by a remarkable sight—here the ghost of Banquo—and it can be the result of witnessing another figure experiencing wonder. Perhaps we can distinguish between what we might call primary or direct wonder and secondary or indirect wonder. Both forms are important. Stage spectacles such as immaterial ghosts or corpses risen from the grave can astound us, and admiring stage characters can effectively cue our own response to a play, guiding us toward a sort of empathetic wonder.

CHAPTER I.4

The Metaphorical Use of the Prodigious Birth Tradition

Lady Anne discovers that the corpse of King Henry VI has begun to bleed. This is a sort of resurrection, a sort of returning to life or the physiological processes of life.

> O gentlemen, see, see! Dead Henry's wounds
> Ope their congealèd mouths and bleed afresh.—
> Blush, blush, thou lump of foul deformity,
> For 'tis thy presence that ex-hales this blood
> From cold and empty veins where no blood dwells.
> Thy deed, inhuman and unnatural,
> Provokes this deluge supernatural. (1.2.55–61)[1]

For viewers of the play who were also aware of the chronicle histories from which Shakespeare drew in writing *Richard III*, the linkage between this unnatural blood flow from a dead corpse and Christ's miraculous resurrection would have been strengthened by the fact that King Henry's corpse bled on the eve of Christ's Ascension Day. As Holinshed writes,

> The dead corpse on the Ascension Even was conveyed with bills and glaives pompously (if you will call that a funeral pomp) from the Tower to the church of St. Paul, and there laid on a bier or coffin barefaced; the same in presence of the beholders did bleed; where it rested the space of one whole day. From thence he was carried to the Blackfriars, and bled there likewise.[2]

Shakespeare modifies this source material in an important way by implying that Richard Gloucester's presence *caused* the corpse to bleed.

Lady Anne emphasizes the wondrous nature of this spectacle by inviting the assembled stage characters and by extension the theater spectators to "see, see!" the blood flowing freshly from King Henry's wounds. One wonders whether or not a special effect could have been employed here to make blood flow through the wounds. It seems more likely that Anne and the assembled stage characters see this wonder themselves, respond to it as a wonder, and cue the audience members to gape in awe with them. While many unnatural or inexplicable occurrences such as the fresh bleeding of a new corpse are open sites—open wounds—for interpretation, Shakespeare's handling of this particular wonder is definitive. It was believed that a murdered corpse often bled when in the presence of its murderer. In essence, then, Shakespeare recasts an ambiguous prodigy as a marvelous confirmation of Richard's guilt.

The scene is particularly arresting because it represents the confluence of multiple prodigies. After referring to Richard as a "foul devil" and a "dreadful minister of hell" Lady Anne describes him as a monstrous birth here, a "lump of foul deformity" (1.2.57). Monstrous or unnatural births represented a major class of prodigies in the early modern period, and a great deal of critical attention has been paid to monstrous births in recent years. Like other prodigies, monstrous births were usually considered portents either of political upheaval or of the Last Judgment. William E. Burns has usefully distinguished between "annalistic" prodigies, which foretold particular political or social events, and "apocalyptic" prodigies, which were related to the end of time itself.[3]

There is a bit of situational irony in this scene of prodigious confluence because immediately before Richard Gloucester appears on the road Lady Anne curses the murderer of Henry VI by wishing him monstrous issue:

If ever he have child, abortive be it,
Prodigious, and untimely brought to light,
Whose ugly and unnatural aspect
May fright the hopeful mother at the view,
And that be heir to his unhappiness. (1.2.21–25)

Though she does not yet know this, the audience members are well aware that in cursing Richard's issue Anne is cursing her own future children with Richard. In production Anne's lines could be given additional weight by having Richard overhear them before he approaches the guards to stop the procession. Anne's curse is an oblique and accidental introduction. Richard is an abortive and untimely monster who brings grief to his mother.

In cursing the murderers of Henry VI Lady Anne inverts the temporal bias of the prodigious birth. Usually the prodigious birth portends or foreshadows a coming catastrophe, but here the prodigious birth is wished as a future punishment for evil acts that have already been committed. This reversal of the natural course of the prodigious wonder makes Anne's curse even more unnatural and strange. A similar temporal inversion of the prodigious birth occurs later in the play when Queen Margaret sees Richard as God's punishment for the Duchess of York's past evils:

> O upright, just, and true-disposing God,
> How do I thank thee that this carnal cur
> Preys on the issue of his mother's body
> And makes her pewfellow with others' moan. (4.4.55–58)

In her final confrontation with her son the Duchess of York seems to confirm that Richard has been a curse since his birth:

> Thou cam'st on earth to make the earth my hell.
> A grievous burden was thy birth to me;
> Tetchy and wayward was thy infancy;
> Thy schooldays frightful, desp'rate, wild, and furious;
> Thy prime of manhood daring, bold, and venturous;
> Thy age confirmed, proud, subtle, sly, and bloody;
> More mild, but yet more harmful; kind in hatred.
> What comfortable hour canst thou name
> That ever graced me in thy company? (4.4.167–75)

Richard was a child prodigy not because of his talent but because of his deformity, and he has remained an unnatural wonder throughout his life.

In his first soliloquy Richard emphasizes that he is a monstrous birth. Lamenting that he will have little to do in a time of peace when "Grim-visaged war... capers nimbly in a lady's chamber / To the lascivious pleasing of a lute" he claims that he is not "shaped for sportive tricks" or "made to court an amorous looking-glass" because he is "rudely stamped" (1.1.9–16). He goes on to describe himself as

> Deformed, unfinished, sent before my time
> Into this breathing world scarce half made up—
> And that so lamely and unfashionable
> That dogs bark at me as I halt by them—(1.1.20–23)

Richard Gloucester is a walking abortion, his gestation cruelly cut short in such a way that he is not smaller of stature but freakishly deformed. His own mother describes him as a monster after she learns that he has maneuvered to plant himself on the throne. She calls him a "cockatrice...whose unavoided eye is murderous" (4.1.54–5).[4]

One of Richard's characteristics, which makes him particularly unnatural even within the scope of the prodigious birth tradition, is that he survives infancy. Monstrous births were often infants with debilitating or life-threatening birth defects. Richard not only survives his bizarre infancy in which he allegedly gnawed a crust of bread immediately after birth, he also continues his unnatural and hideous ways throughout his life. Strangely he is both retarded and precocious, according to the legends that surround him. His mother notes that he grew very slowly as a child: "He was the wretched'st thing when he was young, / So long a-growing, and so leisurely" (2.4.18–19). The young Duke of York is surprised to hear this because he heard that Richard "grew so fast / That he could gnaw a crust at two hours old" (2.4.27–28). Richard's mother challenges the source of this information, but the fact that the legend exists at all reinforces Richard's air of prodigiousness. The concept of the *child prodigy* in use today was not available to Shakespeare, as the OED records its first use in the late seventeenth century, but in his eating habits at least Richard would seem to qualify under the modern definition.

Richard is explicitly described as a prodigy in the horrific scene in *3 Henry VI* in which Queen Margaret tortures and then kills the Duke of York. After capturing York, Margaret begins to taunt him:

> Where are your mess of sons to back you now?
> The wanton Edward and the lusty George?
> And where that valiant crookback prodigy,
> Dickie, your boy, that with his grumbling voice
> Was wont to cheer his dad in mutinies? (1.4.74-78)

Even in deriding him Margaret shows some respect, describing him as "valiant." What exactly does Queen Margaret mean when she describes Richard as a crookback prodigy, and in the Folio a "Crookbackt prodegie"? The OED's entry for the word *prodigy* includes Margaret's statement as the very first historical appearance of sense 2 of the word: "An unusual or extraordinary thing or occurrence; an anomaly; something abnormal or unnatural; *spec.* a monster, a freak." Sense 2 is significant because it is not predictive. It describes something that is wonderful for its own sake, not a sign of some future upheaval. This presentist sense is clear in the OED's citation of the

Puritan Thomas Gataker's commentary on a passage from Jeremiah in which God chides those who read "signs in the sky" as portents of destruction. His *Vindication of the Annotations of Jeremiah* (1653) comments: "What is a prodigie, but some thing that comes to passe besides, beyond, above, or against the course of nature?"[5] Sense 1 of prodigy, by contrast, is "An extraordinary thing or occurrence regarded as an omen; a sign, a portent." This sense had a much longer pedigree, dating back to the middle of the fifteenth century. While I am inclined to agree with the OED's editors that Queen Margaret wishes to smear Richard Gloucester here by describing him as a freak or a monster, it may be useful to consider Richard as a "prodigy" in the sense that would have been traditional to Shakespeare and his audience members—that of an omen or portent of future events, sense 1 of the OED's definition. Tudor historians made Richard into a monster in order to highlight the glorious arrival of the Tudor dynasty with Henry VII. Their smear campaign was intended to celebrate the Tudors, and Shakespeare enthusiastically participated in this fiction.

If we read Richard as a prodigy both in sense 2 (a monster) and in sense 1 (a predictive sign or portent), it seems reasonable to view the play *Richard III* as a *prodigy play*, which highlights a prodigious birth come to maturity whose political rise and fall signals a significant political upheaval—the final battles of the War of the Roses and the establishment of the Tudor dynasty under the Earl of Richmond. One important difference between Richard's story and the monstrous birth tradition is that this particular monster *creates* the political instability that his birth seems to foreshadow. There are several fanciful early modern accounts in the prodigy pamphlets of babies being born, uttering politically charged statements, and then expiring, but Richard's status as monstrous birth and revolutionary force is something unique, and it helps to generate the unique appeal of the play.

While Richard's prodigious birth, life, and death dominate the final two plays of the first tetralogy, references to the prodigious birth tradition can be found throughout the plays. In 2.2 of *King John*, Lady Constance encourages her son Arthur to seek the crown by noting that he is the anti-Richard, a perfectly normal and natural son who is the rightful heir of France. Had he been a crookback like Richard she would not have urged him to assume his rightful regal seat, she insists, but as a beautiful boy the throne is his birthright:

> If thou that bidd'st me be content wert grim,
> Ugly and sland'rous to thy mother's womb,
> Full of unpleasing blots and sightless stains.
> Lame, foolish, crooked, swart, prodigious,
> Patched with foul moles and eye-offending marks,

I would not care, I then would be content,
For then I should not love thee, no nor thou
Become thy great birth, nor deserve a crown. (2.2.43–50)

Instead, according to Constance, Arthur's perfection demands that he usurp his uncle John. The only problem is that Fortune has become a "strumpet" (2.2.61). She is "corrupted, changed, and won from thee; / She adulterates hourly with thine uncle John" (2.2.55–56) in ways that are entirely unnatural. In essence Constance argues that Fortune herself is the unnatural prodigy.

The closing song in *A Midsummer Night's Dream*, which some editors ascribe to Oberon, instructs the fairies to convey good fortune to Hymen's band. They are to bless all the play's newlyweds, and their blessing will protect their issue from the foul blots of nature.

> Now until the break of day
> Through this house each fairy stray
> To the best bride bed will we,
> Which by us shall blessèd be,
> And the issue there create
> Ever shall be fortunate.
> So shall all the couples three
> Ever true in loving be,
> And the blots of nature's hand
> Shall not in their issue stand. (5.2.31–40)

Oberon specifies what these "blots of nature" are in the following lines:

> Never mole, harelip, nor scar,
> Nor mark prodigious such as are
> Despisèd in nativity
> Shall upon their children be. (5.2.41–44)

There seems to be some redundancy here as moles, harelips, and scars were included in the category of prodigious marks.

The concept of the prodigious birth was so ubiquitous in Shakespeare's culture that he was able to use it as a metaphor for various types of ill-fated occurrences. A brief but poignant use of the prodigious birth metaphor to depict a wondrous event occurs at a critical moment in *Romeo and Juliet*. Juliet learns that her new beloved Romeo is a Montague from the Nurse.

The Nurse's news includes a reference to Romeo's lineage—"The only son of your great enemy"—and the idea of generation informs Juliet's response: "My only love sprung from my only hate!" Birth imagery continues in Juliet's final couplet: "Prodigious birth of love it is to me / That I must love a loathèd enemy" (1.5.135–38). Juliet's love is marked, crooked, stained from birth because it is directed toward an enemy. Unlike Lady Constance and other mothers who seek to distance themselves physically or emotionally from their monstrous births, the virginal Juliet nurtures her unnatural love, and disaster ensues.

A more elaborate example of the metaphorical use of the prodigious birth tradition comes from the first play of the second tetralogy. After King Richard II has banished Bolingbroke and departed for Ireland the Queen has vague misgivings about the future. She describes her concerns using a birthing metaphor:

> methinks
> Some unborn sorrow, ripe in fortune's womb,
> Is coming towards me; and my inward soul
> at nothing trembles. With something it grieves
> More than with parting from my lord the King. (2.2.9–13)

Moments later Green enters with devastating news: the banished Bolingbroke has returned, Northumberland, Hotspur, Ross, Beaumont, and Willoughby have joined his rebellion, and Worcester has resigned his office. The Queen describes the news as a prodigious birth:

> So, Green, thou art the midwife to my woe,
> And Bolingbroke my sorrow's dismal heir.
> Now hath my soul brought forth her prodigy,
> And I, a gasping new-delivered mother,
> Have woe to woe, sorrow to sorrow joined. (2.2.62–66)

The description of Bolingbroke as her "heir" is laden with irony because Bolingbroke has forcibly taken the crown from her and King Richard II.

Bolingbroke is the "heir" to the Queen in more ways than one. He uses prodigy rhetoric toward the end of the next play in the tetralogy, *1 Henry IV*, to chide Worcester. After supporting Henry Bolingbroke and helping him to become king, Worcester turned against him. The scene in question opens with a discussion of ominous weather between King Henry and his son Prince Hal. "How bloodily the sun begins to peer / Above yon bulky hill!" says the king, "the day looks pale / At his distemp'rature." Hal concurs that the natural order seems out of joint:

> The southern wind
> Doth play the trumpet to his [the sun's] purposes,
> And by his hollow whistling in the leaves
> Foretells a tempest and a blust'ring day. (5.1.1–6)

Echoing Richard III's optimism in the morning before the Battle of Bosworth Field, King Henry notes that such signs, inherently ambivalent, likely reflect the imminent defeat of his enemies: "Then with the losers let it sympathize, / For nothing can seem foul to those that win" (5.1.8).

Primed to contemplate prodigious wonder by the ominous weather, King Henry goes on to chide Worcester using an elaborate prodigy metaphor. Furious at Worcester for his insurrection, he asks him if he will cease his support of the rebellion and serve him:

> Will you again unknit
> this churlish knot of all-abhorrèd war,
> And move in that obedient orb again
> Where you did give a fair and natural light,
> And be no more an exhaled meteor,
> A prodigy of fear, and a portent
> Of broachèd mischief to the unborn times? (5.1.15–21)

Because meteors were thought to be made of gas emitted from the sun, this particular metaphor indicates Worcester's distance, in amity at least, from the glorious regent. The reference to the "unborn times" also dimly suggests the link between prodigious wonder and unnatural birth.

Prodigies associated with conspiracy also dominate *Julius Caesar*, particularly in act 1, scene 3, where prodigious wonders take center stage. The scene is illuminating for three main reasons. First, it indicates the variety of events that can qualify as annalistic wonders. Second, it indicates that Elizabethan wonders were open to interpretation. Third, it hints at an important debate taking place in Elizabethan England regarding the divine origin and the predictive power of wonders.

Shakespeare encourages the audience to share in Casca's wonder by employing stage effects to create the illusion of thunder and lightning as the scene opens. Cicero notes the signs of admiration in Casca, "Why are you breathless, and why stare you so?" (1.3.2), and Casca relates that he has seen "tempests" that have split oaks and swelled "Th'ambitious ocean" before, "But never till tonight, never till now, / Did I go through a tempest dropping fire" (1.3.7–10). The ambiguity of the prodigious wonder is one of its most distinctive and most troubling characteristics: What does this unnatural event *mean*? Casca offers two possible interpretations: "Either there is a civil strife in heaven, / Or else the world, too saucy with the gods, / Incenses them to send destruction" (1.3.11–13). Casca seems capable of negative capability here, acknowledging that these cosmic wonders may or may not relate to Rome directly. In his next speech, though, he claims that he believes these prodigies predict some sort of judgment on Rome: "For I believe they are portentous things / Unto the climate that they point upon" (1.3.31–32). Cicero goes on to indicate the inherently subjective nature of prodigy interpretation: "men may construe things after their fashion, / Clean from the purpose of the things themselves" (1.3.34–35). Shakespeare is not only interested in presenting wondrous prodigies, he is also interested in the debates going on in his culture about how prodigies could or should be interpreted, a key question given the official Protestant position that wonders (with the notable exception of the coming apocalypse and resurrection of the dead) had long since ceased.

The definitive interpretation of a wonder is very rare in the plays. After Antony's ships have turned with Cleopatra's to retreat from the sea battle with Caesar near Actium, Enobarbus asks Scarus what has happened and Scarus responds that the fight resembles "the tokened pestilence, / Where death is sure" (3.10.9–10). Indeed once one of God's tokens, or red spots, appeared on a plague-stricken individual, death was imminent. Similarly, in the aftermath of Antony's retreat three scenes later Antony thinks that Cleopatra is fawning over Thidias as a way to show her newfound affection for his master Octavius Caesar. Using a prodigy metaphor Antony laments "Alack, our terrene moon / is now eclipsed, and it portends alone / The fall of Antony" (3.13.156–58). The loss of Cleopatra's favor can have, in Antony's mind at least, only one meaning—his utter devastation. These two references to prodigies are unambiguous, but these are merely rhetorical figures, metaphors, not dramatized prodigies. Where a play's plot pivots on a prodigious wonder Shakespeare prefers ambiguity. This preference is particularly clear in *Antony and Cleopatra* in Shakespeare's dramatization of the mysterious music heard in and around Alexandria on the eve of Antony's decisive defeat. Shakespeare's source, North's 1579 translation of Plutarch's *Lives of the Noble Grecians and Romans*, clearly interprets the mysterious music as a sign that Antony has been abandoned by the god who has favored and protected him.

> Furthermore, the selfe same night within litle of midnight, when all the citie was quiet, full of feare, and sorrowe, thinking what would be the issue and ende of this warre: it is said that sodainly they heard a

maruelous sweete harmonie of sundrie sortes of instrumentes of musicke, with the crie of a multitude of people, as they had bene dauncing, and had song as they vse in *Bacchus* feastes, with mouings and turnings after the maner of the Satyres: & it seemed that this daunce went through the city vnto the gate that opened to the enemies, & that all the troupe that made this noise they heard, went out of the city at that gate. Now, such as in reason sought the depth of the interpretacion of this wō[n]der, thought that it was the god vnto whom *Antonius* bare singular deuotion to counterfeate and resemble him, that did forsake them.[6]

North's translation of Plutarch included a marginal note beside this passage: "Straunge noises heard, and nothing seene."

In Shakespeare's dramatization of this passage confusion reigns briefly before any definitive interpretation of the prodigy can be made. "Heard you of nothing strange about the streets?" the Second Soldier asks before the music is heard (4.3.3). By using the word "strange" in the Second Soldier's statement prior to the music being heard Shakespeare seems to pick up on North's marginal note: "Straunge noises heard, and nothing seene." When the First Soldier says that he has not heard that anything extraordinary has taken place the Second Soldier responds, "Belike 'tis but a rumor. Good night to you" (4.3.5–6). This small talk whets the audience's appetite for a wonder. What is the rumor? What has the Second Soldier heard? The soldiers take their positions "in every corner of the stage," and consider their prospects. The Second Soldier says that if Antony's naval fleet succeeds he is confident the land forces will prevail. After a corroborating vote of confidence from the First Soldier the aural wonder manifests itself. "Music of the hautboys is under the stage" notes the stage direction. The use of the oboe seems significant both because of its novelty and because according to some critics its music may have been considered an ill omen. By transforming the wonder of many instruments and many voices described in Plutarch to the music of a single instrument Shakespeare seems to simplify the prodigy somewhat, but the interpretation of the prodigy is more plural, polyvocal, and ambiguous than it is in Plutarch.

The soldiers are amazed by what they hear, but their wonder does not preclude them from seeking an interpretation of this prodigy.

> Second Soldier: Peace, what noise?
> First Soldier: List, list!
> Second Soldier: Hark!
> First Soldier: Music i'th' air.
> Third Soldier: Under the earth. (4.3.9–10)

The first proposed interpretation is a cautiously optimistic one, offered by the Fourth Soldier in what is his only line in the brief scene: "It signs well, does it not?" (4.3.14). Delivered with confidence this line could be a sincerely hopeful prediction, but in performance it could just as easily be a line expressing terror, a concerted effort to whistle past the graveyard. The Third Soldier immediately challenges the optimistic question with a flat "No" before the First Soldier articulates the interpretive crux in which the soldiers find themselves: "What should this mean?" The Second Soldier provides a version of Plutarch's interpretation, with the insertion of Hercules as Antony's patron instead of Bacchus: "'Tis the god Hercules, whom Antony loved, / Now leaves him" (4.3.13–14). This notion of being abandoned by Hercules echoes Antony's claim earlier in the play after witnessing Cleopatra's familiarity with Caesar's ambassador Thidias that his favorable stars have abandoned him:

He makes me angry,
And at this time most easy 'tis to do't,
When my good stars that were my former guides
have empty left their orbs [spheres], and shot their fires
Into th'abyss of hell. (3.13.145–49)

After Antony's troops have tried to make sense of the oboe music they meet others who corroborate the prodigy they have witnessed. Here again North's marginal note seems significant, as both the First Soldier and then all the soldiers collectively describe the noise under the stage as "strange."[7]

Earlier in this chapter I indicated the prevalence and importance of the prodigious or monstrous birth tradition in Shakespeare's England and in his plays. At the other end of the spectrum is what we might call the prodigious death, by which I mean a death that is so disturbing—usually because of the tremendous heroism or virtue of the deceased—that it upsets, at least temporarily, the cosmic order. In the two examples of this, which I will note here, those who grieve the dead anticipate some sort of cosmic irregularity as a reflection of the importance of the individual's demise. This type of thinking is not only characteristic of Shakespeare, a playwright fond of universalizing his protagonists' joy or sorrow, it also reflects his culture's belief in the symmetry or parallelism between the human microcosm and the cosmic macrocosm. Octavius Caesar seems an unlikely mourner for Antony given their political, military, and personal rivalries. His antagonism toward Antony makes his lamentation of Antony's death all the more poignant. Caesar says that Antony's death is so awful, so unnatural, that it should trigger the same types of prodigies that heralded the fall of Caesar:

> The breaking of so great a thing should make
> A greater crack. The rivèd world
> Should have shook lions into civil [city] streets,
> And citizens to their [the lions'] dens. The death of Antony
> Is not a single doom; in that name lay
> A moiety [half] of the world. (5.1.14–19)

Antony's death is more than the demise of a military and political figure; it is the demise of the world order. Of course Caesar's lamentation may be exaggerated here, given their personal animosity and the fact that he stands to gain Antony's moiety. Still there is a sense in Shakespeare's rendition of this portion of Plutarch's history that Antony's death represents a sort of cosmic doom. This sentiment is articulated immediately after Antony stabs himself and is discovered, alone, by his guards and Decretas. One of his guards says, "the star is fall'n" and another adds "And time is at his period" (4.15.106–107). The sense here is that Antony's death is both an annalistic prodigy and an apocalyptic prodigy, the equivalent of the end of time. Ethel Seaton has usefully compared what she calls the "apocalyptic suggestion of the splendid phrases" in the last two acts of *Antony and Cleopatra* with passages from the Book of Revelation.[8]

The expectation that a personal loss will translate into a wondrous prodigy surfaces in many other plays. One notable example is Othello's statement immediately after suffocating Desdemona:

> My wife, my wife! What wife? I ha' no wife.
> O insupportable, O heavy hour!
> Methinks it should be now a huge eclipse
> Of sun and moon, and that th'affrighted globe
> Should yawn at alteration. (5.2.106–110)

This particular passage seems to indicate the importance of wonder not only within the narrative of the play but in the relationship between the stage actors and the audience. Just as the earth yawned or opened up during the earthquake that was thought to follow a solar eclipse, the Globe audiences were expected to stand or sit with mouths agape in wonder as they watched Othello's murder of Desdemona. In this single passage, then, the linkage between macrocosm and microcosm, the linkage between celestial and earthly prodigies, and the connections between the actors and the audience are all suffused with wonder.

While the Second Soldier in Shakespeare's *Antony and Cleopatra* counters the Fourth Soldier's optimistic interpretation of the exotic music with pessimism, Richard Gloucester shifts from ambivalence to pessimism and back to ambivalence again in his interpretation of the sun's failure to rise—perhaps because of an eclipse, but this is not specified—on the morning of the Battle of Bosworth Field. He begins by noting that the lack of sun is an unnatural occurrence, which seems to bode ill for someone: "A black day will it be to somebody" (5.6.10). He then personalizes the prodigy, taking it as a sign that the heavens are biased against him and his troops: "The sun will not be seen today, / The sky doth frown and lour upon our army. / I would these dewy tears were from the ground" (5.6.12–14). After a moment's pause he reverses course, returning to his neutral interpretation: "Not shine today—why, what is that to me / More than to Richmond? For the selfsame heaven / That frowns on me looks sadly upon him" (5.6.15–17). These interpretive shifts are consistent with Richard's protean nature, while his ultimate interpretive position—identical to his initial objective position—seems to reflect his courage and charisma as a military leader.

Aware of the dangerous ambiguity of the prodigious occurrence, Roman authorities created an official body called the College of Augurs responsible for interpreting unnatural events. During the Renaissance in Catholic Europe the Inquisition performed a similar role. Because Protestant authorities largely discounted the divine origin of prodigies, they did not create a corresponding institution devoted to explaining prodigies rationally or theologically. Thus the ambivalence of the prodigies in Shakespeare's *Julius Caesar* is a telling anachronism. In Caesar's day a simple explanation of this type of tempest could have been provided by the College of Augurs, but in Elizabethan England these types of cosmic spectacles engendered confusion, questioning, and ultimately subjective interpretation that could be potentially destabilizing in multiple ways.[9] The frequent use of prodigious elements in the history plays places the audience in a unique position. Knowing the outcome the prodigious wonder predicts, the audience members experience the pleasure of clear interpretation even as they watch the characters in the plays struggle for interpretive clarity. This extreme form of dramatic irony carves out a place for the traditional variety of wonder inherent in prodigies even as it contains or limits its postclassical ambiguity.

Cassius takes advantage of the ambivalence of these signs to condemn Caesar. These prodigies prove, according to this master manipulator, that Caesar himself is a prodigious monster who must be removed from power.

Cassius's interpretation of the prodigies is compelling, and his confidence reveals that the problem of interpretation could and often did lead to a fantasy of clear interpretation.[10] Cassius begins by criticizing Casca for his inability to interpret the signs, claiming that he either lacks or fails to use the intellectual capabilities expected of a cultured man of Rome: "You are dull, Casca, and those sparks of life / That should be in a Roman you do want, / Or else you use not" (1.3.57–59). While he may lack "sparks of life," he does possess the ability to register wonder, and Cassius goes on to describe Casca's physiological, psychological, and affective symptoms of wonder: "You look pale, and gaze, / And put on fear, and cast yourself in wonder, / To see the strange impatience of the heavens" (1.3.59–61). Here wonder is described as a near relative of fear. The notion of casting or throwing oneself in wonder suggests that the experience is all-encompassing and that it is voluntary, but for Casca, of course, it is not.[11] While there is a certain level of openness or susceptibility required to experience wonder inside or outside the theater, it is rarely a state of being that can be consciously chosen. Instead it develops reflexively in response to strange, unnatural, or striking phenomena. In some ways it is akin to surprise, but it is a more profound reaction than surprise because it often entails religious or pseudoreligious awe. Indeed one of the key assertions of this study is that wonder is a response that dominates both religious and secular experience, moving seamlessly across the boundary between the secular and the sacred.

Cassius's critique of Casca's inability to interpret the prodigious signs presents a sort of paradox. On one hand he suggests that the prodigies should not elicit wonder because they are easily explicable, but on the other hand he insists that the prodigies are wonders that mirror the monstrosity of Caesar's rapacious nature. In essence he is attempting to domesticate, or at least explain, the unnatural occurrences that they have seen while preserving an appreciation for their terrible significance:

> But if you would consider the true cause
> Why all these fires, why all these gliding ghosts,
> Why birds and beasts from quality and kind—
> Why old men, fools, and children calculate—
> Why all these things change from their ordinance,—
> Their natures, and preformèd faculties,
> To monstrous quality—why, you shall find
> That heaven hath infused them with these spirits
> To make them instruments of fear and warning
> Unto some monstrous state. (1.3.62–71)

Without mentioning Caesar by name, Cassius then goes on to illustrate the direct parallels between the prodigies that have just occurred and Caesar's own prodigious evil:

> Now could I, Casca,
> Name to thee a man most like this dreadful night,
> That thunders, lightens, opens graves, and roars
> As doth the lion in the Capitol;
> A man no mightier than myself or me
> In personal action, yet prodigious grown,
> And fearful, as these strange eruptions are. (1.3.71–77)

Casca did not mention the raising of the dead among his list of the night's wonders, but with Cassius's mention of opening graves he recalls the special wonders of resurrection and pseudoresurrection that were the focus of chapter I.2. Interestingly, the Q2 edition of *Hamlet* offers a fuller picture of pre-Caesarian resurrection prodigies than *Julius Caesar*. In Q2 Horatio tells Barnardo that "The graves stood tenantless, and the sheeted dead / Did squeak and gibber in the streets" (1.1.106.8–9).

Cassius depicts Caesar in terms that resemble Richard Gloucester, with the important difference that Richard was a monster from birth while Caesar has developed his allegedly monstrous ambition in adulthood. Cassius's interpretation of the prodigies seems straightforward enough, but because this is a Roman history play the audience is already well aware that these portents refer not to Caesar's monstrosity but to the unconscionable conspiracy and murder that will cast the state into chaos.

Casca's list of prodigious events provides a nice overview of the types of occurrences that could be categorized as wonders:

> A common slave—you know him well by sight—
> Held up his left hand, which did flame and burn
> Like twenty torches joined; and yet his hand,
> Not sensible of fire, remained unscorched.
> Besides—I ha' not since put up my sword—
> Against the Capitol I met a lion
> Who glazed upon me, and went surly by
> Without annoying me. And there were drawn
> Upon a head a hundred ghastly women,
> Transformèd with their fear, who swore they saw
> Men all in fire walk up and down the streets.

> And yesterday the bird of night did sit
> Even at noonday upon the market-place,
> Hooting and shrieking. (1.3.15–28)

The literal inflammation of the hand—a secular recapitulation of the miracle of the burning bush recounted in Exodus—suggests a magic trick, the peaceful lion suggests an unexpected but harmless encounter with the exotic and the dangerous like those afforded to Elizabethan visitors to menageries, and the owl reverses its normal biorhythm. The most amazing wonder of all is not something that Casca witnesses. It is something he hears reported by "a hundred ghastly women." This distancing transforms it from a personal experience into a legendary event, in a sense enhancing its affective power.

One of the most interesting passages in the scene—and one of the most instructive in terms of Elizabethan attitudes toward prodigious wonders—is Casca's own commentary on this list of wonders he has seen. He takes a step back from these particular marvels and ponders the competing claims made by early modern English men and women regarding miraculous occurrences in general. His assessment indicates the extent to which official positions on wonders failed to satisfy large segments of the population:

> When these prodigies
> Do so conjointly meet, let not men say
> "These are their reasons," "they are natural,"
> For I believe they are portentous things
> Unto the climate that they point upon. (1.3.28–32)

Casca parrots the official Protestant position on wonders here—that miracles ceased after the time of the early church—and he does so partly by employing the rhetoric of the natural philosopher.

CHAPTER I.5

More of a Prodigy than a Prophecy

Natural philosophers were fascinated by all sorts of strange occurrences, and they avidly collected those exotic *naturalia* and *artificialia* that had a whiff of the marvelous. Even Francis Bacon, who was a proponent of empirical thought and the thinker credited with devising the model for the first scientific society in England, believed that special attention should be paid to all sorts of marvels. Bacon claimed in his *The Advancement of Learning* (1605) that natural history could be divided into three parts: "nature in course," "nature erring or varying," and "nature altered, or wrought."[1] The first category included all naturally occurring flora and fauna; the second included marvels, monsters, and other apparently unnatural creatures; and the third represented works of art made by human beings. Elsewhere he referred to these categories as the "History of Creatures, History of Marvailes, and History of Arts" (3:330). Bacon believed that sufficient progress was being made in the first area, but that the others were deficient. He lamented that there was no "substantial and severe Collection of the Heteroclites, or irregulars of Nature" and he said this should be corrected by the collection and study of marvels (3:331). He offered a nice definition of the wondrous when he claimed that the marvels of interest to him "have a digression and deflection from the ordinary course of generations, productions, and motions" (3:330). Bacon championed the idea of the wonder cabinet as a repository for these types of marvels, telling his colleagues that "we have to make a collection or particular natural history of all prodigies and monstrous births of nature; of everything in short that is in nature new, rare, and unusual."[2] In the next chapter, I will examine some of the relationships between Shakespeare's plays and wonder cabinets.

Casca is not interested in studying wonders for the sake of some sort of totalizing natural philosophical program. He feels that wonders have predictive power and that they are geographically specific. Thus for him and for Cassius as well a wonder is a predictor, a sign from the gods of something to come in a particular "climate" or place. While Casca is uncertain as to the meaning of the ambiguous prodigies he has witnessed, Cassius interprets them as signs of divine displeasure with Caesar's imminent reign.

Because the prodigy was—particularly in the postclassical period—inherently ambiguous, it seemed to invite personal bias. Indeed it became a sort of mirror of the desires and fears of the early modern individual. Early modern wonder pamphlets betray their authors' agendas in a variety of ways. Most commonly they used the wondrous prodigy as evidence for God's support of their religious or political position. A certain cosmic event, monstrous birth, natural disaster, or war among flocks of birds prefigured the collapse of the heretical or corrupt powers. Thus the labeling of any natural or cosmic occurrence as a prodigy was usually politically destabilizing. Indeed those individuals with an axe to grind against the status quo were primed to identify and interpret unusual events of any kind as wonders, and so they were usually the ones to discover and interpret signs and wonders in the first place. A clear example of bias where the identification and interpretation of prodigious wonders were concerned can be found in *King John*. After King John has captured his young nephew Arthur, Cardinal Pandolf tells Louis the Dauphin that King John is preparing to murder Arthur. If he does, Pandolf claims, the people will turn against him and begin to see prodigies in all the usual places such as unusual weather and monstrous births. In addition, Pandolf asserts, people will inevitably start to discover or even invent prodigies in everyday phenomena. Primed to find signs of God's displeasure with King John's tyranny, they will interpret everything, whether ordinary or extraordinary, as an indication that King John is a tyrant who must be removed from power:

> This act [killing of Arthur], so vilely born, shall cool the hearts
> Of all his people, and freeze up their zeal,
> That none so small advantage shall step forth
> To check his reign but they will cherish it;
> No natural exhalation [meteor] in the sky,
> No scope of nature, no distempered day,
> No common wind, no customèd event,
> But they will pluck away his natural cause,
> And call them meteors prodigies, and signs,
> Abortives presages, and tongues of heaven
> Plainly denouncing vengeance upon John. (3.4.149–59)

Cardinal Pandolf believes that King John's tyranny will encourage misinterpretation, the reading of mundane meaningless natural phenomena as reflections of King John's tyranny, which must lead to rebellion, the removal of John from power, and the installment of Louis the Dauphin as king. The phrase "tongues of heaven" is particularly apt, for it suggests that prodigies offer a means of communication between the human and divine, but it also suggests the inscrutability of divine intentions, the sense in which divine forces necessarily resort to speaking in tongues.

Shakespeare recycles much of act 1, scene 3, from *Julius Caesar* in the discussion of the Ghost's appearance in the second quarto edition of the opening scene of *Hamlet*. After Horatio summarizes the recent conflict between Denmark and Norway and indicates that young Fortinbras is preparing an invasion, Barnardo claims that the ghost of King Hamlet is a "portentous figure"—a prodigy, a wonder—which "Comes armèd through our watch so like the king / That was and is the question of these wars" (1.1.106.2–4). Horatio then reminds us of the prodigies reported in *Julius Caesar*. His speech elaborates on the wonders that took place on the eve of Caesar's assassination and it closes with a verbal echo of Casca's conclusion that prodigies are not explicable logically but are instead: "portentous things / Unto the climate that they point upon" (1.3.31–32). Invoking that night, Horatio states:

> In the most high and palmy state of Rome,
> A little ere the mightiest Julius fell,
> The graves stood tenantless, and the sheeted dead
> Did squeak and gibber in the Roman streets
> As stars with trains of fire, and dews of blood,
> Disasters in the sun; and the moist star,
> Upon whose influence Neptune's empire stands,
> Was sick almost to doomsday with eclipse.
> And even the like precurse of feared events,
> As harbingers preceding still the fates,
> And prologue to the omen coming on,
> Have heaven and earth together demonstrated
> Unto our climature and countrymen. (1.1.106.6–18)

In both Q2 and F Horatio decides to ask the ghost for information regarding the future: "If thou art privy to thy country's fate / Which happily foreknowing may avoid, / O speak!" (1.1.114–116). This statement seems to contain a paradox. If the ghost has knowledge of the future, can the imparting of that knowledge change the future? Put another way, to what extent is a harbinger an indication of a definitive future and to what extent is it an indication of one possible future?[3]

This question comes up most prominently in *Macbeth*. After Macbeth is named Thane of Cawdor, Banquo reports that Macbeth is "rapt," possessed with wonder. In this rapt state Macbeth says to himself, "If chance will have me king, why, chance may crown me / Without my stir" (1.3.142–43). Here he grasps that there is a certain inevitability in the witches' prophecy and he seems to suggest that no action is required on his part. Lady Macbeth views the prophecy differently, as an invitation to act in such a way as to gain the crown. One thing that both royals-to-be share is the wholehearted belief in the veracity of the prophecies. Even as things unravel for Macbeth in the final act he clings to the prophecy that seems to convey unassailability, asserting that he lives "a charmèd life, which must not yield / To one of woman born" (5.10.12–13). When Macduff reveals that he was not of woman born Macbeth loses courage and then seems to defy the prophetic witches:

And be these juggling fiends no more believed,
That palter with us in a double sense,
That keep the word of promise to our ear
And break it to our hope. (5.10.19–22)

This is a rich and complex passage, which merits careful analysis. Initially it seems to suggest that one should not believe in prophecies from supernatural agents such as the witches, but Macbeth qualifies this statement by saying that one should not put faith in their statements because they deceive by uttering prophecies that are duplicitous. The literal sense engenders hope in the hearer, particularly if that hearer is susceptible to ambition, while the hidden meaning foretells one's ultimate doom. Macbeth's final epiphany before his death is not that the witches speak falsehood but that they speak the truth in a way that defies expectations. Here again, then, we see that prodigies are both titillating and maddening because even when they seem self-explanatory they offer interpretive cruxes, riddles wrapped in enigmas.

Immediately after Macbeth realizes the duplicity of the witches he refuses to fight with Macduff: "I'll not fight with thee" (5.10.22). Macduff responds by threatening to display the living Macbeth as a wonder, a "show and gaze o'th' time." He threatens to "have thee as our rare monsters are, / Painted upon a pole, and underwrit / 'Here may you see the tyrant'" (5.10.25–27). This threat infuriates Macbeth—"I will not...be baited with the rabble's curse" (5.10.28–29)—and he decides to fight Macduff to the death. In this scene Shakespeare is not only able to show us a satisfying fatal encounter between

Macbeth and Macduff, which fulfills the prophecy; he is also able to offer a sort of moral epitome for his entire play. In a sense the play as a whole does just what Macduff threatens to do: it holds a living Macbeth up to the audience as a spectacle, a living, breathing monument of the suffering tyrant. By offering this perspective on Macbeth Shakespeare secures the moral high ground, intimating that his purpose all along was to show audiences a cautionary tale, a sort of mirror for magistrates in which vice is appropriately punished. But the predictive power of the prodigy is also cryptically present in the hypothetical spectacle with which Macduff threatens Macbeth. The caged tyrant and his suicidal bride are wonders, spectacles unto themselves, and they are also predictions of what will happen to tyrants who let themselves get carried away by the potent combination of suggestive prophecy and overweening ambition.

Prodigies were serious business in part because they were thought to foreshadow destabilizing political upheaval or divine wrath. In the opening scene of Shakespeare's first tragedy, *Titus Andronicus*, Lucius feels compelled to sacrifice Tamora's son Alarbus, the "proudest prisoner of the Goths," in order to avoid prodigious occurrences. He claims that he needs to sacrifice Alarbus so that "the shadows" of his slaughtered Roman brethren "be not unappeased, / Nor we disturbed with prodigies on earth" (1.1.96, 100–101). Despite the deadly serious nature of the prodigies discussed in the tragedies, not all of Shakespeare's references to prodigies deal with such dour topics as revenge and political corruption. For example, the lighter side of the prodigious wonder surfaces in two interesting places in *The Taming of the Shrew*. Petruccio's public humiliation of Kate on their wedding day entails dressing ridiculously, outrageously, and altogether inappropriately. When he appears (intolerably late) in tattered motley the assembled wedding guests are amazed. Petruccio notices this immediately:

Gentles, methinks you frown.
And wherefore gaze this goodly company
As if they saw some wondrous monument,
Some comet or unusual prodigy? (3.2.86–89)

Petruccio is more outrageous than prodigious here, but his appearance here is prodigious in the sense that it is a sign of outrageous behavior to come. In the meantime the mute wonder of the onlookers resembles the response to a cosmic spectacle of ambiguous import.

Prodigious wonder features even more prominently in the play's climactic scene. Petruccio, Hortensio, and Lucentio have placed bets on whose new bride will come first when called. Hortensio's widow and Bianca both refuse to come and Petruccio sends Grumio to "command" Kate to come. She enters, and Baptista responds with awe. "Now by my halidom, here comes Katherina" (5.2.103). Baptista may lack sensitivity or even a basic sense of fair play regarding his daughters, but his earnestness is not in doubt here. He swears by all that he holds sacred because he is amazed. During the course of Kate's life he has never been able to tame her, and here Petruccio has apparently tamed her completely in a relatively short time.

Petruccio sends Kate to retrieve the two disobedient brides and as she is doing this Lucentio provides a sort of coda for the entire play: "Here is a wonder, if you talk of wonders" (5.2.110). Because wonders were so often prodigious Hortensio responds, "And so it is. I wonder what it bodes" (5.2.111). He picks up Lucentio's word "wonder" but transforms its meaning from the sense denoting a highly charged prodigy to the simple denotation of curiosity. His curiosity regarding what this wonder "bodes" indicates how intimately that wonder and prodigy were not only interrelated, but often interchangeable terms and concepts. "Marry, peace it bodes," Petruccio answers optimistically, "and love, and quiet life; / An awful rule and right supremacy, / And, to be short, what not that's sweet and happy" (5.2.112–14). This reference to "awful rule" indicates another synonym for wonder, and the slightly positive connotation of "awful," though obsolete, calls to mind the decidedly positive connotation of the word "awesome" in modern parlance. In this brief and apparently insignificant exchange, then, the key male figures in the play assert that the conclusion of the play is wonderful, indicate some of the emotional and intellectual planes on which the term "wonder" could operate, and invoke religious rhetoric to describe both individual responses to a stunning occurrence and the ideal interaction between a subject/wife and her lord/husband. The centrality of wonder in this particular play is further reinforced in its very last line. After Katherine's shocking aria on a wife's proper subjection, Lucentio comments simply, "'Tis a wonder, by your leave, she will be tamed so" (5.2.193). This taming is a "wonder" in part because its ultimate significance is unclear. To paraphrase Lucentio, we wonder what it bodes. Will Kate continue to behave as the ideal subject-wife? Will she instead revert to her pre-Petruccio ways? This ambiguity is consonant with the inherent ambivalence of the cosmic spectacle or the monstrous birth.

In a previous chapter we noted that the presence of the doubting Thomas significantly enhances the affective power of a revealed wonder. By inserting a professed skeptic into a narrative that pivots on a wondrous occurrence, the narrator is able to acknowledge and manage the reader or viewer's own skepticism. In another comic treatment of prodigious wonder in *1 Henry IV* Shakespeare inserts a doubting Henry—Henry Percy, also known as Hotspur, to be precise—in order to cast doubt on the allegedly supernatural occurrences that took place around the time of Glendower's birth. While Thomas of India, the original doubting Thomas, ultimately accepts that Christ has risen after a personal encounter with him, Hotspur's skepticism toward Glendower's alleged prodigies does not abate by the end of their encounter, leading the play's audience to question these particular prodigies. The effect of this exchange is to encourage audience members to view certain alleged wonders as mere superstition, an attitude that was consistent with the mainline Protestant doctrine on post-Biblical wonders.

Act 3, scene 1, begins with the rebels in amity as they prepare to divvy up Henry IV's kingdom. The Welshman Glendower praises Hotspur's valour and Hotspur returns the compliment. Glendower then insists that miraculous acts of nature occurred at the time of his birth, which marked him as a supremely gifted man.

> At my nativity
> The front of heaven was full of fiery shapes,
> Of burning cressets [metal baskets, suggesting meteors]; and
>   at my birth
> The frame and huge foundation of the earth
> Shaked like a coward. (3.1.12–16)

Hotspur is hardly impressed. He replies that these heavenly spectacles may indeed have taken place, but there is no way of linking them to Glendower's birth: "Why, so it would have done / At the same season if your mother's cat / Had but kittened, though yourself had never been born" (3.1.17–19). Glendower is shaken by this retort and seems unable to proffer an adequate rhetorical response as he simply repeats his original claim: "I say the earth did shake when I was born" (3.1.19). His implication is that there is a cause-effect relationship between these two events, but Glendower never makes this explicit. Hotspur does, however, when he answers, "And I say the earth was not of my mind / If you suppose as fearing you it shook" (3.1.20). This is a witty parry made with a double-edged rhetorical sword. On one hand it asserts that Hotspur is not intimidated by Glendower, and on the other it exposes the unlikely assumption underlying Hotspur's description of the prodigies surrounding his birth. Glendower attempts to regain the field by repetition—"The heavens were all on fire, the earth did tremble"—but Hotspur cuts him off by presenting a rational, scientific explanation of the earthquake that coincided with Glendower's nativity.

> Diseasèd nature oftentimes breaks forth
> In strange eruptions; oft the teeming earth

> Is with a kind of colic pinched and vexed
> By the imprisoning of unruly wind
> Within her womb, which for enlargement striving
> Shakes the old beldam earth, and topples down
> Steeples and moss-grown towers. At your birth
> Our grandam earth, having this distemp'rature,
> In passion shook. (3.1.25–33)

Glendower grows incensed at Hotspur's skepticism, in part because the personal narrative that has sustained him throughout his life is being challenged. In response he adds another prodigy to those he has already mentioned—a stampede of goats—before attempting to prove his extraordinary status by noting that he taught himself to read and that he exceeds all men in the occult arts. In essence he claims wondrous status by asserting that he is a self-made man.

>   Cousin, of many men
> I do not bear these crossings. Give me leave
> To tell you once again that at my birth
> The front of heaven was full of fiery shapes,
> The goats ran from the mountains, and the herds
> Were strangely clamorous to the frighted fields.
> These signs have marked me extraordinary,
> And all the courses of my life do show
> I am not in the roll of common men.
> Where is he living, clipped in with the sea
> That chides the banks of England, Scotland, Wales,
> Which calls me pupil or hath read to me?
> And bring him out that is but woman's son
> Can trace me in the tedious ways of art,
> And hold me pace in deep experiments. (3.1.33–47)

Glendower's impassioned defense of his status as a wonder reveals another key problem with prodigious wonders: they can only be verified after the events that they seem to predict have come to pass. In Glendower's case the prodigies surrounding his birth may have suggested that he would be extraordinary, but the nature of his extraordinary development only became apparent in adulthood. Until a prodigy comes to fruition it remains an ambiguous signifier.

Hotspur gets the better of Glendower in this exchange partly for nationalistic reasons. Shakespeare seems interested here in contrasting the rational (if cantankerous) Englishman against the superstitious and diabolical Welshman. The effect of this confrontation within the context of the play may be minimal, but its significance within Shakespeare's larger body of work is substantial because it validates skepticism in the face of certain types of alleged wonders.

Skepticism gives way to wholehearted endorsement of prodigious wonder in Shakespeare's last history play, *Henry VIII*, or *All is True*. Among theater historians the play is best known for the wondrous spectacle of the Globe's destruction by fire during its third or fourth performance on June 29, 1613. There was a keen irony in the destruction of the Globe by fire and its subsequent reconstruction because the triumphant wonder at the center of the play is explicitly compared to the wondrous resurrection of the phoenix from its own ashes. In one of the most important speeches in the play Cranmer prophesies that Elizabeth "now promises / Upon this land a thousand thousand blessings / Which time shall bring to ripeness" (5.4.18–20). Her reign will be a time of peace, wisdom, and prosperity, and most remarkably of all these benevolent features of her reign will not die with her.

> Nor shall this peace sleep with her, but, as when
> The bird of wonder dies—the maiden phoenix—
> Her ashes new create another heir
> As great in admiration as herself,
> So shall she leave her blessèdness to one,
> When heaven shall call her from this cloud of darkness,
> Who from the sacred ashes of her honour
> Shall star-like rise as great in fame as she was,
> And so stand fixed. (5.4.39–47)

The "one" to whom Cranmer refers is of course King James. It is sufficiently amazing that Queen Elizabeth will be able to establish and rule an ideal English commonwealth, but it is even more astonishing that the glories of her reign will be transcendent, that she will somehow be able to transfer them directly to James, Shakespeare's patron when he and Fletcher collaborated on this play. When this miraculous transfer takes effect,

> Peace, plenty, love, truth, terror,
> That were the servants to this chosen infant, [Elizabeth],
> Shall then be his [James I's], and, like a vine, grow to him.
> Wherever the bright sun of heaven shall shine,
> His honour and the greatness of his name
> Shall be, and make new nations. He shall flourish,

And like a mountain cedar reach his branches
To all the plains about him. Our children's children
Shall see this, and bless heaven. (5.4.47–55)

Cranmer's prophecy transforms Elizabeth's birth into a prodigious wonder by recasting a natural occurrence into a marvelous portent of future events. In part because it took place prior to the official marriage between King Henry and Anne Boleyn, Elizabeth's glorious birth is the result of a miraculous conception, a sort of inverse of the monstrous birth. Cranmer's prophecy is rhetorically complex. It covers multiple generations, touches on political, educational, and ethical issues, and blends Biblical rhetoric with proto-imperialist enthusiasm for expansion. King Henry's response to it, however, is simple and telling, and it indicates the centrality of wonder in any interpretation of the play: "Thou speakest wonders."

Unlike *Hamlet*, *Julius Caesar*, and *Macbeth*, the prodigies at the center of *Henry VIII* are uplifting and clearly optimistic. The most striking prodigy in the play is the celestial dream vision, which Katherine enjoys in the moments before her death. Readers may not like this whole description of the differences between prophecy and prodigy. However, a dream vision may become a prodigy when it is staged in public and is thus subject to public witnessing. This dream is prophetic in that it tells the future, but it is more of a prodigy than a prophecy because it is an unnatural and inherently ambiguous spectacle instead of a divinely inspired narration. As a prodigy it requires not only interpretation but also witnessing. This may be one useful way of distinguishing prodigy from prophecy, though in the early modern period these two terms, along with others such as "sign" and of course "wonder," were related and often overlapping terms and concepts.

Like Richard III's dream vision prior to the decisive Battle of Bosworth Field, Queen Katherine's dream accurately predicts the future, but unlike Richard's vision or the apparitions conjured by the witches in *Macbeth* Katherine's vision eases her heart by indicating that she will enjoy eternal peace and happiness in heaven. The dream vision is described in uncharacteristic detail, which has led scholars to suggest that Fletcher and not Shakespeare authored it. Labeled "The Vision" in the text of the play, its masque-like elements convey a certain ritualism to the scene and the play as a whole.

> *Enter, solemnly tripping one after another, six personages clad in white robes, wearing on their heads garlands of bays, and golden visors on their faces. [They carry] branches of bays or palm in their hands. They first congé [bow] unto [Katherine], then dance; and, at certain changes [dance movements],*

the first two hold a spare garland over her head at which the other four make reverent curtsies. Then the two that held the garland deliver the same to the other next two, who observe the same order in their changes and holding the garland over her head. Which done, they deliver the same garland to the last two who likewise observe the same order. At which, as it were by inspiration, she makes in her sleep signs of rejoicing, and holdeth up her hands to heaven. And so in their dancing vanish, carrying the garland with them. The music continues. (Stage directions following 4.2.82)

Katherine confirms the identity of these angelic visitors upon waking: "Spirits of peace, where are ye?" (4.2.83). This celestial vision comforts Katherine, and it also functions in the play to captivate and amaze members of the theater audience. Theater historians note that Sarah Siddons (1755–1831) was the most compelling Queen Katherine in the modern era. The most impressive staging of the play, though, was Charles Kean's performance in 1855. The show ran for one hundred nights with Kean playing the role of Wolsey and his wife playing the role of Queen Katherine. Kean's production featured an elaborate pageant of London as it was supposed to look in the time of Henry VIII and included a moving barge to create the effect of ship traffic on the Thames. We are lucky to have an account of Kean's production in the form of a diary entry written by Lewis Carroll. Carroll's account reveals that for him and presumably for others this production was not just *like* a religious experience, it *was* a religious experience. Queen Katherine's vision is the highlight of the production in Carroll's enthusiastic account.

Carroll sets the stage for the description of Kean's *Henry VIII* by noting the accompanying theatrical fare, a stark contrast to Shakespeare's play. "The evening began with a capital farce *Away with Melancholy*."[4] Then he launches into a rousing encomium for Kean's masterpiece: "And then came the great play *Henry VIII*, the greatest theatrical treat I ever had or ever expect to have—I had no idea that anything so superb as the scenery and dresses was ever to be seen on the stage" (352). Note the awareness of spectacle here. Carroll adds that Kean was magnificent as Cardinal Wolsey and that Mrs. Kean was "a worthy successor to Mrs. Siddons" as Queen Katherine (352). His focus, though, is on the affective response produced by Katherine's dream vision: "But oh, that exquisite vision of Queen Catherine! I almost held my breath to watch; the illusion is perfect, and I felt as if in a dream all the time it lasted. It was like delicious reverie, or the most beautiful poetry" (352). Carroll goes on to claim that the dream vision was not only impressive in its own right, it was the epitome of the perfect theatrical experience. "This is the true end and object of acting—to raise the mind above itself, and out of its petty everyday cares—never shall I forget that wonderful evening, that exquisite vision" (352). Because he was so deeply moved by the scene he is able to recall it in great detail:

> sunbeams broke in through the roof and gradually revealed two angel forms, floating in front of the carved work on the ceiling: the column of sunbeams shone down upon the sleeping queen, and gradually down it floated a troop of angelic forms, transparent, and carrying palm branches in their hands: they waved these over the sleeping queen, with oh! such a sad and solemn grace. (352–53)

Part of my argument in this study is that Shakespeare's theatrical performances helped to supplement or even replace some of the more wondrous varieties of religious experience that were banned under Elizabeth. Shakespeare seems to suggest as much in the prologue to *Henry VIII* when he writes that among the audience members are some who "give / Their money out of hope they may believe" (1.0.7–8). Clearly a true believer in the wonderful world that Shakespeare and Fletcher have constructed here, Carroll considers whether what Kean has presented on stage may in fact resemble angelic visitation: "So could I fancy (if the thought be not profane) would real angels seem to our mortal vision, though doubtless our conception is poor and mean to the reality" (353). Picking up the detailed description again, he emphasizes the overwhelming emotion felt by Katherine and the subsequent admiration of the theater audience:

> She in an ecstasy raises her arms towards them, and to sweet slow music they vanish as marvellously as they came. Then the profound silence of the audience burst at once into a rapture of applause; but even that scarcely marred the effect of the beautiful sad waking words of the Queen, "Spirits of peace, where are ye?" (353)

Carroll closes his diary entry by offering the highest praise imaginable, writing "I never enjoyed anything so much in my life before—and never felt so inclined to shed tears at anything fictitious, save perhaps that poetical gem of Dickens, the death of Little Paul" (353). If, as the prologue states, one of the goals of *Henry VIII* is to make believers out of the hopeful, the prodigious visitation of the angels of peace during Queen Katherine's dream seems to have had its desired effect on Carroll.

In Carroll's description of Kean's performance he notes that sunbeams broke through the theater's roof and characters rode these sunbeams down to the stage itself. This particular solar effect is not indicated in Fletcher's elaborate stage directions in *Henry VIII*, but a solar prodigy does take place on the stage in an earlier history play, *3 Henry VI*, also known as *Richard Duke of York*. In 2.1, as Richard Duke of York's sons Edward and Richard await news of their father's fate in battle, a celestial prodigy appears to them. After line 20 the stage direction in the 1595 Octavo edition reads, "Three suns appear in the air." Shakespeare's source for this wondrous detail is likely Holinshed's account of the Battle of Mortimer's Cross, which took place on February 2, 1461. Holinshed's account is a nearly identical reproduction of Hall's earlier account. The accounts in Hall and Holinshed are intriguing because they create a direct link between the vision and Edward's victory at the Battle of Mortimer's Cross, and they use a parenthetical statement to maintain a certain level of skepticism regarding this trinitarian prodigy. Here is Hall's account:

> The duke of Yorke, called erle of Marche, somwhat spurred and quickened with these noveltyes [i.e., the news that his enemies were planning a surprise attack] retired backe, & mett with his enemies in a faire playne, nere to Mortimers crosse, not farre from Herford east, on Candelmas day in the mornyng, at whiche tyme the sunne (as some write) appered to the erle of March, like. iii. sunnes, and sodainly joined all together in one, and that upon the sight therof, he toke suche courage, that he fiercely set on his enemies, & them shortly discomfited: for which cause, men imagined, that he gave the sunne in his full brightnes for his cognisaunce or badge. Of his enemies were lefte dead on the ground. iii. M. & viii. C [three thousand eight hundred].[5]

Holinshed's account in the third volume of his 1587 edition of the *Chronicles* reproduces Hall nearly verbatim, maintaining the critical phrase "as some write" in parentheses:

> he [Edward, after receiving news of the planned surprise attack] herewith quickned, retired backe and met with his enimies in a faire plaine neere to Mortimers crosse, not far from Hereford east, on Candelmasse daie in the morning. At which time the sunne (as some write) appeared to the earle of March like three sunnes, and suddenlie ioined altogither in one. Upon which sight he tooke such courage, that he, fiercelie setting on his enimies, put them to flight: and for this cause men imagined that he gaue the sunne in his full brightnesse for his badge or cognisance. Of his enimies were left dead on the ground three thousand and eight hundred.[6]

Shakespeare manipulates his sources in three important ways. First in his rendition Richard and Edward witness the prodigy together. This is significant both because it confirms the vision's veracity and because it helps to foreshadow Richard's ultimate ascent to the throne after Edward's death. Second, Shakespeare excises the prodigy from its precise historical context as noted in Hall and Holinshed. By doing this he subtly recasts an omen for a single victory at the Battle of Mortimer's Cross into an omen of the ultimate rise of the house of York more generally, completed at the end of this play at Tewkesbury. Third, Shakespeare expands upon this prodigious detail in the chronicles. Hall and Holinshed deal with it cursorily, stating the alleged facts and moving on without contemplating their precise significance. Shakespeare dedicates some twenty lines to the witnessing and interpretation of this wonder. He even goes so far as to suggest that Edward adopted the prodigious trinity as his emblem, a departure from Hall and Holinshed, who had claimed that Edward adopted a single sun.

Richard is the first to notice the rising sun in Shakespeare's rendition of this prodigy, and he does so in a lyrical passage that recalls his father's final words in the previous scene.

> See how the morning opes her golden gates
> And takes her farewell of the glorious sun.
> How well resembles it the prime of youth,
> Trimmed like a younker prancing to his love! (2.1.21–24)

At this moment Richard and Edward do not yet know that Margaret has killed their father, but for Shakespeare's theater audience this reference to celestial gates opening wide would have seemed an echo of York's final utterance after being stabbed at the end of the previous scene: "Open thy gate of mercy, gracious God—/ My soul flies through these wounds to seek out thee" (1.4.178–79).

Edward is the first to notice that there are three suns in the sky instead of one: "Dazzle mine eyes, or do I see three suns?" In the sixteenth century the word "dazzle" was often used specifically to describe the loss of clear or steady vision caused by gazing at the sun, but it was also used more generally to mean stupefy, confound, make dizzy, or according to the OED "to strike or surprise with splendour." This more general sense seems to be Shakespeare's goal both in this particular scene and in his plays more generally. Richard confirms Edward's vision and clarifies that it is not caused by mundane effects such as the relative position of sun and clouds. "Three glorious suns," he affirms, "each one a perfect sun; / Not separated with the racking clouds, / But severed in a pale clear-shining sky" (2.1.26–28).

At this point the Oxford editors insert a hypothetical stage direction: "The three suns begin to join" but it is not possible to determine with any accuracy if this was the case. C. Walter Hodges has offered a credible mechanism by which the special effect of one sun dividing into three and then reunifying could occur.[7] Seeing this reunion, Richard comments,

> See, see—they join, embrace, and seem to kiss,
> As if they vowed some league inviolable.
> Now are they but one lamp, one light, one sun.
> In this the heaven figures some event. (2.1.29–32)

Richard's suggestion that this celestial unity symbolizes a "league inviolable" is ironic because the audience knows that the league he will forge with his brothers will, in Shakespeare's rendition at least, be violently severed. His reflex is to view the prodigy as a sign of a future event, as Shakespeare's contemporaries would have done, but ambiguity remains—a hallmark of the prodigious wonder.

That this prodigy evokes wonder is clear in Edward's awestruck response to the spectacle he has just witnessed. "'Tis wondrous strange, the like yet never heard of" (2.1.33). While Richard sees only a vague approximation of a future "league inviolable," Edward in *Henry VI* provides a more precise interpretation.

> I think it cites us, brother, to the field,
> That we, the sons of brave Plantagenet,
> Each one already blazing by our meeds,
> Should notwithstanding join our lights together
> And over-shine the earth as this [prodigious sun]
>   the world. (2.1.34–38)

But the prodigy can never be interpreted with complete certainty, and Edward backs away from this entirely plausible interpretation in the final two lines of this same speech even as he decides to embrace the prodigy as his emblem, saying, "Whate'er it bodes, henceforward will I bear / Upon my target three fair-shining suns" (2.1.39–40). By devising this interpretation Shakespeare recasts this remarkable prodigy a symbol of York family unity, a symbol with a limited shelf-life, as the fourth and final play in this first tetralogy will make clear.

CHAPTER I.6

Wonder, Awe, and Admiration: Shakespeare's Cabinets of Curiosity

Romeo's response to the news of Juliet's apparent death at the beginning of the fifth act of *Romeo and Juliet* has long been considered curious. Balthasar tells Romeo that Juliet's body "sleeps in Capel's monument, / And her immortal part with angels lives." Balthasar adds that he was an eyewitness to her death, noting that he "saw her laid low in her kindred's vault" (5.1.18–20). Romeo defies the stars, the symbols of his fortune, and asks for ink, paper, and horses, telling Balthasar that he will leave that night. Alone, he states matter-of-factly that he will "lie" with Juliet "tonight." "Let's see for means," he says to himself, and quickly crafts a plan (5.1.34–35).

His ensuing soliloquy, which includes a detailed inventory produced from memory of the furnishings of an apothecary's shop, has raised questions among Shakespeare scholars at least since the eighteenth century for two main reasons. First, Shakespeare swerves far from his major source, Arthur Brooke's *The Tragical Historye of Romeus and Juliet* (1562), in providing these details. Indeed in filling the memorially reconstructed shop, he directly contradicts his main source here, which insists that the shop is empty.[1] Second, the speech occurs at a moment of tremendous psychological intensity. Some have claimed that Romeo's detailed account is inappropriate given his duress. Why bother detailing the furnishings of an apothecary's shop at this particular moment when Shakespeare might have provided his tragic protagonist with raillery against fortune, woe in the contemplation of his deceased beloved, or even a modicum of the type of self-pity he displayed upon failing to win Rosaline's favor?

If Shakespeare did not have Brooke's translation of Pierre Boaistuau's adaptation of Matteo Bandello's novella right in front of him as he wrote the speech about the apothecary's shop, he clearly had Brooke's text in mind when he sat down to write the scene, as he recycles multiple phrases from Brooke verbatim. What Shakespeare does with Brooke's text, though, is very interesting. He takes Brooke's intentionally empty space—the shop is described as bare to emphasize the apothecary's penury—and fills it with some of the most wondrous accoutrements of the early modern wonder cabinet. Here is Brooke's translation:

> An Apothecary sate unbusied at his doore,
> Whom by his heavy countenaunce he gessed to be poore,
> And in his shop he saw his boxes were but fewe,
> And in his window (of his wares) there was so small a shew,
> Wherefore our Romeus assuredly hath thought,
> What by no friendship could be got, with money should be
>   bought; (ll. 2566–72)[2]

Brooke's translation of Boaistuau's description of the apothecary—a description, it should be noted, that Boaistuau did not find in his source Bandello but invented himself—notes only a few "boxes" and nondescript "wares" in his "window."

In Shakespeare's description of the scene the apothecary himself serves as the first curio inside the recollected space:

> I do remember an apothecary,
> And hereabouts a dwells, which late I noted,
> In tattered weeds, with overwhelming brows,
> Culling of simples. Meagre were his looks.
> Sharp misery had worn him to the bones, (5.1.37–41)

Brooke's "heavy countenaunce" becomes Shakespeare's "overwhelming brows," and Shakespeare captures his poverty in part by describing him as a skeleton, a wondrous human artifact who has been metaphorically stripped of his flesh.

But it is the second half of this description that has done the most to raise the critics' own eyebrows:

> And in his needy shop a tortoise hung,
> An alligator stuffed, and other skins
> Of ill-shaped fishes; and about his shelves

> A beggarly account of empty boxes,
> Green earthen pots, bladders, and musty seeds,
> Remnants of packthread, and old cakes of roses
> Were thinly scattered to make up a show. (5.1.42–48)

Shakespeare translates Brooke's nondescript account by describing the boxes as "empty." Brooke had not said this, but they are empty from a narrative standpoint because he does not describe what is in them. Similarly, Brooke describes the "wares" as "few" but does not indicate what they are.

While Brooke's description insists on a lack of detail, Shakespeare's Romeo indulges in it, filling Brooke's empty chamber with all manner of strange objects. These objects are not chosen randomly, however. Instead the tortoise, the alligator, and the skins of ill-shaped fishes, which likely represent sea rays, together with the herbs and other flora mentioned here comprise a standard assembly of objects in an early modern apothecary shop. This passage is worth considering carefully in the present study because the early modern apothecary shop doubled as a cabinet of curiosities during the sixteenth century. Indeed Italian apothecary shops served as the earliest and most important examples of the cabinet of curiosities or wonder cabinet genre. These apothecary shops were multiuse spaces (not unlike Elizabethan public theaters, which were known to host bear-baiting among other activities) in which useful medicines were stored and dispersed; natural and artificial wonders were assembled and displayed in order to teach interested visitors about natural philosophy; and objects were gathered to impress wealthy, educated, or politically connected patrons.

Romeo's description of the apothecary shop is critical for the present study not only because it indicates Shakespeare's awareness of curiosity cabinets and wonder cabinets (the terms are often used interchangeably, and I will for the most part follow that practice here), but also because these types of spaces provide a compelling analogy for Shakespeare's theaters. The idea of the "show" in Romeo's catalog mentioned earlier indicates a critical point of intersection. Brooke's description notes that in the apothecary's window "there was so small a shew," and Shakespeare picks up on this when he writes that the "beggarly account" of boxes, pots, bladders, seeds, thread, and roses "were thinly scattered to make up a show." The passages are essentially similar, but there is a subtle difference. Brooke seems to be using the word "shew" as a shortened form of the gerund "shewing" or "showing" to denote lack, as in "a poor showing." Shakespeare, in part I would suggest because of his own professional associations, seems more interested in the idea of performance. His use of the word "show" is affirmative. Though they are meager, the apothecary's assembled wares do constitute a spectacle, a mute performance, a *show*.³ I believe that the careful sifting of Shakespeare's storehouse of words—significantly, the Greek and Latin roots of the word "apothecary" meant storehouse, from the verb meaning "to lay away"—in this catalog is worthwhile in part because it holds within it a key to understanding Shakespeare's dramatic enterprise. I will argue (and hopefully show) that the space of the Shakespearean stage can usefully be compared to a cabinet of wonders in which "*exotica*," "*artificialia*," "*naturalia*," and all manner of wonders were either described or shown. In the same way that sixteenth-century continental apothecary shops were outfitted with the express purpose of teaching natural philosophy, Shakespeare and his company could and did pretend that their primary goal was didactic, to teach or instruct. This provided them moralizing cover in a society that was increasingly hostile to frivolity, idleness, and eventually entertainment of all kinds. In reality, though, the apothecary shops, curiosity cabinets, and wonder cabinets that proliferated throughout Europe during the so-called Age of the Marvelous were intended to delight by arousing amazement, awe, and admiration.

It seems reasonable to assert that the theater can be viewed as a cabinet of wonders in part because apothecary shops, curiosity cabinets, and wonder cabinets were routinely described as theaters or shows. One particularly compelling example of the commensurability of these various types of spaces comes from a description of the Mantuan apothecary Filippo Costa's *studiolino*. Giovan Battista Cavallara asserted that Costa had compiled "a genteel theater of the rarest simples that our age has discovered."⁴ While it is important not to overemphasize historical coincidence, it is noteworthy that this statement was published less than a decade prior to the first production of *Romeo and Juliet* and it depicts a working space in Mantua, the same town in which Shakespeare's apothecary resides in the play. In her study of early modern Italian collecting practices Paula Findlen emphasizes the word "genteel" in Cavallara's description of Costa's shop in order to highlight "the precise social and moral ground in which it should be located."⁵ I would like to emphasize the word "theatre" in Cavallara's statement in order to suggest the overlapping structures and functions of wonder cabinets and theatrical spaces.

The evolution of Italian apothecary display spaces during the late sixteenth and early seventeenth centuries exemplifies the extent to which the apothecary shop became a venue for entertainment in addition to a business office and a resource for the aristocratic student of natural philosophy. Paying special attention to the changing representations of two particular Italian apothecary shops—that of the Veronese Francisco Calzolari and that of the Neapolitan military-leader-turned-apothecary Ferrante Imperato—Findlen sees evidence of a shift around the turn of the seventeenth century from "professional activity to noble pastime."[6] Apothecary shops had long been spaces where wonders were collected and displayed—in 1558 in his *History of Animals* the Swiss naturalist Conrad Gessner told his readers about "apothecaries and others who usually dry rays and shape their skeletons into varied and wonderful forms for the ignorant"—but in the changing descriptions of the spaces and in the changes in the published catalogs describing their contents Findlen sees a gradual increase in theatricality, in the pursuit of entertainment value both for the collector and the observer at the expense of didacticism.[7]

The overarching theme of Brooke's description, and Shakespeare's adaptation of it for that matter, is that the apothecary is destitute and thus desperate enough to sell a deadly poison. While it may not be wise to speculate as to whether Shakespeare may have empathized with the apothecary who combined mysterious herbs to generate cures and poisons, the steady state of the Elizabethan playwright was one of want, of desperation, as the many pleas by playwrights for bail money from debtors' prison confirm. Just as some apothecaries, naturalists, and courtiers used their stunning displays to elevate their social standing, Shakespeare used his theater of wonders to garner for his family a coat of arms. The Imperato family provides a nice analogy to the Shakespeares of Stratford-upon-Avon. Ferrante Imperato was a military captain before turning to the career of an apothecary, and his work as an apothecary and naturalist helped his son secure a political career. Findlen comments, "They and their museum participated in the attempts on the part of the 'principal citizens' (*principali cittadini*) to assimilate themselves into the Neapolitan aristocracy. Possession of a museum was one way to climb the social ladder."[8]

There are records of alligators displayed in English apothecary shops in the mid- to late sixteenth century. Thomas Nashe's *Have With You to Saffron Walden* (1596) includes the passage: "He made an anatomie of a rat, and after hanged her over his head, instead of an apothecary's crocodile or dried alligator."[9] The late nineteenth century critic George Steevens adds,

> I was many years ago assured that, formerly, when an apothecary first engaged with his druggist, he was gratuitously furnished by him with these articles of show, which were then imported for that use only. I have met with the alligator, tortoise, &c., hanging up in the shop of an ancient apothecary at Limehouse, as well as in places more remote from our metropolis.[10]

The literary critic J. O. Halliwell received a note from a Mr. Fairholt, which read in part

Romeo's description of the shop of the poor apothecary may be accepted as minutely accurate, for it was customary with his class "to make a show," according to their means...Dried fishes and marine monsters were suspended from the ceiling; "an alligator stuff'd" was the most coveted and indispensible of all; and we rarely meet with any representation of the shop of the humblest medical practitioner without one. In Dutch art they abound.[11]

Our emphasis here will be on continental cabinets, particularly Italian spaces, both because the apothecary-shop-cum-wonder-cabinet first flourished on the Italian peninsula, and because Shakespeare's play is set in Verona and Mantua. Shakespeare's apothecary shop, while hinting at English trends, also seems to be an attempt to provide some local color.

A central tenet of the present study is that the varieties of wonder that Shakespeare offered on his stages represented a substitute for pre-Reformation English religious practices and traditions intended to generate wonder, awe, and admiration. In England the collection and display of sacred relics was an important element of religious experience prior to the reforms of the 1530s, and these relics were usually objects that generated wonder either through their historical association with a saint or a biblical event. In the same way that the communion wine and wafer generated awe by conjuring the presence of Christ's body and blood, relics of every conceivable stripe were presented either regularly or on special occasions to give the faithful the thrill of being in the physical presence of the miraculous.

Around the year 1314 a treasure trove of objects was "discovered"—perhaps they had been brought out on previous occasions—in the old cross on the steeple of St. Paul's Cathedral. Among the awe-inspiring contents were "a piece of the true Cross, a stone of the Holy Sepulchre, other stones from the place of Ascension and the Mount of Calvary," and "bones of martyred Virgins." These sacred objects were "showed to the people" during a sermon preached by Master Robert de Clothale, who was the chancellor of the Cathedral, and then, presumably with much fanfare, they were returned to the cross.[12] This particular showing would have generated intense awe because it was presented as an unexpected discovery of lost treasure.

The more regular arrival of the summer holiday known as "relic Sunday," usually celebrated in July on the third Sunday after Midsummer's Day, would also have been wondrous in part because its advent was greatly anticipated as a highlight of the liturgical calendar. One account announces the imminent arrival of the holiday by noting that in addition to the worship of God's body in the sacrament the members of the congregation planned to "reverens, honour, and worship...all the reverent relikes of patria[r]cks, prophetes, apostelles, martirs, confessours, and virtuous virgins, and other holy and devoute men and women, whoos belssid bodyes, holy bones, and other relikes" have been "left in erth to cristen mannes socour, comfort and recreacion."[13] In his history plays Shakespeare satisfies some of these same religious urges by resurrecting deceased historical personages that can be admired, feared, or loathed. King Harry's repeated insistence that he will sacrifice his bones rather than pay a ransom indicates his ability to imagine himself as a collection of relics. "Bid them achieve me, and then sell my bones," Harry tells Montjoy after repeated requests for ransom, alluding to the traffic in holy relics that aroused opprobrium among reformers (*Henry V*, 4.3.92).

We have a good deal of information regarding the nature of relics held in religious houses because of the accounts by Thomas Cromwell of his so-called visitations. Less interested in the sacred relics themselves than in the gold and jewel-encrusted settings in which they were encased and the ornate chests, or reliquaries, in which they were held, Cromwell's raid notes such contents as Bath Abbey's girdle of St. Peter; combs of Mary Magdalene, St. Dorothy, and St. Margaret; Bristol's God's coat; Our Lady's smock; "part of God's supper on the Lord's table, part of the stone [of the manger] in which was born Jesus in Bethlehem"; Bury St. Edmunds's "coals that Saint Lawrence was toasted withal, the parings of S. Edmund's nails, S. Thomas of Canterbury's pen knife and his boots"; Dover's Malchus's ear that Peter struck off; Reading's "holy dagger that killed king Henry [VI], and the holy knife that killed saint Edward [the Martyr]."[14] In a sense these relics are peripheral in that they represent an odd assortment of fragments, some of them personal accessories and some of them body parts, but their status as mundane minutiae makes them both portable and comprehensible.

In part because of reformist pressure to desanctify, commandeer, and destroy relics, churches and religious houses gradually began to shift their holdings in ways that brought them more in line with Continental wonder cabinets. Among the few church artifacts that survived Cromwell's raids and subsequent raids under Elizabeth were items that Richard Altick describes as "natural curiosities." This odd assortment of objects had no "direct reference to any biblical or later religious event." They were simply "evidence of the marvelousness of God's creation."[15] Among these were giants' bones and huge teeth. These secular wonders would have fit in nicely in an Italian apothecary shop or in a German *Wunderkammer*.

Still lacking in England at the turn of the seventeenth century, with a few notable exceptions such as Cope's Cabinet, which will be discussed in detail later, were ample sets of rooms inside noble estates dedicated exclusively to the display of strange and exotic naturalia and artificialia. In

Germany elite travelers could gaze at *Wunderkammern* and *Kunstkammern*, and this same aristocratic urge for the collecting and displaying of secular wonders found expression in French *cabinets des curieux*, of which Jean de France, Duc de Berry's collection was an early example. Altick comments on this apparent void, noting that in the late sixteenth and early seventeenth centuries in London "there was little sign of an equivalent cluster of exhibitions appealing to the nominally more sophisticated interests of the handful of scientific and artistic amateurs who were appearing among the aristocracy and higher gentry. In this respect, as in others, the Renaissance came late to England."[16] I will propose in this chapter that theater spaces in general and Shakespeare's theaters in particular picked up the slack in England's wonder economy. Appealing both to aristocrats and to working-class Londoners, theater spaces satisfied the longing for wonder in every way allowable. Both through the secular antiquarianism of the Roman and English history plays and through the amalgamation of exotica in other plays, Shakespeare's performed spectacles satisfied the appetite for wonder that had been fulfilled by the church and were during Shakespeare's career increasingly satisfied by wonder cabinets on the continent. Whereas plays such as *The Tempest, Othello, Antony and Cleopatra*, and to some extent *The Merchant of Venice* fulfilled the passion for exotica that motivated Sir Walter Cope to assemble his cabinet filled with exotica, plays such as *Lear, Cymbeline*, and to a lesser extent even *Julius Caesar* and *Antony and Cleopatra* satisfied the same antiquarian impulse that motivated Sir Robert Bruce Cotton to gather pre-Christian coins, medals, and manuscripts, while the two tetralogies emphasized heroic figures in English history like who could be compared to saints and martyrs. Blocked from dramatizing hagiography directly by reformist authorities, Shakespeare discovered a new outlet for hero worship in his dramatization of larger-than-life historical figures such as Talbot, King Harry, Henry Tudor, and King John; and martyrs such as Julius Caesar, Richard II, the Duke of York, and Joan of Arc. At the same time Shakespeare's plays satisfied the growing interest in exotica that was intensifying with reports of English voyages to East and West Indies, Russia, and America. While theatrical displays of actors, costumes, sets, props, special effects and perhaps most importantly words differed from the reliquaries of the pre-Reformation Church, the precise brand of antiquarianism that motivated Cotton and Cope's exotica was commensurate with the passion for collecting and display in religious and secular spaces. The analogy between the theater and these early prototypes of the museum is complex and in many ways imperfect, but I will suggest in this chapter that more is gained than lost by considering Shakespeare's plays as blueprints for *wunderkammern*.

A useful survey of the various "amusements" available to the London tourist at the turn of the seventeenth century is provided in a travel journal compiled by a Swiss medical student named Thomas Platter in 1599.[17] Platter's account has long been considered important because it contains the first reference to a production of *Julius Caesar* at the Globe. I will suggest here that it is also important because when read in its entirety it casts Elizabethan stage performance at the Globe as one of many wonders available to the London tourist.

After describing his visits to Elizabeth's menagerie at the Tower, Whitehall palace, and the Globe, Platter's narrative reaches its climax with his description of a visit to Walter Cope's wonder cabinet. Platter writes that within Cope's "fine house" is "an apartment, stuffed with queer foreign objects in every corner" (171–73). He lists fifty notable items, many of them exotic artifacts from America, Africa, China, and Arabia such as exotic birds, fish, and even a unicorn's tail. Platter concludes his description by giving Cope himself pride of place as a collector of "exotica." He writes that there are "other people in London interested in curios, but this gentleman is superior to them all for strange objects, because of the Indian voyage he carried out with such zeal" (173). Platter then offers a telling aerial perspective on his visit to London: "This city of London is... brimful of curiosities" (174). The distinct impression created by Platter's account is that the Globe's wooden O is one wonderful space among many.

Steven Mullaney has noted the direct links between the exotica accumulated in Cope's wonder cabinet and Shakespeare's Globe, pointing out that Platter describes the objects in Cope's cabinet as *frembden Sachen*, or strange things, and that he uses the same phrase to describe the English penchant for armchair travel through theater attendance.[18] There is more to Shakespeare's *wundertheater* than geographical exotica, however. In the history plays especially Shakespeare satisfies England's growing antiquarian impulse. In a play like *Antony and Cleopatra*, for example, Shakespeare seems to draw upon two reservoirs of wonder simultaneously: the fascination with exotica that peaked with journeys of exploration and discovery begun in earnest in the late sixteenth century, and the interest in England's classical past, in particular her links to the Roman empire. The confluence of these two major types of wonders is particularly clear in Enobarbus's description of Cleopatra sailing upon the Cydnus River. Shakespeare prepares us for the description of a wonder by having Enobarbus describe her in act 1 as an exotic marvel, more specifically the subject of a compelling travelers' tale. Grieved upon learning of Fulvia's death in 1.2, Antony tells Enobarbus that he wishes he had never seen Cleopatra, and Enobarbus responds, "O, sir, you had then left unseen a wonderful piece of work, which not to have been blessed withal would have discredited your travel" (1.2.139–41). In the climactic description of her beauty, though, her physical features are notably absent. She "beggared all description" (2.2.204) and is more beautiful than the picture of Venus which, in turn, surpasses the beauty of nature. Like the holy pre-Reformation relic, it is her frame that arouses the most admiration because it is so precious. Her "barge" was "like a burnished throne," its upper deck "beaten gold," and her pavilion also was "cloth of gold, of tissue." Her ship's oars are silver, the sails and rigging silk. In *Romeo and Juliet* the apothecary's shop was perfumed with "cakes of roses," and here again the sense of smell intensifies the wondrous spectacle. The sails, dyed purple, were "so perfumèd that / The winds were love-sick with them," one of two references to the delicious smell of her pageant ship. Sound too plays a part, as flutes played to signal the strokes (2.2.197–203). This wonder engages all of the senses.

Shakespeare stays very close to his primary source in this lyrical description. North's translation of Plutarch describes Cleopatra's barge this way:

> the poope whereof was of gold, the sailes of purple, and the owers of siluer, which kept stroke in rowing after the sounde of the musicke of flutes, howboyes, citherns, violls, and such other instruments as they played vpon in the barge. And now for the person of her selfe: she was layed vnder a pauillion of cloth of gold of tissue, apparelled and attired like the goddesse *Venus*, commonly drawen in picture: and hard by her, on either hand of her, pretie faire boyes apparelled as painters doe set forth god *Cupide*, with litle fannes in their hands, with the which they fanned wind vpon her. Her Ladies and gentlewomen also, the fairest of them were apparelled like the nymphes *Nereides* (which are the mermaides of the waters) and like the *Graces*, some stearing the helme, others tending the tackle and ropes of the barge, out of the which there came a wonderfull passing sweete sauor of perfumes, that perfumed the wharfes side, pestered with innumerable multitudes of people.[19]

Much of this language migrates directly into Enobarbus's speech. Shakespeare's primary modification is to break the speech up with exclamations of wonder interjected by Agrippa. "O, rare for Antony!" Agrippa cries at one point, and "Rare Egyptian!" at another (2.2.211, 224).

Of particular interest to us here is the marginal note inserted into North's text right beside his description of the barge on the bottom of page 981: "The wonder-/full sumptu-/ousnes of / Cleopatra, / Queene of / AEgypt, go-/ing vnto An-/tonius." Shakespeare's Cleopatra, like North's, is wondrous here. North's text goes on to describe the feast, at which Antony most "wondred at the infinite number of lightes and torches hanged on the top hanged on the toppe of the house" (982), while Shakespeare steps back from particulars to assert that she is a transcendent figure, defying the ravages of time and religious mores:

> Age cannot wither her, nor custom stale
> Her infinite variety. Other women cloy
> The appetites they feed, but she makes hungry
> Where most she satisfies. For vilest things
> Become themselves in her, that the holy priests
> Bless her when she is riggish. (2.2.240–45)

In short she is a miracle, a singular wonder who defies the laws of nature and religion.

CHAPTER I.7

Transalpine Wonders: Shakespeare's Marvelous Aesthetics

In the penultimate scene of *The Winter's Tale* Shakespeare denies his audience the chance to witness the wondrous reunion of Perdita and Leontes in order to highlight the wonder of Hermione's resurrection in the final scene. Though we never see Perdita's reunion with Leontes, we hear secondhand that it astounds Leontes and Camillo. The first gentleman reports that when Perdita's identity is revealed the changes seen in Leontes and Camillo "were very notes of admiration...A notable passion of wonder appeared in them, but the wisest beholder, that knew no more but seeing, could not say if th'importance were joy or sorrow" (5.2.9–10, 13–16). The third gentleman then relates that the nobles are on their way to Paulina's house to view a marvelous statue of Hermione. He describes the statue as "a piece many years in doing, and now newly performed by that rare Italian master Giulio Romano, who, had he himself eternity and could put breath into his work, would beguile nature of her custom, so perfectly he is her ape" (5.2.86–90).

Shakespeare scholars have long been both baffled and intrigued by this reference to Giulio Romano. Why does Shakespeare specify that this particular Italian painter and sculptor—a significant but not outstanding student of Raphael—was the alleged sculptor of the statue? Romano died in 1546, so Shakespeare could not have met Romano personally. Had Shakespeare ever seen any of Romano's works? Does this reference indicate that Romano had a particularly important reputation in England at the beginning of the seventeenth century? Instead of focusing on the biographical links between Shakespeare and Romano, I would like to pause for a moment to consider the significance of this passage from an aesthetic perspective. Shakespeare's third gentleman seems less interested in the particular artist than in the fact that the work itself is a marvel of verisimilitude. Like the grapes drawn by Zeuxis or the curtain drawn by Parrhasius, this sculpture of Hermione is a wonder because it is indistinguishable from Hermione herself.

In the broader context of the play what is most interesting about this praise of Romano's talents as the sculptor of Hermione's statue is that it is entirely baseless. In fact there is no statue; there is only Hermione herself, who Paulina has artfully hidden away. When she draws the curtain and reveals the figure that they all believe is Romano's statue, Paulina says to the assembled stage characters, "I like your silence; it the more shows off / Your wonder" (5.3.21–22). Leontes confirms that Perdita is amazed by the verisimilitude of the apparent sculpture:

O royal piece!
There's magic in thy majesty, which has
My evils conjured to remembrance, and
From thy admiring daughter took the spirits,
Standing like stone with thee. (5.3.38–42)

Without mentioning Romano by name, Polixenes praises his work: "Masterly done. / The very life seems warm upon her lip," and Leontes adds, "The fixture of her eye has motion in't, / As we are mocked with art" (5.3.65–68). Staring at the statue, he adds "What fine chisel / Could ever yet cut breath?" (5.3.78–79). On one level Shakespeare is using the statue to confirm the capacity of art to produce wonder through verisimilitude, and on another he has placed an actual human being on the pedestal in order to engineer an astounding metamorphosis.

Paulina baits the fish well by telling the assembly that they must either leave—which they seem physically unable to do as they can hardly look away from the wonderful sculpture—or prepare themselves for "more amazement" (5.3.87). The complicity of the stage audience is critical here. Paulina claims that she will make the statue "move indeed, descend, / And take your hand," only "if you can behold it" (5.3.87–89). She emphasizes this complicity again in the last moment before she brings the statue to life: "It is required / You do awake your faith" (5.3.94–95).

If there were any doubt that Paulina is attempting to create a marvel by bringing Hermione's statue to life it is dispelled when she tells Hermione's statue to move, instructing it: "'Tis time. Descend. Be stone no more. Approach. / Strike all that look upon with marvel" (5.3.99–100). Paulina invokes Christian rhetoric when she describes the statue's motion as a resurrection that defeats or cheats death: "Come, I'll fill your grave up. Stir. Nay, come away. / Bequeath to death your numbness, for from him / Dear life redeems you" (5.3.100–103). In her effort to assure the stage audience that she is not conjuring a spirit, she adds "Her actions shall be holy as / You hear my spell is lawful" (5.3.104–105). The apparent resurrection of Hermione is a stunning and awe-inspiring piece of stage business because Paulina is the only one aware of the deception. Unlike *Much Ado* or *Measure for Measure*, where the audience members know that the miraculous reappearances of apparently dead characters are in fact merely masks removed, *The Winter's Tale* builds to a climax in which the audience members are placed on the same footing as the wonder-struck Leontes, Polixenes, Florizel, Camillo, and Perdita.

The conclusion of *The Winter's Tale* is marvelous in its own right, but it is also worth considering closely because it serves as a window into early modern literary theories regarding wonder. As several scholars have pointed out, there was not a great deal of critical discourse surrounding wonder in Shakespeare's England. This may have been because wonder was widely linked to Aristotle's literary aesthetics at a time when Neoplatonism was on the rise, or it may simply have been a by-product of England's overall belatedness in the development of the type of sophisticated debate about literary aesthetics that took place in Italy during the sixteenth century. For a full account of the nature of the early modern literary marvelous, the importance of marvels, and the means by which artists could generate wonder we need to look to Italian literary criticism, where wonder is given a much more prominent place.

Most Italians who wrote about wonder were paraphrasing or responding to Aristotle's statements about wonder in his *Rhetoric*, his *Poetics*—which was recovered in Italy in the mid-sixteenth century—and his *Metaphysics*. As one contemporary scholar has noted, "Renaissance theorists concocted various recipes for wonder, but they almost all shopped at the same store, the texts of Aristotle."[1] In his *Poetics* Aristotle described wonders as surprises, which seemed inevitable, necessary, or fitting in the overall scheme of a tragic or epic work:

> Incidents arousing pity and fear . . . have the very greatest effect on the mind when they occur unexpectedly and at the same time in consequence of one another; there is more of the marvelous in them than if they happened of themselves or by mere chance. Even matters of chance seem most marvelous if there is an appearance of design as it were in them . . . for incidents like that we think to be not without a meaning.[2]

In the first book of his *Metaphysics* Aristotle argues that wonder spurs philosophy since a state of ignorance or puzzlement leads to contemplation, and in his *Rhetoric* he reiterates the philosophical significance of wonder and adds some notes on marvelous style, which includes novel and surprising words and metaphors to make an impression on the audience.[3]

James Mirollo has identified three phases of Italian discourse on wonder between 1550 and 1650. In the first phase authors addressed the use of the marvelous in tragic and epic plots, in the second they affirmed the use of the marvelous as an element of style, and in the third they proclaimed that the marvelous was the end of literary art. When we examine the various phases of Italian discourse on wonder closely we see that wonder was a top priority, in some cases *the* top priority in Italian literature in a variety of genres, but there seems always to have been vigorous debate about the true sources and proper uses of the marvelous. Even the terms used to describe wonders and marvels were highly ambivalent. A careful consideration of the binaries, paradoxes, contradictions, and ambivalences in Italian literary discourse on wonder sheds light on Shakespeare's own dramatic aesthetic. Just as Shakespeare utilized different techniques to generate wonder at the conclusion of *Winter's Tale*, Italian authors and literary critics embraced multiple and often contradictory notions about how and in what circumstances an author could amaze the reader. My hope is that this comparative approach may also offer a new overarching conceptual framework for the analysis of Shakespeare's drama both in his tragic and his comic modes.

In the first decade of the seventeenth century the poet Giambattista Marino asserted that the ability to arouse wonder was the primary criteria for a poet: "The end of the poet is to arouse wonder (I speak of the excellent, not the foolish): Let him who does not know how to astonish go work in the stables! [*E del poeta il fin la meraviglia (Parlo de l'eccellente e non del goffo): Chi non sa stupir, vada all striglia!*]." Giason Denores concurred with Marino's assessment regarding the centrality of wonder when he wrote in a *discorso* of 1586 that "every poem by its nature is based on the marvelous."[4]

Giovambattista Giraldi Cinthio's ideas about wonder are particularly important because his *Hecatommithi* provided direct sources for Shakespeare's *Othello* and *Measure for Measure*. Giraldi agreed with Marino and Denores that a prerequisite for poetry was the liberal use of marvels, particularly in the fable or the story the writer created. According to Baxter Hathaway, Giraldi "took the extreme position that a poet is to be called a poet primarily because of the marvels that he uses," so "it follows that he wanted poems to be filled full of such events as men changing into trees and ships into nymphs."[5]

Giraldi's views on wonder were influential not only because he was one of the first writers of vernacular tragedies modeled on the drama of the ancients but also because he held prominent roles as a scholar and a theorist at the court at Ferrara and at the university. Holding Giraldi up as the model of Italian literary aesthetics, Hathaway contrasts Italian fondness for marvels and wonders on one hand with what he calls the "moral earnestness of Sidney or of the English tradition" on the other.[6] While there may have been a fundamental difference between Giraldi and Sidney or George Puttenham, I believe that Giraldi and his Italian contemporaries expressed the same type of literary approach that Shakespeare used while composing his plays.

At the conclusion of *The Winter's Tale* Shakespeare presents three very distinct types of wonders: the wonder created by verisimilitude; that created by the unexpected, the unnatural, or the strange; and what we might describe as the Christian marvelous. Admiration for verisimilitude dates back to antiquity, and early modern Italian authors often referred to Pliny the Elder and Callistratus as exponents of mimetic wonder. Pliny and Callistratus argued that the best works of art were those that simulated reality with an uncanny exactitude. They often noted that the artfully crafted statue or painting did not just give the appearance of life, it seemed to actually be alive.[7] This is precisely the praise that the characters in *The Winter's Tale* lavish on the statue of Hermione. According to the third gentleman, Romano has crafted a statue that is so verisimilar that "one would speak to her and stand in hope of answer" (5.2.91–92). As Paulina prepares the assembly to see the statue she instructs "Prepare / To see the life as lively mocked as ever / Still sleep mocked death" (5.3.18–20). Literary critics of the sixteenth and seventeenth centuries often referred to the idea of making a work of art seem vividly present as *energeia*. In his *Discorsi* and his *Della poesie* Speroni claimed that wonder was the effect produced by this type of vivid realism.[8]

In 1597 Giovanni Talentoni delivered a lecture before the Milanese academy of the Inquieti entitled "Discorso sopra la maraviglia." In it Talentoni claimed that admiration or wonder was a passion of the soul, which could be produced by the conjunction of the animate and the inanimate, and this is precisely the effect of Hermione's statue in the final scene. Before Paulina cues her to move, Hermione amazes because she seems to straddle the boundary between an inanimate object and a living being. After she begins to move, Hermione seems to definitively cross over that boundary. Talentoni noted that the reaction to the marvelous entailed both a physiological response and a psychological response, and the stage audience, which Hermione amazes, responds both physically and psychologically. While their physical bodies are turned to stone with wonder and their gazes become fixed stares, Leontes and Perdita are psychologically "transported" or "distracted," moved in ways that Paulina fears are dangerous.[9]

Italian art critics often praised works using the same terms that Shakespeare's characters use in their praise of Hermione. Vasari commented that the female figure in Leonardo's *Mona Lisa* seemed so alive that "one would swear that the pulses were beating" and "all those who saw it were amazed to find that it was as alive as the original."[10] This statement closely resembles Leontes's rhetorical question to Polixenes: "See, my lord, / Would you not deem it breathed, and that those veins / Did verily bear blood?" (5.3.62–64). Bernini was said to have made his marble statues of Apollo and Daphne live and breathe, while Caravaggio was both renowned and criticized for his super-realism. The artist's ability to fool the eye was sometimes viewed with suspicion, as a sort of magic that the artist could work on the beholder. Paulina certainly casts a spell on her stage audience and her theater audience when she seems to bring Hermione to life. Leontes confesses that he is spellbound: "O royal piece! / There's magic in thy majesty" (5.3.38–39).

While verisimilitude was often depicted as a means of generating wonder, the majority of Italian authors and critics commented that the wondrous derived not from the realistic portrayal of nature but from the surprising or startling representation of the unusual, the unexpected, or the strange. In 1557 Giraldi wrote that *il maraviglioso* could only be found in "those things that are outside of common experience and outside natural limits."[11] Throughout his critical treatises on romances, comedies, and tragedies he emphasized that marvels were events in narratives, which were both unusual and apparently impossible:

> The wonderful is not to be found in what occurs often and naturally, but is well derived from what appears to be impossible, and, indeed, is taken for what happened, if not for the factual, at least of the fictional...and other like things which, although false and impossible, are nevertheless so accepted in usage that no composition is pleasurable in which such fables are not read.[12]

Giulio del Bene agreed that "a most beautiful ingredient of poetry is the wondrous, which occurs when something unexpected comes about for the audience, for men marvel and take delight in things that are new and beyond their knowledge."[13] Lodovico Castelvetro paid special attention to the role of the unexpected reversal as a means of generating wonder in his *Poetica d'Aristotele vulgarizzata et sposta* (1576), where he dedicated fifteen pages to describing recognitions and reversals that could generate wonder in literature.[14] Hermione's resurrection serves as the key reversal in *Winter's Tale*, generating a very different type of wonder from that of gazing on a lifelike sculpture.

Some Italian authors insisted that the marvelous could be generated either through verisimilitude or through the surprising sudden reversal, but others argued that it was possible for a literary work to generate wonder using both techniques at the same time. Torquato Tasso wrote an essay on the heroic poem in 1594, which sought to validate his *Gerusalemme Liberata*. In the discourse, he argued that a poem could be realistic or mimetic in terms of its focus on a historical event or a key moment in Christian history, and that it could also indulge in the pleasures of the marvelous. James Mirollo has suggested that in laying claim to this dual aesthetic agenda Tasso may have been suggesting a critique of Ariosto's *Orlando Furioso*, a work "whose romance, variety, and marvels outweighed its nominal Christian subject."[15]

I noted earlier that Paulina's resurrection of Hermione resembles a Christian resurrection. When Paulina says to the statue of Hermione "Come, / I'll fill your grave up" (5.3.100–101), she seems to literally mean that she will replace the empty space created by the removal of the casket with dirt, but there is also a hint here—partly because Paulina mentions her own demise in her final speech in the play—that Paulina will herself trade places with Hermione's corpse in a sacrificial act that recalls Christ's bodily sacrifice through death for the sins of humanity. In an early modern Christian context familiar with the medieval legend of the Harrowing of Hell, Paulina's claim "Bequeath to death your numbness, for from him / Dear life redeems you" seems to suggest Christ's voyage to the underworld to defeat Satan and rescue his deceased ancestors (5.3.102–103).

Sixteenth-century Italian assessments of the marvelous often highlighted its linkages to religious awe. Augustine set the precedent for the contemplation of the Christian marvelous. As Peter G. Platt has recently noted, "Augustine Christianized the marvelous by connecting it to miracles, a connection that is expressed etymologically in the embedding of *miror* (Latin for 'to wonder') and *admiratio* in *miraculum* and is linked to the Messiah (*et vocabitur nomen eius Admirabilis*, Isa. 9.6)."[16] Augustine defined "miracle" rather broadly as "anything great and difficult or unusual that happens beyond the expectation or ability of the man who wonders at it."[17] Italian theorists of the sixteenth century embraced the Christianization of the classical marvelous in multiple ways. There is a distinctly religious element, for example, in Giambattista Marino's understanding of wonder. In praise of a painting by Titian in his *Galeria* (1619) Marino seems to be praising God himself: "Oh celestial semblance, oh masterly craftsman, / For in his work he outdoes himself; Eternal ornament of cloth and paper, / Marvel of the world, honor of art!"[18]

Since all wonder was believed to derive ultimately from divine intervention into the mortal realm, it was not unusual for literary theorists to compare the artist directly to God. Emmanuele Tesauro suggested that the artist was God's rival, particularly in his cultivation of his *ingegno*—his wit, genius, ingenuity, or talent. The poet's *ingegno* was analogous to God's creative power because just as God made something from nothing, the artist could produce being from nonbeing.[19] Tesauro even suggested that God and the poet shared some characteristics in terms of their deployment of literary figures: "even God enjoyed being the poet and witty speaker, verbalizing to men and angels with various heroic devices and figurative symbols his lofty conceits."[20]

Shakespeare's attitude toward the Christian marvelous is complicated by the fact that the standard Protestant position on marvels and wonders was that miracles and marvels ceased after the days of the early church. This orthodox position is presented by Lafeu in act 2, scene 3, of *All's Well That Ends Well*: "They say miracles are past, and we have our philosophical persons to make modern and familiar things supernatural and causeless." However, Lafeu's very next sentence suggests that this orthodox position is both inadequate and untenable: "Hence is it that we make trifles of terrors, ensconcing ourselves into[21] seeming knowledge when we should submit ourselves to an unknown fear" (2.3.1–5). Shakespeare was expressly forbidden from writing mystery plays or miracle plays that celebrated the Christian marvelous, but in his secular drama he offered a wide array of wonders that substituted for the daily wonders such as the mass denied to his countrymen during Elizabeth's reign.

To this point we have considered three varieties of the marvelous in Shakespeare's conclusion to *The Winter's Tale* and in early modern Italian discourse about the marvelous. In fact there were many more ways in which authors could and did attempt to generate wonder for their readers or theater spectators. The most comprehensive treatise on the various sources of wonder was Francesco Patrizi's *La deca ammirabile*, published as part of his *Della poetica* in 1587. Danilo Aguzzi-Babagli has suggested that Patrizi's treatise is worth studying because it represents a sort of manifesto on the importance of the marvelous in literature: "the marvellous is seen as the catalyst in the organization of the poem. Patrizi devotes considerable effort to defining the manner by which it operates in the composition: how it can be made to penetrate every component of the structure, from the more outstanding—the subject matter—to the most elementary—the semantic unit."[22] Patrizi thought it was useful to distinguish between two general categories of wonder: one intrinsic and another extrinsic. He referred to the wondrous quality of the poem itself as the *mirabile*, and he described the effect of the wondrous elements on the reader as *la maraviglia*. He believed that there were twelve techniques that a poet could employ to generate wonder: ignorance, fable, novelty, paradox, augmentation, departure from the usual, the verisimilar, the divine, great utility, the very exact, the unexpected, and the sudden.[23] Platt comments that Patrizi's list "is vast and suggests the difficulty of determining any unified definition of the marvelous and isolating its effects in the early modern period. Indeed, there *was* no unified sense in the Renaissance: the marvelous was a concept full of multiplicity and variety."[24] While Giovanni Pontano used the word *admiratio* in his *Actius* to mean something as mundane as "applause," Hathaway notes that "at its highest level," *admiratio* "is practically an access to Godhead or a direct intimation of divinity."[25] Instead of attempting to compress or collapse the full panoply of definitions into a few categories, it seems most useful to accept that we are speaking about an inherently ambivalent, multifaceted category in which the terms and issues denoted were constantly in flux and frequently subject to debate.

Study of the historical usage of the words for wonder confirms the inherent ambivalence of the category we are describing. In English words such as "admire," "awful," and "wonderful" were far more ambivalent during the early modern period than they are today. The OED's first sense of "admire" indicates that it was not only a laudatory term: "this would make you admire, your haire stand [on] end, and bloud congeale in your veynes." Admiration could serve as a synonym for horror. A citation listed in the OED under "wonder" from 1632 confirms that word's sinister potential: "They made a wonderfull massacre of poore afflicted Christians." On the other hand, the word "awful," which today holds only a negative connotation, was in the early modern period a term that could suggest religious awe. It could mean "terrible, dreadful, appalling" or "sublimely majestic."

In the 1612 edition of the *Vocabolario degli Accademici della Crusca*, the word *maraviglia* (or *meraviglia*) is rather loosely defined as a passion of the soul, an astonishment born of novelty or the rare.[26] The Italian words for wonder could take on sinister connotations much as they did in English. According to Mirollo, "there is a marvelous *in malo* as well as a marvelous *in bono*. If the marvelous or wondrous exhilarates because of its size or scope, its rarity, its novelty, its ingenuity, its paradoxicalness, it may also depress because of the fearful destructiveness that religion, nature, and human events may display or promise."[27] An example of the sinister sense of Italian wonder exists in an inscription that Vicino Orsini, the owner and creator of the Sacro Bosco, a mid-sixteenth-century garden at Bomarzo, had carved into a bench in his garden: "You who have traveled the world wishing to see great and stupendous marvels [*maraviglie*], come here, where there are horrendous faces [*faccie horrende*], elephants, lions, bears, orcs, and dragons."²⁸ Vicino's collocation of *maraviglie* and *faccie horrende* indicates the extent to which the definitions of marvels and horrors could be coterminous. Shakespeare captures the ambivalence of wonder in the third gentleman's comment that "A notable passion of wonder appeared" in Camillo and Leontes when the lost Perdita was found, "but the wisest beholder, that knew no more but seeing, could not say if th'importance were joy or sorrow."

The gruesome death of Antigonus in act 3, scene 3, of *The Winter's Tale* and the earlier death of Mamillius have given many Shakespeare scholars pause. To what extent can this play be construed as a comedy if multiple characters meet untimely deaths within it? An appreciation of the play as a showcase for marvels or wonders may shed new light on this question. During the sixteenth century Italian authors and literary critics expanded the generic extent of the marvelous. Whereas Aristotle claimed in his *Poetics* that the marvelous was a necessary element in tragedy and epic, Italian authors argued that the marvelous was also a suitable and indeed necessary component of all literary genres, including comedy. Giason Denores believed that the same types of reversals and recognitions that created wonder in tragedy could create wonder in stage comedy and the novella. In 1549 Gian Giorgio Trissino expanded the domain of the marvelous still further when he noted that the desire to arouse wonder is inherent in any type of narrative: "all those who narrate or who allude to anything always add something of their own in order to arouse more wonder in those who listen."²⁹

Another key issue in Italian discussions of the marvelous was the *res et verba* debate: should the marvelous be limited to the fable or story of a poem, or should it instead be generated by a marvelous style created by lofty diction, strange words, neologisms, ancient words, or unusual syntactical structures? Hathaway has suggested that *res* trumped *verba* in Italian literary aesthetics: "The whole matter of poetic invention centered more upon what was invented than upon how it was invented."³⁰ We see the emphasis on matter over style in several Italian authors. In 1600, right around the time that Shakespeare was writing *Hamlet*, Paolo Beni argued that a play is much better if it contains events "full of variety and inconstancy, crowded with strange and unexpected accidents, in which therefore enter the marvelous."³¹ Not only does this serve as a fitting description of *Hamlet*, it describes *The Winter's Tale* and many of Shakespeare's other plays quite well. When Camillo Pellegrino wrote his *Del concetto poetico* (1598), he emphasized the importance of the *concetti*, by which he meant the idea or content of a composition rather than the type of words chosen to convey it.

In England Sidney concurred that the idea of a literary work was more important than its technique: "the skill of the artificer standeth in that Idea or fore-conceit of the work and not in the work itself."[32]

Despite the critical emphasis on content over style in the creation of the literary marvelous, there were many sixteenth-century Italian authors who claimed that marvelous style was important in literature. Lorenzo Giacomini, a member of the Accademia degli Alterati in Florence, wrote that poets can make their work delightful if they "invent the plot out of marvelous things" and "adorn the diction with strange and wonderful forms of speech."[33] Denores agreed that the marvelous could be created through elevated style, which he referred to as "*la maravigla della parole*," the marvelous in words.[34] He insisted that in tragedy particular characters' diction should be "raised above the way of speaking of private persons."[35] Giovanni Mario Verdizzoti agreed that poetry ought to be written in a high style to generate feelings of the marvelous.[36] Antonio Minturno epitomized the growing sense that marvels derived from both *res* and *verba* when he wrote in his essay *L'arte poetica* (1564):

> It can in no way be doubted that marvelous subject matter delights marvelously... but because both from things and from words the marvelous is born, we repute those things to be marvelous that are feigned prudently, that are invented admirably, and are disposed and arranged in an order worthy of marvel, and so well put together as if one event depended on the other.[37]

What stylistic elements in the *verba* could create wonder? In reading through a litany of these elements one gets the sense that one is reading an analysis of Shakespeare's style. Consider the description of the stylistic marvelous in Torquato Tasso's praise of Homer in his *Scritti Sull'Arte Poetica*: "he transfers words not only from related terms but also from remote ones, just so that he may please the hearer, fill him with stupefaction, and enchant him with wonder."[38] Both neologisms and adaptations or recastings of archaic words could generate wonder, and Shakespeare uses both of these to his advantage throughout his corpus. Ornateness of style was often considered wonderful or marvelous as well. In 1554 Giovan Battista Niccolucci, also known as Il Pigna, wrote that ornateness of narrative style "produces novelty, hence the marvelous, hence an intense pleasure."[39]

Questions of genre and questions of style intersected in discussions of Terence, one of Shakespeare's most significant models for comic drama. Benedetto Grasso criticized Terence for what he believed was a vulgar, mundane style. In his *Oratione contra gli Terentiani* (1566) Grasso conceded that Terence's low-brow, familiar diction was considered appropriate for the comic genre of its time, but he criticized Terence for failing to use eloquence to arouse even a modicum of wonder.[40] Grasso was not alone in his insistence that authors of stage comedies employ lofty style in order to generate wonder. Vincenzo Maggi, Il Pigna, and Giason Denores also demanded that one of the roles of comic stage plays was to astound their audiences via an elevated style.

The notion of decorum seems to guide Shakespeare in navigating these somewhat conflicted stylistic expectations. Whereas the noble characters in his comedies and tragedies ascend to lofty rhetorical heights, low-born or working-class characters indulge in the slang of the countryside or of London. The stylistic contrasts between working-class slang and courtly wit cast each segment of society in bold relief and reveal Shakespeare's mastery of linguistic possibilities.

An in-depth study of Italian literary aesthetics sheds light on the beginning of *Winter's Tale* as well as the end. After highlighting several of the most common techniques authors use to generate wonder in their plots, Castelvetro writes in his *Poetica d'Aristotele vulgarizzata et sposta* (1570) that "Our marvel at deeds deliberately evil grows greater as the cause for committing atrocities diminishes."[41] Leontes has no reason to suspect Hermione at the beginning of the play. Unlike Othello, he is not goaded into jealousy by a cunning deceiver such as Iago. In fact his trusted lord Camillo tries on more than one occasion to convince Leontes that he is acting unreasonably. Iago, Edmund, and Don John also amaze us in part because they lack sufficient justification to destroy their friends, confidants, and relatives. Iago's motive-hunting is unconvincing, and while Edmund and Don John are bastards, their villainy exceeds the indignities that they endure. From reading all of Shakespeare's passages and watching real performances we see and feel wonder in a wide variety of dances, languages, fictions, and multiple forms of imagination.

Notes

I.1 Wonder, Amazement, and Surprise: Beginning a Stunning Story

1. References to Shakespeare are drawn from *The Norton Shakespeare*, ed. Stephen Greenblatt, Walter Cohen, Jean E. Howard, and Katharine Eisaman Maus (New York: W.W. Norton & Company, 1997).
2. Jean E. Howard, *Shakespeare's Art of Orchestration: Stage Technique and Audience Response* (Urbana: University of Illinois Press, 1984).
3. *The Diaries of Lewis Carroll*, ed. R. L. Green, in Gamini Salgado, *Eyewitnesses of Shakespeare: First Hand Accounts of Performances 1590–1890* (New York: Barnes & Noble, 1975), 349. As a footnote, Carroll added, "Miss Carlotta Leclerque made a charming Miranda" (350).
4. *Henry VIII* as a whole seems intended to elicit wonder by representing kingship in all its majesty.
5. Terms such as "rare," "strange," and "monstrous" are important and ubiquitous synonyms for "wonder" throughout all the plays. These words function as barely audible background music to complete the wondrous atmosphere of the drama.

I.2 Resurrections of the Living and the Dead: Natural and Spiritual Bodies and Souls

1. Beatrice Groves, *Texts and Traditions: Religion in Shakespeare 1594–1604* (Oxford: Oxford University Press, 2007), 21. Annabel Patterson has discussed the ways in which censorship provided linguistic and thematic opportunities for early modern authors. See Annabel Patterson, *Censorship and Interpretation: The Conditions of Writing and Reading in Early Modern England* (Madison: University of Wisconsin Press, 1984).
2. In-text citations refer to the following early version of the Bible: *The Geneva Bible: Facsimile Edition of 1560*, ed. Lloyd E. Berry (Madison: University of Wisconsin Press, 1969).

3. Saint Augustine, *The City of God*, Book 22, Chapter 5, trans. John Healey (London: George Eld, 1610), 879.
4. Ibid.
5. Ibid., 879–80.
6. Samuel Gardiner, *A Sermon Preached at Paules Crosse the 9. Of June. 1605* (London: E. Alde for Edward White, 1605).
7. Saint Augustine, *Faith and the Creed*, in Saint Augustine, *Earlier Writings*, trans. John H. S. Burleigh (Philadelphia: The Westminster Press, 1953), 368.
8. Saint Augustine, *Enchiridion*, in Saint Augustine, *Confessions and Enchiridion*, trans. and ed. Albert C. Outler (Philadelphia: Westminster Press, 1955), 392–93. Augustine's most extensive discussion of the nature of bodily resurrection occurs in the final book of *The City of God*, where he takes up a host of challenges to the doctrine by Platonists and others and considers some of the logistical questions surrounding resurrection such as whether the body will rise with all the hair and all the fingernails that have ever grown on it and what will become of bodies that have been eaten by beasts or cannibalized.
9. Athenagoras, *Embassy for the Christians: The Resurrection of the Dead*, trans. Joseph Hugh Crehan, S. J. (Westminster, MD: The Newman Press, 1956), 14.
10. Thomas Aquinas, Saint, Opusc. XIII, *Compendium Theologiae*, 151, in Saint Thomas Aquinas, *Philosophical Texts*, ed. and trans. Thomas Gilby (London: Oxford University Press, 1951), 278.
11. Thomas Aquinas, Saint, IV *Contra Gentes,* 79, in *Philosophical Texts*, 211–12.
12. George England and Alfred W. Pollard, eds., *The Towneley Plays* (London: The Early English Text Society, 1925).
13. Richard Beadle, ed., *The York Plays* (London: Edward Arnold, 1982).
14. Athenagoras, *Embassy*, 103.
15. This notion of the separation between elemental body and airy soul or spirit gets picked up again in Cleopatra's statement as she is about to commit suicide: "I am fire and air; my other elements / I give to baser life" (5.2.280–81).
16. Athenagoras, *Embassy*, 104–105.
17. Ibid., 83–84.
18. *The Resurrection of Our Lord* (Oxford: Oxford University Press for The Malone Society, 1912), line 242, stage direction.
19. *Tudor Royal Proclamations*, ed. Paul L. Hughes and James F. Larkin (New Haven: Yale University Press, 1964–9), 2:115. For more on the popularity and importance of biblically based dramas, see Groves, *Texts and Traditions,* 10–25.
20. *Acts of the Privy Council of England, AD 1589–90*, ed. John Roche Dasent (London: His Majesty's Stationary Office, 1890–1964), 18:215.
21. E. K. Chambers, *The Elizabethan Stage* (Oxford: Oxford University Press, 1923), 4:338–39.
22. The Towneley *Resurrection of the Lord*, rather than warlock, has "tratur" [traitor], a word with political instead of metaphysical associations (449).
23. Jesus uses sleep as a metaphor for death in John 11 when he states, "Our friend Lazarus sleepeth; but I go, that I may awake him out of sleep" (John 11:11). His

disciples take Jesus literally here until he clarifies what he meant: "Then said Jesus unto them plainly, Lazarus is dead" (John 11:11–14).
24. Kaara L. Peterson, "Shakespearean Revivifications: Early Modern Undead," *Shakespeare Studies* 32 (2004): 240–66.
25. John Sadler, *The Sick Woman's Private Looking-glasse* (London, 1636), 62–3, in ibid., 246.
26. In *Confessions and Enchiridion*, 390.
27. King James Version, Acts 2:22.
28. This compares nicely to the film *Shakespeare in Love* to which the audience response when she awakens is an audible gasp of wonder—evidently they think that she has actually died.
29. Qtd in Gamini Salgado, ed., *Eyewitnesses of Shakespeare: First Hand Accounts of Performances 1590–1890* (New York: Barnes & Noble, 1975), 69–72.
30. Ibid., 71.

I.3 "Die to Live": Various Forms of Empathetic Wonder

1. See Barbara Ardinger, "Cleopatra on Stage: An Examination of the *Persona* of the Queen in English Drama, 1592–1898." Southern Illinois University dissertation, 1976 (DA 37 [1976] 3634A), 93.
2. John Minshue, *Ductor in Linguas, The Guide into Tongues* (London: John Browne, 1617).
3. For further study on the ghost of King Hamlet, see Stephen Greenblatt, *Hamlet in Purgatory* (Princeton: Princeton University Press, 2002).
4. The reference to Q2 here comes from *The Norton Shakespeare*, 1671.
5. Just before Romeo hears the news of Juliet's death, he refers to Juliet's appearance in a dream vision as a "shadow." The passage is significant for our purposes because in it Romeo suggests that romantic love can raise one from the dead:
    I dreamt my lady came and found me dead—
    Strange dream, that gives a dead man leave to think!—
    And breathed such life with kisses in [into] my lips
    That I revived and was an emperor.
    Ah me, how sweet is love itself possessed
    When but love's shadows [dreams, images] are so rich
        in joy! (5.1.6–11)
6. Many editors replace "At" with "As" in the final line of this passage because they believe that the use of "At" in Q2 creates the need for another verb, which is not present. I disagree with this. Left alone, the "As" transforms "trains of fire" into a simile, suggesting that the sheeted dead squeak and gibber like comets (i.e., shooting stars), another important category of prodigy.
7. Quoted in John Calvin, *Diuers Sermons of Master John Caluin, concerning the Diuinitie, Humanitie, and Natiuitie of our Lorde Iesus Christe* (London: George Byshop, 1581), 68.
8. This idea of "special wonder" may also distinguish the type of wonder of interest to one from the more mundane uses of the word and the idea.

I.4 The Metaphorical Use of the Prodigious Birth Tradition

1. Q and F have "most unnatural."
2. Raphael Holinshed, *Chronicles*, iii.690, in W. G. Boswell-Stone, *Shakespeare's Holinshed: The Chronicle and the Historical Plays Compared* (New York: Longmans, 1896), 345.
3. William E. Burns, *An Age of Wonders: Prodigies, Politics and Providence in England 1657–1727* (Manchester and New York: Manchester University Press, 2002), 1–2.
4. A cockatrice was a fabulous monster also known as a basilisk, which could kill by glancing at its victims.
5. Thomas Gataker, *Thomas Gataker B.D. His Vindication of the Annotations…Jeremiah* (London: J. L. for Thomas Downes, 1653), 52.
6. Plutarch, *The Lives of the Noble Grecians and Romanes…Translated out of Greeke into French by Iames Amyot…and out of French into Englishe, by Thomas North* (London: Thomas Vautroullier and John Wight, 1579), 1005–1006. Subsequent editions appeared in 1595 and 1603, but after analyzing the various spellings of the editions and comparing them to Shakespeare's most scholars agree that Shakespeare consulted the 1579 edition.
7. For more on Shakespeare's manipulation of his source in this scene, see, e.g., Frederick W. Sternfeld, *Music in Shakespearean Tragedy* (London: Routledge and Kegan Paul, 1963), 222–25; and John H. Long, "*Antony and Cleopatra*: A Double Critical Reversal," *Renaissance Papers* (1964): 33.
8. See Ethel Seaton, "*Antony and Cleopatra* and the Book of Revelation," *Review of English Studies* 22 (1946): 219–20.
9. Burns, *Age*, 3.
10. Another example of the fantasy of transparency can be seen in this play's sequel, *Antony and Cleopatra*, in Antony's outrage at Cleopatra's kind reception of Octavius Caesar's ambassador Thidias: "Alack, our terrene moon / Is now eclipsed, and it portends alone / The fall of Antony" (3.13.157–59). The notion that the eclipsing of the terrene moon, here a symbol of Cleopatra, portends "alone" Antony's fall indicates that the fantasy of transparency was often linked with the fantasy that a prodigy was intended specifically for a particular person or population.
11. Another possible sense of "cast" available to Shakespeare was to put into a mould in order to found. This sense is intriguing because it captures the motionlessness of the wonder-filled individual.

I.5 More of a Prodigy than a Prophecy

1. *The Works of Francis Bacon*, ed. James Spedding, R. L. Ellis, and D. D. Heath (London: Longmans, 1857–74), 3:330.
2. "Translation of the *Novum Organum*," *The Works of Francis Bacon*, ed. James Spedding, R. L. Ellis, and D. D. Heath (London: Longmans, 1857–74), 4:169.
3. While the second quarto may emphasize the status of the ghost as a prodigy more than the Folio edition, both editions highlight its status as a wonder. After

seeing the ghost for the first time Horatio says, "It harrows me with fear and wonder" (1.1.42).
4. Quoted in Gamini Salgado, ed., *Eyewitnesses of Shakespeare: First Hand Accounts of Performances 1590–1890* (New York: Barnes & Noble, 1975), 352.
5. Edward Hall, *The Union of the Two Noble and Illustre Famelies of Lancastre and Yorke*. 1548, in Geoffrey Bullough, ed., *Narrative and Dramatic Sources of Shakespeare* (London: Routledge and Kegan Paul; and New York: Columbia University Press, 1960), 3:179.
6. Raphael Holinshed, *The Third volume of Chronicles, beginning at duke William the Norman, commonlie called the Conqueror; and descending by degrees of yeeres to all the kings and queenes of England in their orderlie successions...* (London: Henry Denham, 1586), 660. For a modern edition, see W. G. Boswell-Stone, *Shakespeare's Holinshed: The Chronicle and the Historical Plays* (New York: Longmans, 1896), 300–301.
7. See Michael Hattaway, ed., *The Third Part of King Henry VI* (Cambridge: Cambridge University Press, 1984), 20.

I.6 Wonder, Awe, and Admiration: Shakespeare's Cabinets of Curiosity

1. For more on the role of memory in this scene and in others like it, see Lina Perkins Wilder, "Toward a Shakespearean 'Memory Theater': Romeo, the Apothecary, and the Performance of Memory," *Shakespeare Quarterly* 56.2 (Summer 2005): 156–75.
2. My reference to Brooke is drawn from *Narrative and Dramatic Sources of Shakespeare*, ed. Geoffrey Bullough (London: Routledge and Kegan Paul; New York: Columbia University Press, 1966), 1:352. For Pierre Boaistuau's description of the "covetous apothecary," see his contributions to François de Belleforest's translation of Bandel's tales, *Histoires Tragiques extraictes des Oeuvres italiens de Bandel* (Paris, 1559). For a discussion of the sources of the Romeo and Juliet tale, see Bullough, *Narrative*, 1:269–83.
3. Barbara Maria Stafford has noted that early modern wonder cabinets and theaters shared a heavy reliance on spectacle. Commenting on a painting by Frans Francken II of a northern wonder cabinet entitled *The Art Collection* (1636), she writes, "the heteroclite items forming this artist's gallery presented a *theatrum* of *visibilia* to be looked at and enjoyed rather than to be fitted into a genealogical narrative... The analogies of these retreats and sanctuaries of the muses to the treasury, microcosm, and theater were founded on their shared reliance on spectacle." Barbara Maria Stafford, *Artful Science: Enlightenment Entertainment and the Eclipse of Visual Education* (Cambridge, MA: MIT Press, 1994), 221–23.
4. Giovan Battista Cavallara, *Lettera dell'eccellentissimo Cavallara all'eccellentissimo Girolamo Conforto* (Mantova, 1586), in Dario Franchini et al., *La Scienza a Corte* (Rome: Bulzoni, 1979), 49. Quoted in Paula Findlen, *Possessing Nature: Museums, Collecting, and Scientific Culture in Early Modern Italy* (Berkeley: University of California Press, 1994), 105.

5. Findlen, *Possessing*, 105.
6. Ibid., 42.
7. Conrad Gessner, *Historia Animalium* (Zurich, 1558), 4:945; quoted in ibid., 305.
8. Findlen, *Possessing*, 41.
9. *A New Variorum Edition of Shakespeare. Romeo and Juliet* , ed. Horace Howard Furness (Philadelphia: J. B. Lippincott & Co., 1871), p. 262n43.
10. Ibid.
11. Ibid.
12. James Gairdner, *The English Church in the Sixteenth Century* (London: Macmillan, 1904), 109, in Richard D. Altick, *The Shows of London* (Cambridge, MA: Harvard University Press, 1978), 6.
13. G. R. Owst, *Preaching in Medieval England: An Introduction to Sermon Manuscripts of the Period, c. 1350–1450* (Cambridge: Cambridge University Press, 1956), 350–51; quoted in Altick, *Shows*, 5.
14. G. H. Cook, *Letters to Cromwell on the Suppression of the Monasteries* (London: J. Baker, 1965), 38, 39–40, 66, 188–89, 200.
15. Altick, *Shows*, 7.
16. Ibid., 8.
17. For an English translation of Platter's narrative, see *Thomas Platter's Travels in England, 1599*, trans. Clare Williams (London: J. Cape, 1937). For a reprint of Platter's travel narrative in the original, see *Thomas Platter des Jungeren Englandfahrt im Jahre 1599*, ed. Hans Hecht (Halle: Max Niemeyer Verlag, 1929). Subsequent references to the English translation of Platter's narrative are cited parenthetically in the text.
18. Steven Mullaney, "Strange Things, Gross Terms, Curious Customs: The Rehearsal of Cultures in the Late Renaissance," in *Representing the English Renaissance*, ed. Stephen Greenblatt (Berkeley: University of California Press, 1988), 65.
19. *Plutarch's The Lives of the Noble Grecians and Romanes* (London: Thomas Vautroullier, 1579), 981.

I.7 Transalpine Wonders: Shakespeare's Marvelous Aesthetics

1. James Biester, *Lyric Wonder: Rhetoric and Wit in Renaissance English Poetry* (Ithaca, NY: Cornell University Press, 1997), 23.
2. Aristotle, *De Poetica, The Works of Aristotle*, vol. 9, chapter 9, trans. Ingram Bywater, ed. W. D. Ross (Oxford: Clarendon Press, 1924), 1452a1–10.
3. For a summary of Aristotle's views on wonder, see James V. Mirollo, "The Aesthetics of the Marvelous: The Wondrous Work of Art in a Wondrous World," in *Wonders, Marvels, and Monsters in Early Modern Culture*, ed. Peter G. Platt (Newark, DE: University of Delaware Press, 1999), 24–44, esp. 30.
4. Ibid., 24, 33.
5. Baxter Hathaway, *Marvels and Commonplaces: Renaissance Literary Criticism* (New York: Random House, 1968), 116.

6. Ibid.
7. For more on verisimilitude, see Joy Kenseth, "The Age of the Marvelous: An Introduction," in *The Age of the Marvelous*, ed. Joy Kenseth (Hanover, NH: Hood Museum of Art, Dartmouth College, 1991), 25–59, esp. 48.
8. For more on Speroni's views, see Hathaway, *Marvels*, 155.
9. For a discussion of Talentoni's lecture, see Bernard Weinberg, *A History of Literary Criticism in the Italian Renaissance* (Chicago: University of Chicago Press, 1961), 1:238–39.
10. In Kenseth, "Age," 48.
11. In Mirollo, "Aesthetics," 32–33.
12. *Giraldi Cinthio on Romances* [*Discorso Intorno al Comporre dei Romanzi* (1554)], intro and trans. Henry L. Snuggs (Lexington, KY: University of Kentucky Press, 1968), 49–50.
13. In Mirollo, "Aesthetics," 33.
14. Hathaway, *Marvels*, 162–63.
15. Mirollo, "Aesthetics," 33.
16. Peter G. Platt, *Reason Diminished: Shakespeare and the Marvelous* (Lincoln and London: University of Nebraska Press, 1997), 8.
17. Augustine, *De utilitate credendi* 16.34. Quoted in J. V. Cunningham, *Tradition and Poetic Structure* (Denver: Alan Swallow, 1960), 204.
18. In Mirollo, "Aesthetics," 24. For more on Marino, see Mirollo, *The Poet of the Marvelous: Giambattista Marino* (New York: Columbia University Press, 1963).
19. Emmanuele Tesauro, *Il Cannocchiale Aristotelico* (Turin, 1670; rpt. Berlin: Verlag Gehlen, 1968), 82–83.
20. In Mirollo, "Aesthetics," 34.
21. This passage may read well as "sheltering ourselves with."
22. Danilo Aguzzi-Babagli, "Humanism and Poetics," in *Renaissance Humanism: Foundations, Forms, and Legacy*, ed. Albert Rabil Jr. (Philadelphia: University of Pennsylvania Press, 1988), 3:138.
23. Francesco Patrizi, *La deca ammirabile*, in *Della poetica*, ed. Danilo Aguzzi-Babagli (Firenze: Nella Sede Dell'istituto Palazzo Strozzi, 1969–71), 2:305, in Platt, *Reason Diminished*, 15.
24. Platt, *Reason Diminished*, xv; emphasis in the original.
25. See Giovanni Pontano, *Actius, I dialoghi* (Florence: Sansoni, 1943), 146; Hathaway, *Marvels*, 58.
26. See *Vocabolario degli Accademici della Crusca* (Venice, 1612; rpt. Florence: Licosa Reprints, 1976), 510.
27. Mirollo, "Aesthetics," 26.
28. See Mark S. Weil, "Love, Monsters, Movement, and Machines: The Marvelous in Theaters, Festivals, and Gardens," in Kenseth, "Age," 159–78, esp. 169.
29. In Mirollo, "Aesthetics," 32.
30. Hathaway, *Marvels*, 151.
31. Paolo Beni, *Risposta alle considerazioni o dubbi dell'Ecc. mo Sig. Dottor Malacreta* (Padova, 1600), 89. The Italian text and an English translation appear in Weinberg, *History*, 2:1098.

32. Sir Philip Sidney, *An Apologie for Poetrie*, in *English Literary Criticism: The Renaissance*, ed. O. B. Hardison, Jr. (New York: Appleton Century Crofts, 1963), 105.
33. Lorenzo Giacomini, "Sopra la purgazione della tragedia," *Orazioni e discorsi* (1597). Quoted in Hathaway, *Marvels,* 157.
34. Quoted in Mirollo, "Aesthetics," 33.
35. Giason Denores, *Discorso intorno a'que' principii, cause, et accrescimenti che la comedia, la tragedia, e il poema heroico ricevano dalla philosophia morale, & civile, & da governatori delle republiche* (Padua, 1587), 26. Quoted in Hathaway, *Marvels,* 157.
36. Giovanni Mario Verdizzoti, *Breve discorso intorno alla narratione poetica* (Venice, 1588), p. 5. Quoted in Hathaway, *Marvels,* 157.
37. Antonio Sebastiano Minturno, *L'Arte Poetica* (Venice, 1564), 41. Quoted in Hathaway, *Marvels,* 156.
38. Torquato Tasso, *Discourses on the Heroic Poem*, trans. Mariella Cavalchini and Irene Samuel (Oxford: Clarendon Press, 1973), 191.
39. Giovan Battista Pigna, *I romanzi* (Venice: 1554), 17, in Kenseth, "Age," 40.
40. Weinberg, *History,* 1:179.
41. Quoted in Hathaway, *Marvels,* 61.

Bibliography

Acts of the Privy Council of England, AD 1589–90. 32 Vols. Edited by John Roche Dasent. London: His Majesty's Stationary Office, 1890–1964.

Aguzzi-Babagli, Danilo. "Humanism and Poetics." In *Renaissance Humanism: Foundations, Forms, and Legacy*, vol. 3, edited by Albert Rabil Jr., 85–169. Philadelphia: University of Pennsylvania Press, 1988.

Altick, Richard, ed. *The Shows of London.* Cambridge, MA: Harvard University Press, 1978.

Archer, William. *The Theatrical "World" of 1895.* London: Scott, 1896.

Ardinger, Barbara. "Cleopatra on Stage: An Examination of the *Persona* of the Queen in English Drama, 1592–1898." Southern Illinois University dissertation, 1976 (DA 37 [1976] 3634A)

Aristotle. *De Poetica.* In *The Works of Aristotle.* Vol. 11. Translated by Ingram Bywater, edited by W. D. Ross, 1445–62. Oxford: Clarendon Press, 1924.

Athenagoras. *Embassy for the Christians: The Resurrection of the Dead.* Translated by Joseph Hugh Crehan, S. J. Westminster, MD: The Newman Press, 1956.

Augustine, Saint. *City of God.* Translated by John Healey. London: George Eld, 1610.

———. *Confessions and Enchiridion.* Translated and edited by Albert C. Outler. Philadelphia: Westminster Press, 1955.

———. *Earlier Writings.* Selected and translated by John H. S. Burleigh. Philadelphia: The Westminster Press, 1953.

Bacon, Francis. *The Works of Francis Bacon.* 14 Vols. Edited by James Spedding, R. L. Ellis, and D. D. Heath. London: Longmans, 1857–74.

Beadle, Richard, ed. *The York Plays.* London: Edward Arnold, 1982.

Belleforest, François de. *Histoires Tragiques extraictes des Oeuvres italiens de Bandel.* 7 Vols. Paris, 1564–82.

Beni, Paolo. *Risposta alle considerazioni o dubbi dell'Ecc. mo Sig. Dottor Malacreta* Padova, 1600.

Bible. *The Geneva Bible: Facsimile Edition of 1560.* Edited by Lloyd E. Berry. Madison: University of Wisconsin Press, 1969.

Biester, James. *Lyric Wonder: Rhetoric and Wit in Renaissance English Poetry.* Ithaca, NY: Cornell University Press, 1997.

Bishop, T. G., *Shakespeare and the Theatre of Wonder*. Cambridge: Cambridge University Press, 1996.

Boaistuau, Pierre. *Histoires tragiques*. Paris, 1554.

Boswell-Stone, W. G. *Shakespeare's Holinshed: The Chronicle and the Historical Plays Compared*. New York: Longmans, 1896.

Bullough, Geoffrey, ed. *Narrative and Dramatic Sources of Shakespeare*. 3 Vols. London: Routledge and Kegan Paul; New York: Columbia University Press, 1966.

Burns, William E. *An Age of Wonders: Prodigies, Politics and Providence in England 1657–1727*. Manchester and New York: Manchester University Press, 2002.

Calvin, John. *Diuers Sermons of Master John Caluin, concerning the Diuinitie, Humanitie, and Natiuitie of our Lorde Iesus Christe*. London: George Byshop, 1581.

Carroll, Lewis. *The Diaries of Lewis Carroll*. Edited by R. L. Green. In *Eyewitnesses of Shakespeare: First Hand Accounts of Performances 1590–1890*, edited by Gamini Salgado, 352–53. New York: Barnes & Noble, 1975.

Cavallara, Giovan Battista. *Lettera dell'eccellentissimo Cavallara all'eccellentissimo Girolamo Conforto*. Mantova, 1586.

Chambers, E. K. *The Elizabethan Stage*. 4 Vols. Oxford: Oxford University Press, 1923.

Cinthio, Giovambattista Giraldi. *Giraldi Cinthio on Romances* [*Discorso Intorno al Comporre dei Romanzi* (Venice, 1554)]. Introduction and translation by Henry L. Snuggs. Lexington, KY: University of Kentucky Press, 1968.

Cook, G. H. *Letters to Cromwell on the Suppression of the Monasteries*. London: J. Baker, 1965.

Cunningham, J. V. *Tradition and Poetic Structure*. Denver: Alan Swallow, 1960.

———. *Woe or Wonder: The Emotional Effect of Shakespearean Tragedy*. Denver: Alan Swallow, 1964.

Denores, Giason. *Discorso intorno a'que' principii, cause, et accrescimenti che la comedia, la tragedia, e il poema heroico ricevano dalla philosophia morale, & civile, & da governatori delle republiche*. Padua, 1587.

England, George, and Alfred W. Pollard, eds. *The Towneley Plays*. London: The Early English Text Society, 1925.

Findlen, Paula. *Possessing Nature: Museums, Collecting, and Scientific Culture in Early Modern Italy*. Berkeley: University of California Press, 1994.

Franchini, Dario et al. *La Scienza a Corte*. Rome: Bulzoni, 1979.

Gairdner, James. *The English Church in the Sixteenth Century*. London, Macmillan, 1904.

Gardiner, Samuel. *A Sermon Preached at Paules Crosse the 9. Of June. 1605*. London: E. Alde for Edward White, 1605.

Gataker, Thomas. *Thomas Gataker B.D. His Vindication of the Annotations...Jeremiah*. London: J. L. for Thomas Downes, 1653.

Gessner, Conrad. *Historia Animalium*. 5 Vols. Zurich, 1558.

Giacomini, Lorenzo. "Sopra la purgazione della tragedia." In *Orazioni e discorsi*. Florence, 1597.

Greenblatt, Stephen. *Hamlet in Purgatory*. Princeton: Princeton University Press, 2002.
Groves, Beatrice. *Texts and Traditions: Religion in Shakespeare 1594–1604*. Oxford: Oxford University Press, 2007.
Hall, Edward. *The Union of the Two Noble and Illustre Famelies of Lancastre and Yorke*. In *Narrative and Dramatic Sources of Shakespeare*, edited by Geoffrey Bullough, 3:172–208. London: Routledge and Kegan Paul; New York: Columbia University Press, 1960.
Hathaway, Baxter. *Marvels and Commonplaces: Renaissance Literary Criticism*. New York: Random House, 1968.
Hattaway, Michael, ed. *The Third Part of King Henry VI*. Cambridge: Cambridge University Press, 1984.
Holinshed, Raphael. *The First and Second Volumes of Chronicles*. 3 Vols. London: Henry Denham, 1587.
Howard, Jean E. *Shakespeare's Art of Orchestration: Stage Technique and Audience Response*. Urbana: University of Illinois Press, 1984.
Jorden, Edward. *A Briefe Discourse of a disease called the Suffocation of the Mother*. London: John Windet, 1603.
Kenseth, Joy. "The Age of the Marvelous: An Introduction." In *The Age of the Marvelous*, edited by Joy Kenseth, 25–60. Hanover, NH: Hood Museum of Art, Dartmouth College, 1991.
Long, John H. "*Antony and Cleopatra*: A Double Critical Reversal." *Renaissance Papers* (1964): 28–34.
Minshue, John. *Ductor in Linguas, The Guide into Languages*. London: John Browne, 1617.
Minturno, Antonio Sebastiano. *L'Arte Poetica*. Venice, 1564.
Mirollo, James V. "The Aesthetics of the Marvelous: The Wondrous Work of Art in a Wondrous World." In *Wonders, Marvels, and Monsters in Early Modern Culture*, edited by Peter G. Platt, 24–44. Newark, NJ: University of Delaware Press, 1999.
———. *The Poet of the Marvelous: Giambattista Marino*. New York: Columbia University Press, 1963.
Mullaney, Steven. "Strange Things, Gross Terms, Curious Customs: The Rehearsal of Cultures in the Late Renaissance." In *Representing the English Renaissance*, edited by Stephen Greenblatt, 65–92. Berkeley: University of California Press, 1988.
Owst, G. R. *Preaching in Medieval England: An Introduction to Sermon Manuscripts of the Period, c. 1350–1450*. Cambridge: Cambridge University Press, 1956.
Patrizi, Francesco. *La deca ammirabile*. In *Della poetica*, edited by Danilo Aguzzi-Babagli, 2.231–368. Firenze: Nella Sede Dell'istituto Palazzo Strozzi, 1969–71.
Patterson, Annabel. *Censorship and Interpretation: The Conditions of Writing and Reading in Early Modern England*. Madison: University of Wisconsin Press, 1984.
Peterson, Kaara L. "Shakespearean Revivifications: Early Modern Undead." *Shakespeare Studies* 32 (2004): 240–66.

Pigna, Giovan Battista. *I romanzi*. Venice, 1554.
Platt, Peter G., *Reason Diminished: Shakespeare and the Marvelous*. Lincoln and London: University of Nebraska Press, 1997.
———, ed. *Wonders, Marvels, and Monsters in Early Modern Culture*. Newark, DE: University of Delaware Press, 1999.
Platter, Thomas. *Thomas Platter's Travels in England, 1599*. Translated by Clare Williams. London: J. Cape, 1937.
———. *Thomas Platters des jüngeren, Englandfahrt im jahre 1599*. Edited by Hans Hecht. Halle: M. Niemeyer, 1929.
Plutarch. *The Lives of the Noble Grecians and Romanes... Translated out of Greeke into French by Iames Amyot... and out of French into Englishe, by Thomas North*. Translated by Thomas North. London: Thomas Vautroullier, 1579.
Pontano, Giovanni. *Actius, I dialoghi*. Florence: Sansoni, 1943.
The Resurrection of Our Lord. Oxford: Oxford University Press, for *The Malone Society*, 1912.
Sadler, John. *The Sick Woman's Private Looking-glasse*. London: Anne Griffin, for Philemon Stephens and Christopher Meridith, 1636.
Salgado, Gamini. *Eyewitnesses of Shakespeare: First Hand Accounts of Performances 1590–1890*. New York: Barnes & Noble, 1975.
Seaton, Ethel. "*Antony and Cleopatra* and the Book of Revelation." *Review of English Studies* 22 (1946): 219–24.
Shakespeare, William. *A New Variorum Edition of Shakespeare's Romeo and Juliet*. Edited by Horace Howard Furness. Philadelphia: J. B. Lippincott & Co., 1871.
———. *The Norton Shakespeare*. Edited by Stephen Greenblatt, Walter Cohen, Jean E. Howard, and Katharine Eisaman Maus. New York: Norton, 1997.
Sidney, Philip. *An Apologie for Poetrie*. In *English Literary Criticism: The Renaissance*, edited by O. B. Hardison, Jr., 99–146. New York: Appleton Century Crofts, 1963.
Stafford, Barbara Maria. *Artful Science: Enlightenment Entertainment and the Eclipse of Visual Education*. Cambridge, MA: MIT Press, 1994.
Sternfeld, Frederick W. *Music in Shakespearean Tragedy*. London: Routledge and Kegan Paul, 1963.
Tasso, Torquato. *Discourses on the Heroic Poem*. Translated by Mariella Cavalchini and Irene Samuel. Oxford: Clarendon Press, 1973.
Tesauro, Emmanuele. *Il Cannocchiale Aristotelico*. Turin, 1670; rpt. Berlin: Verlag Gehlen, 1968.
Thomas Aquinas, Saint. *Philosophical Texts*. Selected and translated by Thomas Gilby. London: Oxford University Press, 1951.
Tudor Royal Proclamations. 3 Vols. Edited by Paul L. Hughes and James F. Larkin. New Haven: Yale University Press, 1964–69.
Verdizzoti, Giovanni Mario. *Breve discorso intorno alla narratione poetica*. Venice: 1588.
Vocabolario degli Accademici della Crusca. Venice, 1612; rpt. Florence: Licosa Reprints, 1976.

Weil, Mark S. "Love, Monsters, Movement, and Machines: The Marvelous in Theaters, Festivals, and Gardens. In *The Age of the Marvelous,* edited by Joy Kenseth, 159–78. Hanover, NH: Hood Museum of Art, Dartmouth College, 1991.

Weinberg, Bernard. *A History of Literary Criticism in the Italian Renaissance.* 2 Vols. Chicago: University of Chicago Press, 1961.

Wilder, Lina Perkins. "Toward a Shakespearean 'Memory Theater': Romeo, the Apothecary, and the Performance of Memory." *Shakespeare Quarterly* 56.2 (Summer 2005): 156–75.

PART II

Six Responses to *Wonder in Shakespeare*

Edited by
*M. G. Aune, Joshua B. Fisher, and
Rebecca Steinberger*

Acknowledgments

Adam Max Cohen died in early January of 2010 having only barely completed the manuscript of *Wonder in Shakespeare*. His family and friends discussed various means by which his final scholarly work could and should be brought to publication. With the input and support of his editors at Palgrave, it was decided to publish his manuscript, but to invite colleagues to contribute brief essays responding to the ideas it brought forth. What you have before you is the product of this unusual collaboration, and one that we believe would make Dr. Cohen proud as we attempt to do exactly what he wants readers of this study to do as they relate his concepts of wonder with their own understanding of Shakespeare. We would like to stress that the entire first part of this book is Dr. Cohen's work and that our contribution is only in the chapters in this second part.

We thank Dr. Cohen's family, Debbie, Hailey, and Lauren, and his parents Max and Leslie for their generous support of this project. We would also like to thank the Reading Room staff at the Folger Shakespeare Library for their invaluable help to Dr. Cohen and ourselves. We also acknowledge the support of the Faculty Professional Development Committee at California University of Pennsylvania, of the faculty and students at Wingate University who provided feedback on wonder in *Othello*, and of the Faculty Research Grants committee and students in studies in Shakespeare at Misericordia University. Most importantly, we thank our families, D. K. Peterson, Catherine McClellan, Isaac Fisher, Eli Fisher, and the entire Steinberger family, for their continuous support of our scholarly endeavors, intellectual pursuits, and love of Shakespeare.

M. G. Aune
Pittsburgh, Pennsylvania
Joshua B. Fisher
Wingate, North Carolina
Rebecca Steinberger
Dallas, Pennsylvania

Introduction

Adam Max Cohen's first published article, "Genius in Perspective: Blake, Einstein, and Theories of Relativity," appeared in the *Wordsworth Circle* in 2000. As the title suggests, it is an ambitious attempt to find commonalities between the writings of Blake and Einstein. Cohen focuses on how both men regarded the universe in potentially opposing ways. He coins the term "perspectival lightness" to describe how they were able to deploy an anti-Newtonian tolerance of instability of point of view – like Keats, finding a way to hold contradictory ideas about a subject and at the same time maintain a coherent conception of it. For Cohen, the first step to comprehending "perspectival lightness" and to comprehending Blake was interdisciplinary, to "understand psychology, literature, mathematics... morals and theology."[1] And so throughout his scholarship, Cohen was fascinated by the ways in which different perspectives or disciplinarities could be brought together to generate new insights into his favorite objects of study: Shakespeare's plays and poems. This is perhaps best seen in his first book, *Shakespeare and Technology*, which carefully traces Shakespeare's sometimes explicit, sometimes nuanced use of technology as both resource and metaphor. *Wonder in Shakespeare* seeks to do similar work, though wonder is a much more abstract discourse than technology.

It is in this spirit of putting different approaches to Shakespeare in conversation with each other that we have titled the section "responses," hoping to create an atmosphere of shifting perspectives and give-and-take that so characterizes Cohen's scholarship. Several sought to extend Cohen's arguments using approaches it does not employ, while others investigate plays that are mentioned only briefly, and still others bring unique conceptions of wonder and its function. In the first chapter, Maura Tarnoff begins with Donna Haraway's explanation of partial perspective and situated knowledge. She draws on Cohen's reading of *Pericles* to examine how the restoration of

Thaisa and Pericles highlights the ecological and technological contexts of embodiment, as the practices by which life and sanity are restored depend, as dramatic events, on the perceived connections between the body's internal and external environments. In both cases, the body and its emotional and cognitive processes are conceptualized as part of a greater, interdependent system that stretches beyond the thresholds of flesh to incorporate the wonder-inducing machinery of the early modern theater and the cosmological order it replicates.

Janna Segal extends Cohen's engagement with *Romeo and Juliet* by following his lead in considering the medieval origins of tragedy, but also employing recent theories of theatrical performativity. The chapter focuses on Cohen's formulation of "pseudoresurrection." In the specific context of a love tragedy, she offers a parallel conception, "aesthetic resurrection," which recognizes that the audience is told from the outset that Juliet and Romeo are "death-mark'd." During the play their narrative status exists in a complex state between living and dead and so their "pseudoresurrection" becomes a much more complex phenomenon for its audience. Segal concludes her chapter by examining the medieval traces of wonder and martyrdom at the end of Shakespeare's play, which distinguishes it from Arthur Brooke's strongly anti-Catholic version.

Taking up a play that Cohen only touches on, *Merchant of Venice*, and a medium that he employed extensively in his teaching, M. G. Aune looks for possibilities of transhistorical wonder. At the core of the chapter is the question of whether Shylock's forced conversion to Christianity and Antonio's surprising rescue at the end of the trial scene of *The Merchant of Venice* provoke wonder for modern audiences. Examining historical attitudes toward Jews and conversion in early modern England, Aune argues that audiences in Shakespeare's time would have responded with wonderment at both the prospect of Shylock's conversion and Antonio's salvation. In contrast, modern audiences tend to view Shylock with a kind of sympathy that deflates the wondrous potential of the trial scene. A case in point is Michael Radford's 2004 film adaptation of the play. While Radford portrays Shylock sympathetically, Aune identifies aspects of the filmic medium including camera work and Al Pacino's cultural capital as an iconic Hollywood actor that imbue the scene with a particular kind of wonder-inducing power.

Cohen's interest in wonder and Shakespeare's histories is largely confined to the presence of prodigies in the *Henry VI* plays. Expanding this scope, Rebecca Steinberger takes up the trope of wonder as a means of characterization in *Richard II*. Like Aune, she sees wonder effects in the way Shakespeare manipulates his audience's feelings for a character. Richard begins the play as an unsympathetic narcissist, but under the pressure of incarceration and impending death, he deploys articulate, forceful rhetoric that forces viewers to reassess their opinions of him. Steinberger then links this instability or blurriness of character to England's identity at the end of the sixteenth century and concludes by wondering about the transitory nature of power across the ages.

Focusing closely on language, Keating and Reynolds argue that the frequent exclamation of "no wonder" and other seeming denunciations of wonder in numerous early modern English texts in fact create structural and conceptual spaces for the possibility of wonder. Framing their discussion within the parameters of negation and "vanishing mediators" (whereby "no wonder" "transubstantiates into wonder"), the authors explore how "no wonder" functions as a positive force in the performative realm of theatrical space where "definitions of rationality are upended, recapitulated, expanded..." Within this space, audience responses, the physical and verbal articulations of the actor, the intricacies of staging, and other elements potentially undermine the wonder-negating power of "no wonder" and other such utterances.

In the concluding chapter "Passing for Truth: Wonder Tales and their Audiences in *Othello*," Joshua B. Fisher draws on Cohen's discussion of Desdemona's murder scene to consider how the word "globe" functions in both a macrocosmic sense (anticipating celestial prodigies) and a microcosmic sense (anticipating the amazed responses of audiences at the Globe theater). While Othello's words in 5.2.106–109 clearly attest to the wonder-inducing power of his actions, they importantly call attention to the broader implications of wonder in the play. Fisher argues that Othello's reaction to Desdemona's death provides a kind of sounding board for the various and wide-ranging responses to wondrous accounts and spectacles from audiences both within and of the play. Fisher provides a concrete history of the wonders of key characters, symbols, and themes in *Othello*, and in doing so, provides the reader with an understanding of the audience response/reception of amazement as the final scene is staged.

Note

1. Adam Max Cohen, "Genius in Perspective: Blake, Einstein, and Theories of Relativity," *The Wordsworth Circle* 31.3 (Summer 2000): 164.

CHAPTER II.1

Embodying Wonder

Maura Tarnoff

In "Situated Knowledges: The Science Question in Feminism and the Privileges of Partial Perspective," Donna Haraway enumerates a "doctrine of embodied objectivity" in which objective vision becomes possible as well as meaningful in a feminist context as a result of "partial perspective."[1] What Haraway refers to as a feminist version of objectivity "is about limited location and situated knowledge," rather than "transcendence and splitting of subject and object."[2] Just as our partial perspectives enable "us to become answerable for what we learn how to see," they also foreground the status of knowledge, and the knowing self, as part of a dynamic process with collaborative as well as ethical possibilities and responsibilities: "The knowing self is partial in all its guises, never finished, whole, simply there and original; it is always constructed and stitched together imperfectly and therefore able to join with another, to see together without claiming to be another."[3] I have found Haraway's explanation of partial perspective and situated knowledge useful for approaching Adam Cohen's work in *Wonder in Shakespeare*, a project that opens with a powerful account of its critical positioning. In the introduction, Cohen locates his study of wonder within an autobiographical narrative of illness, in which the effects of a brain tumor transform and force him to renegotiate, among other things, his relationship with language and his approaches to Shakespeare. This narrative documents what Haraway refers to as "the view from a body," in which the body is revealed not as a stable, uniform entity, but as a configuration that is "complex, contradictory, structuring, and structured…"[4] For Cohen, the breakdown of the body and notions of a unified self alter epistemic approaches as well as the relations between literary historian and the lives and cultural materials under investigation:

> I began to think about how many of the audience members for Shakespeare's plays were in fact illiterates, groundlings, similarly struggling to understand their place in an increasingly confusingly technological, mechanical, and textual world. From the ashes of my studies emerged flesh and blood people on stage in Shakespeare's time with whom my disability allowed me to connect.[5]

Here, the language of Phoenix-like regeneration and reanimation evokes one of the very conventions for eliciting wonder—the raising of the (presumed) dead—that occupies a significant place within Cohen's own study of Shakespeare's dramatic thaumaturgy.

Like the defamiliarizing effects of illness and its treatment, Shakespeare's "pseudoresurrections"—a term Cohen uses to refer to "the raising of those thought to be dead but not actually dead, or the apparent raising—in the form of a ghost, for instance—of the actual dead"[6]—call attention to the porous boundaries between flesh and spirit, humans and machines, bodies and the material worlds they inhabit. In particular, this chapter will draw on Cohen's reading of *Pericles* to explore how the revivals of Thaisa and Pericles highlight the ecological and technological contexts of embodiment, as the practices by which life and sanity are restored depend, as dramatic events, on the perceived connections between the body's internal and external environments. In both cases, the body and its emotional and cognitive processes are conceptualized as part of a greater, interdependent system that stretches beyond its own thresholds of flesh to incorporate and fuse with the wonder-inducing machinery of the early modern theater and the cosmological order it replicates.

Thaisa's astonishing recovery takes place in Ephesus, a location that, as Cohen points out, links this central event and the doctor overseeing it with the apostle Paul, whose raising of Eutichus (who, like Thaisa, is not really dead) in Acts 20:7–12 and the doctrinal account of resurrection in 1 Corinthians 15 offer a rich interpretive framework for the reanimation of the dead as well as the living in *Pericles*.[7] The wonder generated by Thaisa's revival is enhanced through geographic association not only with Paul's ministry, but also with the turbulent and transformative properties of the sea. As Steve Mentz argues, Shakespeare's "oceans span the God-sea of the ancient world, where 'they who go down to the sea in ships' see 'wonders in the deep' (Psalm 107), and the boundless deeps of the early modern globe." From *The Comedy of Errors* to *The Tempest*, "Shakespeare's plays write the sea as opaque, inhospitable, and alluring, a dynamic reservoir of estrangement and enchantment."[8] When she emerges from this strange and tempestuous landscape, Thaisa's body, like that of Eutichus, is a mysterious terrain where life teems beneath the surface, its signs discernible only to those who, like Paul and Cerimon, know to look for it. Gazing upon Thaisa in her coffin, Cerimon marvels at "how fresh she looks" and concludes "They were too rash / That threw her in the sea" (12.77–78).[9] Significantly, Cerimon recognizes the rashness of this act not only in terms of its nearly fatal consequences for Thaisa, but also in terms of its ecological effects: "If the sea's stomach be o'ercharged with gold / 'Tis by a good constraint of queasy fortune / It belches upon us" (12.55–57). As it turns out, the master of Pericles's ship is mistaken about Thaisa as well as the sea—in burying her alive, he disrupts the equilibrium of the oceanic waters he sought to placate by sending her overboard.

Cerimon's medical skills are rooted in an understanding of the correspondences between bodies and their environments reflected in early modern conceptions of the humoral body, including "the relation of macrocosm to microcosm, of world to body, of the movements of wind or water to the movement of the passions."[10]

> 'Tis known I ever
> Have studied physic, through which secret art,
> By turning o'er authorities, I have,
> Together with my practice, made familiar
> To me and to my aid the blest infusions
> That dwells in vegetives, in metals, stones,
> And so can speak of the disturbances
> That nature works, and of her cures, which doth give me
> A more content and cause of true delight
> Than to be thirsty after tott'ring honour,
> Or tie my pleasure up in silken bags
> To glad the fool and death. (12.28–39)

Underlying Cerimon's practice is the recognition that the natural world is both responsive and hostile, its forces and elements are a source of harm as well as healing.

This awareness informs Cerimon's treatment of Thaisa, which involves fire and linen to foster and encourage "the fire of life [to] kindle again" (12.81), a vial of medicine, and musical accompaniment that, in the first quarto (1609), Cerimon characterizes as "the rough and / Wofull Musick that we haue" (1309–10).[11] While subsequent editors, including those of the Oxford edition, render this as "The still and woeful music that we have," Philip Edwards and Roger Warren make a strong case for the first quarto's version, which links the music that accompanies Thaisa's revival with the music that "nips [Pericles] vnto listning" (First Quarto 2228) prior to Diana's descent.[12] While musical accompaniment enhances the wonder generated by Thaisa's recovery, its melancholy roughness is also a reminder of the pain and darkness from which she awakens and into which she may still irretrievably return. As Cerimon warns those who attend to Thaisa, "this matter must be looked to, / For her relapse is mortal" (12.106–107).

In *Pericles*, musical performances signal as well as calibrate the correspondences between human and cosmological bodies. Cerimon's use of music therapy is based on Neoplatonic ideas of harmony as a "regulatory principle" that links the music of synchronized planetary motions to the disposition of bodily elements and humors, which constitutes emotional and physiological health.[13] In his "Mathematicall Praeface" to the 1570 English translation of Euclid's *Elements of Geometrie*, John Dee includes music among the mathematical arts and sciences necessary for the study of cosmography, and lists classical and biblical instances of music's therapeutic application as evidence for its "wondrous effectes":

> *Democritus* and *Theophrastus* affirmed, that, by *Musike*, griefes and diseases of the Minde, and body might be cured, or inferred. And we finde in Recorde, that *Terpander, Arion, Ismenias, Orpheus, Amphion, Dauid, Pythagoras, Empedocles, Asclepiades* and *Timotheus*, by *Harmonicall* Consonācy, haue done, and brought to pas, thinges, more then meruailous, to here of. (biii)

In *Pericles*, the performance of music doubles as a performance of the healing process that renders the body's internal workings accessible as part of the phenomenological experience of the theater. Given that the architectural design of early modern theaters, such as the Globe, stood in mimetic relation to that of the cosmos, the relation of body to world is also represented through the correspondences between the body and the miniature, man-made world of the theater.

As Cohen argues in *Shakespeare and Technology*, Shakespeare's plays incorporate the technological changes and developments within early modern culture through the increasingly mechanical terms in which human identity is articulated, a process Cohen refers to as "turning tech." In *Wonder in Shakespeare*, while Cohen focuses primarily on the theological and medical contexts of Thaisa's pseudoresurrection, his own language takes an intriguingly technological turn when he claims for Cerimon "a Dr. Victor Frankenstein-like moment as he describes the signs of life returning to Thaisa"[14]:

> She is alive. Behold,
> Her eyelids, cases to those heav'nly jewels
> Which Pericles hath lost,
> Begin to part their fringes of bright gold.
> The diamonds of a most praisèd water
> Doth appear to make the world twice rich.—Live,
> And make us weep to hear your fate, fair creature,
> Rare as you seem to be. (12.95–102)

Cohen notes that while the comparison of women to "rich jewels" is commonplace, "there is nothing conventional... about Cerimon's successful attempt to bring Thaisa back to life," an event that the attending gentlemen—the audience onstage—characterize as "strange" and "rare" (12.103–104), thus deploying "two of the more popular adjectives used to describe wonders or marvels during the period."[15] The language of wonder and artifice-in-motion also links Thaisa's reawakening body to the "marvelous self-moving machines, products of art that imitate nature" found in classical and neoclassical depictions of automata.[16] As Alexander Marr points out, such machines were essential to Aristotelian notions of wonder in the *Metaphysics*, where "Aristotle uses the example of automata to illustrate the assertion that it is wondering (thaumazein) about the causes of things that prompts philosophy: 'For all men begin, as we said, by wondering that things are as they are, as they do about wondrous automata.'"[17]

For Cerimon as for Aristotle, self-moving machines inspire curiosity as well as a richer appreciation for the living systems whose designs and movements they replicate. In his *Essayes of certain paradoxes* (1616), William Cornwallis references automata to convey the interdependent relations that comprise as well as connect bodies and their environments.

> In the whole course and frame of Nature, we see that nothing is made for it selfe, but each hath a bond of duty, of vse or of seruice, by which it is indebted to other. The sunne by his splendor to lighten all the world; by his warmth and heate, to cherish and comfort each liuing and vegetable thing. Yea, man himselfe is so framed of God, that not onely his Countrey, his Parents and his friends claime a share in him, but he is also indebted to his dogge, and to his Oxe... Let him but looke into himself,

and see how his constitutiue parts are debters each to other, the soule doth quicken and giue life to the body, the body like an *Automaton*, doth moue and carry it selfe and the soule. Suruey him in his parts, the eye seeeth for the foote, the foote standeth for the hand, the hand toucheth for the mouth, the mouth tasteth for the stomacke, the stomacke eateth for the whole body, the body repayeth backe againe that nutriment which it hath receiued, to all the parts, discharging the retriments by the *Port-Esquiline*; and all this in so comely an order, and by a Law so certain, and in so due a time, as if Nature had rather man should not haue been at all, then not to be a debter in euery part of him... (G2–G3)

As an illustration of the paradox that it is good to be in debt, the comparison of bodies to automata invokes patterns of obligation rather than prospects of autonomy or self-reliance. Cornwallis, like Cerimon, figures the body as an ever-expanding network—what Jeffrey Jerome Cohen, drawing on the work of Gilles Deleuze and Félix Guattari, refers to as an "identity machine," or the notion that "human identity is—despite the best efforts of those who possess it to assert otherwise—unstable, contingent, hybrid, discontinuous; that the work of creating a human body is never finished..."[18]

Shakespeare reiterates Cerimon's marvelous and mechanical description of eyes opening to music in *The Tempest*, when Prospero instructs Miranda to look upon Ferdinand (as Ariel lures him toward her with a song about his father, Alonso, submerged in the ocean's transforming waters), while imagining her eyes as a discovery space in which the beginnings of desire and the hope of a future alliance will be revealed: "The fringèd curtains of thine eye advance, / And say what thou seest yon" (1.2.412–13). As Prospero links Miranda's body with the theater's machinery for wondrous disclosure, he anticipates his dramatic pseudoresurrection of children and parents presumed lost at sea in act 5 when, with Alonso looking on, Prospero "discovers," or draws back the curtain to reveal Ferdinand and Miranda playing chess. Sebastian's characterization of this elaborately staged reunion as "a most high miracle" (5.1.180) underscores the relations among Prospero's art, religious mystery, and the recently prohibited mystery play cycles. As Adam Cohen argues, by evoking the conventions of resurrection drama without actually raising the dead, "Shakespearean theatrical wonder offered an alternative, a substitute, and in some sense even a replacement for the venues of religious wonder that were eliminated under Elizabeth."[19] Along these lines, pseudoresurrections provide an ostensibly secular framework for confronting the forces of death and disorder as well as for occasioning the practices and conventions for constructing life on stage. In locating these conventions within the domain of science, and in relation to the information technologies of the digital age, Henry S. Turner argues for an approach to the early modern theater in terms of a laboratory or machine for producing artificial life: "the theater provided a device with which to experiment with different forms of life according to a variety of codes and 'scripts': to examine its definitions, causes, variety, and significance, to model and to experiment with, in a word, its 'character.'"[20] *Pericles* registers a deep investment in such experiments and in the multimedia networks for communicating the phenomenal lives and transformations of its characters. The marvelous restorations of Thaisa and Pericles provoke wonder not only because of their association with the religious mystery of resurrection, but also because the dramatizations of the healing process are, arguably, the most elaborately theatrical and technologically complex of the play's spectacles. As with Thaisa's return to life, Pericles's restoration is marked by and enacted through music that signals the correspondences between corporeal and cosmological rhythms, as well as the material relations between bodies and environments that, in what Gail Kern Paster refers to as an "ecology of the passions," were understood by early modern cultures as constituting psychophysiological states.[21] This music also associates the practices of interiority with the inner workings of the theater, as the "most heav'nly music" (22.218) that Pericles hears anticipates the culminating spectacle of Diana's descent from the heavens of the stage and, by disguising the din of the pulley system needed to orchestrate the play's theophany, enables it to effect the kind of wonder associated with *sprezzatura*.

Just as the pseudoresurrections of Thaisa and Pericles call attention to the multiple, intersecting systems for generating and sustaining life, Cohen's methodologies emphasize the importance of thinking about scholarly projects as complex ecosystems, as rich accumulations of examples and readings that foster new connections and ongoing conversations: "My approach resembles Shakespeare's work by resisting clear finite forms. Instead Shakespeare and I are trying to generate variety among readers and viewers. Wonder is often scary for scholars... Ambiguity is what we avoid, fear, resist, and fight, but I believe in these things."[22]

Notes

1. Donna Haraway, "Situated Knowledges: The Science Question in Feminism and the Privileges of Partial Perspective," *Feminist Studies* 14.3 (1988): 581.
2. Ibid., 583.
3. Ibid., 583, 586.
4. Ibid., 589.

5. See the introduction to part I of the present volume, p. 6.
6. See chapter I.2, p. 18.
7. See ibid., p. 28.
8. Steve Mentz, *At the Bottom of Shakespeare's Ocean* (London: Continuum, 2009), ix.
9. William Shakespeare, *The Norton Shakespeare*, ed. Stephen Greenblatt, Walter Cohen, Jean E. Howard, and Katharine Eisaman Maus, 2nd ed. (New York: W.W. Norton & Co., 2008). Unless otherwise indicated, all citations of Shakespeare's plays are from this edition.
10. Gail Kern Paster, *Humoring the Body: Emotions and the Shakespearean Stage* (Chicago: University of Chicago Press, 2004), 9.
11. First quarto citations are from the reprint included in the Oxford Shakespeare edition of *Pericles*, ed. Roger Warren (Oxford: Oxford University Press, 2003).
12. Ibid., 164 n. 86.
13. Jeanice Brooks, "Music as Erotic Magic in a Renaissance Romance," *Renaissance Quarterly* 60.4 (2007): 214.
14. See chapter I.2, p. 34.
15. See ibid., p. 34.
16. Alexander Marr, "*Gentille curiosité*: Wonder-working and the Culture of Automata in the Late Renaissance," in *Curiosity and Wonder from the Renaissance to the Englightenment*, ed. R. J. W. Evans and Alexander Marr (Aldershot, UK: Ashgate, 2006), 149.
17. Ibid., 149.
18. Jeffrey Jerome Cohen, *Medieval Identity Machines* (Minneapolis: University of Minnesota Press, 2003), xxiii.
19. See chapter I.1, p. 10.
20. Henry S. Turner, "Life Science: Rude Mechanicals, Human Mortals, Posthuman Shakespeare," *South Central Review* 26.1–2 (2009): 209.
21. Paster, *Humoring*, 25–76.
22. See the introduction to part I of the present volume, p. 7.

Works Cited

Cohen, Adam Max. *Shakespeare and Technology: Dramatizing Early Modern Technological Revolutions*. New York: Palgrave Macmillan, 2006.

Cornwallis, William. *Essayes of certain paradoxes*. London, 1616. *Early English Books Online,* http://eebo.chadwyck.com.ezp.slu.edu.

Dee, John. "Mathematical Praeface." In *The elements of geometrie of the most auncient Philosopher Euclide of Megora*. London: John Day, 1570. *Early English Books Online,* http://eebo.chadwyck.com.ezp.slu.edu.

CHAPTER II.2

The Aesthetic Resurrection of the "Death-mark'd" Lovers in *Romeo and Juliet*

Janna Segal

In chapter I.2, Cohen traces the presence in Shakespeare's drama of "pseudoresurrections," which he defines as "either the raising of those thought to be dead but not actually dead, or the apparent rising—in the form of a ghost, for instance—of the actual dead."[1] Although Cohen identifies Juliet's revival after ingesting a liquid effecting "A thing like death" (4.1.74)[2] as a pseudoresurrection,[3] I find that the Friar's phrasing recalls a morose fact of the "death-mark'd" title characters' existence (1.P.9): they are "a thing like death," theatricalized representations of fictional figures who are introduced as having "take[n] their life" prior to their first entrance (1.P.6). Expanding upon Cohen's examination of the relationship between medieval Resurrection plays and Shakespeare's theaetr, I will first discuss how *Romeo and Juliet* reproduces forms of awe present in the dramatizations of resurrections in the Wakefield cycle. I will then argue that *Romeo and Juliet* frames the title characters as "aesthetic resurrections," rather than as "pseudoresurrections," through the conventions of the stage. This is in part a result of the play's prologues, conclusion, and deathly allusions, which function to maintain the wonder of resurrection drama in the present tense of the love tragedy, where the deceased Romeo and Juliet are brought back to life as living characters by actors even as their deaths continue to haunt the action from an "unaesthecized absent-present affective space" that Bryan

Reynolds and I refer to as a "some-other-where-but-here-space."[4] In conclusion I will consider how *Romeo and Juliet*'s appropriation of the conventions of banned cycle drama and depiction of the title characters as martyrs is a departure from the anti-Catholic sentiments of its primary source text, Arthur Brooke's *The Tragicall Historye of Romeus and Juliet* (1562).[5]

"The fearful passage of their death-mark'd love" (1.P.9)

The resonance of cycle drama in the early modern English theater, especially Resurrection plays, is central to Cohen's examination of the function of wonder in Shakespeare's theater. Cohen argues that in the aftermath of Elizabeth I's May 16, 1559, proclamation prohibiting the public performance of religious plays, Protestant dramatists crafted works to induce wonder in ways that recalled the awe invoked by the medieval Resurrection plays.[6] One means to do so was through a "pseudoresurrection," which Cohen defines as "the plot device of the raising of the undead or the apparently dead."[7] Cohen contends that this "plot device," which functioned to produce "wonder among the stage characters and, by extension, the audience members,"[8] may have been a conscious attempt on Shakespeare's part to reproduce the affects of the now deemed treasonous dramatic material: "He turned to pseudoresurrections because they spoke to the aesthetic tastes of his audiences, they offered a close approximation of the affective and cognitive pleasure of wonder plays, and they were acceptable to the Elizabethan and Jacobean censors."[9]

That Shakespeare's audiences were, as Cohen argues, still inured to the aesthetics of dramatic material officially banned in 1559 is further suggested by the persistent presence of the Wakefield cycle in the wake of Elizabeth I's proclamation against religious drama. In 1576, the Diocesan Court of High Commission wrote in response to learning

> "that it is meant and purposed that in the towne of Wakefeld shalbe plaid this yere in Whitsonweke next or thereaboutes a plaie commonlie called *Corpus Christi* [...] wherein they are done t' understand that there be many things used which tende to the derogation of the Majestie and glorie of God, the prophanation of the sacramentes and the maunteynaunce of superstition and idolatrie."[10]

While there are no records after 1576 of attempts to produce this cycle,[11] this evidence points toward its circulation and potential influence on audiences nearly two decades after its suppression by the court and roughly two decades before the appearance of *Romeo and Juliet*.[12]

Both *Lazarus* (twelfth play) and *The Resurrection* (twenty-eighth play) in the Wakefield cycle[13] stress the both blissful and fearful wonder that resurrection drama sought to produce and that *Romeo and Juliet* endeavors to reproduce. When the deceased Lazarus rises from beneath the "earth," he speaks of the fantastic "wonder" of God that produced the miracle of his resurrection:

> Lord, that all things made of nought,
> All praise be to thee,
> That such wonder here has wrought,
> Greater may none be. (327)

Similarly, Mary Magdalene celebrates the "joyful sight" of Christ reborn at the end of *The Resurrection* (476). On the other hand, when the Centurion in *The Resurrection* reports to Pilate of the "sights of wonder" following Christ's crucifixion (461), such as "dead men" rising from "their grave" (459), he reports that these gruesome "marvel[s]" (ibid.) are threatening and will have tragic consequences: "Sir, I fear me ye have done great wrong / And wondrous ill" (460). *Romeo and Juliet* likewise strives to engender both delightful and frightening, sorrowful awe. This attempt is initiated from the start with the First Act Prologue's pronouncement that the impending action is "The fearful passage of their death-mark'd love" (1.P.9). The audience is hereby directed to celebrate the enormity of the title characters' "love," which endured despite being "death-mark'd," and to tremble at its tragic, "fearful passage." This conflation of pleasurable and "fearful" wonder is continued at the conclusion when Prince Escalus announces, "For never was a story of more woe / Than this of Juliet and her Romeo" (5.3.308–309). Again, the spectator is led to be moved by the advertised as "never" before produced impact of both the tremendous "woe" and the awe-inspiring passion of "Juliet and her Romeo." The title of the Second Quarto (1599), "The Most Excellent and Lamentable Tragedie of Romeo and Juliet,"[14] additionally capitalizes on the play's capacity to offer what is referred to in the Wakefield cycle as both a "joyful sight" and "wondrous ill." "The Most" connotes the marvelous by implying uniqueness and vastness, while "Excellent" and "Lamentable" signify the two wonders that make Romeo and Juliet "the Most" tragic figures: their exceptional "love"; and its "fearful passage" (1.P.9).

"where we lay our scene" (1.P.2)

The suggestion that the play's combo awe-effect recalls that produced in the Wakefield cycle's reenactments of resurrections expands upon Cohen's contention that the pseudoresurrections in Shakespeare's theater "indicate an important form of continuity between his plays and the medieval dramatic tradition, particularly the *Resurrection of the Lord* plays that featured prominently in mystery or miracle cycles."[15] My argument that *Romeo and Juliet*'s narrative structure positions the title figures as resurrected through the conventions of the stage also extends Cohen's claims. Cohen's definition of "pseudoresurrection" delimits it to a "plot device of the raising of the undead or the apparently dead."[16] However, in *Romeo and Juliet*, the title characters are reborn in theatrical form not due to a "plot device"; rather, their return to life as living figures is in part a function of the play's narrative frame, which is, as Davis denotes, bookended by the First Act Prologue and Prince Escalus's final decree.[17] This framework creates what Reynolds and I describe as "a theatricalized transition state between life and death"[18] by introducing the "death-mark'd" lovers (1.P.9) as deceased before reviving them in the form of two actors. Counter to Cohen's designations, the resurrected characters are initially presented as neither "undead," "apparently dead," nor as "the actual dead" in "ghost" form[19]; instead, they appear alive even though "their death," which serves to "bury their parents' strife" (1.P.8), both precedes and marks the culmination of "the two hours' traffic of our stage" (1.P.12). The exchange ("traffic") between actors and spectators ("our") is also what allows for their rebirth as living characters in the "now" of the forthcoming two-hour "stage" representation (1.P.12). Indeed, the audience's complicity is requested by the Chorus: "if you with patient ears attend" (1.P.13). Attentive and attuned to the blurring of time and place effected by the first Prologue, the audience can be transported along with the characters back to a tragic past as represented in a "now" through the conventions of "our stage."

The First Act Prologue creates with the spectators what Augusto Boal refers to as an "aesthetic space."[20] The Prologue highlights the spatiotemporal plasticity of the performance area by situating the audience in bifurcated places and times: "In fair Verona, where we lay our scene" (1.P.2), and simultaneously in the theater, where the "two hours' traffic of our stage" is about to commence (1.P.12); and in the past, where the "star-cross'd lovers" committed suicide (1.P.6), while in the present, where they "take their life" (1.P.6). The capacity of "our scene" to be both "fair Verona" and an early modern English "stage" is in keeping with Boal's conception of the performance area as an "aesthetic space" that "*is* but *doesn't exist.*"[21] This seemingly contradictory space designated by actors and spectators allows for the distortion of spatiotemporal demarcations and socially prescribed codes: "In the aesthetic space one can be without being. Dead people are alive, the past becomes present, the future is today, duration is dissociated from time, everything is possible in the here-and-now, fiction is pure reality, and reality is fiction."²² Having introduced the title characters as previously deceased, the first Prologue draws the audience's attention to an "aesthetic space," where the spectators are confronted with "A pair of star-cross'd lovers" who have "take[n] their life" (1.P.6) and who are reborn in the present "aesthetic space" in part by two actors who serve in, to borrow from Boal, the "aesthetic resurrection" of Romeo and Juliet.

The "aesthetic resurrection" of Romeo and Juliet differs from a "pseudoresurrection" in form and function. It is not a plot device, but a consequence of dramatic and theatrical conventions. It is an effect of the bookended narrative framework that Davis delineates, with the Prince's pseudoepilogue inviting, as Callaghan argues, future retellings of the love tragedy.²³ The title characters' resuscitation in an "aesthetic space" is also dependent on a series of negotiations in the First Act Prologue between the actors and spectators, including a tacit agreement to be transported via the action and performers to the Catholic "fair Verona, where we lay our scene" (1.P.2), and an overt contract to "attend" to the past with "patient ears" in the "now" and in the future "two hours' traffic of our stage" (1.P.12–13). This request for the audience's aural attentiveness also points to the dependence of Romeo and Juliet's aesthetic resurrection on the repeated allusions to their deaths. For instance, both Romeo's and Juliet's first onstage appearance is preceded by their respective fathers associating them with graves: Romeo is described by his father as living a tomblike existence, "Away from light" (1.1.135) in "an artificial night" (1.1.138); and Juliet's father announces that Juliet is the last of his "hopes" to be "swallow'd" by the "earth" (1.2.14). The Second Act Prologue recalls the lovers' "deathbed" (2.P.1) even as it asserts that "passion lends them power" (2.P.13). Moreover, act 2 begins with a direct reference to resurrections with Mercutio's attempt to "conjure" the deceased Romeo "to raise up him" (2.1.29): "He heareth not, he stirreth not, he moveth not: / The ape is dead and I must conjure him" (2.1.15–16). Mercutio's remark that Romeo "is already dead" (2.4.13), the Friar's pronouncement that Romeo was "lately dead" for Juliet's "sake" (3.3.135), Juliet's dissembling insistence to her mother that she "never shall be satisfied / With Romeo, till I behold him—dead—" (3.5.93–94), the Nurse's advice that Juliet marry Paris since Romeo "is dead, or 'twere as good he were" (3.5.224), and Capulet's lament, "martyr'd, kill'd" (4.5.59), upon seeing his seemingly dead daughter all remind the audience of the offstage deaths that continue to haunt the action even before it moves in act 5 into the Capulet crypt, which serves as a visual cue of the "fearful" culmination of their "death-mark'd" lives promised in the first Prologue (1.P.9).

These recurrent references to the fact that Romeo and Juliet "take their life" (1.P.6) before the play begins create more than dramatic irony: they produce what Reynolds and I refer to as a "some-other-where-but-here-space." Named after Romeo's lines, "Tut, I have lost myself, I am not here. / This is not Romeo, he's some other where" (1.1.195–96), which imply the existence of a "real" Romeo alternative to the actor-as-character who exists "some other where" beyond the representation, "some-other-where-but-here-space" is "a non-represented yet aesthetically-invoked dimension conjured through a performance that posits its existence, but cannot confine it to the conventions of a specific performance area."[24] The repeatedly invoked knowledge of the title characters' deaths in *Romeo and Juliet* alludes to this hovering plane outside the aesthetic space from which the actors in a sense channel their roles, inasmuch as they portray characters that remain deceased in this dimension beyond the performance area. Reynolds and I argue that the audience, led to accept the actors as the characters who appear as both dead ("*he's* some other where") and not dead ("*I* am not here"), are temporally and spatially shifted "through their observation of the representational forms from the past to the present portrayal of these figures whose elusive whereabouts are referred to yet not shown."[25] We argue that this oscillation of the spectators through spacetime reveals the negotiability of imagined as concrete, state-supporting boundaries between, for instance, life and death and real and theatrical.[26] What I here refer to as the title characters' aesthetic resurrection only heightens this effect. The actors-as-characters, with the assistance of the spectators' "patient ears" and eyes (1.P.13), bring the deceased back to life for the duration of the play while alluding to their existence "some-other-where," thus continuing to obfuscate Protestant-Church delineated states of existence between life, death and postdeath. Moreover, they do so partly through recourse to dramatic devices and forms of awe that can be traced back to the officially banned Resurrection plays in the Catholic cycle dramas.

"And to this ende (good Reader) is this tragicall matter written" [27]

It has thus far been argued that *Romeo and Juliet*'s commingling of medieval and early modern English theatrical material and of living and nonliving figures undermines official Elizabethan conceptualizations and decrees. This supports Cohen's contention that "Shakespearean theatrical wonder offered an alternative, a substitute, in some sense even a replacement for the venues for religious wonder that were eliminated under Elizabeth."[28] An analysis of the prose note "To The Reader," which initiates Brooke's *The Tragicall Historye of Romeus and Juliet* (1562),[29] shows that Shakespeare's

Romeo and Juliet (1591–95)[30] also provided a countercultural "substitute" to the anti-Catholic sentiments attached to Romeo and Juliet that had been circulated in the period via Brooke's popular poem.

Brooke's address "To The Reader" pronounces the Protestant, antipapist moral of his ensuing narrative. He says he strives "to describe unto thee a coople of unfortunate lovers" in order to "warneth men not to be evyll" (284). In this prefatory account, the "unfortunate lovers" are not the victims of fortune; rather, their deaths are the result of their abuses against the Church and monarchy, including "unhonest desire," conferring with "superstitious friers (the naturally fitte instruments of unchastitite)," and "usying auriculer confession (the kay of whoredome, and treason) for furtheraunce of theyr purpose" (284–85). The poem endeavors to retract its opening depiction of Friar Lawrence as a "superstitious" instrument of "treason." He is situated as an exception to the "Frauncis order": "Not as the most was he, a grosse unlearned foole" (.566–67). He is also described as a "trusty frend" (.1265) who eventually went to a hermitage to die with "no marke of defame" (.2999). Nonetheless, he is "defame[d]" by his preliminary association with the "naturally fitte instruments of unchastitite," and in the narrative by his involvement in an "order" overpopulated with the "grosse" and his hearing of the lovers' "confession," which the Reader is warned is "the kay of whoredome, and treason." Furthermore, the Friar participated in Romeus and Juliet's undoing, which ultimately was a result of their "unhonest desire," blasphemy, and "treason." Brooke tells his readers that the lovers are explicitly presented "to thintent to rayse in them an hatefull lothying of so filthy beastlyness" (285). Thus Romeus and Juliet are framed for the "good Reader" (284, 285) as a Protestant warning against "filthy" acts of "treason."

Bullough correctly notes that Brooke's poem is more sympathetic to the lovers than his opening address[31]; however, this does not negate the possibility that an irreligious stigma remained attached to the figures and was circulated with the poem, which was republished before *Romeo and Juliet* was staged. Bullough cites the text's license for reprinting in 1582 and its reissue in 1587 as evidence of its popularity in the Elizabethan period.[32] The existence of Shakespeare's public stage version[33] also evinces the poem's presence in Elizabethan culture. That the play's Second Quarto title, "The Most Excellent and Lamentable Tragedie of Romeo and Juliet" (1599), is an adaptation of Brooke's title, *The Tragicall Historye of Romeus and Juliet*, implies an attempt to capitalize on the audience's familiarity with Brooke's work and on the notoriety of Romeo and Juliet in the popular imagination. Yet, Shakespeare's analogue to Brooke's note "To The Reader," the first Prologue, renders the figures from the source text's antipapist framework.

Rather than as signs of profane "filthy beastlyness" (285), Romeo and Juliet are introduced as "star-cross'd lovers" whose "piteous overthrows" were an act of martyrdom: "with their death" they "bury their parents' strife" (1.P.6–8). The tragedy's conclusion also counters Brooke's positing of the lovers as sights to engender "hatefull lothyng" (285) by imagining them as secular martyrs to be enshrined in "pure gold" (5.3.298). The play's use of dramatic and theatrical conventions associated with Catholicism to give life and death to the title characters generally undermines the poem's anti-Catholic stance. Romeo points toward the play's "sweet" alternative to Brooke's lesson against the "treason" of papistry (285) when he foretells, "all these woes shall serve / For sweet discourses in our times to come" (3.5.52–53). As their "times to come" have told, Brooke's pro-Protestant "Tragicall Historye" was overshadowed by "The Most Excellent and Lamentable" version, which continues to be resurrected time and again.

Notes

1. See chapter I.2, pp. 17–18.
2. All quotations from *Romeo and Juliet* are from the Arden edition, ed. Brian Gibbons (London: The Arden Shakespeare, 1980).
3. See chapter I.2, pp. 36–37.
4. Bryan Reynolds and Janna Segal, "Fugitive Explorations in *Romeo and Juliet*: Searching for Transversality inside the Goldmine of R&Jspace," in *Transversal Enterprises in the Drama of Shakespeare and His Contemporaries: Fugitive Explorations*, by Bryan Reynolds (New York: Palgrave Macmillan, 2006), 156.
5. Brooke's poem is identified by Geoffrey Bullough as Shakespeare's "main and perhaps sole source" in his introduction to Brooke's "The Tragicall Historye of Romeus and Juliet," in *Narrative and Dramatic Sources of Shakespeare*, vol. 1, ed. Geoffrey Bullough (London: Routledge and Kegan Paul, 1957), 274. Frank Kermode likewise refers to Brooke's text as Shakespeare's "direct source" in "Introduction to *Romeo and Juliet*," in *Modern Critical Interpretations: William Shakespeare's Romeo and Juliet*, ed. Harold Bloom (Philadelphia: Chelsea House, 2000), 118. Bullough also provides a summary of the transmission of the story from fifteenth- and sixteenth-century *novella* to Brooke's poem to Shakespeare's play (269–76), as does Brian Gibbons in his introduction to the Arden edition (32–37).
6. See chapter I.2, p. 27.
7. See chapter I.3, p. 41.
8. See ibid., p. 41.
9. See chapter I.2, p. 27.
10. Quoted in Martial Rose, "An Introduction to the Wakefield Plays," in *The Wakefield Mystery Plays*, ed. Martial Rose (Garden City: Anchor Books, 1963), 17.

11. Ibid., 18.
12. Kermode dates Shakespeare's play around 1595 in "Introduction to *Romeo and Juliet*" (118). Bullough assigns it to 1594–95 in his introduction to "The Tragicall Historye of Romeus and Juliet" (269). Gibbons identifies 1591 as the earliest and 1596 as the latest date possible for the first performance of *Romeo and Juliet* (26).
13. All quotations from the Wakefield cycle are from *The Wakefield Mystery Plays*, ed. Martial Rose.
14. Title quoted in Gibbons, introduction to *Romeo and Juliet* (1). Gibbons suggests that Q2 title's inclusion of the phrase "Newly corrected, augmented, and amended" is a response to the 1597 pirated First Quarto (1).
15. See chapter I.2, p. 18.
16. See chapter I.3, p. 41.
17. Lloyd Davis, "'Death-marked love': Desire and Presence in *Romeo and Juliet*," in *Romeo and Juliet: Contemporary Critical Essays*, ed. R. S. White (New York: Palgrave, 2001), 28–29.
18. Reynolds and Segal, "Fugitive Explorations," 155.
19. See chapter I.2, pp. 17–18 and p. 41.
20. Augusto Boal, *The Rainbow of Desire: The Boal Method of Theatre and Therapy*, trans. Adrian Jackson (London: Routledge, 1995), 18–21.
21. Ibid., 20; emphasis in the original.
22. Ibid.
23. Dympna Callaghan, "The Ideology of Romantic Love: The Case of *Romeo and Juliet*," in *The Weyward Sisters: Shakespeare and Feminist Politics*, eds. Dympna Callaghan, Lorraine Helms, and Jyotsna Singh (Oxford: Blackwell, 1994), 61–62.
24. Reynolds and Segal, "Fugitive Explorations," 156.
25. Ibid., 157.
26. Ibid.
27. Brooke, "The Tragicall Historye of Romeus and Juliet," 284.
28. See chapter I.1, p. 10.
29. Brooke, "The Tragicall Historye of Romeus and Juliet," 1:284. All Brooke citations are from this source.
30. See note 12 in regards to the dating of the play.
31. Bullough, introduction to "The Tragicall Historye of Romeus and Juliet" (277).
32. Ibid., 275.
33. The titles for Q1 and Q2, both of which are provided in Gibbons's introduction to *Romeo and Juliet* (1), imply that the play was initially produced in a public theater. Q1 (1597) advertises that "it hath been often (with great applause) plaid publiquely by the right Honourable the L. of *Hunson* his Seruants," and the Q2 (1599) title announces that the text appears "As it hath bene sundry times publiquely acted, by the right Honourable the Lord Chamberlain his Seruants."

CHAPTER II.3

The "Spectacle of Conversion," Wonder, and Film in *The Merchant of Venice*

M. G. Aune

Adam Cohen writes in depth about moments of internal wonder in *The Tempest*. When Miranda first sees Alonso and the others, she is awestruck by their very existence; they are completely new to her. These men in turn experience their own sense of wonder when Miranda and Ferdinand are discovered playing chess together. Alonso in particular had been convinced that his son was dead.[1] The audience, in contrast, Cohen speculates, would not have had the same experience of wonder as the characters, having been privy to Prospero's machinations throughout the play. Instead, any wonder on the part of the audience would have been external and manifested itself in their reaction to the special effects of the disappearing banquet or to the actions of fantastic creatures such as Caliban and Ariel. *The Winter's Tale* provides an analogous division of wonder experiences, though in this play the audience knows little more than do the characters. They are at the mercy of Paulina as the stage manager. As Cohen observes, she constructs a theatrical wonder when she reveals the living statue of Hermione while carefully treading the line between magic and miracles.[2] The characters are free to gape at the pseudoresurrection; while subject to real-life concerns about heresy and witchcraft, the audience requires an eventual explanation of the deception. In both these instances, the audiences' willingness to believe stage magic is exploited, while their cultural concerns about magic and heresy are alleviated. The theater's role as a place of wonder and safe affirmation of cultural and religious beliefs is reestablished.

A similar example of Shakespeare's use of wonder to alarm and then reassure his theater audience can be found in *The Merchant of Venice*, a play Cohen mentions several times but does not examine in depth. Similar to *The Tempest* and *Winter's Tale*, *Merchant of Venice* is a comedy about a sympathetic character's rescue from a potentially fatal situation through a near-miraculous intervention. The climax of the play, and the locus of much of the wonder, is a courtroom scene replete with accusations, flaring tempers, and surprise guests. The wonder of this scene, for the characters, derives from Antonio's rescue and Shylock's redemptive defeat.

For Shakespeare's audience, Shylock's characterization was conventionally familiar, but his salvation would have reflected an unconventional and marvelous variation on the fate typically reserved for Jews on stage. Modern audiences do not experience Shylock's fall and salvation in the same way. Shylock can be seen as a victim and his forced conversion as an excessive and perhaps puzzling punishment. Is it still possible for modern audiences to experience wonder in the figure of Shylock, or is his status as a victim too firmly fixed? This chapter will begin with a discussion of the Elizabethan experience of wonder in *Merchant of Venice* and then examine how Michael Radford's 2004 film version of the play exploits the medium to provide a modern sense of wonder for its audiences.

Though it occurs well before the end, the trial scene in *Merchant* is perhaps the most wonderful moment in the play, for the surprise verdict as well as for Shylock's forced conversion. In order to facilitate these instances of wonder, Shakespeare first establishes the unusual nature of Shylock and his behavior. In his opening speech, the Duke's language delineates the bizarre and surprising situation. He states:

> Shylock, the world thinks, and I think so too,
> That thou but leadest this fashion of thy malice
> To the last hour of act, and then 'tis thought
> Thou'lt show thy mercy and remorse more strange
> Than is thy strange apparent cruelty. (4.1.16–20)[3]

The Duke is convinced that Shylock is playing a game by pretending to be resolute in his desire for Antonio's flesh and expects that Shylock will relent and show mercy at the last moment. His use of the word "strange" has a double meaning that amplifies itself. The first use of strange meaning "surprising" or "remarkable" reveals the Duke's recognition of the melodramatic suspense that Shylock has created. To make a bond against a pound of flesh is odd enough, but to pursue it into the courts is almost unbelievable. At the same time, the possibility that Shylock might show mercy would be a remarkable exception to the stereotype of the ruthless Jew.[4] The second meaning of strange articulates a central theme in the play: the question of what is unusual or alien in Venice. In that city and that culture, Jews are held to a double standard. Though they are strangers, they are also residents and, for the Duke, such cruelty as Shylock pursues seems atypical of a Venetian, whether Christian or Jew. Shylock cannot escape the double standard linked to the label of "strange." If he is to be considered a resident of Venice, his behavior is unusually cruel. If he relents and shows mercy, he will be acting strangely for a Jew.

Earlier in the play, Solanio also uses "strange" in recounting Shylock's behavior after learning of Jessica's elopement. "I never heard a passion so confused, / So strange, outrageous, and so variable, / As the dog Jew did utter in the streets" (2.8.12–14). At first, Solanio wonders at the fervor and the energy of Shylock's reaction. Indeed, his comments might well be sympathetic, and many critics have seen them as one of few moments of compassion for Shylock.[5] But for Solanio, Shylock's reaction is excessive and not the mourning of a human, but of a dog.[6] He goes on to report Shylock's ravings and how he repeatedly conflates his daughter with his ducats.

In terms of the audience, Solanio here has a function similar to Miranda's in 1.2 of *The Tempest*. He is orchestrating or prompting the audience's (as well as his friends') reactions to Shylock.[7] This mediation of the audience's knowledge and emotions effectively controls its understanding of Shylock. Not only does the audience hear of Shylock's outrageous behavior, it also receives Solanio and Salerio's reactions and has little opportunity to consider or even form an alternative reaction to Shylock's dehumanization.

For Shakespeare's audience, this characterization would have been familiar. The figure of the Jew carried a substantially negative stereotypical weight. As early as the late fifteenth century, Jews on stage were characterized as treacherous, plotting to undermine Christians and Christianity. The *Croxton Play of the Sacrament*, for example, has a group of Jews attempting to desecrate the Host, yet being miraculously and repeatedly foiled.[8] By the late sixteenth century, conditioned by Christopher Marlowe's *Jew of Malta* (1592) and other plays, along with a great range of other libels and myths, viewers were ready to see and wonder at Shylock as a duplicitous, bloodthirsty, and devious character.[9] Very few Jews lived in England at the time and few of them practiced their religion openly, providing few, if any, counterexamples.[10] Much information about Jews came from the Bible and travelers' tales. Most usefully for playwrights, visitors to Venice and other

European Jewish centers reported a variety of information, such as the fact that, as a rule, Jews were required to wear red or yellow caps in public.[11] No evidence exists that Shylock wore such a cap, but Shakespeare suggests another sartorial marker when he has Shylock speak of his "Jewish gaberdine" (1.3.108).[12]

When the trial scene begins, the audience has been prepared to dislike Shylock and to expect that Antonio will be vindicated. Shylock's strangeness has been established, as has his dislike of Antonio and Christians in general.[13] Visually, the tension in the scene increases as Shylock begins sharpening his knife. The Norton editors suggest that he uses his shoe, an interpolation that may originate with Edwin Booth's late nineteenth-century practice or Graziano's pun: "not on thy sole but on thy soul" (4.1.122).[14] As a moment of secondary wonder, Shylock's actions amplify an already tense scene. He seems to have the upper hand, but a glimpse of hope appears in the first surprise of the trial—Nerissa's appearance. None of the characters on stage know why she is there and the sight of the knife and the act of sharpening it must have shocked Antonio and his friends as well as Nerissa.[15]

The trial scene becomes even more unconventional when Portia shows up disguised as Balthasar and awkwardly takes command of the trial. The theater audience experiences a measure of reassurance, but the characters remain silent. Once she establishes her credentials, Portia begins her investigation with a startling question: "Which is the merchant here, and which the Jew?" (4.1.169). After the constant references to the similarities and differences between Shylock and the Christians, this question is remarkable. Portia may be asking sincerely. If so, she is revealing her nescience of Shylock's gaberdine or other visual markers. Even if Portia is well aware of who is who and is trying to appear unbiased, more than a few in the room must have been surprised by her sudden appearance, her ignorance, and her question.

Portia's first tactic in persuading Shylock to change his mind is attributing wonderful characteristics to mercy and suggesting that Shylock may have access to them:

> The quality of mercy is not strained.
> It droppeth as the gentle rain from heaven
> Upon the place beneath. It is twice blest:
> It blesseth him that gives, and him that takes.
> 'Tis mightiest in the mightiest. It becomes
> The thronèd monarch better than his crown.
> His sceptre shows the force of temporal power,

The attribute to awe and majesty,
Wherein doth sit the dread and fear of kings;
But mercy is above this sceptred sway.
It is enthronèd in the hearts of kings;
It is an attribute to God himself,
And earthly power doth then show likest God's
When mercy seasons justice. (4.1.179–92)

Mercy is a wonderful and rare quality. As a gift, it benefits both the giver and the receiver. Monarchs fear it, yet it is a characteristic of God. By showing mercy, Portia suggests that Shylock would wield incredible power. He would be (metaphorically) a king or in this way like a character Shakespeare would create nearly a decade later, Prospero. Cohen points out how Prospero evokes wonder in the "dazed nobles" through the power of his magic, but also through his restraint.[16] But Shylock is actually the opposite of Prospero. Rather than choosing to limit his own power and show mercy to his enemy, he chooses to exert it to its greatest extent, desiring only to destroy his enemy.

Rejecting Portia's offer, Shylock prefers to frame the situation in terms of justice rather than mercy: "My deeds upon my head! I crave the law / the penalty and forfeit of my bond" (4.1.201–202). Portia then follows the letter of the law, but still gives Shylock opportunities to relent. Once these are exhausted, she increases the tension by directing the process step-by-step and giving Antonio occasion to make a final speech. She finally makes the long-awaited intervention saying that if Shylock

> shed[s]
> One drop of Christian blood, [his] lands and goods
> Are by the laws of Venice confiscate
> Unto the state of Venice. (4.1.304–307)

At this point, Shylock attempts to back out while Graziano jeers him.

As Solanio did in the previous act, Graziano prompts the audience to mocking delight at the beginning of Shylock's downfall and at the Christians' triumph: "O upright judge! / Mark, Jew! O learnèd judge!" (4.1.307–308). As Shylock tries to escape the rhetorical and legal net that tightens around him and as Portia stymies his every attempt, Graziano shouts similar phrases five more times. He compares Portia to Daniel, though he admits that he did not know of the Old Testament figure before Shylock mentioned him. By the time Portia delivers her final judgment, Graziano has established and reiterated Shylock's failure and abjection for the audience.

A second surprise comes as Shylock tries to exit. Because he is an alien and has sought

> the life of any citizen,
> The party 'gainst the which he doth contrive
> Shall seize one half his goods; the other half
> Comes to the...state (4.1.346–49)

Finally, "the offender's life lies in the mercy / Of the Duke only" (4.1.350–51). The Duke pardons Shylock and accepts the fines. After Shylock protests that without his money he is helpless, Portia invites Antonio to show mercy. He does, promising to give half of Shylock's money to Lorenzo and, most importantly, demanding that Shylock "presently become a Christian" (4.1.382). Shylock finally leaves saying he is ill but content. Graziano is not entirely satisfied, and calls after Shylock, "In christ'ning shalt thou have two godfathers. / Had I been judge thou shouldst have had ten more, / To bring thee to the gallows, not the font" (4.1.394–96). The audience's and characters' attentions are quickly diverted from the trial's triumph and wonder by the shift to a comic register when the disguised Portia confronts the unknowing Bassanio. Shylock is never seen again, and the audience, if it remembers him, can only assume that he converts.

In early modern England, the conversion of a Jew would have had a particular resonance and probably would have elicited a particular sense of awe for characters and audiences alike. James Shapiro in *Shakespeare and the Jews* describes a "spectacle of conversion" that occurred occasionally in sixteenth- and seventeenth-century England, where Jews would be ceremonially converted to Christians.[17] These conversions were wondrous events. They acknowledged Christianity's superiority and Christ's status as the messiah.[18] Perhaps more importantly, Christian eschatology found evidence in the Bible, in Daniel, Paul's letter to the Romans, and the book of Revelation, to indicate that the conversion of the Jews was necessary for the Parousia.[19] Shapiro does not go as far as to suggest that an Elizabethan audience would have understood Shylock's conversion as a purely positive event. But keeping in mind that the play is a comedy and that Antonio seems to see Shylock as a potential fellow Christian, Shylock's conversion must have struck some as a wonderful event for him and for Christianity. As a Christian, Shylock would be able to enter heaven and his soul would be saved, and as a convert he would help hasten the Second Coming.

Other contexts may also be relevant to the wonder of Shylock's rise and fall. Numerous critics have used the trial and execution of Roderigo Lopez to frame discussions of Shylock. Lopez, a Portuguese Jew, had moved to

London to escape the Inquisition, converted to Protestantism, and assimilated into English society.[20] He became a physician whose patients included courtiers and eventually Elizabeth. Implicated in a conspiracy to poison the queen, Lopez was arrested for treason, convicted, and executed in 1594.[21] Lopez's final words, claiming that he loved the queen as he loved Christ, drew cheers and laughter from the assembled crowd, according to contemporary records.[22] Though no evidence existed that he was anything but a practicing Protestant, the prosecutor described him as "a perjured murdering traitor, and Jewish doctor, worse than Judas himself [who] undertook to poison [the Queen]."[23] Despite his travels and enculturation, Lopez could not escape the specter of his Jewish past and the stereotypes attached to it.

At the end of the nineteenth century, Sidney Lee suggested that although Shakespeare may not have intended it, "the perception of a significant relation between [Lopez and Shylock] is, effectively, inevitable."[24] Stephen Greenblatt took up this idea in his biography of Shakespeare, *Will in the World*. Discussing the cultural knowledge of Jews in Shakespeare's England, he writes, "Jews, like modern wolves in modern children's stories, played a powerful symbolic role in the country's imaginative economy."[25] Often echoing Shapiro, Greenblatt traces the presence of Jews though Shakespeare, and especially Marlowe's *Jew of Malta*. In this play, he sees the adventures of the titular Jew, Barabas, as a "homicidal reverie" that for some in the audience made the irrationality of anti-Semitism clear. At the same time, Greenblatt allows, it could well have pandered to audiences' worst beliefs and confirmed their notions about Jews.[26]

Into this context, Greenblatt reads *Merchant of Venice* as Shakespeare's response to the Lopez execution. Rather than simply repeating Marlowe's anti-Semitic stereotypes for the benefit of a crowd that had recently laughed and cheered at Lopez's execution, Shakespeare made Shylock sympathetic by giving him a daughter who runs away to convert and marry a Christian. What is more, rather than being executed at the play's end, Shylock is redeemed by his conversion. In so doing, Greenblatt contends that Shakespeare brings the audience "too close for psychological comfort to the suffering figure."[27] This proximity to such strong emotions provides them with a surprising, wonderful, and thrilling theatrical experience.

If the Elizabethan experience of wonder at *Merchant of Venice* depended upon anti-Semitic cultural constructions of Jews and the importance of their conversion, how then might modern audiences experience wonder in the play, if at all? Modern productions have attempted to make Shylock sympathetic by cutting some of his more inflammatory lines and some of the Christians' more vicious characterizations.[28] As a result, Shylock appears victimized by Venetian culture and attitudes and his conversion becomes an ironic and cruel punishment. Manipulating the text in another way, productions shift the setting to times and places that render Shylock more familiar and the Christians' attitudes more intolerant.[29] In either case, the sense of wonder associated with Shylock's embodiment of anti-Semitic stereotypes and his eventual conversion is lost. The play becomes less a comedy than a morality play. The first commercial Hollywood film of *Merchant of Venice* (2004) fits comfortably into these performance trends, rendering Shylock a sufferer rather than an instigator. At the same time, it manages to generate a particularly filmic wonder by exploiting audiences' familiarity with movie star Al Pacino who portrays Shylock.

Nearly everyone who has written about the film notes that director Michael Radford attempts to evoke a sense of historical authenticity by setting the film in Venice in 1596. It opens with a montage of anti-Semitic violence, including the burning of a Torah, a mob inspired by a friar throwing a red-capped Jew into a canal, and Antonio (Jeremy Irons) spitting on a startled Shylock. Intercut with these images are lengthy titles explaining how Venetian culture of the time both valued and abhorred its Jewish residents. In so doing, Radford projects the representation of anti-Semitism past Shakespeare and onto Venice and, most importantly, by showing Antonio spitting on Shylock, indicates that the prejudice was a personal matter for Shylock and his fellow Jews.[30] To extend the moral distinction between the Christians and the Jews and set the stage for Shylock's victimization, the film goes on to use images of decadence and excess that highlight the Christians' hypocrisy and corruption.[31]

As with the play, the trial scene is central to the characterization of Shylock and the evocation of wonder. By invoking the film's opening, the scene, arguably, manages to recoup some of the wonder that Radford's adaptation has drained from the film. At the beginning of 4.1, the text calls for the entrance of the Duke, the Magnificoes, Antonio, Bassanio, [Salerio], and Graziano. When Shylock enters after about fifteen lines, he is the lone Jew, isolated, outnumbered, and set up to be the villain. Radford subverts this effect by including a large crowd of agitated onlookers, men and women, Christians and Jews. Their presence provides an audience for Shylock and Portia to play to, increases the tension, and through their responses and reaction shots carefully shape the audience's response.

The opposition of Shylock and Antonio, the Christians' bigotry, and the presence of a vocal crowd again call to mind the stark distinctions established by the film's first scene.[32] The set is a large room with windows along one side providing illumination. Bailiffs use staves to hold the boisterous crowd back and clear an area in front of the ducal throne. Into this claustrophobic space, Pacino enters carrying a bag with his knife and scales.

A gruff, worldly, and crafty old man, he dominates the initial exchange with the Duke, having clearly anticipated the arguments and prepared his responses.

Though Pacino never laughs or even smiles, his jokes and arguments generate scattered laughter and murmurs suggesting some level of sympathy for Shylock. The tone shifts, however, when Pacino ends his first speech with "Are you answered?" (4.1.61). The crowd shouts "No!" as the camera pans away from him and around the room, pausing on a man who spits on him. Pacino calmly wipes it off and turns away.

The crowd continues to shape the audience's response to the events. When Pacino mentions the "purchased slave" (4.1.89) and points widely into the assemblage, the camera cuts to a Venetian being fanned by a (presumably) African slave. As Pacino draws and begins to sharpen a long knife, the shouts nearly drown out his quietly triumphant line "Shall I have it?" (4.1.102). The crowd also provides a convenient explanation for Portia's opening question: It is not that she is unable to tell the Christian and Jew apart, it is that she is not sure which Christian and which Jew are involved in the dispute.

Once Portia (Lynn Collins) enters, the mood in the courtroom settles. As she walks around and deliberates with Shylock, the room becomes quiet and the reaction shots are limited to Bassanio (Joseph Fiennes) and Graziano (Kris Marshall). The crowd noise increases only when Pacino speaks and returns to silence when Antonio is strapped to the chair and during his conversation with Bassanio (4.1.259–82). The only reaction shots at this point are from Shylock, Portia, and Nerissa (Heather Goldenhersch).[33] As he prepares, Pacino appears intent, but never vindictive or triumphant. He even pauses for what seems to be a brief prayer. But several minutes later, once Shylock has been defeated Graziano is both triumphant and vindictive in his comments, though the crowd remains quiet. When Collins tells Pacino to beg mercy of the Duke, Pacino slowly sinks to his knees. Somehow evading the bailiffs, Graziano slips up to hiss "Beg that thou mayst have leave to hang thyself!" (4.1.359) into Shylock's ear. The camera remains largely on Pacino for the rest of the scene as he squirms pathetically on the floor, wringing his hands. No reaction shots of the crowd are provided except a brief close up of Tubal (Allan Corduner) who looks stunned at his friend's fate. As Pacino exits alone, he is again spat upon and his cap is thrown off—symbolically enforcing the conversion. The camera cuts back to close-ups of Portia and Bassanio, both of whom look grim and concerned. The mood at the scene's end contrasts starkly with its beginning. Rather than spirited and excited, the crowd is oddly quiet and contemplative. They do not by any means find any triumph or redemption in Shylock's fate. Instead, their quietude emphasizes Shylock's disappointment and defeat rather than Antonio's escape from a gruesome death.

The camera marginalizes Shylock and favors Portia in more ways than one. Pacino begins the scene triumphant, yet measured. Though he is central to the scene, the camerawork and *mise en scène* reinforce his characterization as a victim and Portia's as the hero. The camera tends to hold Pacino in a medium shot, highlighting his short, slightly stooped stature and includes the people behind him, while reaction shots of the crowd tend to be tighter concentrating on their faces. Where Collins tends to be photographed from a high angle, remains in the center of the frame without the presence of the crowd, and is followed by a mobile camera, Pacino is confined by a largely stationary camera and is frequently shot from low angles. As a result, the scene "manages to capture Shylock's victimization by Venetian society without blaming Portia."[34]

The Elizabethan reception to the scene would have included several aspects of wonder: surprise, triumph, and delight. The film, however, prompts distinctly different reactions. Though Irons's Antonio is largely a sympathetic character, his escape from a painful death is subordinated to Shylock's loss. The trial scene and much of the film become about Shylock's victimization rather than his villainy, defeat, and redemption.[35] This receives its final iteration in an interpolated scene placed after the reunions of Bassanio and Portia and Graziano and Nerissa. Through a doorway, a bare-headed Shylock is shown standing outside a synagogue as congregants enter. After the last one passes, a close-up of Pacino's haggard face is shown; then the door is closed against him. Because of his conversion, Shylock no longer wears his red cap and is no longer welcome in his community. Because of his past, he is not welcome among the Christians. Because the audience is repeatedly prompted to see Shylock as a victim of Venetian biases, the wonder of Antonio's escape, his forgiveness of Shylock, and Shylock's conversion are eliminated.

If we focus closely on the character and actor, as film invites audiences to do, we can find distinct elements of wonder in Pacino's portrayal of Shylock. Initially, this wonder is an a priori element of the medium; showmanship and virtuosity are aspects of the spectacle of film, which in turn can "evoke wonderment and pleasure."[36] The quality of Pacino's performance and his reputation as an actor amplifies the audience's sympathy for Shylock as victim. Samuel Crowl articulates a contrarian position, arguing that Pacino gives Shylock a dignity that helps the character avoid being seen simply as a victim.[37] In addition to being one of the most famous stars in Hollywood, Pacino carries with him the cultural capital of having performed Shakespeare on stage and screen several times and he has stated how important Shakespeare is to him as an actor.[38] As Shylock, Pacino is recognizable, though heavily made up with sagging flesh and a long gray beard and hair. His delivery is strong, gruff, and deliberate and his costuming, posture, and age invite sympathy.[39] He is shorter than most around him, which his long robes and stooped posture accentuate. A weight from a set of scales that hangs around his neck on a chain indicates his profession and foreshadows the pound of flesh. Though he has moments of anger, his age and manner inevitably elicit a certain fondness.

Along with this grouchy grandfather characterization, Pacino also brings a considerable weight of intertextuality to the film, recalling some of his earlier and dynamic characters: *Dog Day Afternoon*'s tragic bank robber Sonny Wortzik, the whistle-blower police detective Frank Serpico, and most notably *The Godfather*'s ruthless and charismatic Michael Corleone.[40] In some ways even more relevant is Pacino's Cuban gangster character in *Scarface*, "an immigrant outsider scrapping for power and touched by an element of paranoia produced by a life time of vigilant self-preservation and opposition to the enfranchised."[41] The intertexual traces of these characters combine with Pacino's capacity to give Shylock "dignity," and help the character resist the role of victim.[42] Pacino's Shylock is sympathetic, but he is also commensurate with the humiliations that the Duke, Bassanio, and Graziano visit on him. He has been spat on before.

This dignity is evident perhaps mostly profoundly in Shylock's final, interpolated, scene. Clearly the outsider, he looks through the doorway into the synagogue as his former friends and congregants shut him out. The close-up shows him staring and his eyes move once, but he never speaks and never makes a gesture of appeal. Pacino is not quite defiant (and certainly not in the manner of Tony Montana at the end of *Scarface*), but neither does he seem defeated. His somewhat ambiguous expression, combined with Pacino's movie star status generates an element of wonder for the audience. While the audience sees Shylock's rejection, it also sees another starring role for Pacino. It is through the movie-star element of the Hollywood film rather than Shylock's actions or his conversion that Radford's *Merchant of Venice* creates wonder for its audience.

Cohen argues, as have others, that wonder was a central part of the early modern theater experience, occupying a space vacated as "the venues of religious wonder that were eliminated under Elizabeth."[43] Susan Sontag makes a similar argument that wonder is a fundamental element of film: "cinema began in wonder...All of cinema is an attempt to perpetuate and re-invent that sense of wonder."[44] Differences in time and culture may have stripped *Merchant of Venice* of much of its capacity for generating surprise or delight through the figure of Shylock. At the same time, the advent of film as a dominant medium over the past century has created new means for that lost wonder to be recreated. One of the most subtle but effective strategies is the talent and the intertextual potential of the movie star. Seeing the man who played Michael Corleone and Tony Montana embody Shylock allows viewers to experience their own sensations of wonder at a film that otherwise lacks the surprise that Shakespeare and his culture provided.

Notes

1. See chapter I.1, pp. 9–11.
2. See chapter I.2, pp. 28–29.
3. All quotations are from *The Norton Shakespeare*, ed. Stephen Greenblatt, Walter Cohen, Jean E. Howard, and Katharine Eisaman Maus, 2nd ed. (New York: W.W. Norton, 2008).
4. For more on these stereotypes, see note 9.
5. For example, Arthur Quiller-Couch and John Dover Wilson, introduction to *The Merchant of Venice,* by William Shakespeare (Cambridge: Cambridge University Press, 1953), xix–xxi. And as Dennis Kay points out, sympathy for Jewish characters in Elizabethan drama seems contingent on their first conforming to a stereotype. Dennis Kay, *Shakespeare, His Life, Work, and Era* (New York: Morrow, 1992), 223.
6. Shylock is referred to as a dog several times. He refers to Antonio's calling him a dog again in 3.3.6–7. Graziano uses it as an epithet, "damned, inexecrable dog," in 4.1.127. For more on this, see Paul Yachnin, "Shakespeare's Public Animals," in *Humankinds: The Renaissance and its Anthropologies,* ed. Andreas Höfele and Stephan Laqué (New York: De Gruyter, 2011), 185–98.
7. Cohen adapts this term from Jean E. Howard (see chapter I.1, p. 11). Jean E. Howard, *Shakespeare's Art of Orchestration: Stage Technique and Audience Response* (Urbana: University of Illinois Press, 1984).
8. Similar to *Merchant of Venice*, at the play's end, the Jews voluntarily convert rather than being executed. See Osborn Waterhouse, ed., "The Croxton Play of the Sacrament," in *The Non-Cycle Mystery Plays* (London: Early English Text Society by Kegan Paul, Trench, Trübner and Co., 1909), 54–87.
9. Stephen Gosson mentions seeing a play called *The Jew* at the Bull Theatre and admires its critical portrayal of usury. *Schoole of Abuse* (London, 1579), C6v. These myths and images are further documented by James Shapiro in *Shakespeare and the Jews* (New York: Columbia University Press, 1996), esp. 43–113. Also John Gross, *Shylock: A Legend and Its Legacy* (New York: Simon and Schuster, 1994), 16–17; and Jay Halio, ed., introduction to *The Merchant of Venice* (Oxford: Oxford UP, 1993), 10. An extant broadside, "The Ballad of the Cruel Jew," seems to be based on *Merchant* and follows its plot closely. H. H. Furness, ed., *The New Variorum Merchant of Venice* (Philadelphia: J. B. Lippincott, 1895), 288–92. For a near-contemporary summary of libels against Jews, see Thomas Calvert, *The Blessed Jew of Morocco* (London, 1648), 16–20. Charles Edelman

argues that not all Elizabethans were anti-Semitic and that Shylock could potentially have been portrayed sympathetically. Charles Edelman, "Which is the Jew That Shakespeare Knew?: Shylock on the Elizabethan Stage," *Shakespeare Survey* 52 (1999): 99–106.

10. Robert Wilson's play *The Three Ladies of London* (*ca.* 1584) provides a curious example of a Venetian Jew whose generosity is used to contrast a villainous Italian merchant's deceit.
11. Thomas Coryate, *Coryats Crudities* (London, 1611), 321. Fynes Moryson writes that the Jews have to wear red caps because the color is closest to that of Christ's blood. *Shakespeare's Europe: A Survey of the Condition of Europe,* ed. Charles Hughes (New York: Benjamin Blom, 1967), 489.
12. According to the *Oxford English Dictionary*, "gaberdine," in the sixteenth and seventeenth centuries referred to a loose outer garment, often associated with Jews or other groups.
13. Most notably, when he speaks of Antonio:
    I hate him for he is a Christian;
    But more, for that in low simplicity
    He lends out money gratis, and brings down
    The rate of usance here with us in Venice.
    If I can catch him once upon the hip
    I will feed fat the ancient grudge I bear him. (1.3.37–42)
    And when he speaks of going to dinner with Bassanio. "But yet I'll go in hate, to feed upon / The prodigal Christian" (2.5.14–15).
14. See Furness, *New Variorum*, 204n131.
15. Patrick Stewart, writing about his performance of Shylock in John Barton's 1978 Royal Shakespeare Company production, sees Shylock as "black humorist" and speculates that his actions are intended to scare Nerissa in particular. "Shylock in *Merchant of Venice*," *Players of Shakespeare: Essays in Shakespearean Performance,* ed. Philip Brockbank (Cambridge: Cambridge University Press, 1985), 25.
16. See chapter I.1, p. 10. Though Cohen does not cite it, Prospero clearly refers to his own mercy in his consideration of his enemies and Ariel:
    Let [Trinculo and Stephano] be hunted soundly. At this hour
    Lie at my mercy all mine enemies:
    Shortly shall all my labours end, and thou
    Shalt have the air at freedom. (4.1.258–61)
17. Shapiro, *Shakespeare,* 130.
18. Ibid., 132.
19. Ibid., 132–65. See, e.g., Romans 11:11–28. In the Geneva Bible, a series of glosses interpret these verses as calling for conversion.
20. Edgar Samuel, "Lopez, Rodrigo (c.1517–1594)," *Oxford Dictionary of National Biography* (Oxford: Oxford University Press, 2004), http://www.oxforddnb.com/view/article/17011.
21. Numerous accounts of the trial and execution are extant. See Sir Francis Bacon, *The Letters and Life of Sir Francis Bacon,* ed. James Spedding (London: Longman,

Green, Longman, and Roberts, 1861), 1:274–87. A manuscript account of the trial is contained in British Library Additional Manuscript 871, 50–51r and 58v–59v and British Library Stowe Manuscript 166–77. Most editors date the composition of *Merchant* to several years after the event, ca. 1596/7.
22. William Camden, *Annals or The Historie of the Most Renowned and Victorious Princess Elizabeth*, 3rd ed., trans. R. N. (London, 1635), 430–31.
23. Mary Anne Everett Green, ed., *Calendar of State Papers, Domestic Series, of the Reigns of Edward VI, Mary, Elizabeth, 1547–1580: Elizabeth 1591–1594* (London: Longman, Green, Reader, and Dyer, 1867), 446.
24. Sidney Lee, "The Original of Shylock," *The Gentleman's Magazine* 248 (1880): 192.
25. Stephen Greenblatt, *Will in the World: How Shakespeare Became Shakespeare* (New York: W.W. Norton, 2004), 259.
26. Ibid., 266–67.
27. Ibid., 284.
28. For example, Shylock's "I hate him for he is a Christian" (1.3.37) is frequently omitted, see note 11 and Jay Halio, *Understanding Shakespeare's Plays in Performance* (Manchester: Manchester University Press, 1988), 12–13.
29. For a useful survey of recent approaches, see James Bulman, *Shakespeare in Performance: "The Merchant of Venice"* (Manchester: Manchester UP 1991), esp. 117–42; and more recently James Bulman, "Shylock, Antonio, and the Politics of Performance," in *Shakespeare in Performance: A Collection of Essays*, ed. Frank Occhiogrosso (Newark: U of Delaware P, 2003), 27–46.
30. In his director's commentary, Radford explains that the sequence "sets up everything." Thomas Cartelli, "Redistributing Complicities in an Age of Digital Production: Michael Radford's Film Version of *The Merchant of Venice*," in *A Touch More Rare: Harry Berger, Jr., and the Arts of Interpretation*, ed. Nina Levine and David Lee Miller (New York: Fordam UP, 2009), 61; Samuel Crowl, "Looking for Shylock: Stephen Greenblatt, Michael Radford and Al Pacino," in *Screening Shakespeare in the Twenty-First Century*, ed. Mark Thornton Burnett and Ramona Wray (Edinburgh: Edinburgh University Press, 2006), 117–18; L. Monique Pittman, "Locating the Bard: Adaptation and Authority in Michael Radford's *Merchant of Venice*," *Shakespeare Bulletin* 25.2 (2007): 15; Milla Cozart Riggio, "Filming Shylock: Radford and Miller," in *Shakespearean Performance: New Studies,* ed. Frank Occhiogrosso (Madison, NJ: Fairleigh Dickinson University Press, 2008), 189; Yong Li Lan, "Spectacle and Shakespeare on Film," in *Shakespeare's World/World Shakespeare*, ed. Richard Fotheringham, Christa Janson, and R. S. White (Newark: University of Delaware Press, 2008), 186; and Laury Magnus, "Michael Radford's *The Merchant of Venice* and the Vexed Question of Performance," *Literature/Film Quarterly* 35 (2007): 109–10, 113.
31. Cf. Lan, "Spectacle," 187; Magnus, "Michael Radford," 110; and Pittman, "Locating," 17.
32. Lan notes how various groups of characters in the film provide multiple layers of spectatorship ("Spectacle," 188).

33. Collins and Goldenhersch, both look at the floor in shame when Bassanio and Graziano mention them, and their asides (4.1.283–84, 288–89) are cut, preserving the glum tone of the moment.
34. Pittman, "Locating," 16. Pittman's (ibid., 19–20, 25–26) and Crowl's ("Looking," 122–24) observations on this scene are detailed and insightful.
35. Radford refers to Shylock as one of Shakespeare's tragic characters, an interpretation that influences the film heavily. See Cartelli, "Redistributing," 60–61; Magnus, "Michael Radford," 112; Pittman, "Locating," 26; and Riggio, "Filming," 191.
36. Lan, "Spectacle," 184.
37. Crowl, "Looking," 120.
38. See M. G. Aune, "Star Power: Al Pacino, *Looking for Richard* and the Cultural Capital of Shakespeare on Film," *Quarterly Review of Film and Video* 23.4 (2006): 353–67. In the summer of 2010, Pacino revisited his role of Shylock in a Public Theater Shakespeare in the Park production of *Merchant of Venice*, directed by Daniel Sullivan. It transferred to Broadway that fall.
39. Pittman notes Pacino's style and identifies an element of a Bronx accent ("Locating," 19) while Crowl evinces great admiration for Pacino's voice and overall approach ("Looking," 118-19).
40. Crowl, "Looking," 118.
41. Pittman, "Locating," 19.
42. Ibid., 120.
43. See chapter I.1, p. 10.
44. Susan Sontag, "The Decay of Cinema," *New York Times Magazine,* February 25, 1996, 6.

CHAPTER II.4

God Save the King: *Richard II* in Wonder-land

Rebecca Steinberger

In his introduction to *Wonder in Shakespeare*, Adam Max Cohen argues that scholarship on wonder and the plays of Shakespeare has been "limited" as it focuses on the late romances or the tragedies.[1] While I agree with Cohen's assertion, his argument opens up a space for the largely excluded history plays; in fact, the very texts that he highlights as being tragedy- and romance-centric[2] can be used to support the presence and value of wonder in the history cycles. This can be achieved, in part, by examining "wonder" or the "marvelous" through the marriage of tragic elements in historical literature. One play where this is profoundly important is *The Tragedy of King Richard II*, for it begins with an indictment of the hapless ruler and ends with a surge of sympathy and wonder (from both the audience and the characters) as he meets his sorrowful end. In this first play in the *Henriad*, Shakespeare's *Richard II* offers the Elizabethan audience a blend of Tudor history with the tragic consequences of a challenge to the divine right of kings. With a nod to Cohen, then, I consider the concept of wonder as it relates to three specific aspects in *Richard II*: first, through the shift in audience perception of the hapless monarch, whose own identity is blurred; second, in the blurring of English identity and Queen Elizabeth in particular; and third, through Richard's final scene. As in Shakespeare's day, the resulting cocktail is served to modern audiences in an attempt to both praise and critique the concept of an English national identity.

This Second Fall of Curs'd Man: Why Do We Marvel at Richard?

Written around the same time as Edmund Spenser's pro-Tudor/anti-Irish propaganda piece *A View of the Present State of Ireland* (ca. 1595), Shakespeare counteracts with a politically potent history that depicts the rise of one monarch (Henry IV) and the fall of another (Richard II). Succumbing to the praise and opinions of flatterers, Bushy, Bagot, and Green, the regent fails the people and land he rules—as well as his queen. The play is laced with prelapserian imagery, and the "sea-walled garden" has become a perverse type of the Garden of Eden. England, the "blessed plot, this earth, this realm... that was wont to conquer others, / Hath made a shameful conquest of itself" (2.1.50; 65–66),[3] as John of Gaunt professes on his deathbed. Shakespeare repeats metaphors of disease, waste, and lack of growth, and in a final attempt to persuade his nephew to recuperate the land *and* his reputation, Gaunt offers the following chastisement:

> Why, cousin, wert thou regent of the world,
> It were a shame to let this land by lease;
> But for thy world enjoying but this land,
> Is it not more than shame to shame it so?
> Landlord of England art thou now, not king... (2.1.109–13)

Sadly, Gaunt's wake-up call to Richard goes unheeded, and he quickly turns his attention to "Irish wars" (2.1.155) and taking "the plate, coin, revenues, and moveables / Whereof our uncle Gaunt did stand possess'd" (2.1.161–62). In fact, Richard appears unaffected as England falls from "demi-Paradise" (2.1.42) to "pelting farm" (2.1.60). However, once the king's flatterers abandon him, Bullingbrook's campaign to usurp the throne is catapulted into the forefront with promises to "weed and pluck away" (2.3.167) the parasitic court favorites that distracted and negatively influenced Richard.

By act 3, though, Shakespeare pronounces a shift in Richard and as he recognizes his own blurred identity, the audience's perceptions undergo a similar blurring. It is a universal fact that we like to cheer for the underdog. When the odds are stacked up against us, don't we rally, and if victorious in our conquest, does that not make the win all the more sweet? Arguably, it does indeed. Just as Richard accepts the reality of his foolish past and the severe impact it has on the island nation, the audience stops cheering for Bullingbrook's rogue government policies and supports the thwarted regent. Shakespeare provides us with a wonderful turn of events. While at the onset of the play Bullingbrook appears the hero, the audience develops a sympathy for the devil—a sense of wonder, if you will.

Early in act 3, a king focused on his nation returns to English soil, and although he is warned that Bullingbrook "grows strong and great in substance and in power" (3.2.35), he responds, "not all the water in the rough rude sea / Can wash the balm off from an anointed king" (3.2.54–55). A self-confident Richard comforts himself with the assurance that the "divine right of kings" protects him. The confidence dissolves rather quickly, however. Upon hearing that his supporters have fled to Bullingbrook's side, his identity begins to blur. "I had forgot myself, am I not king? / Awake, thou coward majesty! thou sleepest" (3.2.83–84), Richard reminds himself. As it becomes clearer to him that too much damage has been done for the divine right to protect him, he wonders aloud to his supporters:

> Cover your heads, and mock not flesh and blood
> With solemn reverence, throw away respect,
> Tradition, form, and ceremonious duty,
> For you have but mistook me all this while.
> I live with bread like you, feel want,
> Taste grief, need friends: subjected thus,
> How can you say to me I am a king? (3.2.171–77)

These are the words of a man who comes to know himself. Finally, Richard has the revelation that his identity—as he has perceived it and as the people of England have perceived it—is a fallacy. Furthermore, his identity mirrors that of his nation: "we are barren and bereft of friends" (3.3.84).[4]

The Mirror has Two Faces: Richard/Elizabeth, or a View of the Present State of England

In his Introduction to *Shakespeare and the Theatre of Wonder*, T. G. Bishop writes, "plays desire and expect audiences to be 'overwhelmed' by what they hear and see. Such fraught moments have a way of making us feel a curious mixture of pain and elation, whether their circumstance be happy or sad."[5] This is especially applicable to *Richard II* as both a history play and also a tragedy because its message resonated with traitors as well as Elizabeth herself. First, if we recall Elizabeth's expenditures in Ireland,[6] we may deduce that Shakespeare's Richard is a construction of Elizabeth. As Philip Edwards argues, "the nation which is sometimes seen marching towards its deliverance and realisation under the Tudors is most often seen as a threatened or a suffering land looking for a spiritual kingship which it can never find."[7]

Shakespeare's portrayal of the troubled Richard can be read as a direct warning to Elizabeth.

Therefore, it is important to, first, look at Elizabeth's *personal* reading of the character of Richard and, second, then consider the impact of the request by Essex to stage a special performance of *Richard II* on the eve of the Rebellion.[8] In addition to the connection of both English rulers with Irish affairs,[9] Elizabeth also endured scrutiny over the divine right of kings because of her sex, her parentage, and her religion. Undeniably, the traitors' sentiments of "wonder" with Shakespeare's play and the act of treason that they were about to commit relate to both Bishop's and Cohen's assertions about the audience's emotional response. And while several history plays examine the life and reign of Richard II, only Shakespeare's depicts the murder of the monarch on the stage.[10] In another entry from the *Elizabethan Journals* dated August 22, 1597, the writer indicates, "Mr. William Shakespeare's play *The Tragedy of Richard the Second* that was publicly acted by the Lord Chamberlain's Men is being printed, but without the scene of the deposing of King Richard."[11] Allegedly, Queen Elizabeth became distraught over this crucial and emotional segment of 4.1, and as Jonathan Dollimore explains, "[she] anxiously acknowledged the implied identification between her and Richard II, complaining also that "this tragedy was played 40 times in open streets and houses."[12] The fact that a play written around 1595 was used to motivate Elizabeth's conspirators in 1601 further validates Cohen's assertion that "it is reasonable to consider whether the pursuit of the wondrous served as an overarching aesthetic for Shakespeare as his imagination 'bodie[d] forth / The forms of things unkown...Turn[ed] them to shapes, and [gave] to airy nothing / A local habitation and a name.'"[13]

To stage *Richard II* on the eve of the Essex rising was an overt political act in February 1601. During the last decade of Elizabeth's reign, and the final three years in particular, numerous anxieties surfaced in London. First, the elderly queen still refused to name an heir to the throne; and the plague—as well as Popish plots—remained a constant threat. Perhaps most importantly, the conflict with Spain was not entirely resolved in 1588, and in the waning years of the 1590s England was afflicted with inflation and distress caused by poor harvests.[14] James Shapiro writes that in 1599, English soldiers were training

> once again in and around London as they had in 1588 in preparation for the Spanish invaders, and...the prayers designed for the pulpits in 1588 were dusted off and read again in 1599 (Archbishop Whitgift proposed that "the same which were used in the year 1588 are also fit for this present occasion and cannot be bettered").[15]

Londoners responded accordingly with alarm and fear, and John Stow provides glimpses of the growing anxiety in his *Annales*, writing that by royal commandment "the chains were drawn [throughout] the streets and lanes of the city, and lanthorns with lights of candles hanged out at every man's door, there to burn all night, and ... great watches kept in the streets."[16] Considering the anxiety-riddled climate in the Metropolis, cause for near-hysteria was certainly understandable.

We must consider, then, the Earl of Essex's motivation for having this special performance of *Richard II* staged with the deposition scene. I believe that he strived to invoke a sense of wonder in both his followers and citizen supporters. Just as Henry showed "a little touch of Harry in the night" on the eve of the great Battle of Agincourt in Shakespeare's *Henry V*, Essex desired that his own "troops" would be inspired for the pending rebellion by wondering at the parallel and noting the surprising victory of Bullingbrook over the monarch.

"Now mark me how I will undo myself": Deposing the Divine King

Clearly a history play, *Richard II* is also a tragedy as it tells the "sad stories of the death of kings" (3.2.155) who prioritize personal gain and narcissism over the needs of the citizens. What is the importance of the interplay between wonder and tragedy? As J. V. Cunningham defines,

> Wonder is, first of all, the natural effect of a marvelous story, and hence of those myths which furnished the plots of ancient tragedy and epic ... in the second place, [it is] the result of a surprising and unexpected turn in events, and is thus intimately involved in the tragic catastrophe and in its proper effect.[17]

We see this with the shift in audience sympathies toward Richard. As he appears alone on the stage in his Pomfret prison, moments before his execution, he muses,

> Thoughts tending to ambition, they do plot
> Unlikely wonders: how these vain weak nails
> May tear a passage thorough the flinty ribs
> Of this hard world, my ragged prison walls;
> And for they cannot, die in their own pride. (5.5.18–22)

What are the "unlikely wonders" that Richard alludes to at this juncture? It could be that the "thoughts tending to ambition" put him in his current state as he waits for Exton to fulfill Bullingbrook's plot. On the other hand, these thoughts could allude to the "unlikely wonders" of his escaping this sorrowful end. Whatever the case, the poetic postdeposition Richard woos his audience with words. His manipulation of rhetoric is pungent and noticeable from the beginning of the play; but once the shift in the universe denotes a shift in power,[18] Richard's speeches become all the more poignant and mesmerizing. He is a statesman; he is a weaver of words; he is a polished poet. Certainly, they invoke a sense of wonder in all who hear him. Northrop Frye writes,

> It is the mastery of rhetorical language that makes a figure in a play heroic... In the clash between [Richard] and Bolingbroke near the end of the play, Bolingbroke seems to be winning everything, the crown, the title, the mastery of the kingdom, and yet Richard continues to put on his own show, and that is the one thing that Bolingbroke cannot steal. After we leave the theatre, it is Richard II, with his gazing into a mirror and his wonderful speech in prison that we remember: he is still hero of the play.[19]

The fading monarch's gift of rhetoric in Shakespeare's play makes him an object of awe and admiration, something that Bullingbrook—even after he becomes Henry IV—never attains. In fact, as soon as Richard dies, Exton regrets the deed and foreshadows things to come for his nation, "As full of valure as of royal blood! / Both have I spill'd; O would the deed were good!" (5.6.113–14).

It is important to note here that Elizabethan audiences may have been aware that the meaning of the Latin word *admiration* is, in fact, "wonder."[20] Near the closing of the play, a Groom tells Richard how grieved he was when he watched "In London streets, that coronation-day, / When Bullingbrook rode on roan Barbary, /...so proudly as if he disdain'd the ground" (5.5.77–78; 83). Despite the admiration the English originally heaped on Henry IV for his ability to redress the sea-walled garden that was overcome with weeds on account of Richard's poor leadership, he now "disdain'd the ground." The very sociopolitical chaos that was a direct result of what I call the blurring of Richard will obviously not be mended by Henry. Even the newly minted monarch recognizes his mistake and repents his crime immediately following Richard's murder: "I'll make a voyage to the Holy Land, / To wash this blood off from my guilty hand" (5.6.49–50). Evidence of the ramifications for Henry's actions can be seen in *2 Henry IV* (1.3.100–107) when the Archbishop of York asks Hastings, Mowbray, and Bardolph:

> What trust is in these times?
> They that, when Richard liv'd, would have him die,
> Are now become enamor'd on his grave.
> Thou, that threw'st dust upon his goodly head

> When through proud London he came sighing on
> After th' admired heels of Bullingbrook,
> Cri'st now, "O earth, yield us that king again,
> And take thou this!"

The Archbishop's passionate yearning here fails to consider the "tardy, apish nation" (2.1.22) under Richard, with "empty lodgings and unfurnish'd walls, / Unpeopled offices, untrodden stones" (1.2.68–69). With the blurring of Richard's identity, Shakespeare portrays the blurring of an English national identity. This blurring may be precisely what caused the heightened anxiety preceding the Essex rising and his own transformation from court favorite to traitor. Admiration for Richard continues throughout this history cycle, in fact, and it is Bullingbrook's son, the foppish Prince Hal, who brings England to a state of prosperity. The Gardener's cry in *Richard II* that "All must be even in our government" (2.4.36) is lost on Henry IV, too. In the final component of the *Henriad*, Shakespeare complicates the issue of "Englishness" even more and in doing so, questions the concept of a unified, national identity.

As previously addressed, it is not until 3.2 that Richard wonders about the threat of Bullingbrook, largely due to the notion that, under the divine right of kings, he is protected. The Bishop of Carlisle even attempts to reassure, "Fear not, my lord, that Power that made you king / Hath power to keep you king in spite of all" (3.2.27–28). Richard certainly buys into this, and reaffirms his position:

> The breath of worldly men cannot depose
> The deputy elected by the Lord;
> For every man that Bullingbrook hath press'd
> To lift shrewd steel against our golden crown,
> God for his Richard hath in heavenly pay
> A glorious angel; then if angels fight,
> Weak men must fall, for heaven still guards the right. (3.2.56–62)

Bullingbrook's opportunity to insert himself in the role of ruler of England is a direct result of Richard's blurred identity. This blurring is also related to nation formation, for Shakespeare offers a critique of Elizabethan foreign policy *through* his portrayal of Richard and his preoccupation with Ireland and with the "lining of his coffers" (1.4.61). However, Richard serves as a microcosm of the land itself. As he muses on his death, he further questions his identity:

> Sometimes am I king;
> Then treasons make me wish myself a beggar,

> And so I am. Then crushing penury
> Persuades me I was better when a king;
> Then am I king'd again, and by and by
> Think that I am unking'd by Bullingbrook,
>   And straight am nothing. (5.5.32–38)

By once again reinforcing his nothingness, Richard takes his divine right with him to the grave. It is, in my opinion, a scene of wonder—the seemingly weak Richard stands up to armed men and even kills a few. As the main assailant, Exton, closes in on him, he warns, "That hand shall burn in never-quenching fire / That staggers thus my person. Exton, thy fierce hand / Hath with the King's blood stain'd the King's own land" (5.5.108–10). The Elizabethan audience would know that any person who interferes with the divine right of king has committed a damnable offense. It is also interesting to note in this section that the lines are not succinct or balanced in meter. The frenetic dialogue appears once the Keeper enters Richard's prison with poisoned meat. Shakespeare reflects a fragmented nation—and with it, a fragmented identity—through disjointed speech. Order is not truly restored, and the play ends with a sense of woe.

Bishop remarks,

> It is not the purging or conversion of wonder into something else that theatre seeks, but the placement of that emotion in relation to an audience's understanding of the action. In particular, wonder registers not the audience's analysis of the action, but something more like their sense of its significance. Wonder, that is, is less directed to the acquisition of knowledge than to the perception of meaning.[21]

As we see with the crescendo of action in Shakespeare's *Richard II*, the audience is certainly left with a sense that the curtain has not closed on the issues raised in this history play. In light of the events on the world stage today, I wonder if Shakespeare's tale can serve as a warning for those in power just as it did in his lifetime. Surely, Elizabeth I would not be the only ruler to remark, "Know you not that I am Richard?"

Notes

1. See the introduction to part I, p. 7.
2. See J. V. Cunningham, *Woe or Wonder: The Emotional Effect of Shakespearean Tragedy* (Athens, OH: Swallow Press, 1964); and T. G. Bishop, *Shakespeare and the Theatre of Wonder* (New York: Cambridge University Press, 1996).

3. All quotations are from *The Riverside Shakespeare*, ed. G. Blakemore Evans (Boston: Houghton Mifflin, 1974).
4. For a detailed examination of the concept of the monarch as inextricably linked to the land, see Ernst H. Kantorowicz's discourse, *The King's Two Bodies: A Study in Medieval Political Theology*, pref. William Chester Jordan (Princeton, NJ: Princeton University Press, 1997).
5. Bishop, *Shakespeare*, 2.
6. As Phyllis Rackin ascertains: "Richard's outrageous fiscal exactions as well as his confiscation of Gaunt's estate are motivated by his need for money for Irish wars, the same need that constituted queen Elizabeth's major financial burden in the late 1590s." *Stages of History: Shakespeare's English Chronicles* (Ithaca, NY: Cornell University Press, 1990), 100.
7. Philip Edwards, *Threshold of a Nation: A Study in English and Irish Drama* (Cambridge, UK: Cambridge University Press, 1983), 129.
8. The unfolding of this plot appears in an entry in the *Elizabethan Journals* dated February 7, 1601 [*The Elizabethan Journals: Being a Record of Those Things Most Talked of During the Years 1591–1603*, ed. G. B. Harrison (Ann Arbor, MI: University of Michigan Press, 1955), 144]:

    Yesterday Sir Charles Percy, Sir Joscelyn Percy, the Lord Mounteagle and some other of my Lord Essex's followers, came to some of the Lord Chamberlain's players and would have them play that play of the deposing and killing of King Richard II, promising to give them 40 s. more than their ordinary to play it. The players answered that the play of King Richard was so old and so long out of use that they should have little or no company at it. Nevertheless, at their request, and in consideration of 40 s., they played it this afternoon at The Globe, when many of my Lord of Essex's followers were present.

9. According to Christopher Highley, "The Royal Image in Elizabethan Ireland," in *Dissing Elizabeth: Negative Representations of Gloriana*, ed. Julia M. Walker (Durham and London: Duke University Press, 1998), 60:

    Elizabeth's preoccupation with Irish affairs was most intense in the last decade of her reign, when her former ward and ally Hugh O'Neill, the Earl of Tyrone, galvanized resistance among a coalition of Gaelic and Old English forces to the "Newcomers": the New English planters, administrators, and soldiers whose collective mission was to consolidate, and when possible to extend, the queen's authority in Ireland.

10. Rebecca Lemon, *Treason by Words: Literature, Law, and Rebellion in Shakespeare's England* (Ithaca and London: Cornell University Press, 1996), 52.
11. Harrison, ed., *Elizabethan*, 206.
12. Jonathan Dollimore, *Political Shakespeare: Essays in Cultural Materialism* (Ithaca, NY: Cornell University Press, 1985), 8.
13. See the introduction to part I, p. 7.
14. Carol Levin, *The Heart and Stomach of a King: Elizabeth I and the Politics of Sex and Power* (Philadelphia: University of Pennsylvania Press, 1994), 90.

15. James Shapiro, *Rival Playwrights: Marlowe, Jonson, Shakespeare* (New York: Columbia University Press, 1991), 97.
16. Qtd in ibid., 98.
17. Cunningham, *Woe*, 66.
18. In 2.4, the Welsh Captain notes,
    'Tis thought the King is dead; we will not stay.
    The bay-trees in our country are all wither'd,
    And meteors fright the fixed stars of heaven,
    The plae-fac'd moon looks bloody on the earth,
    And lean-look'd prophets whisper fearful change...
    These signs forerun the death or fall of kings. (7–10; 15)
19. Qtd in Jennifer Ann Bates, *Hegel and Shakespeare on Moral Imagination* (Albany: State University of New York Press, 2010), 123.
20. Cunningham, *Woe*, 60. See also J. E. Gillet, "A Note on the Tragic 'admiration,'" *Modern Language Review* 13 (1918): 233–38.
21. Bishop, *Shakespeare*, 4.

CHAPTER II.5

A World of (No) Wonder, or No Wonder-wounded Hearers Here: Toward a Theory on the Vanishing Mediation of "No Wonder" in Shakespeare's Theater

Kristin Keating and Bryan Reynolds

It is no wonder that so many scholars are fascinated by the wonders and marvels of the early modern stage, for assuredly Shakespeare was as well. He peoples his worlds with a plethora of marvelous characters: fairies, sprites, monsters, magicians, fools, apothecaries, witches, ghosts, kings, queens, actors, and so on. He elevates and devastates them with love, betrayal, confusion, war, prophecy, shipwrecks, and poisons. He births, kills, and resurrects them at will. The wonder-cabinet of Shakespeare's collected work resonates with the preciousness, rarity, and profundity of both the worlds he creates and his own virtuosity as a conjurer and craftsman of wonder. To be sure, for centuries, scholars have invested a remarkable amount of time and energy into their attempts to understand wonder, often referred to in early modern texts by the similarly used words "wonder" and "marvel" and their derivatives, as it is experienced and imagined not just in Shakespeare, but also in the early modern English society of which Shakespeare was both a part and a product. Given Shakespeare's eminence as an enabler and affecter of wonderment, it is no marvel that, in this research, theater has emerged as a primary object for the desire to make sense of the phenomena of wonder.[1] Alternatively seen as a surrogate for the religious wonder that was suppressed under Queen Elizabeth, a bulwark for theological wonder in spite of doctrinal change, an exploratory site for the possibilities and limitations of theological and theatrical wonder alike, or as a champion for the supernatural and the improbable, as various scholars have argued, the theater was a central locus for the production and experience of wonderment.[2] Other sources of wonderment in early modern England outside of theater included faith healings, demonic possessions, exorcisms, magic shows, astrology, monstrous births, sorcery, ghostly appearances, and miraculous recoveries. With copious supply and demand, the economy of wonder thrived and continues to thrive.

Wonder fascinates the authors of this chapter too. We enjoy it. We desire it. We wonder about it. Wonder often inspires transversal movements beyond the controllable limits of established parameters for subjective experiences, and we delight in such excessive wonderment, for it is through these experiences that subjectivity can crystallize with intensity and grace. Nevertheless, rather than investigate accounts of wonderment and the marvelous, as so many others have done productively,[3] we want to explore the previously unattended to exclamations of "no wonder," "no marvel," and other related idiomatic expressions that ostensibly seek to bracket, negate, diminish, or obviate the wondrous.[4] Whereas these interjections might seem like innocuous expressions, mere colloquialisms intended to convey obviousness or obvious lack of surprise, we want to consider the invocation of wonder and affective presence that they might suggest. It is our hypothesis that the exclamation "no wonder" and similar expressions, structurally and conceptually, always create space for the possibility of wonder. In other words, under certain circumstances, they produce conditions for wonderment, even if wonderment itself cannot be reduced to these conditions; through their temporal suspension of wonder, like a form of diversion in the face of imminent danger, they may even intensify the effects of wonder on the distracted subject.

We want to consider, particularly in spaces where wonderment is the expectation or hope, such as the theater or faith healings, that exclamations of "no wonder" and similar expressions exceed negation as they become a "vanishing mediator" for positive emergences. That is, they become a kind of dialectical, intermediary structure that preconditions its own transubstantiation and thereby allows a new structure or structures to emerge from the stuff of its disappearance, like a torrent of information downloading bits from the listener's previous experiences with the concept of wonder. It may even be the case that what emerges from the vanishing mediation of "no wonder" is an occurrence that surpasses the phenomenological; experience exceeds, and might happen despite, the interpretive structuring of semiotics and perspective.[5]

Wonderknot

To begin with an account of negation,[6] from James Calderwood's critical immersion in dialecticism in Shakespeare while writing *To Be and Not to Be: Negation and Metadrama in Hamlet* emerges positively the postulate that negation "introduces a paradox into language: the verbal presence of conceptual absence."[7] The negative "cannot destroy without at the same time creating something to destroy."[8] For Hamlet, then, "Not to Be" inevitably entails, and gives life to, "To Be."[9] Calderwood maintains, however accurate the comparison may be, that "killing words with words" is a linguistic version of Heisenberg's uncertainty principle, for just as electrons will not betray both their position and velocity at once, "words [will not] yield outright to other words."[10] Wolfgang Iser presents a similar understanding of the effects negations have on readers of literary texts:

> The various types of negation invoke familiar and determinate elements or knowledge only to cancel them out. What is canceled, however, remains in view, and thus brings about modifications in the reader's attitude toward what is familiar or determinate—that is, he is guided to adopt a position *in relation* to the text.[11]

Thus, in the very instant that it attempts to cancel out wonder, the expression "no wonder" simultaneously contracts and expands the concept of wonder as it brings attention to it. The dialectic of wonder/no wonder destabilizes the subject's cognitive positioning, and the affective result might be the bewilderment that is intrinsic to wonderment, the characteristic symptom of the wonderstruck.

But the negation and invoked dialectic of wonder/no wonder does something more important, particularly with regard to the wonderworks of theater. The dialectic of wonder/no wonder opens up spaces for critical reflection as a result of wonder's vanishing mediation through the exclamation of "no wonder." The most powerful of these circumstances might be those in the context of theater performances, delivered verbally or physically (such as through the physiognomy of the actor) by a character on stage. In the theater, the concept of "no wonder" ostensibly denies the wonderwork that scholars of wonder most celebrate. With metatheatrical force, "no wonder" imposes rationality and rationalization on a space that is ontologically designed to produce and sustain wonder. Accordingly, through its stimulation of "reflexive-consciousness," the means by which consciousness regards itself in relation to its operations and progressions,[12] "no wonder" can position the subject/audience member outside of wonderment. It can prompt the subject/audience member to bracket or suspend her experience of wonder. It can forestall the subjunctive movements that wonder precipitates and situates the subject/audience member within a self-aware cognitive cartography. Put differently, on an immediate level, one that might persist, "no wonder" can disrupt the effects of wonder, and of theater, in the interest of order, sense, or compensatory subjective mapping.

Early modern England's antitheatricalists were masterful technicians of "no wonder" rhetoric, often employing the phrase directly to combat the transversal power of theater—that was in many ways epitomized by its wonderwork—and to circumvent any further wondering on the part of their own audiences.[13] The following examples from John Northbrooke and William Prynne are representative:

> Feastings out of time, and pleasant sportes, and delicate pastime bringeth always Dauncing in the last ende. So that Dauncing must needes be the extreme of all vices. But wee nowe in christian countries haue schooles of Dauncing, howbeit that is no wonder, seeing also we haue houses of baudrie.[14]
>
> And no wonder, that he putting on of womans apparell, and the wearing of long haire should make men abominable unto God himselfe, since it was an abomination even among Heathen men...[15]
>
> And no wonder is it, that Players are so transcendently vitious and unchaste, since *they are trained up from the-r cradles, in the very art, the Schoole of Venerie, lewdnesse and prophannesse*; which quickly *eates out all their honesty, their modestie, their virtues, and fraughts them full with vice.*[16]

In these examples, the expression "no wonder" vanishes mediation itself, allowing Northbrooke and Prynne to assert certain conclusions without fully revealing the man (or premises) behind the curtain. In these cases, the deductive logic of "no wonder" is only effective if it correctly identifies and appeals to the opinions of its targeted audience, and this effectiveness is enhanced by quick movement from premise to conclusion. In this sense, "no wonder" can be likened to the abbreviated syllogisms that ancient Greek philosophers termed enthymemes, which Aristotle asserts are essential to public rhetorical persuasion (*Rhetoric* I, 1, 1355^{a}4–8). When employing an enthymeme as proof, the orator leaves one or more of the arguments' premises unstated. The assumption is that the vanished premises are commonly held beliefs and thus do not need to be overtly stated (*Rhetoric* I, 2, 1357ª17–19). Proof by enthymeme has more flair than proof by example, and therefore, Aristotle writes, it "excites the louder applause" (*Rhetoric* I, 2 1356ᵇ24–5). The enthymematic art seduces its listeners by suggesting that something has already been demonstrated and proved.

Likewise, in Northbrooke and Prynne, we can see that conclusions concerning the tenacious endurance of dancing in a Christian country, the abomination of theatrical cross-dressing, and the corruption of actors are based upon presumptions that the reader already believes in the wickedness of whorehouses, cross-dressing, and the theater. "No wonder" is only rhetorically effective if the reader or listener accepts the connections without wondering about the elided assumptions; the more obviously the reader experiences the connections, the more persuasive the assertions. Aristotle implies as much when he suggests that the adept rhetorician keeps his enthymemes as compact as possible so that even "untrained thinkers" will be able to mentally supply the unstated propositions themselves (I, 1357ª11–12, 16–17). Surely, Northbrooke and Prynne as well were banking on the ability of "no wonder" to circumvent wondering. "Well duh" (abundant obviousness) becomes the appropriate response to assertions about the connections between dancing and prostitution or the wickedness of cross-dressing and theater, rather than, say, "but what about...?"

In distinguishing between cognitive approaches to negation that focus on rhetoric from approaches for which semantics is the focus, Todd Oakley emphasizes that, like the enthymeme, the context of the utterance and the common beliefs, presumptions, and value judgments at work in the discourse of the participants are crucial to determining significance.[17] Utterances such as "he is no scholar," "she is no beauty queen," or "you are no Jack Kennedy" are only rhetorically powerful insofar as they resonate with the beliefs of their intended listeners. Whereas "not" negations are often used to overturn actual or supposed beliefs, "no" negations typically serve to reinforce these actual or supposed beliefs.[18] Furthermore, "no" negations are often more inflammatory than their anti-inflammatory "not" counterparts[19] because they intentionally, sometimes maliciously, remove certain positive qualities from the subject and place her unwillingly in a negatively defined space. For example, the phrase "he is not a scholar" makes an analytical observation on an individual's career-path with little presumed value judgment involved in the words themselves, although variability in vocal inflection and context might charge this phrase with more suggestive meaning. But to say "he is no scholar" is to decisively ensnare the subject of this sentence in a vast wealth of historical and cultural presumptions about the scholarly art and the unfortunate subject's inability to be positively defined according to such values. Following Oakley's cognitive rhetorical approach, phrases such as "not a wonder" and "no wonder" are complex constructions because "wonder," particularly in the medieval and early modern periods, carries with it deep-seated religious and cultural peculiarities, as has been addressed briefly here and attended to extensively elsewhere.[20] To say "the earthquake was not a wonder" could alternatively mean, just to give a couple of examples, that the earthquake had God's hand in it, and therefore is a "miracle" by Thomas Aquinas's standards, and not a "wonder," or that the earthquake was of natural rather than supernatural origins, if wonder is being defined as a supernatural effect.

If the "not" construction with wonder is complex, the "no" construction, as we have seen, is even more so. Whereas expressions of "no wonder" are often dismissed today as almost involuntary pronouncements of the previously unrecognized obviousness of a situation and have perhaps lost some of their rhetorical effectiveness as a result of idiomatic overuse, we can see in the examples given above that expressions of "no wonder" are not simply transitional expressions, but that they rhetorically dance with various conceptual mappings of wonder and attempt to vanish them in the process. But as Calderwood, Iser, and Oakley demonstrate in their respective accounts of negation, wonder categorically cannot be dissipated through the invocation of its dialectical counterpart. It continues to resonate semantically, rhetorically, and cognitively, and like a temporary fix that leaves the wonder-addict craving more, "no wonder" may actually serve to remind its listeners of wonder's affective, subliminal, and transliminal powers; perhaps it even propels them back to the theaterspace, where, as we will attempt to demonstrate, "no wonder" takes on new significance.

Wonderpause

Wonderment can inspire "paused consciousness," which is when one is so captivated by sensory input that they become unaware of where they are physically and mentally in space and time[21]; they are "swept away" by the "flow," and are "transported" elsewhere, such as into the fictional world of the theatrical performance of a play. This experience can result in the immediate experience of what we term "inarticulatory space," a fractured, nonsensical, and usually ephemeral cognitive space of dumbfoundedness where the gap between experience and its articulation through language reaches a crisis of incoherence and aphasia. The incoherence of wonderment is perhaps especially relevant to a study of early modern wonder because, as Adam Cohen notes, terms such as "awful" and "wonderful" had much more ambivalent meanings in Shakespeare's time. They could emerge from a variety of causes and they could be charged with either positive or negative meaning. Therefore, in the early modern English theater, neither characters nor audience members may ever be sure how to ascribe affective significance to the wonder they encounter.[22] The subject reels indecipherably. Subsequently and in retrospect, however intrinsic or immediate to the recovery of consciousness and awareness in spacetime, the subject usually transitions into a subjunctive space of contemplation of the what-ifs and as-ifs that might have come into play in the causes and effects of the "eventualization" achieved by and through the experience. By "eventualization," we refer to the duration of the event in conjunction with its affective progression on a subject or subjects.

In contrast to "awful" and "wonderful," "no wonder" serves as an articulator for the incoherence of affective wonderment. Expressions of "no wonder" announce with certainty that an underlying cause for the wonder is present or has been unearthed, a cause presumably so shallowly buried that the wonderer is often deemed a fool for not having seen its signs before. Thus, in the first instance, "no wonder" necessitates an "ah-ha! moment," a sense of surprise involving recognition, what we might also call a "wonderpause" because this moment is also caught up with wonder, if only for an instant. In the second instance, "no wonder" implies a "duuuh moment," what was recognized is considered obvious to the point of stupidity, or possibly the conveyance of "I told you so" in some contexts. It is here that the metatheatrical reflections generated by the dialectic of wonder/no wonder catalyzed by "no wonder" supersedes the direct wonderworks of theater and rationality or rationalization. Depending on the circumstances and perspectives at play, the metatheatrical reflections have an opportunity to emerge, if only through the interstices of performativity, and therefore contemplate both the fictions performativity couches and the realities it elides.

We might even go so far as to argue that "no wonder," albeit ironically, enables and affects wonder, not just through phenomenological bracketing (when wonder is temporally suspended) andor positive processes of vanishing mediation (by which "no wonder" transubstantiates into wonder), but also because irony begets wonder. It is the combination of the exclamation of "no wonder" in theater, a context designed to produce wonder, and the vanishing mediation that negation involving explicit presence of the thing negated can attain, that gives so much power to the irony in this case. It is precisely because of irony that the event of its theatrical appearance so easily gives way to, at the very least, subjunctivity, and, most radically, transversality. "No wonder" can deprive audience members of the immediate experience of wonder and therefore prevent them from becoming what Hamlet calls "wonder-wounded hearers," victims of melodrama, as Hamlet insists Laertes produces with his exaggerated sorrow.[23] Yet "no wonder" never operates in perfect opposition to wonder, for wonder and "no wonder" share vital similarities: both contain an element of surprise, both are revelatory processes, and both are positive, creative forces. To be sure, through its irony and vanishing mediation, "no wonder" can exceed as well as expand the experiential and articulatory limits of wonder.

Wonderation

Wonder is that which surprises, mesmerizes, andor unsettles us before we find a nonmarvelous solution to whatever it is we are wondering about. It is a bedazzlement, an impasse, a progressive quagmire of sorts that one must overcome on the path to comprehension and clarity, a condition or precursor to the satisfaction that comes through learning.[24] It is philosophical meditation. For Aristotle, wonder is the impetus of all philosophy; it is a recognition of an ignorance that can be resolved through the pleasurable process of learning (*Metaphysics* I, 2, 982^{b}12–17). Like Aristotle, Aquinas emphasizes that the dissolution of wonderment is the ultimate goal of the philosopher or theologian, arguing that the only pleasure to be derived from wonder lies in its ability to generate hope for future understanding (*Summa theologiae* I–II.32.8). Left to its own devices, wonder can expand promiscuously into uncharted mental territories, and so, in this Aristotelian philosophical tradition that was so important to early modern English thought,[25] the supreme goal of wonder became its own disappearance. For commentators on Aristotle such as Albertus Magnus, poetry and theater are exemplary genres for wonder-reduction because these arts excite wonder, and this wonder in turn excites scientific inquiry.[26] Whether Shakespeare himself subscribed to this model of wonder, by which wonder is diminished by reason, is a matter of scholarly debate.[27] Many of his characters, at least, share the perspective both that wonder can be dispelled through a reasoning process, what we refer to as "wonderation," and that "no wonder" can contribute significantly to a wonderless outcome.

Such a process can be observed in *Cymbeline* when Imogen contemplates why she has been misdirected by a couple of beggars:

> Two beggars told me
> I could not miss my way: will poor folks lie,
> That have afflictions on them, knowing 'tis
> A punishment or trial? Yes; no wonder,

When rich ones scarce tell true. To lapse in fullness
Is sorer than to lie for need, and falsehood
Is worse in kings than beggars. (3.6.8–14)

Imogen is confronted with a situation she cannot initially explain: beggars would lie despite knowing that their miserable state is a punishment or trial that further sins would only exacerbate. Through a process of wonderation, Imogen experiences an ah-ha! moment and discovers what to her is a rational resolution of her prior uncertainty: "Yes; no wonder"; poor people lie out of need. "No wonder," therefore, is crucially participant in a certain phenomenological process, a means of hermeneutic bracketing by which humans make sense of their world. This moment of wonder affects not only Imogen, but also the audience privy to her thought process. "No wonder" serves as a wonder-check. It interrupts wonder's trance and facilitates examination.

As is the case with wonder, the rationality of "no wonder" is always specific to the speaker, audience, and context, and the context of Imogen's utterance of "no wonder" highlights its performativity. Imogen invokes "no wonder" during self-reflection, in which she serves as both speaker and immediate audience. In dialogue with herself, Imogen is able to rationalize a relationship between monetary poverty and diminished scruples that suddenly seems obvious to her. Yet the effect her logic has on the performance's audience is dependent upon each audience member's stance on such social and ethical issues, and while Imogen may have satisfied her own desire for a reasonable solution, her assertion of "no wonder" may only serve to activate further wonderment in the audience: doubts about Imogen's logic, questions about ethical responsibilities, speculations about social injustices, and so on.

But while the example above illuminates some of the rhetorical interventions of "no wonder," it does not serve to distinguish the specific potential of "no wonder" in theaterspace from its intercession in other situations involving a speaker and an audience. For this, we might look to the play-within-a-play presentation of *Pyramus and Thisby* in *A Midsummer Night's Dream*. Theseus, as audience member, thinks aloud, "I wonder if the lion be to speak," and his companion Demetrius replies, "No wonder, my lord: one lion may, when many asses do" (5.1.154–55). Demetrius's response illuminates how definitions of rationality are upended, recapitulated, expanded in the theater: for in the play they watch, talking animals are not only plausible but expected, and in the world they inhabit, Bottom has literally been turned into a donkey and the characters cannot help but make asses of themselves. A loquacious donkey might be no wonder on the Shakespearean stage, but that same donkey would not last long on the streets of London before being swept up into a sideshow of wonders and marvels. Hence, the marvelous world of *A Midsummer Night's Dream*, and the theater in general, can expand the parameters of what might be considered reasonable, or, of "no wonder." Whereas even early modern thinkers aligned with a more Longinian model of wonder for wonder's sake, such as the Italian Francesco Patrizi, could often not resist categorizing the techniques and potential effects of wonder,[28] theaterspace catalyzes the expansion of the meanings of both wonder and "no wonder." The subjunctive portals opened by wonder need not be resolved by scientific reasoning, or even resolved at all. Like Michel de Montaigne's "spirited mind," theater has "impulses beyond its powers of achievement" (818).

Wonderwit

The theatrical deployment of wonder as a powerful and persuasive rhetorical tool frequently functions complementarily with its invocation by imaginative means. Shakespeare's plays are often equipped with verbal cues for wonder (perhaps necessarily so, given the minimal sets and special effects) that invite the audience to share in the stage characters' wonderment. A measure of a play-text's potential, such "wonderwit" is integral to the dramaturgy of all plays inasmuch as the production of wonder is a goal. Verbal invitations to wonder abound in Shakespeare. To give some powerful examples: in *As You Like It*, when Celia attempts to excite wonder where it otherwise does not exist by teasing Rosalind with concealed knowledge of the author of the love poems, exclaiming, "O wonderful, wonderful, most wonderful wonderful, and yet again wonderful, and after that, out of all whooping!" before she reveals Orlando to be Rosalind's wooer (3.2.149–50); in *Hamlet*, when Horatio's harrowment with "fear and wonder" (1.1.50) at the ghost's appearances, "O day and night, but this is wondrous strange!" (1.5.170), is likely intended to ravish the audience's sensibilities as well; and, perhaps most significantly, in *The Winter's Tale*, when Paulina coaches the awakening "statue" of Hermione to "strike all that look upon with marvel," presumably including the theatrical spectators as well in the object of this sentence (5.3.122). Desdemona is a prime example of a wonder-wounded hearer completely overtaken by aural wonder: she falls head over heels for Othello simply through listening to and imagining his adventurous exploits (*Othello* 1.3.141–84). These accounts inspire both pain and pleasure in the masochistic Desdemona,[29] an ambivalent reaction that, as noted earlier, is central to the aesthetic experience of the early modern wonderstruck.

We believe that just as verbal invocations of wonder possess magical powers on the Shakespearean stage, potentially unleashing transversal movements, wonder's dialectical counterparts, "no wonder" or "no marvel," can enact similar witchcraft, disrupting and reschematizing wonder itself. For example, in *The Tempest*, Miranda enters the stage in a state of wonder-provoked distress at the disastrous consequences of Prospero's storm, exclaiming, "O, I have suffered / With those that I saw suffer..." (1.2.5–6). So deeply affected is Miranda that Prospero, a magician of spectacles and wonders, must invoke the rhetorical power of "no wonder," advising her to "Be collected: / No more amazement. Tell your piteous heart / There's no harm done" (1.2.14–16). Here, Prospero's interruption redirects the potentially dangerous processes of wonder that Miranda seems to be undergoing: an emotional spiraling into as-if and what-if scenarios. Miranda soon does the same for Ferdinand upon his arrival, correcting Ferdinand's involuntary exclamation of wonder—"O you wonder!—/ If you be maid or no?"—with, "No wonder, sir; but certainly a maid" (1.2.494–95, 96–97). Miranda and Ferdinand had both initially mistook each other for divine wonders, but Miranda sets limits on Ferdinand's wondrous ventures. "No wonder" carries with it the power to redirect a current train of thought, regardless of whether the alternative it invokes is "rational." It introduces a new trajectory by invoking rationality capable of bringing a wonderer out of her paused-consciousness, possibly hampering her becomings-wondrous. Yet, through vanishing mediation facilitated by the negation—the limit-setting attempted by Miranda—the enraptured Ferdinand is spurred on to further wonder: What would it be like to get to know this beautiful Italian virgin ("maid") on a deserted island? What mysterious wonders does she possess? The titillating irony of this moment is signified by Miranda's proper name. She calls herself "no wonder" even though her name means "to be wondered at."

Wonderwhelmed

"No wonder" does not need Aristotelian logic, rationality, scientific method, or any other type of processes we might set up in opposition to wonder in order to be effective. Rather, it calls upon what we want to call the "powers of the obvious": the stress-relieving comfort one feels in effect of obviousness, when anxiety surrenders to familiarity, however real or imaginary; the calming clarity one enjoys without obstruction or resistance. Nevertheless, in the context of theater, where the wonder/no wonder dialectic operates differently, the powers of the obvious from which "no wonder" draws power can offer false security, and in fact make the wonderer more vulnerable to the wonderworks of the performance. This phenomenon operates in conjunction with the vanishing mediation, and subsequent transposition, that "no wonder" inaugurates. The wonderer is disarmed by the duuuh moment, rendered defenseless by the obviousness it implies, and becomes all the more vulnerable to the wondrous.

"No wonder" creates a temporary disruption, however slight, in the wonder-process that enables the marvels to be viewed from a different perspective or situated in a different framework, allowing the paralyzing anxiety of the wonderstruck to be at least partially relieved through the acknowledgment that their distress is appropriate or "obvious" given the circumstances. In *Richard III*, when the Duke of Clarence awakes from his hellish dream inside the Tower of London and reaches out to the jail keeper for comfort, the keeper's first impulse is to soothe him: "No marvel, my lord, though it affrighted you, / I am afraid, methinks, to hear you tell it" (1.4.64–65). The keeper acknowledges Clarence's right to be distressed at the dream—it is obviously frightening—and enters into a kinship with him as he acknowledges, like Desdemona, the transversal power of a wondrous tale. But given that Clarence has just delivered a lengthy description of the wondrous content of the dream involving his own drowning at the hands of his brother Richard, visits from those who he had previously murdered, and brutal torture from the fiends of hell, the keeper's instinctive cognitive reach to "no marvel" must be viewed with special significance. "No marvel" soothes both the keeper and Clarence by validating their frightened reactions as appropriate responses. While it does not deny the marvelous potentials of the dream, it incorporates them in a framework that acknowledges the wonder and rationalizes the effect. Its simultaneous disavowal and acknowledgment of the wonder hearkens back to the mutually creative and destructive wonder/no wonder dialectic. "No marvel" destabilizes and reframes the wonders in this instance, temporarily bracketing them, but under the pressure of existential implosion that the keeper's "no marvel" eventually and ironically exacerbates, it cannot prevent wonders from spilling over into waking existence, reminding Clarence of his sins, subjunctively foreshadowing future spectacles, and infecting the keeper as well with prodigious dread.

Rewonder

As scholars of theater, we often presume that theater effects, perpetuates, and is intimately intertwined with wonder. We debate the peculiarities of wonder on the early modern stage, conjecture about Shakespeare's metaphysical and theological leanings, draw distinctions between *coup de théâtre* and "genuine" miracle,[30] and make historical arguments about theater's mimetic potential. Underlying all of these musings, postulates, and rhetoric, much of which qualifies as enthymematic, is the vanished premise that theater is intrinsically and necessarily a producer of wonder. Perhaps we want theater to produce wonder. Or, and more likely, we hope that the wonderworks of theater are overwhelmingly powerful because we desire and believe that one can always experience more wonderment, and since wonderment can be both euphoric and ecstatic, we pursue more wonder. By entertaining the amazing powers of desire as well as the fantasies it can generate, in no way do we wish to resist connections between theater and wonder, for we believe that the two are in fact deeply connected, and that the success of the former depends on its ability to inspire the latter. More to the point, as we have been trying to demonstrate, we think that when expressed in a location where the expectation is for wonder, such as during a theater performance, "no wonder" operates differently than in contexts where the general expectation is not for wonder. The metatheatricality of the player who stands upon a stage and declares "there is no play here," or the witticism of the clockmaker who announces he will have a customer's watch repaired in "no time," or the preacher who warns that the devil is up to "no good" help to emphasize the point that even idiomatic phrases can resonate differently in different contexts. The point is that, taken to its extreme, if wonder is so integral to theater, then the actor that stands about the stage and declares "there is no wonder here" is akin to the preacher on his pulpit who, surrounded by all the material and atmospheric trappings of Christian theology, declares "there is no God here." To further demonstrate this, we need to expand the theoretical and theatrical implications of "no wonder" beyond its philosophic, rhetorical, and idiomatic functions.

It would be tempting to argue that moments of surprise and marvel require contrasting impulses of banality, certainty, or rationality in order to be experienced as wondrous. Or, in other words, that there can be no wonder without expressions of "no wonder." But theater reverses these expectations. In a world of wonder, "no wonder" becomes the distinctive moment. Or, to invoke Samuel Taylor Coleridge's well-known axiom concerning the "willing suspension of disbelief" to which the participants in the theatrical fiction subscribe, to insert a reference to "no wonder" in the theater is to insert a moment of "disbelief," that is, it prompts critical reflection challenging wonder's ability to suspend and enrapture. But while awareness might be a first step to avoidance, it cannot diminish, as Prynne notes, the effects of exposure to the intoxicating effects of theater:

> No wonder therefore if Play-haunters discover not the hurt they receive from Playes, because it creepes thus on them by imperceptible gradations,

though faster upon some then others. But albeit Play-haunters feele no hurt at first, (no more then those who drinke downe poyson in a sugered cup, which yet proves fatall to them at the last, though it were sweet and luscious for the present,) yet when terrors of conscience, death, and judgements, when crosses and afflictions shall thorowly awaken them.[31]

As in the examples discussed earlier from Northbrooke and Prynne, Prynne deploys the expression "no wonder" to invoke the powers of the obvious, and what is "obvious" here is that the natural ends of succumbing to theater's sweet poison are the terrorizing thoughts of damnation. For Prynne, this is a nightmare of reflexive-consciousness, when the eventualizations of wonder-strikes torment the unsuspecting audience member through the wonderation that is their by-product or symptom. In this case, denial of theater's wonder-powers surrenders unwittingly to their insidious impact; "disbelief" of theater's wonderwork is disillusioned and counterexperienced by "imperceptible gradations."

Expressions of "no wonder" within theater resonate with special poignancy insofar as the potential opportunities for wonder-strikes on a willing and therefore susceptible audience are plethoric. The more unpredictable, the more powerful the strikes might be, however predisposed the audience is to receiving them. At the very least, great theater involves surprise, if not wonder; and theater, by definition, is not wonder in itself, although wonder may be its goal. Moreover, unlike in a church where the oxymoronic prospect of an evil miracle is unlikely, if not unthinkable, wonder-strikes are not inherently good or evil, positive or negative. Their value is determined by context and the wonderpauses and wonderation they stimulate.

Wonderstruck scholarly discussions of the Shakespearean corpus tend to gravitate—as if discovery of miracles, or nonmiracles, is the goal—toward the preponderance of marvelous recognitions, reunions, pseudoresurrections, quasi-resurrections, and failed resuscitations in his plays.[32] As has often been noted, in no fewer than fourteen of Shakespeare's plays, characters are reunited with loved ones previously presumed to be dead. In many of the tragedies, namely *Romeo and Juliet*, *King Lear*, and *Othello*, it is moments of near-resurrection or almost-reunion, moments that open spaces of wonder and doubt for both the characters and spectators, that exponentially deepen the tragic conclusion. For the dead body on the stage is always both an object of wonder, in that it can undergo a process of theatrical transubstantiation and become "live," and an object of "no wonder," in that the actor is alive all along. This doubt, this capacity of theater to expand realms of possibilities lays the foundation for experiences that can exceed the phenomenological through the wonderment and wonderpauses by which an audience member moves transversally.

We find dramatic potential for such magnificent wonderwork in the final scene of *King Lear* when Lear enters the stage with the broken Cordelia in his arms. He vacillates in his speech between rational certainty and wondrous hope:

> Howl, howl, howl! O, you are men of stones
> Had I your tongues and eyes, I'd use them so
> That heaven's vault should crack. She's gone for ever!
> I know when one is dead and when one lives:
> She's dead as earth. Lend me a looking-glass:
> If that her breath will mist or stain the stone,
> Why, then she lives. (5.3.264–70)

Bewildered, wonderstruck, Lear reels on the stage and Kent and Edgar, as onstage observers, provide a framework for the theatrical audience that pushes to the very limits of wonder: the apocalypse, with Kent asking, "Is this the promised end?" and Edgar amending, "Or image of that horror?" (5.3.271–72). For the first audiences of Shakespeare's *Lear*, perhaps as yet unacquainted with Shakespeare's tragic revision of the legend's conclusion, the associations between theater and wonder work to heighten the tragedy, for the inadvertent breathing of the actor playing Cordelia, perhaps the inadvertent stirring of a feather, provides hints at resuscitation. In his final speech, as he tries to cope with the fact that Cordelia possesses "no, no, no life," Lear enters a phase of emphatic negation, repeating the word "never" three times in the Quarto version and five times in the Folio (5.3.322, 325). Here, the wonder/no wonder dialectic accentuated by exclamations of "no wonder" dynamically energizes vanishing mediation. While in the Folio version, Lear dies at the conclusion of his speech, the Quarto version tortures Lear with ambivalent life for just a bit longer: he expires after Kent pleads, "O, let him pass! He hates him / That would upon the rack of this tough world / Stretch him out longer" (5.3.332–34). Kent's metaphor is an appropriate one, for at least in the Quarto version, Lear is stretched out longer in suspense somewhere between the realms of wonder and "no wonder," so that when Kent declares "The wonder is he hath endured so long: / He but usurped his life" (5.3.336–37), the wonder of Lear's endurance has more resonance; the point may be that not only has Lear managed to live for so long in such a cruel world, but also that his heart has managed to hold on so long during a period of such uncertainty.[33] In this moment, Kent's wonderation works to both reduce wonder by rationalizing a reason for it and expand and transform phenomenological wonder into something more metaphysical, enabling Albany to join with Edgar and Kent on a deeper level, as "friends of [his] soul" (5.3.340). There is the genesis of new wonder, or "rewonder," in "no wonder": as vanishing mediator, it is not as a negative force disappearing into the abyss of intervention, but a positive force still actively at work. When the actor who plays Cordelia stands and greets the audience during the curtain call, she realizes, in an implicit metatheatrical epilogue, the rewonder emergent through the vanishing mediation of her death, the echoes of Lear's "no, no, no life" resounding in the liveness everywhere apparent in a theater busy with actors and audience members, but free of characters and fictions. "No wonder," this is theater.

Notes

1. See Sean Benson, *Shakespearean Resurrection: The Art of Almost Raising the Dead* (Pittsburgh, PA: Duquesne University Press, 2009); T. G. Bishop, *Shakespeare and the Theatre of Wonder* (New York: Cambridge University Press, 1996); Dolora G. Cunningham, "Wonder and Love in the Romantic Comedies," *Shakespeare Quarterly* 35.3 (1984): 262–66; J. V. Cunningham, *Woe or Wonder: The Emotional Effect of Shakespearean Tragedy* (Athens, OH: Swallow Press, 1964); Huston Diehl, "Strike All that Look Upon with Marvel: Theatrical and Theological Wonder in *The Winter's Tale*," in *Rematerializing Shakespeare: Authority and Representation on the Early Modern English Stage*, ed. Bryan Reynolds and William West (Basingstoke, England: Palgrave Macmillan, 2005), 19–34; H. W. Fawkner, *Shakespeare's Miracle Plays: Pericles, Cymbeline, and the Winter's Tale* (Rutherford, NJ: Fairleigh Dickinson University Press, 1992); Stephen Greenblatt, "Resonance and Wonder," in *Learning to Curse: Essays in Early Modern Culture* (New York: Routledge, 1990), 161–83; Marco Mincoff, *Things Supernatural and Causeless: Shakespearean Romance* (Newark, DE: University of Delaware Press, 1992); Peter G. Platt, *Reason Diminished: Shakespeare and the Marvelous* (Lincoln, NE: University of Nebraska Press, 1997); David Richman, *Laughter, Pain, and Wonder: Shakespeare's Comedies and the Audience in the Theater* (Newark, DE: University of Delaware Press, 1990); Gareth Roberts, "'An art lawful as eating'? Magic in *The Tempest* and *The Winter's Tale*," in *Shakespeare's Late Plays: New Readings*, ed. Jennifer Richards and James Knowles (Edinburgh: Edinburgh University Press, 1999), 126–42; Kenneth J. Semon, "Fantasy and Wonder in Shakespeare's Last Plays," *Shakespeare Quarterly* 25.1 (1974): 89–102; Elizabeth Williamson, "Things Newly Performed: The Resurrection Tradition in Shakespeare's Plays," in *Shakespeare and the Religious Change*, ed. Kenneth J. E. Graham and Philip D. Collington (New York: Palgrave Macmillan, 2009), 110–32.

2. To give some examples, Adam Cohen argues that "Shakespearean theatrical wonder offered an alternative, a substitute, and in some sense even a

replacement for the venues of religious wonder that were eliminated under Elizabeth" (see chapter I.1, p. 10). Elizabeth Williamson asserts that Hermione's reappearance in *The Winter's Tale* breaks with medieval resurrection drama ("Things Newly Performed," 129), while Huston Diehl points out that numerous scholars, T. G. Bishop included, situate this pseudoresurrection scene in a Catholic theological tradition ("Strike All," 19–20). Diehl herself argues that Shakespeare "aligns the wonder his theater arouses with a kind of theological wonder endorsed by the Protestant English Church" (21). Gareth Roberts contends that Shakespeare uses magic and wonder to explore the limits of the poet's creative powers in the face of God's higher power ("Magic," 142), and Dolora Cunningham maintains that the contrived conclusions to Shakespeare's comedies give us access to wondrous events beyond the scope of normal human existence ("Wonder and Love," 266).

3. See note 1.
4. "No wonder," "no marvel," and other related idiomatic expressions, such as "small wonder," "little wonder," "what wonder," and "what marvel," were well established in the English language by the late medieval period, and appear with great frequency in early modern English texts. Our search on the EEBO database, an incomplete collection of early modern English works, rendered 2,898 results for the phrase "no marvel" and 465 for "no wonder" in works published during Shakespeare's lifespan.
5. For a related discussion of "vanishing mediation," see Courtney Lehmann & Bryan Reynolds, "Awakening the Werewolf Within: Self-help, Vanishing Mediation, and Transversality in *The Duchess of Malfi*," in *Transversal Enterprises in the Drama of Shakespeare and his Contemporaries: Fugitive Explorations,* ed. Bryan Reynolds (Houndmills, Basingstoke: Palgrave Macmillan, 2006), 227–39.
6. We would like to express our sincere thanks to Todd Oakley, Bill Ladusaw, and Dan Donoghue for their illuminating input on the linguistic, rhetorical, and etymological intricacies of negation and "no" and "not" constructions.
7. James L. Calderwood, *To Be and Not to Be: Negation and Metadrama in* Hamlet (New York: Columbia University Press, 1983), 55.
8. Ibid., 57.
9. Ibid., 58.
10. Ibid., 56.
11. Wolfgang Iser, *Prospecting: From Reader Response to Literary Anthropology* (Baltimore: John Hopkins University Press, 1993), 34; emphasis in the original.
12. For more on "reflexive-consciousness," see Bryan Reynolds, "Transversal Poetics and Fugitive Explorations: Theaterspace, Paused Consciousness, Subjunctivity, and *Macbeth*," in Reynolds, *Transversal Enterprises,* 21–22; Bryan Reynolds (with additional dialogue by George Light & Bryan Reynolds), "Subjective Affects: Surveying with Shakespeare, Husserl, and Derrida into the Twentieth-First Century," in *Transversal Subjects: From Montaigne to Deleuze*

after Derrida, ed. Bryan Reynolds (Basingstoke, England: Palgrave Macmillan, 2009), 16, 52; Adam Bryx & Bryan Reynolds, "The Masochistic Quest of Jean-Jacques Rosseau: Deleuze and Guattari to Transversal Poetics with(out) Baudrillard," in Reynolds, *Transversal Subjects,* 85–92, 110, 121; and "Glossary of Transversal Terms," in Reynolds, *Transversal Subjects,* 286.

13. As an additional note, "no wonder" is also a phrase commonly used in early modern religious debates, often in a more literal sense, and we can certainly infer that the employment of this phrase in these documents is rhetorically oriented toward defining, limiting, or combating the "wonders" associated with a Catholic theological tradition. See, e.g., Stephen Gardiner, *An explicatio[n] and assertion of the true Catholique fayth, touchyng the moost blessed sacrament of the aulter with confutacion of a booke written agaynst the same* (Rouen, 1551); John Calvin, *Sermons of Master Iohn Caluin, vpon the booke of Iob* (London, 1574); and Thomas Cranmer, *An aunsvvere by the Reuerend Father in God Thomas Archbyshop of Canterbury, primate of all England and metropolitane, vnto a craftie and sophisticall cauillation, deuised by Stephen Gardiner Doctour of Law, late Byshop of Winchester agaynst the true and godly doctrine of the most holy sacrament, of the body and bloud of our sauiour Iesu Christ* (London, 1580).

14. John Northbrooke, *Spiritus est vicarius Christi in terra. A treatise wherein dicing, daucing, vaine playes or enterluds with other idle pastimes [et]c. commonly vsed on the Sabboth day, are reproued by the authoritie of the word of God and auntient writers* (London, 1577), 132. *Early English Books Online,* http://gateway.proquest.com/openurl?ctx_ver=Z39.88-2003&res_id=xri:eebo&rft_id=xri:eebo:citation:99848594.

15. William Prynne, Histrio-mastix The players scourge, or, actors tragaedie…besides sundry otherparticulars concerning dancing, dicing, healthdrinking, &c. of which the table will informe you (London, 1633), 882. Early English Books Online, http://gateway.proquest.com/openurl?ctx_ve =Z39.88-2003&res_id=xri:eebo&rft_id=xri:eebo:citation:99850535.

16. Ibid., 142.

17. Todd Oakley, "Negation and Blending: A Cognitive Rhetorical Approach": www.google.com/site/toddoakley/negation.pdf, 2.

18. Ibid., 11–12.

19. Ibid., 17.

20. See note 2.

21. For more on "paused consciousness," see Bryan Reynolds, "Transversal Poetics and Fugitive Explorations: Theaterspace, Paused Consciousness, Subjunctivity, and *Macbeth*," in Reynolds, *Transversal Enterprises*, 13–16, 21; Bryan Reynolds, "Subjective Affects: Surveying with Shakespeare, Husserl, and Derrida into the Twentieth-First Century" and "Glossary of Transversal Terms" in Reynolds, *Transversal Subjects,* 16; 281.

22. See chapter I.7, p. 105.

23. In response to Laertes's melodramatic mourning speech at Ophelia's grave, Hamlet responds:

> What is he whose grief
> Bears such an emphasis? Whose phrase of sorrow
> Conjures the wand'ring stars, and makes them stand
> Like wonder-wounded hearers? This is I, Hamlet the Dane. (5.1.207–11)

24. On the relationship between surprise and learning in the experience of theater, see Bryan Reynolds, "Subjective Affects: Surveying with Shakespeare, Husserl, and Derrida into the Twentieth-First Century," in Reynolds, *Transversal Subjects*, 19–39.
25. See chapter I.7, pp. 99–100.
26. See Cunningham's discussion and translation of a portion of Albertus Magnus's *Commentary on the Metaphysics of Aristotle* in *Woe or Wonder*, 77–80.
27. See Bishop, *Shakespeare and the Theatre*, 40–41; and Platt, *Reason Diminished*, xi–xiii.
28. See chapter I.7, pp. 104–105.; and Platt, *Reason Diminished*, 12–18.
29. On Desdemona's masochism, see Joseph Fitzpatrick & Bryan Reynolds (with additional dialogue by Bryan Reynolds & Janna Segal), "Venetian Ideology or Transversal Power? Iago's Motives and the Means by which Othello Falls," in *Performing Transversally: Reimagining Shakespeare and the Critical Future*, ed. Bryan Reynolds (New York: Palgrave MacMillan, 2003), 71.
30. Understandably enough, Hermione's reemergence in *The Winter's Tale* has received a great deal of scholarly attention in this respect, serving as a focal point for theological debates over the Catholic or Protestant leanings of Shakespeare or his critical respondents, as well as inquiry into the distinction between theatrical sleight-of-hand and bona fide supernatural wonder.
31. Prynne, Histrio-mastix, 958.
32. Examples might be Benson, *Shakespearean Resurrection*; Fawkner, *Shakespeare's Miracle Plays*; or Williamson, "Things Newly Performed."
33. In an often-quoted passage from his *Commentary on the Metaphysics of Aristotle*, Albertus Magnus highlights the palpable biological repercussions of wonder: the "constriction and suspension of the heart caused by amazement at the sensible appearance of something so portentous, great, and unusual, that the heart suffers a systole." We are indebted to J. V. Cunningham for this translated passage in *Woe or Wonder*, 77.

Works Cited

Aristotle. *Metaphysics*. In *The Complete Works of Aristotle: The Revised Oxford Translation*, Vol. II. Edited by Jonathan Barnes. Princeton, NJ: Princeton University Press, 1984.

———. *Rhetoric*. In *The Complete Works of Aristotle*, Vol. II.

Aquinas, St. Thomas. *Summa Theologiae: Latin Text and English Translation, Introductions, Notes, Appendices, and Glossaries*. Cambridge, England: Blackfriars, 1964.

de Montaigne, Michel. "Of Experience." In *The Complete Essays of Montaigne,* translated by Donald M. Frame. Stanford, CT: Stanford University Press, 1976.

Shakespeare, William. *As You Like It*. In *William Shakespeare Complete Works*, edited by Jonathan Bate and Eric Rasmussen. New York: The Modern Library, 2007.

———. *Cymbeline*. In *William Shakespeare Complete Works*, edited by Bate and Rasmussen.

———. *Hamlet*. In *William Shakespeare Complete Works*, edited by Bate and Rasmussen.

———. *King Lear*. In *William Shakespeare Complete Works*, edited by Bate and Rasmussen.

———. *A Midsummer's Night Dream*. In *William Shakespeare Complete Works*, edited by Bate and Rasmussen.

———. *Othello*. In *William Shakespeare Complete Works*, edited by Bate and Rasmussen.

———. *Richard III*. In *William Shakespeare Complete Works*, edited by Bate and Rasmussen.

———. *The Tempest*. In *William Shakespeare Complete Works*, edited by Bate and Rasmussen.

CHAPTER II.6

Passing for Truth: Wonder Tales and their Audiences in *Othello*

Joshua B. Fisher

In his diary entry for October 11, 1660, Samuel Pepys records the following brief impression of that evening's performance of *Othello*: "Here, in the Park, we met with Mr. Salisbury, who took Mr. Creed and me to the Cockpit to see *The Moor of Venice* which was well done. Burt acted the Moor; by the same token, a very pretty lady that sat by me, called out, to see Desdemona smothered."[1] While the performance venue is the Cockpit rather than the Globe, the utterance by Pepys's fellow theatergoer resonates with Othello's fraught state after suffocating Desdemona:

> My wife, my wife! What wife? I ha' no wife.
> O insupportable, O heavy hour!
> Methinks it should be now a huge eclipse
> Of sun and moon, and that th'affrighted globe
> Should yawn at alteration. (5.2.106–109; emphasis mine)[2]

Indeed as Adam Cohen points out in his discussion of the play, "globe" here functions both in a macrocosmic sense (anticipating celestial prodigies) and in a microcosmic sense (anticipating the amazed responses of audiences at the Globe theater).[3] Othello's words certainly attest to the wonder-inducing power of his actions, but perhaps more importantly they call attention to the broader implications of wonder in a play comprised at nearly every level of improbable stories and audiences' reactions to them. I will argue that such reactions to Desdemona's death provide a kind of sounding board for the various and wide-ranging responses to wondrous accounts and spectacles from audiences both within and of the play. Numerous characters react with astonished wonderment to orally transmitted stories ranging from sensational traveler's tales and yarns about magical handkerchiefs to unsubstantiated news of alleged infidelity. In turn, Desdemona's demise is itself the culmination of a sequence of episodes in which potentially commonplace stories, household objects, and familiar situations are manipulated in order to ensure that the viewers'/listeners' reaction is one of surprise, suspicion, amazement, or any number of other revelatory responses. Principally through Iago's rhetorical, theological, and theatrical manipulations, the familiar comes to seem wondrous, thereby inverting post-Reformation efforts to make marvels (miracles, relics, and other previously wondrous signs) seem commonplace and ordinary. Increasingly subjected to Iago's manipulations, Othello comes to externalize Desdemona as a wondrous spectacle to behold. Possessed by wonder, Othello himself becomes an object of wonder in the eyes of his audiences. While the play would seem to present a cautionary tale about the dangers of such wondrous possessions, the theatrical spectacle itself complicates any straightforwardly didactic resolution. Both the rapt responses of audiences beyond the stage to Desdemona's death (among the only surviving accounts of audience reactions to specific performances during the seventeenth century) and the unsettled way in which the play ends (leaving tale-tellers to report "marred" stories that may induce further wonderment) suggest that wonder is not so easily exorcised from this play. At the same time, Desdemona's death and its aftermath are part of the contrived fiction of the dramatic representation itself and in this context, the awestruck responses of audiences off-stage (including that of Pepys's seatmate) can be understood as resulting much like the responses of their onstage counterparts from theatrical manipulation.

The status of the marvelous and audiences' reactions to it in *Othello* (ca. 1602–1603) reflect shifting attitudes toward wonder in the sixteenth and seventeenth centuries. In the realm of theology and religion, Protestant reformers rejected Catholic adherence to sacramental signs and symbols (including the power of relics and other objects to generate wonder) by arguing that the age of miracles had ended after New Testament times. As Lorraine Daston explains,

> Protestants challenged by Catholics to produce miracles in attestation of their reformed faith retorted that there was no need for God to confirm the revelation of Christianity anew, for the Protestants meant to reinforce, not break from the teachings of the Bible. Although there was some

internecine wrangling as to when miracles had ceased, that they had done so many centuries ago was above dispute for Protestant authors.[4]

Such sentiment is expressed in several of Shakespeare's plays. In the opening scene of *Henry V*, the Archbishop of Canterbury anachronistically conveys the idea in response to Hal's wondrous transformation from impetuous prince to sensible king. Agreeing with Ely's assessment that such a metamorphosis can be understood by natural rather than divine or supernatural causes, Canterbury exclaims anachronistically that "it must be so, for miracles are ceased, / And therefore we must needs admit the means / How things are perfected" (1.1.68–70). Lafew's lines in *All's Well That Ends Well* suggest a similar trajectory from an earlier age of miracles to an age in which skepticism shifts the focus to explanations grounded in natural causes: "They say miracles are past, and we have our philosophical persons to make modern and familiar things supernatural and causeless. Hence is it that we make trifles of terrors, ensconcing ourselves into seeming knowledge when we should submit ourselves to an unknown fear" (2.3.1–5). Lafew's assessment aptly sums up the official attitude toward marvels and wonders during the reign of Elizabeth. As Dennis Kay has demonstrated, skepticism about astrological influences and prodigies was becoming "the orthodoxy in the final third of the sixteenth century"[5] at least among learned university men.[6] Such views influenced Elizabeth herself, who famously dismissed the prodigious potential of signs such as comets, and reflect a broader effort in the post-Reformation period to make wonders seem familiar.[7]

A similar effort can be seen in early modern writings focusing on natural history, where marvels are often grounded in some form of familiarity.[8] Edward Grimestone's translation of Simon Goulart's *Admirable and Memorable Histories* (1607), for example, includes numerous accounts of wondrous events and phenomena ranging from notable overeaters and "appetites strange" to "visions in the aire, strang and wonderfull." Yet the text makes a number of efforts to situate its encyclopedia of marvels within familiar contexts. As a physician, Goulart was himself an apparent eyewitness to many of the wondrous bloodlettings, notable births, remarkable recoveries from injuries, extraordinary cures, and other episodes compiled in the volume. Many more of the entries cite as their sources authorities both classical and modern. Grimestone highlights this factor in his opening epistle, reminding readers that the improbable nature of marvels can be tempered if one recognizes how the stories are couched in the familiar space of textual authorities:

> The title...shewes the subject to be extraordinarie, and if many of these Histories shall seem very strange, miraculous, and it may be fabulous,

for that they exceed our common sense and apprehension, I must with Monsieur Goulart referre them to the Authors, out of whose writing they are collected, who being learned and iudicious, it is to be presumed would not incurr so foule an imputation, as to be reputed Liars. (2)

In Grimestone's assessment, truth telling is closely aligned with authorial place. To be a well-regarded and familiar author is to ensure that one's writing is reputable no matter how far-fetched and unbelievable the tales may sound. As the notice "From the printer to the reader" makes clear in a parallel effort to reassure skeptical readers, "these from good authors to good purpose are in good sort set downe."

Along with the emphasis on authorities, the meticulous cataloging of wonders stands as another effort to make marvels seem familiar during the post-Reformation period. In *Admirable and Memorable Histories*, the book's "table of the chapters," which scrupulously inventories and cross-references every kind of wonder to be encountered in the volume, exemplifies such cataloging as Dennis Kay has shown.[9] This impulse to catalog and compile marvels as a way to make them seem familiar is also evident in numerous travel diaries and journals by foreign visitors to England during the late sixteenth and early seventeenth centuries. Accounts by visitors such as the Pomeranian Lupold Von Wedel, the German Paul Hentzner, the Swiss Thomas Platter, and the Bohemian Baron Waldstein each catalog wondrous sights, events, people, and places encountered during their travels in England, but, perhaps surprisingly, many of the same wonders are remarked upon from one account to the next. The Thames swans, the Windsor unicorn's horn and bird of paradise, the spectacle of the monarch at a private meal, Drake's *Golden Hind*, wild animals including England's only living wolf at the Tower, the Westminster "monuments"—these and many other wondrous sights reappear from one travel account to the next. While repetition would seem to detract from the singularity and uniqueness of these wonders, the inventorying of English wonder serves a different purpose in these travel accounts. By treating England itself as a kind of *wunderkammer* (curiosity cabinet) to be opened and exhibited, foreign travelers cataloging English wonders acknowledge their own inclusion within a community of outsiders who have come to know England and to witness its sights.[10] Providing an objective catalog of England's material riches—including Royal treasures and curiosities—symbolically enables foreign travelers to circumscribe England's emerging mercantilism within a contained, familiar, and nonthreatening space. More importantly, the fact that the foreign travelers' catalogs of wonders are predominantly secular rather than sacred reinforces England's close proximity to other Protestant countries (from which the majority of foreign visitors came during the period) and confirms the travelers' own identities as secular rather than religious pilgrims.

This kind of cataloging of the marvelous within authoritative and orderly spaces reflects the conflicted and contested status of the marvelous during the sixteenth and seventeenth centuries. At once the subject of growing fascination during the reign of James I, wonders found themselves increasingly circumscribed and secularized within curiosity cabinets, travel inventories, and theatrical spectacle itself. Indeed, as Richard Wilson has summarized Stephen Greenblatt's argument, in the wake of the Reformation, the performance of sanctified spectacle moved from the space of the church into the space of the theater, "substituting for audiences who 'vow to them subjective duty,' secular saints for spiritual martyrs."[11] As such, theatrical display and its power to induce wonder come to replace the visual spectacle of Catholic ceremony. Thomas Heywood, in his *Apology for Actors* (1612), describes the wonder-inducing power that theatrical performance has on audiences: "So bewitching a thing is lively and well-spirited action that it hath power to new-mould the hearts of the spectators and fashion them to the shape of any noble and notable attempt."[12] At the same time, it is important to recognize how the theater provides a realm of contestation and disputation to explore competing ideologies and epistemologies—including the very status of the marvelous in the early modern English imagination. Such contestation works against the view that there was an "orderly progress from primitive superstition to rational optimism" during this period. So too does this problematize the claim set forth by some recent critics that the theater becomes a space to exorcise the wonder-inducing power of spectacle altogether. As we will see, attending to the wondrous responses of audiences both within and of *Othello* underscores the fraught and contested status of wonder within the space of early modern drama.

Over the centuries, the wonders of *Othello* have become critical commonplaces and it is easy to take for granted the marvelous status of Othello's tale telling, of his handkerchief, and even of the union between Desdemona and Othello itself. Yet, as I will argue here, none of these are a priori wonders—that is, none are remarkable for audiences both within and of the play outside the particular realm of Iago's rhetorical, theological, and theatrical manipulations that transform the potentially mundane, ordinary, and familiar into the stuff of wonder (even to the extent that audiences—including readers and critics—take as a given the status of wonders in the play). Iago's power to possess audiences with wonderment reflects anxieties about the theological stakes of wonder during the period. The iconophilic strategies that Iago employs along with an emphasis on works rather than faith alone to confirm belief resonate with the beliefs and practices of Catholics (particularly Jesuits), at least as they were critiqued in the eyes of post-Reformation Protestants. At issue in the play is an enacting of one of the chief theological conflicts of the period: "whether to accept heavenly love as an irreversible miracle of charity or instead to measure it as the contingent reward of demonstrated merits."[13] By transposing Martin Luther's doctrine of *Solifidianism*—salvation by faith alone—into the realm of marriage, the play makes clear that "Shakespeare was at least subliminally attuned to Protestant valuations of faith and Protestant fears about Jesuitical seductions."[14] Critics have long commented on the fact that Iago's name is linked to Catholic belief by virtue of its resonance with St. James the Apostle (fittingly known as "the Moor-slayer"). But more telling perhaps is Luther's own critique of St. James's epistle (2:14–26), which "contains the clearest scriptural obstacle to Solifidianism" and leads Luther to denounce those among the faithful who "run to St. Iago for help instead of trusting Christ's love…"[15] Indeed, as Robert Watson points out, the opening lines of *Othello* find Iago angry that "God has not honored his good works with the ascendancy he thought he had purchased."[16] More importantly (and perhaps at the heart of his motivation), Iago recognizes in Othello's privileging of Cassio a tendency to distinguish merit not by ocular proof (which would emphasize deeds over other estimable factors) but rather based on "bookish theoric" and "mere prattle without practice" (1.1.23, 25)—the very criticisms that Catholics leveled against Protestants for their emphasis on scriptural authority over the physical performance of the sacraments. Iago's plot thus involves transforming Othello into a believer whose faith rests on a "doctrine of works" using an "adulterated blend of logocentric rhetoric and iconocentric truth-fashioning."[17] It is through this heady mixture that the familiar, ordinary, and domestic can be translated and transformed into the wondrous, thus ensuring that words, objects, and images take on the power to possess audiences both onstage and beyond. To illustrate this thesis about the status of wonder in *Othello*, I will explore three episodes in the play in which audiences are possessed with wonder as a result of Iago's technical wrangling of words, objects, and images. These include Iago's efforts to convince both Roderigo and Brabantio of Othello's alterity in the opening scenes, Othello's report to the Senators of his tale telling to Desdemona, and the handkerchief and its associated tales. In each case, it is chiefly through Iago's manipulations that something potentially ordinary, commonplace, familiar, domestic, or otherwise unremarkable becomes marvelous and capable of inducing wonder.

As Catherine Nicholson has argued in her discussion of the play, the subject of each of the early scenes is persuasion, specifically "the work of translating an initially dubious response into a profession of faith."[18]

To accomplish such ends, Iago uses and abuses wonder to possess his listeners. In the opening scene, Iago counters Roderigo's skepticism ["Tush, never tell me!" (1.1.1)] by transforming the rather banal news that Desdemona has married Othello into an almost unbelievably nightmarish scenario ["If ever I did dream of such a matter, abhor me" (1.1.5)] that centers on Othello's threatening status as "other." Iago builds his case against Othello by distancing Othello from the familiar space of Venice and from the even more familiar space of the self. Iago begins his rhetorical assault by calling attention to the support that Venetians of high status have given to Iago's bid for the position of lieutenant: "Three great ones of the city / In personal suit to make me his lieutenant, / Off-capp'd to him…" (1.1.8–10). By "evading" those local officials who would support Iago's promotion by choosing instead the Florentine Cassio (another outsider no less), Othello distances himself from the standards and values of Venice by privileging "his own pride and purpose" over those of the hegemonic community. Building on this critique, Iago proceeds to demonstrate how Othello's selection process similarly severs Othello from the community as he favors the hypothetical realm of "bookish theoric" over the more certain realm of the visual (or *verba* prioritized over *res*), the latter process resonating for early modern English audiences with the theological implications of Catholic belief and practice.[19] By adding that "preferment goes by letter and affection / And not by old gradation, where each second / Stood heir to th' first" (1.1.35–37), Iago further distinguishes Othello's leadership from the conventional and familiar by showing how his selection of Cassio breaks from more traditional processes of determining merit.

Once he has established Othello's distance from the familiar realm of Venetian community in the area of martial leadership, Iago proceeds to highlight Othello's alterity in the more sequestered realm of individual subjectivity. Iago's cryptic lines, "It is as sure as you are Roderigo, / Were I the Moor, I would not be Iago" (1.1.56–57), decisively cleave Iago's own autonomous personhood from its seemingly associate status in relation to Othello. While Iago's willingness to wear his heart on his sleeve "for daws to peck at" suggests the fleeting, nebulous, and artificial status of any kind of inward subjectivity, the crucial point here is that any self that Iago fabricates will diametrically serve to oppose Othello and ultimately reinforce the Moor's otherness outside of Iago's subjective framework. On a general level, Iago's notorious "I am not what I am" speaks to the indeterminate status of his own inward subjectivity, but on a more pragmatic level, it simply distinguishes his own subject-position (a willfully acting *self*) from its seeming status as Othello's confederate (a *self* in service of an *other*). Tellingly, Roderigo's response directly references Othello's racial alterity

["What a full fortune does *the thick-lips* owe..." (1.1.66; emphasis added)], thereby underscoring the impact that Iago's initial rhetorical assault has had on its primary audience. By the time Roderigo confidently describes Othello to Brabantio as "an extravagant and wheeling stranger / Of here and everywhere" (1.1.137–38) later in the opening scene, Iago's work of possessing Roderigo with the wonder of Othello's alleged alterity has been realized. In turn, Roderigo becomes a speaker imbued with the power to induce wonder in audiences of his own.

In the case of Brabantio, Iago transforms a potentially mundane piece of news about interracial union (particularly within the cosmopolitan context of Venice) into a wondrous story about intimate animal/human couplings and transformations. Othello's racially and geographically positioned alterity is clearly in view as Iago announces that "even now, now, very now, an old black ram / Is tupping your white ewe" (1.1.88–89). Iago's admonition that such a union must be prevented "or else the devil will make a grandsire of you" speaks to fears of miscegenation, which may have been less pronounced in early modern Venice than they were for early modern English audiences.[20] Nevertheless, such stories resonate with travel yarns and travelers' encounters with half-human, half-animal wonders such as the relation from Pliny the Elder that "Indians engender with beasts, of which generation are bred certain monstrous mongrels, half beasts and half men."[21] Tellingly, Iago's words about confronting Othello at the Sagittary—"lead to the Sagittary the raisèd search / And there I will be with him" (1.1.159–60)—reinforce the image of Othello as half-human, half-animal (the astrological Sagittarius is represented by the half-human, half-horse centaur) and yoke Othello to the space of the inn—a symbol of "transnational movement...leading to radical proximities," as Ian Smith suggests.[22] As it had for Roderigo earlier in the scene, the force of Iago's rhetorical attack (here the metaleptic substitution of animal/human hybrid for the union of Othello and Desdemona) transforms Brabantio's initial skepticism (questioning Iago's "terrible summons," calling him "villain," and chastising Roderigo for his seemingly drunken raving) into a response imbued with wonder. Brabantio marvels at how much this news of Desdemona's elopement is "not unlike my dream" and then proceeds to explain the wondrous union between Othello and Desdemona as the result of "charms / By which the property of youth and maidhood / May be abus'd..." (1.1.72–74). Even as Brabantio commends Roderigo for bringing the situation to his attention, it is Iago's one-two rhetorical punch (possessing first Roderigo and then Brabantio with wonder) that proves transformative in the scene.

When Brabantio brings the news of his daughter's elopement to his fellow senators and attempts to prosecute Othello as a result, the expectation is that the hegemonic community of Venice will be sympathetic to his charges and follow "the bloody book of the law" (1.3.67) in seeking justice. So why does this not play out? Numerous readers and critics have grappled with this question, especially given that Othello's ensuing explanation about how his relationship with Desdemona came to be seems to reinforce the very anxieties about charms and witchcraft that Brabantio has come to associate (by way of Iago and Roderigo) with Othello. Part of the answer here may involve recognizing that audiences in this scene both onstage and off are not hearing the tales themselves. They are hearing a narrative about the tales, a narrative in which outcome (specifically the romance and subsequent marriage of Desdemona and Othello) overshadows the individual episodes and anecdotes to which Othello only briefly alludes in his speech. Given the distinction being drawn, it is instructive to consider Greenblatt's claim about the possessive power of travel stories from the late medieval and early modern periods. As Greenblatt argues, "the discourse of travel in the late Middle Ages and the Renaissance is rarely if ever interesting at the level of sustained narrative and teleological design, but always gripping at the level of anecdote."[23] Othello's account of his travels and exploits indeed points to anecdotes (the anthropophagi and the like) and he underscores the episodic nature of his storytelling: "Whereof by parcels she had something heard / But not intentively [continuously]." Yet it is really at the level of teleological design ["the story of my life / From year to year...from my boyish days / To th'very moment that he bade me tell it..." (1.3.128–29, 131–32)—the progression from traveler to captive to stranger to convert to integrated Venetian soldier] that the story proves persuasive to the senators, leading them not so much to wonder at the details as to sympathize with the plight of Othello's narrative trajectory.[24] Underscoring both Othello's travail/travel between "here and everywhere" and his ability to contain a potentially "outsider" identity within the familiar space of persuasive and decorous oratory, the speech reassures its onstage audience about Othello's own qualifications for serving in his present duties against the Turks. While there is no doubt that the wonder-inducing anecdotes and stories have had the power to possess Desdemona (seconded by the Duke's expectation that "this tale would win my daughter, too" (1.3.170), it is the senators' responses to both Desdemona's and Othello's versions of the tale of their union that is important to consider here.[25] Most telling is the way in which the Senators' skeptical rejection of Brabantio's accusations parallels their response early in the scene to the news reports about the Turkish fleet. The First Senator carefully and adroitly dismisses the Turks' apparent strategy as "a pageant / To keep us in false gaze" (1.3.20–21) and his speech leads the Duke to speak with certainty about the Turkish fleet: "Nay, in all confidence, he's not for Rhodes" (1.3.32). Such measured responses contrast with the reactions of both Roderigo and Brabantio in the opening scene where, as we have noted, potentially ordinary or banal news becomes wonder-inducing in Iago's hands. In act 1, scene 3, potentially wondrous news and tales are met with the temperate and reasonable responses usually reserved for the familiar and commonplace. As such, the scene provides a corrective to the misguided responses of listeners to tales in the first scene.[26] And yet, it is the failure of audiences within the play to heed this model of skeptical response to wondrous and improbable news that accounts most directly for the tragic consequences of the drama. As the handkerchief will demonstrate, the urge to imbue with wonder a mundane or commonplace sign is at the very heart of the play's overlapping theological, epistemological, and metatheatrical concerns.

While it is tempting to read Othello's handkerchief as a wondrous object given Othello's own tales about it (and in light of the play's critical legacy), it is helpful to heed Paul Yachnin's reminder that the handkerchief is first and foremost an "altogether practical and commonplace stage property."[27] More specifically, Yachnin explains that the object would have likely been perceived by audiences in Shakespeare's London as "marketable goods, a square of embroidered cloth in a nation whose primary industry was the production of textiles, a stage property in a theatre whose largest operating expense was for the purpose of costumes and draperies."[28] Despite the handkerchief's potentially unremarkable status as a prop, one could certainly argue that Othello's account of its provenance imbues the object with wonder. However, this is problematic given the two conflicting stories about the object's origins. In the first, the handkerchief was a gift to Othello's mother from "an Egyptian charmer" and was made by a two hundred-year-old sibyl. The second version of its origins suggests that the handkerchief was a gift from Othello's father to his mother, a kind of heirloom passed from husband to wife. Beyond the question of which of these accounts is the correct one (or what the inconsistency might say about Othello's own penchant for story-telling), the wonder-inducing power of such tales underscores the handkerchief's own travels as a mutable and inconsistent signifier within the play. Yachnin presents the relationship this way:

> Given the invisible influence that the handkerchief wields in its travels through the play, the claims Othello makes about both its sacred, feminine origins and its magical powers to bind husband to wife through male desire seem not to belong to an enchanted world entirely foreign to Venetian civility, but rather to constitute a somewhat outlandish explanation of the handkerchief's actual operations.[29]

While the handkerchief never becomes "convincingly magical," it is through Iago's rhetorical and theatrical manipulations that a "trifle light as air" comes to seem that it has "magic in the web of it." As such, Desdemona's "sure there's some wonder in this handkerchief" (3.4.97), in response to Othello's tirade upon learning that it has been lost, speaks less to the handkerchief's perceived magical properties and more to the hitherto undiscovered process by which the object has come to possess Othello.

By the time Othello describes the handkerchief as a wondrous portent in act 4, scene 1, when he exclaims, "O, it comes o'er my memory / As doth the raven o'er the infectious house, / Boding to all!" (20), he has become almost entirely confident in the object's status as "ocular proof" to substantiate his doubts about Desdemona's faithfulness. Such confidence attests to the handkerchief's power as a visual object, working much like the relics and sacramental artifacts of the Catholic Church to induce emotional responses imbued with awe and wonder. Richard Wilson underscores the association between the handkerchief and Catholic (especially Jesuit) relics as he cites Gary Wills, remarking that

> Shakespeare's stage handkerchiefs inevitably carry such "Romany" connotations, as "handkerchiefs were associated with the emptying of all a man's blood in the savage castrating, disemboweling, and quartering of hanged bodies of traitors," when because "there could be no containment" of the bloodbath, pious Catholics felt compelled to "dip handkerchiefs and other bits of cloth" in the precious fluid to salvage every drop. Thus, whether or not he witnessed the execution of Jesuits like Campion, "the picture of people trying to sop up blood for relics with handkerchiefs, or any cloth at hand," was clearly "napkins enough" for this dramatist, which explains why these "trifles" are made to carry an "earnestness" in his work that would have been suspect to Protestants. For what Shakespeare stages is what also appalls historians, namely the effluvium of excess meaning from items that look "embarrassingly domestic," or even, "from a *politique* angle, tragically absurd."[30]

The handkerchief, improbably and opportunely falling into the wrong hands at the right times, gives Othello the ocular reassurance that will substantiate his faith as he had earlier demanded: "I'll see before I doubt; when I doubt, prove; / And on the proof, there is no more but this: / Away at once with love or jealousy" (3.3.194–96). As Iago implores Othello to "stand you a while apart" in order to observe the conversation that will both confirm Cassio's guilt and provide the "ocular proof" of the handkerchief in Othello's mind, the Ensign deftly manipulates the boundaries between words and images:

> Do but encave yourself,
> And mark the fleers, the gibes and notable scorns
> That dwell in every region of his face.
> For I will make him tell the tale anew,
> Where, how, how oft, how long ago, and when
> He hath and is again to cope your wife.
> I say but mark his gesture. (4.1.79–85)

Such advice underscores the key element of Iago's transformative power: by muddling the distinction between *verba* and *res*, Iago insists that attending to the visual (Cassio's facial expressions and gestures) can "tell the tale" and substantiate Cassio's crime.

It is quite telling that Othello frequently employs the exclamation "now" as he witnesses the ensuing dialogue between Cassio and Iago. Such exclamations echo Iago's "now, even now" that he had earlier used to rile up his audiences with tales of bestial sexuality and barbarous brawls. As in those earlier scenes, Iago here manipulates words and images to make the familiar (in this case a casual conversation about Cassio's relations with a supposed courtesan) into the stuff of wonder at which Othello marvels. The set piece that Iago orchestrates and stage-manages here parallels the "pageant / to keep us in false gaze" produced by the Turkish fleet in act 1, scene 3, of the play.[31] Unlike the skeptical and cautious Senators though, Othello is thoroughly taken in by the performance. Answering Othello's doubts about the provenance of the handkerchief that he has just seen pass from Bianca to Cassio in the course of the conversation, Iago assures that it is "yours, by this hand." He goes on to conflate promiscuous object and promiscuous spouse as he exclaims, "And to see how he prizes the foolish woman your wife. She gave it him, and he hath given it his whore" (4.1.169–70). Othello's resolutely violent response ("I would have him nine years a-killing") confirms that this is all the "ocular proof" needed to confirm the crime.

Once imbued with such signifying power, the handkerchief in turn transforms Desdemona into a wonder in Othello's eyes. The highly ceremonial language of the murder scene testifies to Iago's power to transform potentially commonplace anxieties about adultery—"There's millions now alive / That nightly lie in those unproper beds / Which they dare swear peculiar" (4.1.65–67)—into the wondrously sacrosanct. Most strikingly, Othello's description of Desdemona's white skin as "monumental alabaster" renders her body into statuary, thus completing Iago's master narrative of

Catholic iconophilia and effecting a wondrous alteration from the mundane (life to death) into the fantastic (life to statue), which would enable Othello to sacrilize his love for Desdemona and purify it of the corruptive influences of sexuality.³² Desdemona's physical body here parallels the handkerchief as both have become objects "whose capacity to arouse wonder in the beholder is seen to underwrite the beholder's selfhood."³³ As Yachnin makes clear, both the handkerchief and Desdemona herself become fetishized possessions that possess Othello with wonderment. Yet even as he is subject to such wonder-inducing manipulations primarily as a result of Iago's diabolical enterprise, Othello himself becomes an object of wonder. Prioritizing *res* over *verba* shatters Othello's confidence in his own narrative self-fashioning (as Greenblatt and others have shown) and transforms him into a wonder in his own eyes and in the eyes of his audiences.

Early in the play, Othello makes several notable efforts to define himself within the realm of the familiar and domestic in terms of martial, marital, and oratory frameworks. Confident that "[my] parts, my title, and my perfect soul, / Shall manifest me rightly" (1.2.31–32), and not yet converted to the idea that absolute faith rests on the ocular rather than aural, Othello provides for the Senators narrative reassurance of his conformity to a decidedly Venetian cosmopolitanism (as we have seen and as Brabantio, charged up by Iago's manipulations, has attempted to challenge). Later, roused by the brawl that has disrupted the consummation of his marriage, Othello once again asserts his place as a familiar countryman rather than an outsider:

> Why, how now, ho? From whence ariseth this?
> Are we turned Turks, and to ourselves do that
> Which heaven hath forbid the Ottomites?
> For Christian shame, put by this barbarous brawl. (2.3.152–55)

Perhaps more so than in Venice, the stakes in Cyprus are higher in terms of clearly defining the boundaries of cultural alterity. Othello voices this concern in the aftermath of the brawl:

> What, in a town of war
> Yet wild, the people's hearts brimful of fear,
> To manage private and domestic quarrel
> In night, and on the court and guard of safety!
> Tis monstrous. (2.3.196–200)

And it is this anxiety that Iago preys upon as he proceeds to unsettle the boundaries between self and other, between familiar and stranger, and between commonplace and marvel within Othello's own mind. Indeed, stirring up Othello's own self-doubts is the first step to unmooring Othello from a familiar Venetian identity:

> Haply for I am black,
> And have not those soft parts of conversation
> That chamberers have; or for I am declined
> Into the vale of years... (3.3.268–71)

As doubts about inferiority based on race and age begin to materialize, so too does a skepticism about the power of language to "manifest me rightly." By the time Othello recovers from his trance (overpowered by the swirling concoction of aural and visual conjurations that Iago's promptings have cooked up), he describes his own status as potential cuckold this way: "a horned man's a monster and a beast" (4.1.59), echoing and confirming Iago's earlier imagery of animal/human hybridity in his efforts to rouse Brabantio's ire.

Becoming a wonder unto himself, Othello proceeds to arouse wonder in his audiences. Lodovico exclaims, "My lord, this would not be believed in Venice, / Though I swear I saw't" (4.1.237–38) and the reactions of audiences to Desdemona's murder call attention to the marvelous or unfamiliar. Gratiano exclaims that "Tis a strange truth" and Montano calls it a "monstrous act." Emilia's racially charged pronouncements—"the more angel she, and you the blacker devil!"; "O dolt, / As ignorant as dirt!... The Moor hath killed my mistress" (5.2.140, 170–71, 174)—work to undermine Othello's previous efforts to distinguish himself from "other." Most tellingly, it is the story that Othello himself narrates to the assembled onlookers that firmly secures his status as wonder. Othello's divided (cloven?) subjectivity, situated as both the chief actor and the victim in a story that shockingly proclaims the triumph of a dominant cultural hegemony, marks him as a wonder to behold.[34] So too does the shocking death that is both the culmination and "bloody period" of Othello's narrative. But it is Gratiano's words more than Lodovico's that prove revelatory in terms of the wondrous import of what has just been witnessed. Before Lodovico promises to report the events "to the state," Gratiano exclaims, "all that is spoke is marred" (5.2.367) after witnessing Othello's suicide. On one level, the words suggest that any effort on Othello's part to retain the kind of dignity argued for in his final speech is undermined by the act of committing suicide. On another level, the statement emphasizes the unsettled relationship between seeing and reporting (between *res* and *verba*), which recapitulates rather than eradicates the power of wondrous possession in the play. Seen in this light, Lodovico's confident words about reporting the news to the state are undercut by the reminder that he might very well become just another tale-teller left to report "marred" stories that may induce further wonderment. So too does the fact that the play itself is a fabricated visual spectacle that generates rapt responses from audiences through the engineering and manipulating of verbal and ocular "certainties" including scripts, actors playing roles, and rhetorically engaging, if not convincing, plots. To conclude, let us consider once again such audience responses to the play itself in order to illuminate more clearly how the wonder inducing powers of theatrical spectacle at once deludes and possesses audiences.

Henry Jackson of Corpus Christi College witnessed a performance of *Othello* at Oxford by the King's Men in 1610, which he describes this way:

> They also had tragedies which they acted with propriety and fitness. In which [tragedies], not only through speaking but also through acting certain things, they moved [the audience] to tears. But truly the celebrated Desdemona, slain in our presence by her husband, although she pleaded her case very effectively throughout, yet moved [us] more after she was dead, when, lying on her bed, she entreated the pity of the spectators by her very countenance.[35]

On the one hand, the description underscores the power of dramatic representation to induce wonder in audiences. In her discussion of the description, Sasha Roberts suggests that Jackson's use of decidedly female pronouns might indicate "how the illusion of the boy actor as woman could be so convincing that Jackson treats the boy actor as though he were female."[36] On the other hand, as Yachnin points out, the description emphasizes how audiences are moved by the *image* of the dead Desdemona so that "the audience response mirrors the shift within the play from the language-based relationship between the lovers at the outset to Othello's subsequent attempt to gain visual mastery over Desdemona."[37] Thus, the scene affects for spectators what Iago has managed to do to Othello—namely, to insist that ocular witnessing eclipses any other form of representation in its power to induce to wonder. However, lest we conclude too hastily that the play simply presents a cautionary (and decidedly Protestant) warning about the dangerous allure of ocular enticements, it is useful to return once more to Pepys's brief description of the 1660 *Othello* performance with which we began in order to reflect upon the ambiguity of wonder-effects by focusing on the female spectator's ambiguous gesture of "call[ing] out." We might ourselves wonder about the nature of the response. Was this in sympathy with Desdemona's plight (something like "Noooo!"), was it something more bloodthirsty and malicious (more like "haha!"), or was the gesture altogether more emotionally innocuous (a wooden "oh!" perhaps not altogether different from the "wooden O" that the Chorus in *Henry V* is referring to since both would underscore the limitations of the theatrical space to enrapt audiences)? The words cry out for a visual referent—leaving us (much like Othello) desiring some kind of ocular proof to substantiate an otherwise hollow idiolectic performance that only hints at the wonder-effects of the dramatic spectacle.

Notes

1. Qtd in Gāmini Salgādo, *Eye-Witnesses of Shakespeare* (London: Chatto and Windus, 1975), 49.
2. In William Shakespeare, *The Norton Shakespeare based on the Oxford Edition*, 2nd edition, ed. Stephen Greenblatt, Walter Cohen, Jean E. Howard, and Katharine Eisaman Maus (New York: W.W. Norton, 2008). All subsequent citations of Shakespeare's work come from this edition.
3. See chapter I.4, p. 64.
4. Lorraine Daston, "Marvelous Facts and Miraculous Evidence in Early Modern Europe," in *Wonders, Marvels, and Monsters in Early Modern Culture*, ed. Peter Platt (Newark: University of Delaware Press, 1999), 91.
5. Dennis Kay, "Who Says 'Miracles are Past'?: Some Jacobean Marvels and the Margins of the Known," in Platt, *Wonders*, 164.
6. For a seminal study on the shifting ideological landscape of popular superstition and belief in relation to religious devotion and doctrine, see Keith Thomas, *Religion and the Decline of Magic* (New York: Scribner, 1971).
7. Henry Howard, Earl of Northampton, *A defensatiue against the poyson of supposed prophecies* (London, 1583). See Kay, "Who Says," 164.
8. See, e.g., *The boke of secretes of Albertus Magnus* (London?, 1560); Edward Fenton, *Certaine Secrete wonders of Nature* (London, 1569); Ambroise Pare, *Des Monstres et Prodiges* [*Deus livres...*] (Paris, 1573); Thomas Lupton, *A Thousand Notable things of sundry sortes* (London, ca. 1590); Edward Topsell; *The historie of foure-footed beastes* (London, 1607); and Edward Grimestone, *Admirable and Memorable Histories* (London, 1607).
9. See Kay, "Who Says," 164–86.
10. On the idea of the *wunderkammer* and other precursors to the museum, see especially Oliver Impey and Arthur Macgregor, eds, *The Origins of Museums: The Cabinet of Curiosities in Sixteenth- and Seventeenth-Century Europe* (Oxford: Clarendon Press, 1985). See also Paula Findlen, *Possessing Nature: Museums, Collecting, and Scientific Culture in Early Modern Italy* (repr. Berkeley: University of California Press, 1996); Joy Kenseth, ed., *The Age of the Marvelous* (Hanover: Hood Museum of Art, 1991); and Lawrence Weschler, *Mr. Wilson's Cabinet of Wonder* (New York: Pantheon, 1995). On the relationship between collecting and travel, see especially Lorraine Daston, "The Factual Sensibility," *Isis* 79.3 (September 1988), in which she observes, "Travel was the alpha and omega of

collecting, being both the source of the bulk of the objects—the voyages of exploration and subsequent trade with newly discovered lands created a steady flow of exotic—and the occasion for inspecting them in Amsterdam, Oxford, Venice, Paris, Augsburg, Uppsala, or wherever the curious and peripatetic tourist might land" (455).

11. Richard Wilson, "Dyed in Mummy: *Othello* and the Mulberries," in *Performances of the Sacred in Late Medieval and Early Modern England*, ed. Susanne Rupp and Tobias Doring (Amsterdam: Rodopi, 2005), 137.
12. Thomas Heywood, *An Apology for Actors* (London, 1612), B4.
13. Robert N. Watson, "*Othello* as Reformation Tragedy," in *In the Company of Shakespeare*, ed. Thomas Moisan and Douglas Bruster (Madison, NJ: Fairleigh Dickinson University Press, 2002), 65.
14. Ibid, 65–66.
15. Ibid., 69.
16. Ibid.
17. Ibid, 72.
18. Catherine Nicholson, "*Othello* and the Geography of Persuasion," *English Literary Renaissance* 40.1 (2010): 64.
19. Interestingly, as we have already seen, audiences in Jacobean England would potentially recognize the theological underpinnings of Othello's strategy as the more familiar one, while Iago's would resonate with abhorred Catholic practices (as discussed earlier).
20. On the question of Venetian cosmopolitan attitudes toward interracial coupling, see Emily C. Bartels, *Speaking of the Moor: From "Alcazar" to "Othello"* (Philadelphia: University of Pennsylvania Press, 2008). See also Paul A. Canter, "The Erring Barbarian among the Supersubtle Venetians," *Southwest Review* 75.3 (1990): 296–319.
21. Qtd in Philip Collington, "Othello the Liar," in *The Mysterious and Foreign in Early Modern England*, ed. Helen Ostovich, Mary V. Silcox, and Graham Roebuck (Newark: University of Delaware Press, 2008), 197.
22. Ian Smith, "The Queer Moor: Bodies, Borders, and Barbary Inns," in *A Companion to the Global Renaissance*, ed. Jyotsna G. Singh (Oxford: Wiley-Blackwell, 2009), 190–91.
23. Stephen Greenblatt, *Marvelous Possessions* (Chicago: University of Chicago Press, 1992), 2. Greenblatt's earlier point that "in *Othello* the characters have always already experienced submission to narrativity [thus making them ripe for Iago's 'narrative fashioning']" (237) further underscores the function of narrative in this episode. See Greenblatt, *Renaissance Self-Fashioning* (Chicago: University of Chicago Press, 1980).
24. The wonder-inducing power of Othello's tales is further diminished when we consider that the anecdotal marvels sound like rehashed stories from Pliny and Mandeville. By the early seventeenth century, such accounts were met with skepticism and yawns by audiences even as recent voyages to the "New World" led to a reassessment of Pliny and Mandeville. In his *Discoverie of Giuiana*, e.g., Ralegh describes the place as "such a nation was written of by Mandeville,

whose reports were holden for fables many yeeres, and yet since the East Indies were discovered, we find his relations true of such things as heretofore were held incredible" (qtd in Greenblatt, *Renaissance,* 122).
25. Considering the impact of Othello's tales from this angle also shifts the focus away from the concern with the "truth" of Othello's stories (a concern going all the way back to Thomas Rhymer and voiced by much more recent critics including Philip D. Collington, Mark Thornton Burnett, and Andrew Hadfield).
26. The Duke's gesture of offering familiar *sententiae* to Brabantio in hopes of providing a "grece or step" to "help these lovers into your favour" stands as another instance of transforming the wondrous—here registering as Brabantio's xenophobic diatribe against Othello's bewitching words and actions—into the familiar and commonplace.
27. Paul Yachnin, "Wonder-effects: Othello's handkerchief," in *Staged Properties in Early Modern English Drama*, ed. Jonathan Gil Harris and Natasha Korda (Cambridge: Cambridge University Press, 2002), 316.
28. Ibid., 324.
29. Ibid., 326.
30. Richard Wilson, "Dyed in Mummy: *Othello* and the Mulberries," in *Performances of the Sacred in Late Medieval and Early Modern England*, ed. Susanne Rupp and Tobias Doring (Amsterdam: Rodopi, 2005), 144–45.
31. In *"Othello* as Reformation Tragedy," Watson points out the parallel between the Turkish fleet and the 1588 Armada defeat, further linking the Turks—and Iago—to a nebulous Catholic threat in the early modern English imagination.
32. This is in a sense the reverse of Hermione's transformation in *The Winter's Tale* where the wondrous spectacle of a statue coming to life is undergirded by both Leontes's contrition and Hermione's potential forgiveness. See *The Winter's Tale*, 5.3.
33. Yachnin, "Wonder-effects," 324.
34. The "base Judean"/"base Indian" textual crux stands as another iteration of such wonder in the passage.
35. Qtd in ibid., 328.
36. Sasha Roberts, "'Let me the curtains draw': The Dramatic and Symbolic Properties of the Bed in Shakespearean Tragedy," in Harris and Korda, *Staged*, 167.
37. Yachnin, "Wonder-effects," 329.

Suggested Reading

Altman, Joel B. *The Improbability of Othello: Rhetorical Anthropology and Shakespearean Selfhood*. Chicago: University of Chicago Press, 2010.
Cantor, Paul A. "The Erring Barbarian among the Supersubtle Venetians." *Southwest Review* 75.3 (1990): 296–319.
Collington, Philip D. "Othello the Traveler." *Early Theatre* 8.2 (2005): 73–100.

Deats, Sara. "The 'Erring Barbarian' and the 'Maiden Never Bold': Racist and Sexist Representations in *Othello*." In *Women, Violence, and English Renaissance Literature: Essays Honoring Paul Jorgensen*, edited by Linda Woodbridge and Sharon Beehler, 189–215. Tempe, AZ: Arizona Center for Medieval and Renaissance Studies, 2003.

Grinnell, Richard W. "Witchcraft, Race, and the Rhetoric of Barbarism in *Othello* and *I Henry IV*." *Upstart Crow* 24 (2004): 72–80.

Highley, Christopher. "'The Lost British Lamb': English Catholic Exiles and the Problem of Britain." In *British Identities and English Renaissance Literature,* edited by David J. Baker and Willy Maley, 37–50. Cambridge: Cambridge University Press, 2002.

Hunt, Maurice. *Shakespeare's Religious Allusiveness. Its Play and Tolerance.* Aldershot: Ashgate, 2004.

Jacobs, Margaret. *Strangers Nowhere in the World: The Rise of Cosmopolitanism in Early Modern Europe.* Philadelphia: University of Pennsylvania Press, 2006.

Loomba, Ania. "'Delicious Traffick': Alterity and Exchange on Early Modern Stages." *Shakespeare Survey* 52 (1999): 201–14.

McQuade, Paula. "Love and Lies: Marital Truth-Telling, Catholic Casuistry, and *Othello*." In *Shakespeare and the Culture of Christianity in Early Modern England,* edited by Dennis Taylor and David Beauregard, 415–38. New York: Fordham University Press, 2003.

Mallette, Richard. "Blasphemous Preacher: Iago and the Reformation." In *Shakespeare and the Culture of Christianity in Early Modern England*, edited by Dennis Taylor and David Beauregard, 382–414. New York: Fordham University Press, 2003.

Menon, Madhavi. *Wanton Words: Rhetoric and Sexuality in English Renaissance Drama.* Toronto: University of Toronto Press, 2004.

Parker, Patricia. "Shakespeare and Rhetoric: Dilation and Delation in *Othello*." In *Shakespeare and the Question of Theory*, edited by Patricia Parker and Geoffrey Hartman, 54–74. New York: Methuen, 1985.

Sell, Jonathan, *Rhetoric and Wonder in English Travel Writing 1560–1613.* Aldershot: Ashgate, 2006.

Smith, Ian. "Barbarian Errors: Performing Race in Early Modern England." *Shakespeare Quarterly* 49.2 (1998): 168–86.

Yachnin, Paul. "Magical Properties: Vision, Possession, and Wonder in *Othello*." *Theatre Journal* 48.2 (1996): 197–208.

Bibliography of Works by Adam Max Cohen

With David B. King. "Afterword: Post-Posthumanist Me: An Illiterate Reads Shakespeare." In *Posthumanist Shakespeares*, edited by Stefan Herbrechter and Ivan Callus. Houndmills, Basingstoke, Hampshire: Palgrave Macmillan, 2012.

"Technology in and around Shakespeare." In *The Oxford Handbook to Shakespeare*, edited by Arthur Kinney. Oxford: Oxford University Press, 2011.

"Transalpine Wonders: Shakespeare's Marvelous Aesthetics." In *Shakespeare and Renaissance Literary Theories: Anglo-Italian Transactions,* edited by Michele Marrapodi, 89–104. Aldershot, Hampshire, England: Ashgate, 2011.

Wonder in Shakespeare. New York: Palgrave Macmillan, 2011.

Review of Paula Blank. *Shakespeare and the Mismeasure of Renaissance Man. Shakespeare Yearbook.* Lewiston, NY: Edwin Mellen, 2010. 190–96.

Technology and the Early Modern Self. New York: Palgrave Macmillan, 2009.

"Tudor Technology in Transition." In *A Companion to Tudor Literature*, edited by Kent Cartwright, 95–100. Malden, MA: Wiley-Blackwell, 2009.

Review of *Transversal Enterprises in the Drama of Shakespeare and His Contemporaries: Fugitive Explorations,* by Bryan Reynolds. *Early Theatre* 11.1 (2008): 137–41.

"The Mirror of All Christian Courtiers: Castiglione's Cortegiano as a Source for Henry V." In *Italian Culture in the Drama of Shakespeare & His Contemporaries: Rewriting, Remaking, Refashioning,* edited by Michele Marrapodi, 39–50. Aldershot, Hampshire, England: Ashgate, 2007.

"Englishing the Globe: Molyneux's Globes and Shakespeare's Theatrical Career." *Sixteenth Century Journal: The Journal of Early Modern Studies* 37.4 (Winter 2006): 963–84.

Shakespeare and Technology: Dramatizing Early Modern Technological Revolutions. New York: Palgrave Macmillan, 2006.

"Hamlet as Emblem: The *Ars Memoria* and the Culture of the Play." *Journal for Early Modern Cultural Studies* 3.1 (Spring/Summer 2003): 77–112.

Review of *Romantic Dynamics: The Poetics of Physicality,* by Mark S. Lussier. *The Wordsworth Circle* 31.4 (Fall 2000): 230–31.

"Genius in Perspective: Blake, Einstein, and Theories of Relativity." *The Wordsworth Circle* 31.3 (Summer 2000): 164–69.

Review of *Maids and Mistresses, Cousins and Queens: Women's Alliances in Early Modern England*. Edited by Susan Frye and Karen Robertson. *The Virginia Quarterly Review* 75.4 (1999): 4.

Review of *Playing With Desire: Christopher Marlowe and the Art of Tantalization*, by Fred B. Tromly. *The Virginia Quarterly Review* 75.4 (1999): 124.

Review of *The Shape of the River: The Long-term Consequences of Considering Race in College and University Admissions*, by William G. Bowen and Derek Bok. *The Virginia Quarterly Review* 75.2 (1999): 61.

Contributors

M. G. Aune is an associate professor of English at California University of Pennsylvania. His research interests include Shakespeare and performance, Shakespeare and film, and early modern travel writing. His articles and reviews have appeared in *Shakespeare Bulletin, Quarterly Review of Film and Video, Shakespeare,* and *Renaissance Quarterly.*

Joshua B. Fisher is an associate professor in the English Department at Wingate University. He has published on a wide range of topics, including early modern literary appropriations of broadside ballads, the domestic travel writing of John Taylor the Water-Poet, recent developments in the canon of early modern literature, and food and nation in Shakespeare's *Henry IV* plays. He is currently working on a book about the development of familiar English space in the early modern period.

Kristin Keating is an associate instructor and doctoral student in the Joint Program in Drama and Theatre at the University of California, Irvine, and University of California, San Diego. She has previously worked in the Literary Department at the Shakespeare Theatre in Washington, D.C. and as a graduate researcher in the Folger Institute at the Folger Shakespeare Library. She is a contributor to the forthcoming *Encyclopedia of Women and American Popular Culture*, and her research currently deals with digital performance and avatar identity, as well as intersections of popular culture, spirituality, mysticism, and technology in the digital age.

Bryan Reynolds is professor of drama at the University of California, Irvine. He is also the artistic director and resident playwright of the Amsterdam-based Transversal Theater Company. He is the author of *Transversal Subjects: From Montaigne to Deleuze after Derrida* (2009), *Transversal Enterprises in the Drama of Shakespeare and his Contemporaries: Fugitive Explorations* (2006), *Performing Transversally: Reimagining Shakespeare and the Critical*

Future (2003), and *Becoming Criminal: Transversal Performance and Cultural Dissidence in Early Modern England* (2002). He is the coeditor of *The Return of Theory in Early Modern English Studies: Tarrying with the Subjunctive* (2011), *Critical Responses to Kiran Desai* (2009), *Rematerializing Shakespeare: Authority and Representation on the Early Modern English Stage* (2005), and *Shakespeare Without Class: Misappropriations of Cultural Capital* (2000).

Janna Segal is an assistant professor in the Theatre Department at Mary Baldwin College. She received her PhD in drama and theatre from the UC Irvine/UC San Diego joint doctoral program. Her dissertation, *Shakespearean-Becomings: Transversal Explorations of Amorous Desire on the Shakespearean Stage*, is an analysis of the transversal representation of amorous desire in Shakespeare's theater and its historical impact on Western cultures through critical and dramatic reconceptualizations. She has published single and coauthored articles on *Othello, Romeo and Juliet, The Roaring Girl, As You Like It*, and Dario Fo and Franca Rame's *Elisabetta*. Janna is also a dramaturg whose production work includes Shakespeare (*As You Like It*), Shakespearean adaptation (*Love's Fire*), and contemporary theater (Sarah Ruhl's *Eurydice*).

Rebecca Steinberger is professor and chair of the English Department at Misericordia University. In addition to Shakespeare and early modern cultural studies, her research interests include broadside ballads, contemporary Irish drama, Gothic literature, and literary treatments of terrorism. She is the author of *Shakespeare and Twentieth-Century Irish Drama: Conceptualizing Identity and Staging Boundaries* (2008) and the contributing editor of *The Renaissance Literature Handbook* (2009). Currently, she is a working on a four-hundred-year literary history of terrorism in literature written in and about London.

Maura Tarnoff is *una profesora de filológia inglesa* at Saint Louis University's Madrid Campus, where she teaches courses on medieval and early modern literature and culture. She has published articles on poetic fame and the domestic arts in John Skelton's *The Garlande or Chapelet of Laurell* and on disability studies approaches to Shakespeare in performance. She is currently working on a book-length study of the interrelations between literature and the domestic arts in sixteenth-century England.

Index

Aaron 43, 45, 50
Acts, Book of 28, 32, 35, 111, 132
Aesthetic resurrection 128, 139, 143
Aesthetic space 142–44
Agincourt, Battle of 169
Aguzzi-Babagli, Danilo 104, 115
Ah-ha! moment 181, 183
Alien 151, 154
All's Well That Ends Well 197
Altick, Richard D. 91–92, 114
Altman, Joel B. 212
Amazement 10, 12, 13, 26, 28, 42, 88, 98, 129, 185, 193, 196
Anti-Catholic 128, 140, 145, 146
Anti-Semitism 155–56
Antitheatricality 178–79, 187–88
Antony and Cleopatra 24, 44–45, 61–64, 65, 93, 94–95, 112
Apocalypse 20, 44, 54, 61, 64, 189
Apothecary's shops 85–90
A priori 158, 199
Aquinas, Saint Thomas 23, 25, 110, 180, 182
Archer, William 38
Ardinger, Barbara 45, 111
Ariel 10, 12–14, 136, 149, 161
Ariosto, Ludovico, *Orlando Furioso* 103
Aristotle, *Metaphysics* 99–100, 135, 182; *Poetics* 99, 106, 114, 135; *Rhetoric* 99–100, 178–79
As You Like It 14, 46, 184

Athenagoras, *Embassy for the Christians* 22–25, 110
Augustine, Saint 25, 103, 115; *City of God* 19, 110; *Enchiridon* 21–22, 34, 110; *Faith and the Creed* 21–22
Awe 9, 11–13, 15, 29, 36, 54, 66, 74, 83, 88–89, 99, 139–41, 144, 149, 153, 154, 170, 196, 205; religious 103, 105

Bacon, Sir Francis 161; *Advancement of Learning* 69, 112; definition of wondrous 69
Bale, Bishop John, *Resurrection of Our Lord* 26–27, 35, 110
"Ballad of the Cruel Jew" 160
Bandello, Matteo 86
Baron Waldstein 198
Bartels, Emily C. 211
Bates, Jennifer Ann 174
Becomings-wonderous 185
Bene, Giulio del 102
Beni, Paulo, *Riposta alle considerazioni* 106, 115
Benson, Sean 190, 193
Bernini, Gian Lorenzo 102
Bible 20, 109, 151, 153–54, 161, 196
Biester, James 99, 114
Bishop, T. G. 167–68, 172, 173, 174, 190, 191, 193
Boaistuau, Pierre 86, 113

Boal, Augusto 142–43, 147
Body, the 132, 133–34
Booth, Edwin 152
Brooke, Arthur, *Tragicall Historye of Romeus and Juliet, The* 85–87, 89, 113, 140–46, 147
Brooks, Jeanice 138
Bryx, Adam & Bryan Reynolds 192
Bullough, Geoffrey 113, 145, 146, 147
Bulman, James 162
Burns, William 54, 112

Cabinet of curiosity 69, 87–88, 91–93, 198; and Shakespeare's plays 92–93, 175
Cabinet of wonder, *see* Cabinet of curiosity
Calderwood, James 177, 180, 191
Calendar of State Papers, Domestic 162
Caliban 11, 14, 149
Callaghan, Dympna 147
Callistratus 101
Calvert, Thomas, *The Blessed Jew of Morocco* 160
Calvin, John, *Diuers Sermons* 111, 192
Calzolari, Francisco 88
Camden, William, *Annals* 162
Cantor, Paul A. 212
Caravaggio 102
Carroll, Lewis 12, 79–80, 109, 111, 113
Cartelli, Thomas 162, 163
Castelvetro, Lodovico 102–3, *Poetica d'Aristotele* 108
Catholic/Catholicism 26, 143, 146, 191, 192, 196, 199–201, 205, 207, 211, 212; drama 27, 144
Cavallara, Giovan Battista 88, 113
Cerimon 30–35, 133–36
Christ 17–18, 35, 41, 103, 112
Christian/Christianity 16–20, 22–26, 28–30, 33, 41, 46, 49, 98, 101, 103, 105, 128, 151–58, 161, 162, 178, 179, 187, 196, 207; marvelous 104; pre- 48, 92

Cleopatra 24, 44–45, 61, 63, 92–95, 110, 111, 112
Cockpit, the 195
Cohen, Adam Max, *Wonder in Shakespeare* 131–32, 134–37, 139, 140, 144, 149, 153, 168, 180, 190–91, 195; *Shakespeare and Technology* 134
Cohen, Jeffrey Jerome 138
Coleridge, Samuel Taylor 187
Collington, Philip 211, 212
Comedy of Errors 38, 132
Conceptual mapping 180
Conversion 128, 150, 154–59, 161, 172
Cook, G. H. 114
Cope, Walter 92–93
Cornwallis, William, *Essayes of certain paradoxes* 135–36, 138
Coryate, Thomas 161
Costa, Filippo 88
Cotton, Sir Robert 92
Cromwell, Thomas 91
Crowl, Samuel 158, 162, 163
Croxton Play of the Sacrament 151
Cunningham, Dolora G. 190, 191
Cunningham, J. V. 115, 169, 172, 174, 190, 193
Cymbeline 36, 37, 38–40, 92, 182–83

Daniel, Biblical story of 153–54
Daston, Lorraine 196–97, 210
Da Vinci, Leonardo 102
Davis, Lloyd 147
Deats, Sara 213
Dee, John, *Elements of Geometry* 134, 138
Dehumanization 151
Deleuze, Gilles and Félix Guattari 135
de Montaigne, Michel "Of Experience" 184; "On Cannibals" 14
Denores, Giason, *Discorso intorno* 100, 106, 107–8, 116
Desdemona 64, 129, 184, 186, 193, 195–96, 199, 201–3, 205–9

Diehl, Huston 190, 191
Divine Right of Kings 165, 167–68, 171
Dog Day Afternoon 159
Dollimore, Jonathan 168, 173
Donoghue, Dan 191
Drake, Sir Francis 198
Duuuh moment 179, 181, 186

Edelman, Charles 161
Edwards, Philip 134, 167, 173
Elizabethan 27, 60, 65, 68, 87, 89, 93, 140, 144, 145, 150, 154–55, 158–59, 160, 165, 167–68, 170–72, 197
Elizabethan Journals 168, 173
Enthymemes 178–79, 187
eschatology 41, 154
Essex, Earl of 168–69, 171
Essex rebellion 168, 171
Eventualization 181, 188

Fawkner, H. W. 190, 193
Fenton, Edward 210
Findlen, Paula 88–89, 113, 114, 210
Fitzpatrick, Joseph & Bryan Reynolds 193
Frye, Northrop 170

Galen 33
Garden of Eden 166
Gardiner, James 114
Gardiner, Samuel, *An Explication* 192; Sermon on June 9, 1605 19–21, 22, 30, 110
Gataker, Thomas, *His Vindication*. 57, 112
Gessner, Conrad, *Historia Animalium* 89, 114
Ghosts 18, 23, 45–52, 66, 112–13, 132, 139, 142, 175, 176, 184; Banquo's 46, 50–52; Holy 27; King Hamlet's 46–50, 71, 111, 113
Giacomini, Lorenzo, "Sopra la purgazione" 107, 116

Gibbons, Brian 146, 147
Giraldi, Giovambattista (Cinthio) 100–3, 115
Glendower 75–76
Globe Theater 77, 93, 129, 134, 164, 173, 195
Godfather, The 159
Golden Hind 198
Gosson, Stephen 160
Goulart, Simon, *Admirable and Memorable Histories* 197–98
Grasso, Benedetto, *Oratione contra gli Terentiani* 107–8
Greenblatt, Stephen 111, 155, 191, 199, 203, 207, 210, 211
Grimald, Nicholas, *Christus Redivivus* 26
Grimestone, Edward (translator) 197–98, 210
Grinnell, Richard W. 213
Gross, John 160
Groves, Beatrice 18, 109

Halio, Jay 160, 162
Hall, Edward 81–82, 113
Halliwell, J. O. 89
Hamlet 14, 33, 42, 45, 46–52, 67, 71–72, 78, 106, 111, 181–82, 184, 192–93
Hamlet 5, 45–52, 67, 71, 177, 181–82, 184, 191–93
Handkerchief 19, 196, 199–200, 204–7, 212
Haraway, Donna 131, 137
Harrowing of Hell 30, 37, 103
Hathaway, Baxter 100–1, 105, 106, 114, 115, 116
Heisenberg's uncertainty principle 177
Heminge, John and Henry Condell 17
Henriad 165, 171
1 Henry IV 59–60, 74–77
2 Henry IV 170
Henry V 169, 197, 210

1 Henry VI 29
3 Henry VI 56, 81–83
Henry VIII 24, 77–80; Charles Kean 79–80, 109; Sarah Siddons 79
Hentzner, Paul 198
Heresy 27, 149–50
Hermione 27–32, 45, 97–99, 101–3, 108, 149, 184, 191, 193, 212
Heywood, Thomas, *Apology for Actors* 199, 211
Highley, Christopher 173, 213
Hodges, C. Walter 83, 113
Holinshed, Raphael, *Chronicles* 53, 81–82, 112, 113
Holy Land 170
Homer 107
Horatio 33, 46–49, 67, 71, 113, 184
Howard, Henry, Earl of Northampton, *A defensatiue against the poyson of supposed prophecies* 210
Howard, Jean 11, 109, 160
Hunt, Maurice 213

Imperato, Ferrante 88–89
Impey, Oliver and Arthur Macgregor 210
Inarticulatory space 180
Inquisition 65, 155
Interpolation 152, 159
Intertextuality 159–60
Inward subjectivity 201
Irish/Ireland 166–68, 171, 173
Isaiah, Book of 18
Iser, Wolfgang 177, 180, 191

Jackson, Henry 209
Jacobs, Margaret 213
James, St. "the Moor-Slayer" 200
Jesuits 200, 205
Joan of Arc 29
John, Book of 18, 49–50, 110
Jorden, Edward, *Suffocation of the Mother* 33

Judaism 150–52, 154–57
Juliet 5, 11, 36–37, 58–59, 85, 111, 139, 141, 143–46
Julius Caesar 51, 60–61, 65–68, 70, 71, 78, 93

Kantorowicz, Ernst H. 173
Kay, Dennis 197–98, 210
Kenseth, Joy 115, 116, 210
Kermode, Frank 146, 147
King James I 199; Act to Restrain the Abuses of Players 27
King John 57–58, 70–71
King Lear 14, 44–45, 92, 108, 188, 189–90
King's Men 209

Ladusaw, Bill 191
Lan, Yong Li 162, 163
Last Judgement (York Cycle) 23–24, 27
Lazarus 19, 32, 35, 110–11, 141
Lazarus (Wakefield Cycle) 141
Lee, Sidney 155, 162
Lehmann, Courtney & Bryan Reynolds 191
Lemon, Rebecca 173
Levin, Carol 173
Loomba, Ania 213
Lopez, Roderigo 154–55
Lord Chamberlain's Men 147, 168, 173
Luke, Book of 49
Lupton, Thomas 210
Luther, Martin 200

Macbeth 45, 50–52, 72–73, 78, 191, 192
Macbeth 45, 50–52, 72–73, 78
Maggli, Vincenzo 108
Magnus, Albertus 182, 193, 210
Magnus, Laury 162, 163
Mallette, Richard 213
Malone, Edmund 24
Marino, Giambattista 100–1, 103–4

Mark, Book of 49
Marlow, Christopher *Jew of Malta*
  151, 155
Marr, Andrew 135, 138
Marvel/marvelous 12–15, 28–30,
  48–49, 54, 68–69, 78, 80, 91,
  93, 97–108, 133, 135–37, 141,
  150, 165, 166, 169, 175–76,
  182, 184–88, 191, 196–200,
  202, 206, 208, 211; age of
  88; Christian 111, 114;
  non- 185–86, 191
Matthew, Book of 48, 49
McQuade, Paula 213
Measure for Measure 29, 99, 100
Menon, Madhavi 213
Mentz, Steve 132–33, 138
Merchant of Venice, The 17, 92, 150,
  155–56, 159
Mercy 82, 149, 150–54, 157, 161
Midsummer Night's Dream, A 58,
  183–84
Mincoff, Marco 190
Minshu, John, *Ductor in Linguas*
  45, 111
Minturno, Antonio, *L'arte Poetica*
  107, 116
Miracle 10, 16, 18–20, 28–29, 31, 35,
  68, 95, 103–4, 136, 141, 149, 180,
  186, 188, 196, 197, 200
Miranda 9–12, 15, 34, 35, 40, 109,
  136, 149, 151, 185
Mirollo, James 100, 103, 105, 114,
  115, 116
Miscegenation 202
Moor 195, 200–1, 208, 210
Much Ado About Nothing 29,
  41–43, 99, 108
Mullaney, Steven 93, 114
Music 14, 32, 36, 61–63, 65, 79,
  109, 133–37

Nashe, Thomas, *Have With You to
  Saffron Walden* 89

Negation 129, 176–77, 179–81, 185,
  189, 191–92
Negative capability 61
Neoplatonism 99, 134
Niccolucci, Giovan Battista (Il Pigna),
  I romanzi 107–8, 116
Nicholson, Catherine 200, 210
Northbrooke, John, *Spiritus est
  vicarius* 178–79, 188, 192

Oakley, Todd 179–80, 191, 192
Orsini, Vicino 105–6
Othello 12, 64–65, 92, 100, 108, 184,
  188, 195–96, 199–200, 209
Othello 12, 64, 108, 129, 184,
  188, 193, 195–96, 200–13
Ovid, *Metamorphosis* 21, 25
Owst, G. R. 114

Pacino, Al 156–59
Papal 168
Pare, Ambroise 210
Parker, Patricia 213
Parrhasius 98
Paster, Gail Kern 137, 138
Patrizi, Francesco 104–5, 115, 184
Patrizi, Francesco, *La deca
  ammirabile* 104–5, 184
Patterson, Annabel 109
Paul, 1 Corinthians 18, 20–21, 27,
  30, 35, 37, 132; in Acts 132
Paulina 28–32, 45, 97–99, 101–3,
  149, 184
Paused consciousness 180, 185,
  191, 192
Pellegrino, Camillo, *Del concetto
  poetico* 106–7
Pepys, Samuel, *Diaries* 195–96, 209
Performativity 128, 181, 183
Pericles 30–36, 132–37
Peter, Apostle 35
Peterson, Kaara L. 33, 111
Pigna, Il, *see* Niccolucci,
  Giovan Battista

Pilgrims, The, (Towneley Cycle) 27
Pittman, L. Monique 162, 163
Platt, Peter G., 103, 105, 115, 190, 193, 210
Platter, Thomas 93, 114, 198
Pliny the Elder 33, 101, 202
Plutarch, *Lives* 61–62, 94, 112, 114
Poel, William 38
Pomfret prison 169
Pontano, Giovanni 105, 115
Popish plots 168
Powers of the obvious 185, 188
Prelapserian imagery 166
Prince Hal 59–60, 171, 197
Prodigy 14, 53–83; "annalistic" vs. "apocalyptic" 54; death 63; play 57; vs. prophecy 78
Progressive quagmire 182
Prospero 9–16, 17, 136, 149, 153, 161, 185
Protestantism 11, 18, 26, 27, 35, 61, 65, 68, 75, 104, 140, 144–46, 155, 191, 193, 196–98, 200, 205, 209
Prynne, William, *Histrio-mastix* 178–79, 187–88, 192, 193
Pseudoresurrection 17–18, 26, 27, 39, 41, 42, 44, 132, 136, 137, 139, 140, 149, 188, 191
Puttenham, George 101

Queen Elizabeth I 10, 27, 77–78, 80, 91, 93, 104, 136, 144, 155, 159, 167–68, 172, 173, 176, 191, 197; 1559 proclamation 27, 110, 140; Censorship Commission 27, 110
Quiller-Couch, Arthur and John Drover Wilson 160

Rackin, Phyllis 173
Radford, Michael 150, 156, 159, 162
Ralegh, Sir Walter 211
Reason 10, 22, 62, 182, 184
Reflexive-consciousness 178, 188, 191
Reformation 196–97, 199–200

Relics 91, 94
Relic Sunday 90
Renaissance 25, 65, 92, 99, 105, 203
Res et verba debate 106, 107, 201, 206, 207, 209
Resurrection, The (Wakefield Cycle) 141
Resurrection 18–40, 97, 98–99, 103, 136; aesthetic 128, 139, 143; Biblical 31–32, 53
Resurrection of the Lord (miracle play) 18, 26–27, 29, 142
Resurrection plays 26, 139, 140, 144
Revelation, Book of 64
Rewonder 186–90
Reynolds, Bryan 191, 192, 193; & Adam Bryx 192; & Courtney Lehmann 191; & Janna Segal 139–40, 142, 144, 146, 147; & Joseph Fitzpatrick 193
Richard II 59, 165, 167–69, 171–72
Richard II 59, 92, 128, 165–72
Richard III 46, 53–57, 67, 78, 111, 186
Richard III 46, 54–57, 60, 65, 67, 78, 81–83, 186
Richman, David 190
Riggio, Millia Cozart 162, 163
Roberts, Gareth 190, 191
Roberts, Sasha 209, 212
Romano, Giulio 97–98
Romeo and Juliet 11, 36–37, 41, 58–59, 85–87, 94, 111, 114, 139–46, 188; Second Quarto 141
Rose, Martial 146, 147

Sacraments 196, 205
Sadler, John, *The Sick Woman's...* 33, 111
Salvation 128, 150, 200
Scarface 159
Seaton, Ethel 64, 112
Segal, Janna & Bryan Reynolds 139–40, 142, 144, 146, 147

Self-fashioning 207
Sell, Jonathan 213
Semon, Kenneth J. 190
Shakespeare in Love 111
Shapiro, James 154, 155, 160, 161, 168, 174
Shylock 128, 150–63
Sidney, Sir Philip, *An Apologie* 101, 107, 116
Sign 9, 10, 29, 33, 34, 35, 44, 56, 57, 60–83ff, 92, 133, 135, 146, 174, 181, 196, 197, 204
Skepticism 10, 74–77, 81, 197–98, 201–4, 206, 208, 211
Smith, Ian 202, 211, 213
Solifidianism 200
Some-other-where-but-here-space 144
Sontag, Susan 159, 162
Spain 168
Spectacular effects 13, 26
Spenser, Edmund, *A View of the Present State of Ireland* 166, 167
Speroni, Sperone 101, 115
Sprezzatura 137
Stafford, Barbara Maria 113
Steevens, George 89
Sternfeld, Frederick W. 112
Stewart, Patrick 161
Stow, John, *Annales* 169
Subjective mapping 178
Subjunctive movement 178
Surprise 9, 11, 12, 34, 56, 66, 81–82, 99, 150, 152, 154, 158–60, 176, 181–82, 187–88, 193, 196

Talentoni, Giovanni 101, 115
Taming of the Shrew, The 73–74
Tasso, Torquato, *Gerusalemme Liberata* 103; *Scritti Sull'Arte Poetica* 107, 116
Tempest, The 9–16, 92, 132, 136, 149–50, 185
Terence 107–8
Tesauro, Emmanuele 104, 115

Thaisa 30–35, 40, 128, 132–35, 137
Theaterspace 180, 183–84, 191, 192
Thomas, Keith 210
Thomas of India (Towneley Cycle) 23, 27, 50
Titian 103
Titus Andronicus 43–45, 73
Topsell, Edward 210
Transliminal power 180
Transversality 146, 181, 191
Transversal movements 176, 185, 189; enterprises 146, 191; poetics 191, 192; power 186, 193; subjects 192, 193
Treason 155
Treasure cabinets (*schatzkammern*) 12
Trissino, Gian Giorgio 106
Tudor Myth 57, 165–66
Tudors 92, 165–67
Turks 203, 206
Turner, Henry S. 137, 138
Twelfth Night 17, 25, 46

Vanishing mediation 129, 175–77, 181, 185–86, 189–91
Vasari, Giorgio 102
Venice 151, 201–4, 207–8
Verdizzoti, Mario 107, 116
Visitatio Sepulchri 25–26
Vocabolario degli Accademici della Crusa 105, 115

Wakefield cycle 139, 140–41, 146, 147; *Lazarus* 141; *The Resurrection* 141
Waldstein, Baron 198
Warren, Roger 134, 138
Watson, Robert 200
Wedel, Lupold Von 198
Weil, Mark S. 115
Weinberg, Bernard 115, 116
Weschler, Lawrence 210
Wilder, Lina Perkins 113
Williamson, Elizabeth 190, 191, 193

Wills, Gary 205
Wilson, Richard 199, 205
Wilson, Robert, *Three Ladies of London* 161
Winter's Tale, The 11, 27–31, 45–46, 97–104, 106, 108, 149–50, 184, 191, 193
Wonder 149–52, 155–56, 158–59, 165–70, 172, 196–202, 204–5, 207–10; Christian 18, 103, 104; Longinian 184; primary or direct 52; Protestant view 11, 18, 61, 65, 68, 75, 104, 176; secondary or indirect 52
Wonderation 182–84, 188, 189
Wonder cabinet, *see* Cabinet of curiosity
Wonder-check 183
Wonderknot 177–80
Wonderment 128, 158, 175–78, 180–83, 187, 189, 196, 199, 207, 209
Wonder/no wonder dialectic 177, 181, 185, 186, 189
Wonder pamphlet 70
Wonderpause 180–82, 188, 189
Wonder-reduction 182
Wonderstruck 26, 177, 184, 186, 188, 189
Wonder tradition, religious 9, 10; secular 9
Wonderwhelmed 185–86
Wonderwit 184–85
Wonderwork 177, 181, 185, 187–89
Wonder-wounded 175, 182, 184, 193
Wunderkammer, *see* Cabinet of curiosity

Yachnin, Paul 204, 207, 209, 212, 213

Zeuxis 98

```
PR          Cohen, Adam Max.
3069
.W65        Wonder in
C64           Shakespeare.
2012

                        35019000035005
```

DATE			

BAKER & TAYLOR